STONE THE DEAD CROWS

STONE THE DEAD CROWS

CARRIE MAGILLEN

Little Robin
PRESS

First published in Great Britain by
Little Robin Press Ltd, 2021
This paperback edition, 2021

A CIP catalogue record of this book is available
from the British Library

e-Book ISBN: 978-1-913692-07-0
Paperback ISBN: 978-1-913692-08-7
Hardback ISBN: 978-1-913692-09-4
Audiobook ISBN: 978-1-913692-10-0

Typeset in the UK by Watchword Editorial Services
Printed and bound by Lightning Source LLC

Little Robin Press Ltd
Kemp House, 160 City Road
London EC1V 2NX
United Kingdom

Little Robin
PRESS

For Jenny

> whose strength and courage inspire me every day

And for Linda

> who goes above and beyond anything any editor
> should do for any writer

ONE

MAGGIE

THERE'S SOMETHING in the trees.

I can't see it, but I can feel it. Its presence has a weight; the air is heavy with it.

We're not alone.

Ahead, the forest path climbs, narrowing on the horizon where the trees huddle, colluding in some conspiracy I'm not a part of.

The blood pulsing in my ears blocks out every other sound. And, although we're not moving, it's as if our fear propels us along the path towards its vanishing point on the skyline.

If we reach it, we'll disappear.

The trees crowd in, herding us in that direction, and I don't want to go. I'm afraid to stay. And I'm afraid to run.

A twig snaps.

I spin around, expecting to find someone standing there, but there's no one. The path is empty. And yet, instinctively, I reach behind me. My palms find Alfie's shoulders and I pull him close, making myself a wall between him and whatever's out there. He hides his face in the backs of my thighs as if he senses the danger too.

Mist clings to the trees and to my left and right, like a petrified army, their silhouetted torsos fade into the distance. The scent of damp pine, moss and resin is cloying.

It's hard to breathe.

My jeans stick to my legs, and beneath my jumper my T-shirt's damp against my spine. I don't need this wax jacket or these Gore-Tex-lined boots; I'm too hot. Light-headed. Running a hand up the back of my neck, I lift the hair beneath my wax hat and pull it away from my skin. What little breeze there is barely cools me, so I let it go and its razored ends graze my shoulders. I tuck it behind my ears which burn as though someone is talking about me.

As I scan the shadows – the dark spaces between the lichen-covered trunks – my voice trembles. 'Is someone there?'

Alfie slips his fingers, marshmallow-soft, into my hand. They're freezing. Somewhere at the back of my mind I register that his gloves are in my pocket, but I can't drag my attention from the forest. Cold hands can wait; his safety can't.

Something – someone – is out there.

Not only can I feel him, I can still hear him. His breath comes thick and fast, rasping. It drowns out the heartbeat in my ears. His eyes are fixed on me, I know it. They travel up and down my body, clawing like fingernails that leave red marks in my white skin.

This is private land. There are no public footpaths and I've never seen a soul trespassing here. But, because it's privately owned, it's not as well maintained as the local country parks and nature reserves. The trees are closely packed, the undergrowth dense with rotting leaves and fallen branches. The air is musty and dank, starved of sunlight by the crowded canopy.

Another twig snaps and I spin again. Gripping Alfie's hand, I take a few steps backwards in the direction of home, and his soft flesh squirms against my palm. I'm squeezing him too tightly. But I can't let go. Left and right, right and left, my eyes sweep the empty wood for the slightest movement between the trees.

Nothing.

But still it breathes.

He breathes.

I take another few steps away but I don't run. I'm afraid to turn my back on whoever is out there.

'Cairo!' I shout her name into the canopy and the crows take flight. She disappeared between the trees ten minutes ago when she caught sight of a deer. 'Cairo, come!'

She won't come.

Cairo's a Blenheim Cavalier King Charles spaniel, chestnut-red and white, quiet and fragile. She spends most of her life sleeping on a large pillow by the wood-burner in the cabin. But if she catches sight of prey, even ten times her size, that fragility evaporates. She bolts into the trees, disappears in a flash, and stays on the hunt for hours. She's her own mistress, responds to commands when she feels like it, and doles out affection on her own terms. She's more cat than dog.

I whistle but the sound doesn't carry. In my mind's eye, my silver dog-whistle, on its leather lanyard, swings from a hook on the storeroom door back at the cabin. Luc always laughs at me. With his melodic intonation (a tinge of the French Loire Valley where he lived till he was five), every T and S ringing with a sherbet-sweet-and-sour tone, he says cooling hot soup isn't whistling. Then, with two fingers in his mouth, he'll whistle loud enough to hurt my ears.

I wish he were here now.

The breathing gets louder, draws closer, as if the stranger's lips are pressed to my ears. Then, like a crackling fire, dead leaves crunch underfoot. The sound comes from the trees to our right.

Finally, I turn and run.

3

The stranger's breath rasps in my ears as I drag Alfie along behind me. Heavy exhalations chase us down the narrow woodland path, but I can no longer tell if it's coming from the trees or my own lungs. Fear clouds my judgement and I swear I hear my name on the wind, trapped in bubbles of sound, caught in his breath.

Alfie can't keep up. And when his little legs trip and stumble, forcing me to grip his hand even tighter, I'm convinced his wrist will snap. So, still running, I scoop him up and stagger a few paces, balancing him on my hip until I find my rhythm again. I'm out of shape, carrying the last stubborn pounds of pregnancy fat along with the child who put it there. And tears of anger sting my eyes at my inability to get him out of danger any faster when I've had more than enough time to get fit again.

Ahead of us, the trees break and, finding a burst of energy from deep inside, I sprint for the lake. I can just make it out in the distance. When we finally stumble into the clearing it's as if the stranger's stale breath reaches out for us: a disembodied smoke-grey hand, determined to pull us back into the forest's darkness. Twisting to look behind, I stumble and fall to my knees.

The path between the trees is empty. The wood is still, the breathing silenced.

There's nobody there.

Alfie squirms in my arms, desperate to be set free, and I don't have the energy to fight him. So, reluctantly, I release my wriggling child, who breaks free of my embrace and runs for the lake, his clumsy wellington boots crunching the gravel. As if nothing has happened, he points to the still water and says, 'Stones, Mumma, stones,' with his eighteen-month-old lisp that sounds as if he's blowing bubbles.

And suddenly I feel stupid. I stare back down the path, searching for the slightest movement, but there's nothing there.

4

'Stones, Mumma!'

'Not now, sweetie.' I catch up with him and take his hand again. 'Let's go and say hi to Daddy.'

Alfie yanks his hand away and totters sulkily along the lakeshore towards the cabin.

I follow.

And all the way, I check behind me.

TWO

ROSE

FINGERS GRASPING the door handle, I pause at the unexpected sight. The open integral blind in the door's small, square window reveals a strange man looming over Daisy. He's dressed in a black shirt with a mandarin collar, and is clearly not a doctor.

Tenderly, almost lovingly, he brushes her red curls back from her face, and although I can't hear a sound through the door I know he's talking to her because his lips are moving.

He leans further forward and his shirt falls open slightly; the four contrasting red buttons that end beneath his breastbone are just for show. He has dark chest hair, a salt and pepper close-cropped beard, and salt and pepper hair. He's strikingly handsome but not in a conventional way: soft around the edges, with a kind face.

I've never seen him before.

Who is he?

Nobody talks to my sister but me.

All right, that's not strictly true. Zesiro, one of the hospital porters, and Dionne, the catering assistant for this floor – they speak to Daisy. But they're different. They're special. They're born of that rare breed of humans who genuinely, deeply care about other people. Even people they don't know. But they don't have long conversations with her like this, they just utter a few words of encouragement.

Nobody *really talks* to Daisy but me.

My sister makes people uncomfortable.

Because she doesn't talk back.

So who is this man? What could he possibly have to say to her that's taking so long? And why isn't *he* uncomfortable?

There are two things I know about my sister: she doesn't have any friends left; and there's no way on God's earth she would have formed a romantic attachment before ending up in here.

I'm about to throw the door open when he brushes back her hair again, his evident affection stopping me. I pause – I don't want to deprive Daisy of this rare moment. Her bed faces the door but slightly off to the left, so I lean sideways to get a better view, my nose almost pressed to the cool glass. A tug of longing, as if I'm outside peering in on a warm room, pulls at the base of my ribs. But then my phone pings in my handbag, a text message alert, and I duck as if I've been caught snooping through someone's kitchen window. I back away, keeping my head low. Once I know I can't be seen, I pretend I wasn't spying and stride towards the door, opening it as if I have no idea anyone's in there.

The door's squeaking swoosh startles the man and he stands bolt upright, turning towards me. I guess he didn't hear my phone after all.

'Can I help you with something?' The undertone of hostility wasn't intentional and I almost apologise for it. It's all those wires and tubes, stuck on Daisy with adhesive pads or pinned into her with needles: they bring out a fierce protective side of me that I didn't know existed.

7

As the man comes out from behind her bed, I glance down at his shirt. It almost reaches his knees. Beneath it, he's wearing matching black cotton trousers and sturdy leather sandals. It's far too early in the year for sandals.

'I am Dr Sharif.' He holds out his hand for me to shake. But I don't take it; my mind is still reeling. Who is he? And what's he doing in Daisy's room? She's been stuck in that bed for three years and I've never seen this man – or any man for that matter – visit her before.

But then I register he said he was a doctor. He must be off duty.

Across his outstretched forearm, exposed to the elbow by the rolled-up sleeves of his shirt, thick veins charm their way over taut muscles. He has a slim but strong frame. Prominent biceps and pectoral muscles strain the seams of his thin cotton shirt. And he has a conspicuous Adam's apple.

When my eyes finally meet his, my presence of mind returns; I have no idea how much time has passed. But, in spite of my rudeness, he's still holding out his hand for me to shake, almost laughing at the discomfort.

'Sorry...' I take the hand. 'Sorry. I'm Rose.'

Although he's clearly very strong, his grip is surprisingly gentle, his skin soft. 'Of course! Rose. Daisy's younger sister. She spoke of you often. You were very close, I understand. I seem to recall her saying you were not just sisters but best friends as well.'

And the moment I hear the precision in his words, the lyrical, almost Dickensian phrasing, all the pennies drop. He *is* a doctor, but not of medicine.

My mind's eye drifts back three years. It fixes on the clean lines of Daisy's lips as this man's name trips from them. In Daisy's pruned and serious tone, his name has rung in my ears dozens of times.

When she was still with us.

When she was still conscious.

8

When her life was so horribly grave.

Her description of the fine-looking Indian man who pronounced every word in full comes back to me. I remember her laughing about it with affection – and she rarely laughed back then. Back then, this man was the only thing keeping her together.

'Saeed,' I say. 'Saeed Sharif. Daisy's therapist.'

'Psychologist. You must have a good memory for names.'

'She talked about you a lot.'

My phone pings in my handbag, reminding me of the unopened text message. And, realising he hasn't let go of my hand, Saeed says, 'Oh! I am sorry. You can have that back now.'

I don't have to look in the mirror to know there's an orb of red in each cheek. So I brush my hair back, lift my face and pretend I'm standing in the snow, a cool breeze blowing over my face. It works almost every time to stop the perpetual cycle of a chronic blush: blushing because you're embarrassed and then embarrassed by the blushing. It doesn't help that I have pale pink lips, ice-blonde hair and baby-powder skin; I wear my emotions like clown paint. But over the years I have learned to manage my condition.

Dr Sharif points at Daisy. 'They say the stimulation of both sound and touch are helpful… I hope you do not mind—?'

'No, of course not.' He's worried he's overstepped the therapist's line by touching Daisy, but I'm grateful he's doing everything he can. We both look at her then and I say, 'She stopped breathing on Monday. They've been keeping her on the ventilator while they run tests.'

'I know,' he says. 'I am sorry. I went to see Dr Anderson when I arrived. He told me that Daisy's condition has worsened.'

He picks up her chart, hanging from the foot of her bed, and runs a finger down the page, nodding as he reads. Clearly the chart makes sense to him when, to me, it's written in an alien language. Of course, he could be showing off, trying to impress me with his intelligence by pretending he understands it. But he doesn't strike me as the type of man who would do something like that. He seems grounded, comfortable in his own skin, certain of himself but not conceited.

'You're a proper doctor?'

He looks up at me with a broad smile.

'Sorry...' I add. Beneath concealer, my cheeks burn, my heart flutters, and my hands tremble as if I've committed some unforgivable sin for which I'm to be sent to the scaffold. 'You know what I mean.'

When he nods, a disproportionate relief washes over me, as if he's exonerated me. What *is* that? I've always been a shy and flighty sort of person – like a robin – not afraid of people but cautious and careful – yet these days I'm on eggshells all the time. Self-conscious about everything I say and do. Is it Daisy? The overwhelming emotion of being here?

I wish I were more like her: bold and self-assured. But I'm not. And stupidity is a self-fulfilling prophecy: walking on eggshells at the thought of something stupid coming out of my mouth always makes something stupid come out of my mouth.

Yet Dr Sharif doesn't seem to mind. He says, 'I *was* a proper doctor. In a previous life. A neurosurgeon. I switched to psychology and neuroscience three years into my speciality training.'

'Why?' I blush again, unprovoked, and do the exercises – snow and cool breezes – while trying to keep my mind on the conversation.

'I prefer the mystery of the mind over its biology.'

'I see. I think I would too. I wouldn't want to be cutting up brains. It's icky.'

He laughs.

'Daisy's chart makes sense to you, then?' I ask.

'It does. And I believe this is only a temporary glitch. They will perform a tracheotomy if she needs the breathing tube for too long – it is easier to maintain – but I suspect, when they remove the tube, she will breathe on her own again. There are no changes to her MRI or CT. And in fact her EEG shows an increase in brain activity, not a decrease.'

He looks more closely at the chart and then flips the pages back and forth, cross-referencing something that makes his eyebrows draw together and a deep crease form between them.

'What's wrong?'

He stares at the chart.

'Dr Sharif?'

He glances up at me, then back at the chart again. 'Oh. Nothing. Just...um....'

'Just?'

'Nothing.' He smiles. 'There is nothing to worry about here. It is all good.' He hangs the chart back on the end of the bed.

'That's a relief. I was so worried when she stopped breathing. I don't know what I'd do without Daisy.' I move to the bed and straighten her blankets even though they're straight already; it's not as if she tosses and turns.

After a moment of uneasy silence, I fill the void by saying, 'You're not at all what I imagined. Daisy never said you were so...'

Eggshells cut the soles of my feet. I'm doing it again: speaking before my brain is in gear and having to check myself before the rest of the sentence falls out. And now I have no idea how to finish it without sounding like a silly schoolgirl. I'm not sure it *is* Daisy making me feel this way. And I don't think it's Dr Sharif either. On the contrary, I feel calm in his company – calmer than I've felt around anyone in a very long time. At the same time, it's as though he's altered the chemical balance of the air in the room and I can't quite catch my breath.

'So...*Indian?*' he rescues me with a boyish smile.

'Yes,' I lie. 'She never said you were from India.'

'Rajasthan.' He moves to stand on the opposite side of Daisy's bed, his movement intentional. As if he senses my need for protection, for a barrier between me and the strange

11

man I've never met. 'Although I have been in England most of my life.'

'I've never been. To Rajasthan, I mean. Of course I've been to England!' I fiddle with the blankets again, face burning at my own idiocy, then add, 'I've never even seen pictures. But I've always thought it sounded romantic.'

'It is. The Water Palace, the Palace of Winds, Mehrangarh. You should go some time.'

I laugh. The idea of Nathan taking me anywhere like India seems absurd. Paris is more his style. Monaco. Vienna. 'One day. Maybe.' Then I ask, 'So what brings you to the hospital? Why have you come to see Daisy?'

'I come every week. Usually on a Friday – her regular lunchtime appointment – but a patient no longer needs this slot, and it is easier to visit Daisy on my way home. So for the last few weeks I have come on a Thursday afternoon.'

'Committed, or cured?' Oh, God. What kind of question is that?

'Cured, actually. It turned out there was nothing wrong with her. At least, nothing a radical exorcism could not cure.'

'You perform exorcisms too?'

'Sometimes.' He laughs. 'Metaphorically.'

'Of course…metaphorically…I didn't imagine…' I pick up one of Daisy's ginger curls and twirl it around my finger, mesmerised by its orange-peel vibrancy and shine. My mind races and time stretches until I finally blurt out the question that's been plaguing my mind for three years.

'Do you think she did it on purpose?'

'What?'

'Took sleeping pills and underdosed on her insulin?'

My question hangs in the air for a moment, then Saeed says, 'I am sorry, Rose. I have no idea. It came as a shock to me too. I saw her just two days before she was admitted and observed no suicidal tendencies. On the contrary, she was very much at peace. I cannot say much, obviously, but she said she had found happiness again. That makes me think it was a mistake. If she had wanted to kill herself she would have taken the whole bottle of pills and no insulin at all. Perhaps she had not calibrated her glucometer for some time and the pills were because she was having trouble sleeping.'

I reach out and touch his arm. 'I can't tell you what a comfort it is to hear you say that. All these years, I've wondered whether it was my fault, whether she was crying out for help and I just didn't hear it.'

'It is not your fault. Do not even think it. When she first came to me, she was broken. I remember the day she first walked into my office: I thought she was ill. Physically, I mean. She was so pale, so fragile. But after a year of sessions she was finding her way again. If she did do this to herself and either one of us could have seen it coming, it should have been me, not you. I *have* to believe it was an accident. If I thought...'

His voice trails off and I understand why he can't say the words. The guilt is too much. And now I know what he's doing here, why he comes to see her every week even though, now, he's the only one doing the talking.

I realise my hand is still on his arm and try to conceal my awkwardness by teasing him with the line he used on me earlier. 'Oh, I'm sorry. You can have that back now.'

It comes out stilted; I don't usually tease people I've just met. My cheeks flush yet again from the warmth of his laugh, but for once I don't mind. Most people who notice my excessive blushing either point it out with a condescending remark or stare, which inevitably makes it worse. But Saeed pays no attention to it, and so it quickly goes away.

'Shall we sit?' He points to the chair by Daisy's bedside. 'They say it is helpful for the patient to hear familiar voices. And it will be much easier to talk to you than to have my usual one-sided conversations. I have very little time for a social life and I run out of things to tell her, since I cannot talk about my cases.'

13

'Why not?' I move to fetch the chair by the door but Saeed darts in front of me, bringing the chair to the bedside and pushing it beneath my knees as if seating me at a restaurant table.

'Patient confidentiality.' He takes the seat on the opposite side of the bed.

I laugh. 'Daisy's pretty good at keeping secrets these days.'

We rest our elbows on the blanket either side of her and it does feel a little like we're out to dinner, albeit with shocking waitress service.

Nathan springs to mind then, and for some strange reason I feel guilty. That's silly, of course. We haven't been married long and it's a situation I have yet to encounter. But Nathan is hardly the sort of person to be jealous over me talking to another man, especially in circumstances as innocent as these. Nathan is supremely confident and wouldn't be intimidated by a man like Saeed. I can't imagine him being intimidated by anyone.

'You never know what she can hear,' Saeed says. 'Imagine Daisy waking up and knowing the details of all my cases. That would not do at all.'

'I see what you mean. So what *shall* we talk about, then?'

'I am afraid the nature of my job means I am much better at listening than talking. So why don't you tell me about yourself? Are you married? Children?'

'Children, no. Married, yes. Actually, the reason we haven't run into each other before is because I was on my honeymoon. I'm usually here on a Thursday afternoon.'

'Congratulations. And who is the lucky man?'

'Thank you. It's Nathan Winter. He's one of the divisional directors. Do you know him?'

'I have heard his name.'

'He used to be a paediatric surgeon but was promoted at the end of last year.'

'I hear the paediatricians here are some of the best in the country. He likes children, then?'

14

'Yes. He'd have had me knocked up by the third date if he'd had his way. But I'd like to be married for at least a year first. What about you?'

'Not married – and no children, no. I moved to Oxford nearly twelve years ago when I took a position as a research scientist at the Sleep and Circadian Neuroscience Institute here. And I run my own practice on the side. As I said, I have very little social life. Where did you meet Nathan?'

'Here, at the hospital. I used to see him around when I was visiting Daisy and then, one day, we ran into each other in the café. It was one of those whirlwind romances. I fell for the charming doctor who swept me off my feet.'

'You are a teacher, yes? I seem to remember Daisy—'

'Not any more. I was finding it difficult to manage; Nathan has a big house. Plus, we don't need two incomes and I wanted to spend as much time as I could with him and Daisy.'

'Do you miss teaching?'

'Desperately. I miss the kids especially. But in a year or so I'll have one of my own to look after. That will help, I hope. Do you want children?'

'I would have to find a partner first. Besides, I already have one: a baby girl.' Saeed gets out his phone.

'I thought you said—'

He turns the lock screen towards me and on the front is the most adorable dog I have ever seen. She has golden hair, bead-black eyes and a shiny black nose. With her head resting on a pillow, paw tucked under her chin, asleep, she looks almost human.

I say, 'She's a little hairier than your average child.'

'Yes. But parents who place too much emphasis on their children's appearance usually land them in therapy.'

I laugh. 'She looks like a teddy bear!'

He puts his phone back in his pocket and, as he does, mine pings another message alert. Reaching down for my handbag, which I'd dropped on the floor at the foot of Daisy's bed, I pull

out my phone. The texts are both from Nathan, and his words
– like string – tug at the corners of my mouth as I struggle to
conceal a broad smile.

> My delicate Rose, I love you more
> than I did this morning, as much as is
> possible right now, but still less than I
> will tonight. Your Doctor of Love. Xxx

The text that arrived while I was hiding behind the door,
watching Saeed, is followed by another:

> Rose? Are you there, my darling? I'm
> thinking of you. I don't need a special
> day to tell you I love you. Every day
> is special when I'm with you. Your
> Doctor of Love. Xxx

'Good news?' Saeed catches my smile and the twinkle in
my eyes.

'Just Nathan being Nathan.' I swipe the messages away
and turn the phone around so that Saeed can see the photo on
my lock screen. 'That's him.'

Saeed looks at it, then points at my phone as if something
on it needs my attention. I turn it back around and realise I
didn't properly clear the messages. So I swipe them away again
and turn it back to Saeed.

'Very handsome,' he says. 'And romantic too, it seems.'

I squirm with embarrassment over the schoolgirl crush I
still have on my husband. 'He sends messages like that every
day. And he's so busy with patients, I don't know how he
finds the time. Or the creative energy for that matter. I'm one
of those people who writes "Love from Rose" in every card
because I can't think of anything witty. It takes me an hour to
think of anything vaguely interesting to say back to Nathan.
Most of my day is wasted composing replies to him.' I put

16

my phone down on the blanket and then pick it up again. 'I'd better… Do you mind?'

'No. Of course. Take your time.'

It takes me ages to think of what to say – I have to keep deleting parts and rewording others – but, finally, I press send.

> I love you too, Doctor of Love!
> Can't wait for this day to end
> so we can curl up together.
> Your delicate Rose.

'How long have you been married?'

'Only a month. But we've been together a year. Lived together for eleven months.'

One of Saeed's eyebrows lifts but he readjusts his expression so quickly I question whether it even happened.

'I said it was a whirlwind. We met on the 14th of January, moved in together on Valentine's Day, and got married on the 14th of December.'

'You must have been very sure of each other.'

'When you know, you know. That's what Nathan says. Before we met in the café – when I'd seen him around the hospital – I thought a man like that would never look twice at me. So tall and scrumptious in his scrubs. But he did.' I laugh at the memory of what I was like around him. Shy and giggly, barely able to look him in the eye, as if he were Ryan Gosling or something. Actually, he's better-looking than Ryan Gosling, and there aren't many men you can say that about.

Saeed says, 'A man would have to be blind to only look once.'

Having forgotten what I'd said and lost my train of thought, at first I think Saeed is talking about Nathan. But then I realise he's talking about me and laugh. 'Nathan's in a different league. He has The Allure.'

'The allure?'

17

'You've never watched *Miranda*?'

'Who is *Miranda*?'

'It's a TV show. You should watch it, it's very funny. The Allure is the *je ne sais quoi* that makes *everyone* look twice.'

'Is he human?'

'I'm not sure. I'll check when he gets home tonight and let you know. The odd thing is that men like him are usually only interested in themselves, but Nathan's not like that. You should have seen him with the kids here – sweet, kind...funny. He gets all this attention from the nurses and still makes *me* feel as if I'm the only woman in the world. I don't know why I'm telling you all of this... Tell me something about yourself.'

'I think you can gather that a man who has never seen *Miranda* is probably not very interesting. I spend most of my life between the four walls of my office.'

'What about before that?'

'Still not very exciting, I am afraid. My parents moved to London when I was eighteen and – whether I liked it or not – enrolled me in a medical degree. I did my postgraduate study and three years of neurosurgery, only to discover that cutting people open...it was not for me. But I could not disappoint my parents when they had done so much, so I waited until they moved back to India – that was the end of 1999 – and enrolled in a psychology and neuroscience degree at St Andrews.'

'New millennium, new start?'

'Exactly. It took me two years to tell my parents that their son was no longer a neurosurgeon.'

'How did they take it?'

'Badly, at first. But they came around. Then, after my doctorate, I took a job at a small practice in the Lakes. But I only treated one patient before...' He fumbles for the words. 'Well... It is complicated... A long story for another day. But I met a marvellous doctor there and have been working with him at the Institute ever since. For more than ten years now.' He looks down at the blanket. 'I told you: a man who inhabits

18

the subconscious and dreams of other people is never going to be very exciting.'

'I disagree. I find the subconscious fascinating. And you've dedicated yourself to your work. You help people. That's exciting. I miss helping people every day.'

'You will go back to teaching, yes? At a better time? You are still young.'

'I hope so.'

My phone, lying on the blanket, pings again, and Nathan's face lights up on the lock screen.

> I have a surprise for our anniversary. Pack a bag! I'll be counting the moments until my pale Rose is in my arms. I'll do things that will turn her red. Your Doctor of Love. Xxx

I turn the phone over.

'Please,' Saeed says. 'Do not mind me. I can entertain Daisy with tales of fake patients who mistake their umbrellas for their husbands.'

'You're funny.'

'Not really. I was stealing from *The Man Who Mistook His Wife for a Hat.*'

I frown, then say, 'Of course! That was a book. Did he really think she was a hat?'

'Yes. He had visual agnosia. He could see objects and faces but was unable to interpret what he saw.'

My phone pings again, reminding me of the unanswered text, but I ignore it while making a mental note to pack a bag, wondering what Nathan has in store for us. Just the thought gives me butterflies. The last time he whisked me away for a romantic weekend was after we'd had Cairo staying with us for a while. I was missing her company so much, he'd taken me to the Jack Russell, a dog-friendly inn in the North Wessex

19

Downs, where all the rooms are named after different breeds and the pub is wall-to-wall dogs. He'd said, since I'd got so attached to her and we couldn't have a dog of our own, I should be able to get my fix somehow. He's so sweet like that. So thoughtful. It was only after Cairo had come to stay that Nathan had realised he was allergic; he'd never had a problem before. We'd had to rush her back home. But he risked having another flare-up, just so I could spend a weekend near dogs.

I compose a quick reply and drop the phone back on the bed. 'Sorry. He has a surprise for our anniversary and wants me to pack. So...' I rummage around for interesting topics, something a little more personal; I'm intrigued by this man who cares enough about my sister to show up every week and have long conversations with her. 'You're not married, but is there not even a girlfriend?'

He shakes his head.

'Surely you've stepped out of your office long enough to go on at least one date?'

'One or two. But they ended in disaster.'

'What sort of disaster? Tell me about the worst one.'

'I am afraid my worst date is not very funny either.'

'I don't care. Besides, it'll entertain Daisy. And that's what we're here for, isn't it?'

'True. All right, then. It was a blind date. A mutual friend set us up and I met her at a nice restaurant in London. I arrived first; she was a little late. The waiter showed her to the table and there was this long moment where she did not speak or sit down. And, when she finally did speak, she said, "Darren should have said you were black." I tried to lighten the moment and said, "Or, more accurately, that I was brown!" But she did not find that at all amusing. She barely looked at me. It was obvious there would be no second date but she still ordered a twenty-pound cocktail and the lobster with a side of soft-shell crab.'

'That's unbelievable. What did you do?'

'While she was giving the waiter a list of sides longer than either of us could possibly eat, I excused myself to go to the bathroom. I paid for my beer and left.'

I can't fight the giggles, saying, 'I really shouldn't laugh, it's not funny. But leaving must have felt great!'

'Yes and no. I felt bad about it afterwards. I understand why they say revenge is bittersweet. I doubt you have had dates like that?'

'Actually… I think I can beat it.'

'Not a chance. You really think you can beat the gourmet racist? It will have to be something really shocking.'

I nod. 'I see your gourmet racist and I raise you one exhibitionist slob.'

'Check.' Saeed taps the blanket with a boyish grin.

'Well… we met in a club, danced for a bit, and he asked me out for the following Saturday. But on the day he texts to ask if I'll pick him up – turns out he doesn't drive – so I drive us to the cinema and afterwards he suggests a pub that apparently serves great burgers—'

'Classy.'

'So I drive us there too and watch him down several beers while nursing a flat lemonade.'

'Did he at least pay?'

'No, we went Dutch. I seem to remember him using feminism as an excuse for me picking up half the tab. It crossed my mind to ask him for half the petrol but I wasn't brave enough.'

'He sounds charming.'

'Wait – it gets better. So…I drop him home and he invites me in for a coffee. I naïvely say yes because I've always struggled with no. But I make a point of saying I'll only stay for one coffee…you know…in other words: *there's no way I'm having sex with you on the first date.*'

Saeed nods as if that didn't need explaining.

'So, we get inside and his entire flat is wall-to-wall with piles of boxes, clothes and junk. He even has two bicycles standing upright on the sofa. He apologises for the mess and guides me through the clutter to the back of the flat, where there's one room that just happens to be immaculate.'

'Let me guess: the bedroom.'

'Funnily enough, yes! Not a single thing out of place. He says he's going to make the coffee and then reappears a few minutes later, leaning on the doorframe in this ridiculous catalogue pose. And he's completely naked.'

'You are not serious?'

'Deadly. I swear I've never run for a door so fast in my life! I had to fight my way through the mess, tripping over piles of junk, apologising all the way, saying it was late and I had to go.'

Saeed laughs.

'You haven't heard the best bit yet. I get outside, shut the front door behind me and realise I've left my handbag on his bed with my car keys inside.' We're both laughing then, tears rolling down our cheeks. 'Oh, my God, it was so humiliating! I had to knock on the door and he opened it only wearing boxer shorts. And he pulled that same catalogue pose on the doorframe while I asked for my handbag.'

'What did he say?'

'He just scoffed and said, "I thought you'd changed your mind."'

'You win.' Saeed's still laughing. 'I fold. I take it this was not Nathan Winter, the Doctor of Love?'

'Absolutely not! Nathan was the complete opposite of the exhibitionist slob. He took me to The Feathers.'

'A little classier than a burger joint.'

I nod heartily. 'While I was in the bathroom, he ordered pink champagne – which he guessed would be my favourite, he said, because I'm *bubbly, beautiful, and always blushing*. And, for dinner, he didn't order any main courses, but starter after starter until we couldn't eat any more. It was the best meal I've ever had. I've always found appetisers more fun than mains, haven't you?'

'Absolutely.'

'It was like we were made for each other; we have so much in common. When he picked me up – no driving for me this time – he turned the stereo on and his phone automatically connected to the car radio and started playing my favourite song, which he'd been listening to on his headphones earlier in the day. I mean, what are the chances? It was like kismet or something. And when he dropped me home, he didn't even hint at being invited in.'

'Unlike your exhibitionist slob.'

'No, a perfect gentleman. He just asked if we could spend the next day together. He'd switched shifts with another doctor, and planned a picnic in Florence Park.'

'Perhaps I should stay away from the dating scene if this is the standard these days.'

'You haven't heard the best part yet: he'd hired a Glenn Miller tribute band to play in the bandstand at the park.'

'That seals it. I am never dating again. Who is this man putting the rest of us to shame? He sounds too good to be true.'

'Sickening, isn't it? He's like a male Mary Poppins: practically perfect in every way.'

'And no doubt he buys you flowers for no reason at all.'

I grin. 'All the time. I used to get to work and find flowers and bow-tied gifts on my desk. Or sometimes just an apple for the teacher. But he still brings me flowers, even now, a year later.'

'What was the song?' he asks.

'Sorry?' My forehead crumples before I realise what he means. 'Oh, "Sunset". Kate—'

'Bush,' he interrupts. '*Aerial*. Beautiful. One of her best.'

'Isn't it? Though I have a soft spot for *The Hounds of Love*. And *The Sensual World*. And *The Dreaming*. And—' I laugh. 'Let's face it: all of them. Which is your favourite?'

'Song or album?'

'Song.'

'Too difficult,' he says. 'Ask me something else.'

I pick up Saeed's phone, turn it on, and point a finger gun at the photo on the lock screen. 'Choose, or the puppy gets it.'

'All right then… "Lily"…. No, "This Woman's Work"… No, "Heads We Are Dancing".'

'You're as hopeless as I am. I think the puppy's dead. And it's not "Heads We Are Dancing", it's "Heads We're Dancing".'

'Old habits… Did you go to the concert?'

'No, I couldn't get tickets. Did you?'

'I tried,' he says. 'I got into one of the holding rooms and watched that spinning thing for ages, not realising it was spinning because the whole page had hung – too many people trying to buy tickets at the same time – and when I finally got back in they were all gone.'

'That's what happened to me! And I'd taken a bloody day off so I could be sitting at my computer when they went on sale.'

'They say the entire tour sold out in less than fifteen minutes.'

'Nathan got a ticket. I wish I'd known him back then; he could have taken me!'

'I am really starting to hate this man.'

'I hate him too – how dare he get tickets when I didn't?'

Saeed checks his watch, then says, 'Well, missing *Before the Dawn* has clearly had a deep impact on your psyche. Undoubtedly that is something that needs a good deal of therapy. But I am afraid we are approaching the hour. Perhaps we can address these profound issues in our next session?'

'I told you you were funny.'

His smile meets his eyes and I notice, for the first time, that they're a strange grey, dark and animated, like molten metal.

We both get up, and as he's heading for the door I say, 'It's been really nice to talk.'

And he turns and looks at me with an intensity I've never seen in anyone I've ever met. 'For me, too. The most enjoyable session I have had all day. I forget, sometimes, that people do exist in contentment, with their lives just as they would wish. It is a rare pleasure to talk to a normal person.' He checks himself and, although it's barely noticeable on his olive skin, it's now his turn to blush. 'I mean someone who is not a client. Usually, I am so tired of talking by the end of the day, I just want to go home and be alone.'

'I have the opposite problem. Too much time alone. And, much as I love Daisy, she's very tight-lipped these days.' Saeed smiles but I feel sad suddenly. 'It's been so hard without her. One-way conversations are exhausting when the person who always had all the answers suddenly has nothing to say. These visits are always difficult, but today...' I rest my hand on his folded arms. 'Thank you for coming to see her.'

Saeed looks through me, as if a memory is playing like a film on the wall behind me.

'What is it?'

'Sorry,' he says. 'I just remembered the first day Daisy mentioned you. Something she said.'

'What?'

A hint of a smile brushes his lips. 'It would be wrong to repeat—'

'You can't do that. You can't say my sister said something about me and then not tell me what it was. I won't be embarrassed if it's something awful.'

He looks directly at me. 'It is not awful. Not at all. She said...'

He blushes again and it draws me to him like a kindred spirit, which is just silly, I know. But I like it when people blush: it makes me feel more human, more present with the person, because I'm less concerned for my own condition and can focus entirely on them.

'She said there was something ethereal about you. Magical. As if you were hatched from a delicate egg rather than born. As if something as traumatic as a natural birth would have

25

shattered you to pieces. But, she said, when you look in your birdlike brown eyes you see power there.'

I stare at him with my birdlike brown eyes and imagine Daisy saying something like that. I always saw her as the one with all the power.

Compared to the woman she was before, I have no power at all.

THREE

MAGGIE

'IT WAS PROBABLY a stag.' Luc swivels in his office chair, his songful tones not reassuring me as much as it usually does. His smile is warm but his fingertips, massaging the thick roots of his black hair, betray mild frustration; he doesn't like to be interrupted when he's writing unless it's really important.

'A stag? Heavy-breathing?'

'*Mais oui.* They make snorting noises when they're threatened.'

Luc holds his index fingers to the sides of his head like two horns and scrapes his toe over the wooden floorboards, baying and panting. And, in spite of what happened in the woods just a few moments ago, I laugh.

Alfie laughs too. Then he climbs on to his daddy's lap and grabs Luc's fake antlers. And Luc pretends to impale his marshmallow hands until Alfie has to dive for cover, burying his face in Luc's thick jumper. When he reappears, he sticks his fingers in his daddy's mouth and Luc pretends to eat them, huffing and puffing through his nose, saying, '*Miam miam!*'

And then all of us are giggling.

That's the thing about having a child – they make you hark back to your own childhood and rediscover your innocence, find laughter and pleasure in the silly things, and not take life so seriously.

I can be guilty of that: taking life too seriously.

Alfie tugs at Luc's beard while I stroll around his desk and stare out of the cabin window at the lake. The water is clouded behind my pale reflection, distorted by the hand-blown glass of the paned window. But the lake, beautiful as it is, doesn't keep my attention for as long as it usually would. I'm drawn to the break in the trees. And it's only through the dark arc of my chestnut hair that I can clearly make out the path that leads into the woods. I feel stupid now. Frightened by a deer.

This cabin is miles from anywhere, which is why Luc rents it. He stayed here two years ago when he was editing the final draft of his first novel. We didn't have Alfie then and I didn't join him. I couldn't get the time off work. If I'm honest with myself, I didn't really try.

This year he's working on the first draft of his second book, and I pressed harder for a sabbatical so I could take care of Alfie while he focused on his writing. Up until now, childcare has been Luc's job.

His first novel sold enough copies to earn back his advance – just – which retained his publisher's interest. But now he's under the pressure of the sophomore slump: the expectations of a second novel set too high by the success of the first. And he wears it on his sleeve as he does all his emotions. It's one of the things I love most about him: I never have to guess how he's feeling.

Luc calls himself 'Maggie's little investment' because I've supported him for the past ten years. Neither of us expected writing to be so time-consuming or to pay so little. But earning a living as a writer isn't a short-term gig; we understand that now. And Luc will need a decent backlist before he can expect to make anything like his solicitor's salary.

I'd like to get out of the rat race too, start my own business as a consultant, but someone has to feed us. This six-month sabbatical is good for both of us: it's giving me the time I need to think about what I want for my own future, and I'm able to help Luc. Keep him buoyed up. Stop him worrying about anyone's expectations and remind him to just enjoy the writing as much as he did the first time. And, all that aside, who could wish for more than their own cosy lakeside cabin in their very own private wood? Well...not our very own... Not yet anyway. It belongs to John, a friend of Luc's, but he's getting tired of the rental administration and is thinking of selling it. I can't countenance the idea of anyone owning it but us.

'How are you getting on?' I ask, my attention still on the path.

'Struggling,' Luc says. 'This is the hard part. Plotting is fun, so it's difficult to tear yourself away from that and face the graft of actually putting words on a page. Five hundred and thirty-seven down, only 89,463 to go.'

'You'll do it. You always do.'

Luc sets strict deadlines, writes to daily word counts, and won't leave this room until he's hit his target. I respect him for that and trust him to get the draft finished and submitted in time. This is actually the third novel he's written; he couldn't even get an agent for the first one, let alone a publisher. But they say most novelists have an unpublished manuscript or two hiding under their bed. I guess it's like any job in the arts: you can't play piano without bumming a few notes, and you don't become a virtuoso without years of practice. They say a writer has to write a million words before they even find their voice, and, with so many rewrites, Luc's easily done that by now. I know this book will be a success; he's a good writer.

Movement in the treeline catches my eye and my heart skips a beat. That strange encounter in the woods has me on edge. I don't like this feeling. I'm not a naturally nervous woman; it takes a lot to get me rattled. But something feels wrong suddenly. Changed irrevocably. As if the three months of peaceful days we've enjoyed lie behind that moment in the woods, and something else lies ahead.

The undergrowth moves again. I rest my palms on the windowpanes and claw the glass as if I can pull apart the stems and leaves and uncover what's hiding in the bracken.

Just like before, I feel as if we're being watched.

The sun reflects my pale face in the glass like a white mist over the watcher, so I move closer until the prominent bones in my cheeks fade away and the sharp angles of my upper lip disappear, the glass cooling the tip of my nose. Half-expecting an animalistic brute to crawl out of the undergrowth – wild-eyed and unshaven, like some scene from a horror film – I strain my eyes on the quivering bushes. I'm not imagining things. Something's out there.

I jump back from the glass when the bushes spring apart and reveal . . . Cairo. Finally she's come back from her hunting expedition through the woods.

I exhale.

She stops at the lake for a long drink before skipping across the stones towards the cabin. Her tail spins in circles as she runs; she's clearly pleased with herself, almost smiling. Realistically, I can't imagine her killing anything. So I don't know what she would do if she ever caught up with her quarry. She caught a baby rabbit once and just stood there, holding it gently between her jaws. I had to prise them open. And when I placed the little thing on the path it just sat there, either stunned or oblivious to the danger, and I had to shoo it into the undergrowth.

'These damn boots,' says Luc.

'Damboots,' Alfie repeats in bubble-talk.

I turn to find Luc struggling to hold Alfie on his lap while pulling off one of his bright yellow wellies. So I move away from the window, kneel down on the floor, and tug.

'They're too tight,' Luc says.

'His toes aren't touching the tips.' I tug some more. 'They're just tight round the ankles.'

'Vas-y! Tire! Plus fort!' Luc pulls Alfie playfully in the opposite direction while I pretend he's the rope in our tug of war. 'Heave!'

The welly gives way and I throw myself backwards, dramatically clutching it to my chest and breathing heavily as if the feat was all too much. Alfie lets out a full-belied bubble-laugh and Luc tickles him.

I get to my knees, give my brow a melodramatic wipe and say, 'I don't think I've got it in me to go again.'

'Buddy...' Luc grabs Alfie's right knee and lifts his leg in the air. 'It seems you're going to have to live in this one.'

'King Alfred the MonoWellie.' I bow to my giggling son.

'Here.' Luc lowers Alfie into my lap. 'Let's switch ends.' And he grabs the welly, making a great show of the tug-of-war, wheeling his chair in reverse while Alfie chortles and I heave in the other direction. When the second boot gives way, I roll backwards on to the floor with Alfie in my arms, tickling his tummy.

'Well,' Luc says, 'that's enough fun for one day; I have to get back to it. Those words won't write themselves.' And he upturns the welly and places it on Alfie's head, before spinning back around in his chair.

'Come on, let's leave Daddy in peace.' I lift Alfie on to his feet before struggling on to my own and tucking the wellies under my arm. Then I run my fingers through Luc's hair, tug his head back by the soft roots, and kiss him on the forehead. 'Type, good man, type!' And I shut the study door quietly behind us.

'Stones!' Alfie points across the lounge at the rear window, in the exact opposite direction to the lake.

'We've just got these wellies off!' I hold them out to him. 'Why don't we play inside?'

'Stones!'

I wince at his voice, bright and loud in the cabin's high-ceilinged open-plan living space. The last thing I want to do is go back outside, but I feel guilty enough as it is for interrupting Luc's flow. The last thing he needs now is a screaming tantrum. Not that Alfie is prone to tantrums but, if pressed, I would have to admit that that's largely because he gets his own way most of the time. When you raise a kid while working full-time, you seriously have to pick your battles.

'All right, then.' Reluctantly, I get down on my knees and hold the wellies steady while Alfie uses me as a leaning post, stepping into them one by one. But then the phone rings on the sideboard while he's only half in the second one and I let it go. That'll be Rose. She always calls on a Thursday for a sisterly catch-up. She talks about Nathan, her voice trembling with butterflies of love, and I swear I can almost hear her heart beating through the receiver. And it makes me feel better about being here with Luc and Alfie instead of there with her. I take comfort from knowing she doesn't need me; she has someone else there to take care of her.

Anxious to speak to Rose, I hurry Alfie into the welly, but he steps on the back of it and it collapses. Then he loses his footing, topples over and I just catch him before he falls. By the time I get to the phone the line is dead, the black vintage handset cold and quiet in my palm.

Alfie whines about stones and I glance up the split-level floor to Luc's study door, then back at the phone.

Damn. I really needed to hear Rose's voice.

I scour the shoreline while Alfie, bent down on his haunches, golden-brown hair flopping into his eyes, flicks pebbles left and right. You'd think he was panning for gold, an experienced prospector who knows just what he's searching for.

Because we've skimmed so many stones across the lake over the last few months, finding flat ones gets harder each day. I picture a great pile of them in the centre of the lake, so tall it almost touches the surface. And I fantasise that, one day, I'll skim a stone and it will bounce six times before stopping dead, coming to rest on the top of the pile as though it's floating on the glassy water.

Toeing the shoreline, I spot the perfect pebble and bend to pick it up, smoothing my thumb over its polished surface as I stand. Then I turn it over and over, bouncing it on my palm to assess its weight and viability.

'I've got one!' I announce, and Alfie comes bounding over.

'Do, Mumma, do!'

'Stand back, then. Give Mumma room.'

Alfie does as he's told and I take a few steps closer to the shore. Bouncing from foot to foot, I bend low and arc my arm to and fro to ready myself. Then I snap my arm forward, releasing the stone at just the right moment. It flicks off the surface, skips into the air, and bounces another five times before skimming the last metre and finally sinking.

'Aaay!' Alfie jumps up and down in his cumbersome wellies.

'Your turn.' And I beam at him with a love so strong it creates a physical pain in my chest. Alfie picks up a stone and holds it up to me on his flat palm. His golden eyebrows arc over his questioning eyes, which are a strange combination of ours: flecked brown in the centre like mine, but rimmed with blue like Luc's. 'Looks good,' I say.

And, with the stone approved, he waddles to the waterline. Then, bending down, he sticks out his little bottom and launches himself off his feet while throwing both hands up at the sky. And only when his feet touch the ground again does he let go of the stone, which flies a ruler's length into the air before landing a few centimetres from his right toe.

Yet I clap and laugh. 'You'll be world champion one day! Let's find some more.'

Sauntering away from the waterline, I scan the shore as I go, but all the pebbles are either too big, too small or too jagged. I toe them around, hoping to find just the right one buried beneath the rest. The perfect stone.

There's a loud crack.

Spinning around, I scan the shore for the source of the sound. Alfie's back on his haunches, sifting through pebbles, oblivious to the noise. Through the cabin window, Luc's face is hidden by his computer screen and all I can make out is a mop of thick hair. Cairo's asleep on the cabin's wide wooden porch. Even she didn't stir.

It's as if I'm the only person who heard it.

The sound comes again, like a cracking branch, and I jerk my head to the left, to the break in the trees where the pathway leads into the wood.

Heavy, rasping breaths fill my ears, as loud as my own breathing. And, although it's too far away, I know it's coming from the trees. It can only be my imagination: the frightening memory of this morning.

Nothing moves in the forest but I can't tear my eyes from the shadows between the trunks. One tree in particular steals my attention. Something about it is all wrong, the shadow behind it darker than the rest, as if someone's hiding there.

The shadow moves.

I jump.

Stepping back, my heel catches a stone and I stumble, stagger and then fall on to my backside, but still I don't break my gaze.

It slinks away.

'Come on, Alfie.' I get to my feet and reach a hand out to my son, my voice hardening as he resists. 'We're going back inside.'

34

FOUR

ROSE

'WHERE ARE we going?'

Nathan takes an unexpected exit from the motorway. His anniversary surprise was a weekend away in Winchester and we had lunch at the Hotel du Vin, where we're staying tonight. I thought we were having dinner at the hotel too but Nathan said he wanted to take me out. It's too early for dinner, so I guess we're going for drinks somewhere first.

Given the direction, I'd guessed at another historic town, like Chichester, but now we're heading into the middle of nowhere.

'It's another surprise.' He turns away from the road and grins at me with that movie-star charm. Then he glances back at the road and then at me again before reaching across and tucking my hair behind my ear with a soft and affectionate touch. 'You look beautiful tonight,' he says.

I look down and my hair falls from behind my ear back over my face, hiding flushed cheeks behind the pale strands.

I have no idea where we're going but feel overdressed in this skirt, blouse and kitten heels. Nathan picked it out from the few outfits I brought with me. I hadn't been planning on packing it, but he'd added it to my suitcase at the last minute. He'd bought it for me on a weekend away in Paris. It felt right for Paris. But it doesn't feel right for an English January: too sheer, pale pink and summery. I fiddle with the fine diamonds that encrust the neckline.

Nathan laughs.

'What? What's so funny?'

'You.'

'Me? Why?' I glance sideways at his beaming smile, the perfectly symmetrical laughter lines around his eyes.

'You're so nervous. Anyone would think you'd got into the car with a complete stranger who's driving you into the woods to bump you off and bury you.'

'What, that's not the surprise?'

'Well, if I told you, it wouldn't be a surprise, would it?'

It's been a clear afternoon and now it's almost dark, with scant clouds like smoke above a horizon of burning embers. Wild fields and brush stretch out on either side of the narrow road and the salt smell of the sea drifts in on the air through the grilles. It's surprisingly warm for January, scarily warm actually, the kind of temperature that makes you doubt our planet's future.

'There's a bar all the way out here?' I look around for signs of life.

'After a fashion.'

I stare at him, eyebrows drawn down in suspicion.

'What?' He takes his eyes off the road for a moment to look back at me.

I reach across and gently push his chin away. 'Keep your eyes on the road.'

'There's no one out here.'

'I'd still rather you kept your eyes on the road.'

The wild fields fall away and trees close in on either side, obscuring the sunset. Dusk claws at the windows and I shuffle forward in my seat to peer through the windscreen in search of a sign or a building, some clue as to where we're going. I glance at Nathan but his eyes are now fixed on the single-lane road.

I twist my wedding ring, a new habit that beats chewing my bottom lip. My finger has yet to adjust to its presence, in the same way I have yet to adjust to Nathan's. There's still so much we don't know about each other. A year is a strange length of time in a relationship. Even though we're married now, that feeling of deep trust – which brings with it the peace of reassurance – doesn't simply leach out of the ink on a marriage register or materialise with the forging of a wedding ring.

It comes with time.

It comes with tin, porcelain and pearl. Not paper and cotton.

It's not that I regret getting married so quickly – I couldn't love anyone the way I love Nathan, or be more sure of anyone – but putting this much trust in someone you barely know is like jumping out of an aeroplane, pulling the deployment handle and finding that the chute doesn't open. So you fall like a stone, hoping the automatic release system will kick in, not knowing whether it's going to.

Nathan gives me that feeling of falling, like going over a bridge too fast. That feeling of pure joy and anxiety rolled into one.

If we weren't married I wouldn't worry so much, because the relationship wouldn't have the same gravitas. I'd still be in the plane wondering whether or not to jump. I know marriage is just a societal construct – a ring and a piece of paper – but relationship failures outside of marriage can be dismissed with barely a mention.

Marriage ends with a branding.

A hot D burned into your haunch.

A scar that never goes away.

And I already have one of those.

Marriage made Nathan the focal point of my life, blurring everything else into insignificance. I love him. But I don't love the weight of responsibility, the pressure to live up to the idealised wife he sees when he looks at me. Perhaps I love him too much; I'm not quite myself around him, so afraid of putting a foot wrong and spoiling what we have.

Suddenly, my head is thrown against the headrest and I grab the edge of the seat for support as Nathan puts his foot to the floor and the trees blur past as we accelerate down the narrow lane.

'Nathan! What are you doing?'

He ignores me, his steely eyes on the road.

'Nathan! Slow down!'

He smiles and accelerates instead.

The treeline ends sharply and the road opens up on to a paved area. A small, empty car park. But I only catch a glimpse of that before it's behind me. To my left, a high grassy bank obscures the red sun and leaves little light to make out my surroundings.

It takes a moment for my eyes to adjust.

To my right, the road falls away suddenly: a boat slipway that descends into the sea. On either side, it's banked by fifteen-foot-high stone jetties, bastions that have weathered the waves for years. Nathan brakes hard and the seatbelt cuts between my breasts as I'm hurled forward. Then he spins the wheel to the right and I'm thrown against him as the back tyres drift across the concrete. And before I've had a moment to compose myself he accelerates again, heading straight for the jetty that runs along the left side of the slipway. It's barely wider than the car, with a steep drop on either side of us.

And directly in front of us there's a five-metre plunge into the ocean.

'Nathan!' I scream, grabbing the seat edge with one hand and bracing myself against the roof with the other, as we fly towards the drop-off at full speed.

Then, at the last second, Nathan slams on the brakes and the car comes to a stop so close to the edge that I can't even see the concrete beneath the bonnet.

Only dark water.

My heart slams against my ribs, thrums my ears and pulses in my throat, a percussive accompaniment to Nathan's laughter. Then he switches the headlights to full beam and illuminates the black sea.

It's crowded with white swans.

As quickly as the last embers of sunlight burn out, the moon rises above the water while we dangle our legs over the edge of the jetty. Nathan brought a thick fur rug for the ground and a warm blanket to huddle under. A winter picnic is certainly a surprise, just as the picnic in the park was a year ago. And luckily, just as it was the first time, the evening is unusually mild: nine or ten degrees.

If I didn't know any better, I'd think he controlled the weather.

I look out across the chequerboard of white birds on the black water and say, 'I didn't think swans swam in the sea.'

'Why not?'

'I don't know. Salt water.'

'Oh, Rose! You're so funny. You think they'll rust?'

My cheeks burn and I turn away, pretending to survey the contents of the basket Nathan has laid down on the rug behind us. I help myself to what looks like a smoked salmon sandwich, clear my throat and ask, 'Where did you get the picnic?'

'The hotel made it up for us.'

'I don't suppose they get many requests for picnics in January.'

'I did have to ask twice.' He surveys the basket too and pulls out a truckle of cheddar wrapped in black wax. Needing

39

a plate to cut it on, he struggles with the leather straps that hold them in place on the underside of the basket's lid. The buckles are fancy but fiddly and he swears under his breath.

'Leave it, baby.' I take his hand and squeeze it gently. 'I'll do it for you.' And, with a little more patience than he has, I manage to free the plates and cutlery from their straps. The hotel didn't think to include a cheese knife and getting through a wax coating with a dinner knife is clearly going to be a challenge, so I do that for Nathan as well.

'Thanks.' He transfers pieces of cheese to his plate as I slice them.

'How did you even know this place was here?' I hold my hand over my mouth as I speak through a bite of sandwich.

Nathan smiles, a little painfully, waiting for me to swallow before he answers. As if he can't speak while my mouth is full. 'I lived in Petersfield for a few years and worked at QA just up the road. I used to come here after work sometimes for a bit of peace and quiet.'

'A friend of mine works at QA. She's a medical secretary. I haven't seen her for ages, I wonder if she's still there.'

'I'm sure she would have called you if she'd wanted to see you.'

'Maybe. But you know what life is like. It gets in the way.'

'In my experience, people who really care about you make the effort to stay in touch.' He takes the half-eaten sandwich from my hand and rests it on the pile in the basket. 'Like me.' He runs a hand over my thigh, around my waist and on to the small of my back, then eases me down on to the blanket. 'I would never let life get in the way of seeing you.' And then he leans over and kisses me, pulling the blanket up and over our shoulders.

'You're so beautiful, Rose.' He straddles me, kissing my neck. 'I remember the first time I saw you at the hospital. I couldn't take my eyes off you.' He runs a hand up under my skirt, finds the strap of my G-string and pulls it down over my hip. 'It took so much restraint not to take you on our first date. I thought I was going to die of deprivation.'

I break away from the kiss, push him back gently and look around. It's not that late and it is a public slipway. 'Not here, Nathan.'

He lifts himself up on his palms and looks around. 'Why? There's no one here.'

'Someone might come.'

He laughs. 'Yes – you. And there won't be any *might* about it.'

Before I know it my panties are off and a few moments later he's inside me. The cold stone seeps through the rug, chilling my back, as Nathan rocks in and out of me, slowly, taking his time. His thick blond hair falls forward over his face, which is tanned and blemish-free. And instead of concentrating on the moment I find myself wondering if he's ever had a zit in his life. The perfectly proportioned features of his broad face are so well defined, it's as if he was crafted from fine bone china instead of mashed together from cells and chromosomes like the rest of us. I often find myself staring at him.

This is exciting for him.

He likes making love in public places where there's a chance of getting caught: cars, aeroplanes, hospital bathrooms. But I can't relax and it takes longer to get in the mood.

I talk to the Rose inside me, the timid girl who frets too much, and tell her not to be so unadventurous. She's such a worrywart. And so ordinary compared to this man who'd never let a little cold weather or the chance of a passer-by put a stop to a romantic picnic. I should be more grateful for having so much excitement and adventure in my life; if it weren't for Nathan, I would never do anything like this.

So the timid girl wraps her arms around his neck and her legs over his. And she kisses him deeply, darting her tongue in his mouth as if she's as thrilling and sexy as him. The kind of woman he thinks she is. When she finally comes, she glimpses Nathan's satisfied smile before he lets go of all restraint and comes too.

And when he does, she feels like his prize.

FIVE

MAGGIE

'Mumma?'

'Yes, sweetie?'

'Sock.' Alfie has pulled his dinosaur slipper off and is pointing at his big toe, which pokes through a hole in the well-worn fabric. His toenail, in desperate need of clipping, makes me squirm; I hate cutting his nails. Once, I didn't realise I'd caught his skin between the blades, and, when I pressed down, he screamed out in so much pain that I still hear it every time I pick up the clippers. I can't help but picture its bladed teeth biting through his precious skin and blood spurting out.

'Sock!' He points, more urgently this time.

'It's all right, sweetie. Come on, we'll get you another pair.' I hold out a hand to help him up off the lounge rug but he slaps it away and rolls on to his knees. Sticking his bottom in the air, he struggles to his feet, and only then reaches out his hand as he waddles after me.

Alfie doesn't like being carried upstairs any more. With one hand he grips the banister spindle and, with the other, holds my hand. He grunts as he struggles to lift his weight up each step then totters like a drunk before composing himself enough to take the next one. It's slow going. As is the case with everything in my life now, even the smallest tasks take hours.

Luc has far more patience than I do. And I'm not sure whether that's from eighteen months of practice or whether he's just a better person than I am.

In Alfie's bedroom, I take the baby nail clippers from the top drawer and catch my reflection in his stegosaurus mirror. I've always had deep-set eyes, hooded and dark, but they look more sunken than usual. I'm cold, stiff, and tired. Leaning over the dresser, I stare between my eyebrows, which are crying out to be tinted and plucked. There's a swollen lump as if I've been hit with a baseball bat and I push my fingertips into the flesh, wincing at the bruised bone. I try to remember banging my head over the previous days, on one of the kitchen cupboard doors perhaps, or one of the low beams in the bedroom.

'Sock!' Alfie shouts from behind me.

So I turn away from the mirror and rummage through the drawer for a clean, hole-free pair. I thought I'd packed dozens to last the winter months but the only ones left are either too small or greying; his feet have gone through a growth spurt.

Settling on the best of a bad bunch, I lead Alfie to our bedroom, knowing the long-winded task of cutting his toenails will be easier if he can stretch out on our big bed.

I stop in the doorway.

Our bedroom's in darkness, exacerbated by the red cedar walls and low, beamed ceiling. Without thinking, I rub my thumbs over my fingers and recall the soft tartan fabric as I pulled the curtains open only a few hours ago, the muscle memory still stored in my fingertips.

I definitely opened them.

44

Luc must have come upstairs and closed them while we walked Cairo around the lake this morning. Maybe he took a nap and forgot to open them again. Does he do that often – sneak away from his desk while I'm out with Alfie and Cairo and go back to bed just hours after getting up? Then pretend he's been working all morning?

That doesn't sound like Luc. He's such a grafter.

Unable to navigate in the darkness, I have to turn on the light before opening the curtains. The woollen fabric caresses my fingers like *déjà vu*.

But I cast the sinking feeling aside, lift Alfie on to the bed, and remove his bright red socks. I have to pretend there's a farm animal hiding under each toenail, otherwise he won't sit still long enough for me to clip them. And who can blame him after I cut him? First there's a pig, then a cow, then a cockerel. And I have to make the noises for each one as I clip.

'These'll have to do for now.' I stretch a greying white sock on to his left foot.

I'm about to start on the other foot when Alfie screams, 'No!' and pulls the first sock off.

'Well, it's these or the ones with the hole.'

Alfie grabs his red socks, balled up on the patchwork quilt, and thrusts them at me. So I concede, switching them around so the hole is near his little toe instead of his big. Pick your battles, I remind myself.

'Maggie!' Luc's panicked voice reverberates up the staircase and I grab Alfie under the armpits, manoeuvring him on to my hip before running for the door. 'Maggie!'

Bolting down the stairs with a struggling Alfie, who's wailing because he wants to do it himself, I throw back the door to Luc's study, breathless. 'What?'

'My computer crashed, and when it booted back up it had this on the screen.'

I glance at the black glass, emblazoned with a grey utilities box and an option for a system reinstall. Then I turn back to my husband and glare at him. 'Jesus Christ, Luc. I thought someone had died!'

'*Putain de merde!* Somebody has! My whole bloody novel!'

'I thought you said you'd only written a thousand words or something.'

'Who gives a fuck about a thousand words!?'

'Luc!' I put a hand over Alfie's ear and press his head to my chest to shield the other. 'We agreed! No more swearing. He repeats every word!'

'Sorry. I meant, who gives a duck about a thousand words? There's six months of planning on there. All my research, character outlines, setting descriptions, photographs. Not to mention the entire ducking plot outlined scene by scene. That *is* the whole book! Without it I can't write a pram word.'

'Pram,' says Alfie.

'Well, where's your back-up?' I scan the room for the bright red external drive but can't see it anywhere, and when I turn back to Luc he's sheepish. 'Jesus, Luc. I bought you that drive so you could back up your work. You didn't do it?'

He shakes his head.

'Not even once?!'

He shakes his head again.

'Get up. Take Alfie.' I bundle him into Luc's arms, plonk myself down in his swivel chair, and hold down the power button to reboot the system. 'As an intelligent ex-solicitor, you really should be ashamed of yourself.'

'What can I tell you? I was a terrible solicitor. Hence the ex.'

The system chimes as it powers on and I hold down the shift key to boot it into safe mode before bringing up a terminal window to try a disk repair. Luc leans over my shoulder as I type, white text filling the black screen every time I press Enter on a command.

'Do you actually know what any of that gobbledygook means? Or are you just typing in random words to impress me?'

'It's a file system check and repair, Luc, not an operating system recode.'

'It looks like an operating system recode to me.'

'The disk's failed.'

'What!? You mean I've lost it all?'

'Possibly. I'll take it out, put it in my machine, and see if I can recover anything. That'll be faster than making a thumb drive to boot from. And since we'll have to replace the disk anyway, I may as well just get on with it. You're lucky we have the spare.'

'All I heard was thumb and boot. It sounds complicated.'

'Not complicated, just time-consuming. You'll have to keep an eye on Alfie for the afternoon.'

Luc's eyes droop. He looks fried.

'Don't look at me like that. If you'd backed up your work, you'd be on my machine by now tapping away while I replaced the drive for you.'

'We need internet out here. Then it would have backed it up to the cloud like it does at home.'

'Well, you wanted a remote place to work. That's what the external drive was for.'

'How could I know the disk was gonna fail?'

'For duck's sake, Luc, how many times have I told you which part gets replaced most often in a computer?'

'Never. You have never said *anything* like that.'

I laugh and then sigh. 'Look, it's got to be done so let's not waste any more time. You take Alfie out to the lake and I'll get to work.'

❧

By the time I've fetched the tools from my desk in the bedroom and a towel from the linen cupboard to protect the iMac's screen while disassembling it, Luc's already skimming stones with Alfie.

47

I stand there for a while, towel over my shoulder, staring out of the window, distracted. It's so perfect here. Everything is just as it should be.

I used to love my job. I thought I had it all: a challenging and well-paid career with a stay-at-home husband. Not many women have that kind of opportunity; it's usually the man who's the primary wage-earner, so then it makes sense for the woman to stay at home. But I'd always struggled with that idea. After Dad died, Mum fell apart. She's just like Rose: too gentle, too fragile. So it fell to me to take care of us all.

I didn't want to be a mother any more; I'd done it for too long. But I still wanted a child. Luc made all that possible. But now, I realise how much I've missed out on. And if I had my way I'd never go back. Luc would make enough money from this second book to support us all and we'd stay here forever: him writing, me being a mother again.

Luc skims a stone across the lake but it only bounces twice before sinking. He's releasing it too soon.

Every once in a while I imagine what life might be like with a strong, masterful man. Someone like Rose's new husband, Nathan. Someone who looked after me instead of the other way around. He'd be tall. Well dressed. Muscular. Strikingly intelligent and powerful.

Of course it wouldn't last five minutes. Unlike Rose, I'm not the type of woman who needs looking after. Within months we'd be at each other's throats, each of us convinced we knew what was best. Luc's helplessness is frustrating sometimes, but I wouldn't want him any other way.

As I watch, he grabs his sweater by the neckline, pulls it up over his head and chases Alfie around the shore, pretending to be a headless monster.

I giggle.

Luc's always in cords and soft knitted jumpers, and my palms warm at the thought of cuddling up to him later in front of the wood burner.

48

'Perfect.' I say out loud to myself. 'At least, he would be if he backed up his fucking computer.'

Laying the towel over his desk, I flip the iMac on its back and set about unscrewing the RAM access door at the base of the machine. But, as I'm mounting the suction cups to remove the glass, I glance out the window.

I can't see Luc or Alfie any more.

Scanning the lakeshore, I lean across the desk to get a better view through the window. They aren't anywhere in sight. Then something else catches my eye. At the head of the path, close to the treeline, almost camouflaged by his surroundings, stands a figure.

A man.

Am I mistaken? The path is a long way from the cabin so, from my spot at the window, he's no more than a shape.

No. I'm not mistaken.

It's definitely a man.

I blink, focusing my eyes like a telephoto lens to take in the details over this distance. Dressed in a khaki rain mac, he leans against a tree by the side of the path. Even though it's a fine day, the hood of his mac is up, and where there should be a face there's only a black, shadowed oval.

It stares directly at me.

SIX

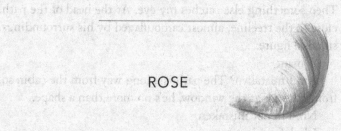

ROSE

'HERE AGAIN, Dr Sharif?'

I step into Daisy's room with the butterflies I've had all morning at the thought of seeing her. Only her curtains are drawn and the nurse's rubber soles squeak softly from inside. Saeed sits in the chair closest to the door – the chair I usually sit in – waiting patiently. She must be running late today; Daisy's physiotherapy is usually finished by now.

Popular culture would have you believe that being in a coma is like taking a long nap, but the reality is that caring for Daisy is a staggering amount of work for the nurses. Along with physio to prevent muscle atrophy and stiffness, she needs regular bed baths, catheter and nutrition bag changes, bed linen changes, and she needs to be moved every two hours to prevent bed sores. In three years, Daisy's never had a bed sore because her care is so scrupulous and regimented. Despite the mundanity of the tasks, the nurses treat her with dignity and respect, as if she's a member of their family.

And, after being here so long, she no doubt feels like one.

I was aiming for airy, cool and carefree as I breezed into the room. As if it wouldn't have bothered me one way or the other whether Saeed was here. But when you suffer from idiopathic craniofacial erythema – chronic blushing – pretence is impossible.

Despite also being fair, Nathan never blushes, and I'd love to be able to control and conceal my emotions the way he does. You can have surgery for chronic blushing and it did cross my mind when I was in my twenties, unable to control it and suffering with social anxiety as a result. But the side effects are too frightening to consider.

It was actually my friend at Queen Alexandra Hospital – the one I lost touch with – who helped me through it. She was the only person who had realised that my strange behaviour in public – ending conversations rudely and abruptly, or suddenly checking my mobile and feigning an emergency to get myself out of a room – were because I was embarrassed by my condition. One day, she took a video of me while saying the most embarrassing things to me until my face was on fire, and then played it back to me. When I saw it, I realised it felt far worse inside than it looked on the outside. And, once I knew that, I knew that I just needed to keep it under control and, beneath make-up, people would barely notice.

That was when I learned self-hypnosis techniques. I cut off all my hair, too, into a long pixie cut that's razored at the base of my neck. It helps keep me cool when I start overheating.

'Here again.' Saeed gets up like an old-school gentleman. And even though he doesn't appear to notice – or pretends not to notice what's written all over my face in red ink beneath this make-up – for a brief moment I struggle to look him in the eye.

The physio nurse throws back the curtains, smiles at each of us in turn and leaves. It's then that I notice the second chair on the far side of the bed. Saeed's already moved it into the same position as last week. I point at them in turn.

'You knew I'd be here?'

'You said so, last week. You do not remember? You were surprised that we had never met on a Thursday before. So I gathered...I hoped that you would come.'

'I hoped you'd be here too.' I drop my handbag on the floor and take my usual seat, still warm from Saeed's presence. 'Like you said last week, it's easier to talk to someone than keep up a one-way conversation with Daisy.'

He walks around the bed and takes his usual seat but there's something off about his demeanour, the way he sits, as if his body's weighed down by heavy stones and he has to take the chair more cautiously than usual.

'Is something wrong? You seem sad.'

'I had to say goodbye to a friend this morning. She is moving away. Well...an old patient, actually. But she became a good friend.'

'The one you exorcised?'

'Yes... Well, not exactly. It is complicated.'

He doesn't want to talk about it, or he can't talk about it, so I just ask, 'Will she be all right?'

'She will. Eventually.' He's lost in thought for a moment, then says, 'I checked Daisy's chart. They did another EEG yesterday and her brain activity is still strong.'

'They haven't removed the breathing tube, though.'

'No, but I expect they will soon. Try not to worry.'

'Why haven't you taken another patient to fill this spot? There isn't much you can do for Daisy now.'

'It is not only my patients' conscious minds I am interested in. I like to keep an eye on them whether they are asleep or awake.'

'But she can't be paying you now, surely? Is she going to wake up to an enormous therapy bill?'

He laughs. 'Of course not. It is not about the money. Until Daisy has recovered, she is my responsibility. I feel responsible for...'

His voice trails off and I know exactly what he feels responsible for because I feel it too. 'You can't make people want to live, Dr Sharif. They have to want it too.'

'Saeed, please.'

'Saeed… I worry that, even if it was an accident, Daisy doesn't have the *will* to live. Most people either die from the injuries that put them in the coma in the first place or wake up within a few weeks or months. When Daisy first came in, they caught the swelling in her brain and operated quickly. Her scans don't show any damage and you said yourself that they're unchanged. So why is she getting worse? Why didn't she wake up the moment they treated her injuries and stabilised her blood glucose? I think it's because she doesn't want to be here any more, no matter what she told you. I worry that what she meant by finding happiness was taking her own life.'

I remember finding her that day. Drugged up on sleeping pills and on the border of a diabetic coma, Daisy had fallen. Her head smashed straight through her glass coffee table. There was so much blood. If I hadn't stopped by… I had to put a brick through her patio door.

'I worry about that too,' Saeed says. 'After I saw you last week, I went back over Daisy's notes to see if I had written down exactly what she said. She did not say she had found happiness again, as I thought. Her precise words were that she had found *a way* to be happy again. But I am reluctant to even consider that an overdose – or a diabetic coma – was what she meant by that.'

'If that's the case, I feel selfish for wanting her to live. I want it for myself. But if she doesn't… God, I don't want to let her go.'

My phone pings in my handbag and I reach down for it. It's Nathan.

My dainty Rose. We have only been apart for seven hours but it feels like seven years. Your Doctor of Love xxx

I read it from the lock screen and put the phone face down on the blanket without responding.

'Please,' Saeed says, 'if you want to reply...'

'I will in a bit.'

'How was the surprise?' he asks.

'Surprise?'

'Your anniversary. You said your husband had a surprise for you.'

'Oh, yes.' I twiddle Daisy's curls while I talk. Now it's no longer subjected to dyes, blow-dryers and straighteners, her tangerine hair shines. 'He took me to Winchester for the weekend. It was lovely.'

'It is a beautiful city. I think that Oxford and Winchester are two of the most beautiful cities in England, do you not agree?'

'I do now. I hadn't been to Winchester before. It was smaller than I expected but I liked that. I find Oxford too busy sometimes. Too many people. And don't get me started on London.' I shiver at the thought of the crowded streets.

My phone pings again, reminding me of the unopened text from Nathan, but I leave it face down on the blanket.

'I know what you mean,' he says. 'I am far more comfortable one-to-one than around a lot of people.'

'Me too. Nathan's colleagues' wives are all social animals. They're constantly organising get-togethers, which I obligingly agree to and then dread the moment they arrive. Nathan keeps suggesting I organise another one myself, but I nearly had an aneurysm the first time. And these women all have high-powered careers. I have all day to organise parties and they still put me to shame. It's so humiliating; I have no idea how they manage it.'

'I think you will find that most people are like ducks on a pond: underneath, their feet are doing this.' He paddles his hands frantically and I laugh.

'I guess some people are just better at hiding it.'

My phone pings with another message and I scan it in my peripheral vision while trying to keep my attention on Saeed. 'Sorry. I've always judged people who look at their phones constantly while someone's trying to have a conversation with them. It's so rude. And now I'm doing it.'

'It is really no problem. Please...' He gestures towards my phone and I pick it up, reading the message properly.

> My blushing Rose. It makes my day when I hear from you. My heart skips a beat every time you reply to one of my messages. Your Doctor of Love.

'He is very attentive,' Saeed says.

I nod. 'Sometimes I think I'm all he thinks about. I wonder how he gets any work done. I'll reply in a little while. I'm here for Daisy now. I think our visits help her. I wonder if she can hear us. Do you think she can?'

'It is hard to know. Many patients are misdiagnosed as PVS—'

'PVS?'

'Persistent vegetative state.'

My chest tightens and my mouth turns down.

'Sorry. It is a dreadful term, I agree. But it is *persistent*, not *permanent*, and that is the word to cling to. A study ten years ago found that as many as fifty per cent of PVS patients are misdiagnosed. They are treated as such when they are, in fact, acutely aware of everything around them.'

'Like locked-in syndrome?'

'Exactly.'

I reach across the bed and touch his arm, anxious for him to confirm what I've hoped for for so long.

'Do you think Daisy might be locked in? Do you think she might be aware of her surroundings, able to hear everything we're saying?'

55

'It is entirely possible. As I said last week, I will not even discuss my patients with her in case she can hear me.'

'I'd better watch what I say as well, then.'

'I do not imagine you have many secrets from Daisy.'

'That's true, I don't. She knows everything about me. Or at least, she did.'

Saeed and I jump as the door swings open and we both turn to find Nathan standing there. He looks at us, then at the bed, and I follow his gaze to my hand, still resting on Saeed's arm. It slips away as we both get to our feet. And suddenly, no amount of make-up or self-hypnosis can arrest the blood flow to my face. My chest warms, my neck flushes and my cheeks burn. I brush back my hair and lift my face to the imaginary cool breeze but it does nothing. I try to redirect the heat to my hands by pretending I'm warming them by a fire, but none of the techniques I've learned have any effect. My face must look like an advert for a dubious establishment in Amsterdam. And, combined with my hand on Saeed's arm, at the very least a misleading advert for something clandestine going on between us.

I'm about to tell Nathan *it's not what it looks like* when I realise that will only make it worse.

'Nathan,' I say. 'This is Dr Sharif. He was treating Daisy before…'

Saeed takes a few steps in Nathan's direction, reaching out his hand, but when Nathan doesn't take it he lets it drop to his side. Nathan looks him up and down, glaring at his grey kurta, black cotton trousers and leather sandals, the lack of hospital scrubs conspicuous. It's exactly what I did when Saeed said he was a doctor. But only someone who knows Nathan very well would notice the subtle curl of his lip. It's not something I've ever seen before.

'Treating Daisy for what?' Nathan asks. 'Who are you?'

'I am Dr Sharif.'

'I didn't ask your name. I asked who you are.'

'Nathan,' I say sweetly, 'Saeed is Daisy's psychotherapist.'

Nathan still doesn't offer Saeed his hand. 'Dr Sharif, is it? I think you'll find psychotherapy more effective when the patient is conscious.'

Saeed's grey eyes darken.

I say, 'Dr Sharif thinks it's helpful for Daisy to hear familiar voices, Nathan. We've been talking to her.'

'That's very kind of you,' Nathan says. 'Are you being paid to continue Daisy's treatment?'

'I am not here to collect. And, until Daisy decides she is no longer in need of my services, she is still my patient.'

'You're far too generous, Dr Sharif. Perhaps you should bill me here at the hospital; I'm happy to pay for her treatment. I wouldn't want you to be out of pocket.'

'Thank you. But I am here of my own free will and, given there is little I can do for Daisy other than be a familiar voice, I would not feel comfortable taking money for my services.'

'I insist. Rose...are you heading home now?'

'I've only just got here.'

'I was hoping you might pick up my dry-cleaning. I need the blue pinstripe for a staff meeting tomorrow. It's not too much trouble, is it?'

'No, of course not.'

'Thank you, darling.' He kisses me on the lips, lingering. 'It was nice to meet you, Dr Sharif.' And this time he shakes Saeed's hand before leaving us in the room's suddenly oppressive silence.

57

SEVEN

MAGGIE

I BANG ON the window, hoping that Luc and Alfie are just out of sight and they'll hear me. That they'll see the man. And Luc won't be able to say it's a stag or my overactive imagination because he's right there, watching us from between the trees.

I expect him to run at the sound of my knuckles rapping the glass, but he doesn't even stir. He just stands there.

The minutes lengthen as the man and I stare at each other until I can't take it any more. I bolt from Luc's study, jump the two steps to the lounge, and grab the shotgun from its high rack above the fireplace. Then I throw back the cabin door so hard it crashes into the log wall, strains on its hinges and swings back in my direction. So I slam my palm against it and march on to the deck – where Luc and Alfie sit on the steps, tickling Cairo's tummy.

'Maggie?' Luc turns. 'What the fu— duck?'

'It's not a stag.' I leap from the deck. 'It's a man.'

And I brandish the shotgun, cradling it between my ribs and elbow as I stride away from Luc and Alfie.

'Maggie! What the hell?'

My feet crunch the shingle as I round the cabin, mounting the gun when I get a clear view of the trees, pointing the barrel in the stranger's direction. But then my footsteps slow.

There's nobody there. Just a gnarly old tree.

Little by little, the barrel slips through my palm until it's resting feebly by my side, muzzle-down in the stones. Luc comes to stand behind me, staring over my shoulder in the direction I'd been aiming the gun.

'There's nothing there,' he says.

'There was! A man. He was right there. Next to that tree, to the right of the path.'

'Are you sure?'

'Of course I'm sure! I'm not bloody blind.'

'Buddy,' says Alfie.

'Shit,' I whisper under my breath. I hadn't realised he was right behind us.

Luc's full of mirth. 'We agreed, no more swearing. You know he repeats every word.'

I turn on him, pointing behind me at the path. 'I swear it, Luc. He was standing right there, watching us.'

'That's almost fifty metres. You wouldn't know the difference between a man and a tree from that distance, let alone whether he was watching us.'

Luc's right. I can't be sure that he was looking in our direction, at the cabin, at us.

At me.

But, crazy as it sounds, I *felt* it. I've read in books, dozens of times, how a person's eyes can bore into you, pierce right through you. But I've never actually experienced it. Not like that. The weight of his stare was like being buried alive beneath six feet of earth. And I wanted – needed – to claw my way out of it, away from it.

59

No lifeless tree would make you feel like that.

'Besides,' Luc adds, 'we're miles from anywhere. There are no trails. Any hiker would have had to wander fifteen miles in the wrong direction and scale the forest fence. And even then – what...? He was that lost but didn't ask for directions?'

'He isn't lost.'

'Maggie! You can't know that. Unless you think you know who he is?'

I look at him but don't say anything.

'You think it's Ryan, don't you?'

Again I don't speak.

'You honestly think Rose's ex-husband would come all the way out here just to stalk you? Maggie! Seriously! If Ryan had a problem with anyone it would be with Nathan, not you.'

'He just got out of prison, did you know that? Early release for good behaviour.'

'How do you know?'

'Rose told me.'

'You spoke to her?'

'Last week. She phoned. The guy's a psycho, Luc. He won't have forgiven me for getting Rose out from under his boot. He's always hated me because I knew what he was from the start. And because I was there for her at the end.'

'Maggie – if Ryan wanted to hurt you, he wouldn't linger around in the trees. You know what he's like. The guy's temper's so quick, it doesn't even have a fuse. Do you think the isolation might be—'

'Don't even go there, Luc. Isolation? You act like you're not here. Like Alfie's not here. I'm not isolated.'

'I'm not suggesting you're going crazy or anything. It's just that Alfie and I have been playing on the deck for the last fifteen minutes and we didn't see anyone. It was probably just tree branches blowing in the wind.'

Doubt burrows its way in. Luc has been saying things like that a lot lately. That my not having a clear head is a product of spending too much time alone in the woods with only a child for company. And up until now – right up until I saw that tree where I thought the man was standing – I hadn't even entertained the idea that he might have a point. I'm not the kind of person whose mental stability is so fragile that it can be shaken by a little solitude.

I say, 'Maybe you're right.' But I'm not sure who I'm trying to appease.

I'm surprised he's not more bothered by the possible presence of a stalker in the woods. I'm not used to Luc being the grounded one of the two of us. Sure, he's dependable and caring, but he's also a writer, given to fanciful flights of the imagination. His mind is always elsewhere, holed up in his world of fiction, detached from whatever's happening in the real world. I always joke that if the bomb ever went off he'd be wheeling a trolley around Tesco wondering why it was so empty.

Since we came to the cabin at the beginning of November, our roles seem to be slowly and imperceptibly reversing.

That makes me uneasy.

I'm logical. Self-possessed. But is there some truth in what Luc is saying? That I don't realise it's slipping a little more each day, like the bark that peels from the giant eucalyptus behind the cabin. The wind blows it from the trunk strip by strip.

Everything's been so perfect recently that perhaps I haven't noticed the effect that months of isolation can have. Like looking at yourself in the mirror every day, not noticing you're ageing, until one morning, out of the blue, you notice deep pockets in the corners of your eyes, as if your face collapsed overnight.

Luc's been working such long hours on the book. Is it possible that spending so much time with an eighteen-month-old, lacking the stimulation of adult conversation, is turning my brain to mush?

61

I'm not quite myself, I do know that much.

Little cracks are opening up in the perfection of our escape to the woods and real life is peering through. Its sharp eyes remind me that all holidays must come to an end. You have to go back to where you came from, return to who you were. And for me that's a woman in a business suit, commuting to London three days a week to resolve Level-4 service requests that leave even my best engineers stumped and keep me working through the night.

I don't want to go back.

Scrabbling around for my logical self, I say, 'You're right. Who would make it all the way out here? I'm probably still spooked by the noises in the woods the other day.'

'You thought it was your heavy breather, come back to get you?' Luc wraps his arms around my shoulders and pulls me back towards him. 'What were you going to do, shoot him for being out of breath?'

I laugh, but it's empty.

I feel stupid.

But I can't take my eyes off the path.

EIGHT

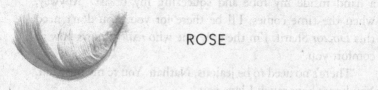

ROSE

'I'M JUST SAYING you came across a bit rude, that's all.' Against my white robe and pale skin, grey circles under my eyes stand out in the mirrored wardrobe door. I turn away quickly, not liking what I see, and unzip the carrier for my silk dress before hanging it on the dressing screen.

'I'm sorry if you thought that.' Nathan buttons his cuffs. 'I didn't think I was rude. On the contrary, I offered to pay the guy just to sit and talk to your sister. I thought that showed incredible restraint. To be so generous to a man I catch you holding hands with.'

'We weren't holding hands. He'd been comforting me and I thanked him for it, that's all. There was nothing in it.'

'Comforting you? Why? Did Dr Anderson say something about Daisy's life support?'

'No. Should he have?'

'No. It's just…he mentioned something to me in passing about it getting to that time…'

'I'll decide when it's getting to that time.'

'You should think about it, Rose – start adjusting to the idea of saying goodbye. If you leave it too long, Dr Anderson will make the decision for you. Besides, three years is a long time and it's a lot of emotional pressure on you to keep visiting her. I know how much you love Daisy but I'm worried about you. Dr Anderson thinks, in the long run, it might be the best thing for both of you.'

I ignore him. I'm not ready to discuss withdrawing life support from Daisy.

Nathan comes over and puts his arms around me, sliding a hand inside my robe and squeezing my breast. 'Anyway, when the time comes, I'll be there for you. You don't need this *Doctor* Sharif. I'm the only one who *really* knows how to comfort you.'

'There's no need to be jealous, Nathan. You're my husband. You know how much I love you.'

'Do I? When you don't reply to my texts because you're too busy holding hands with another man?'

'*We weren't holding hands!* And I didn't reply to your texts because we were talking and I didn't want to be rude.'

His hand stills but he doesn't take it out of my robe. 'So, you don't want to be rude to him, but you don't mind being rude to me?'

'What are you talking about?' I pull away and peel back the carrier from the dress.

'You won't ignore the shrink for the few seconds it takes to send a text, but you're quite happy ignoring your husband for half an hour.'

'I wasn't ignoring you. I was going to reply.'

'When?'

'When we'd finished talking.'

'Which makes him your priority. How am I supposed to feel about that?'

'Nathan, this is silly, we're going in circles.'

I sit down at the dresser. Its mirrored surface is covered in fingerprints, smudges of oil, and tiny hairs from Nathan's goatee. I spin around on the padded seat. 'I just polished this today. If you're going to trim and oil your beard at my dressing table, you could at least clean it up afterwards.'

He ignores me. 'We're going in circles because you won't admit that another man was your priority today.'

'I won't admit it because it's not true. You're *always* my priority and you know that. But Saeed was right there in front of me. Having a conversation with me. And it would have been rude to keep looking at my phone.'

'Well, *some of us* have important jobs. We only have time for a quick text, not hour-long conversations.' He reaches into the wardrobe and pulls out his tan leather brogues. '*Some of us* don't have the luxury of swanning around a hospital wasting time talking to unconscious patients.' Sitting down on the edge of the bed, he unties the lace of one shoe before resting it on the floor and going to work on the next. 'I can't be with you as much as I'd like, Rose. And I rely on those texts to make up for the hours we spend apart.'

'I *know* that.'

'I don't think it's too much to ask my wife to take ten seconds out of her day – out of a conversation with another man – to reply to me before I have to go back into surgery.' He tugs hard at the thin shoelace he's managed to work into a knot. It happens a lot because he takes his shoes off with a boot jack instead of unlacing them. 'For fuck's sake!'

Knowing he's about sixty seconds from hurling the shoe across the room, I get up from the dressing table and go over and sit next to him. At first he won't let go but I ease it from his grip, speaking softly. 'Leave it, baby. I'll do it for you.' With his shoe resting on my lap, I free the knot by twisting the loose ends and then pushing them back into their loops. 'You have to be kind to a knot. You can't pull at it, that just makes it tighter. You have to push it together.'

He takes the unlaced shoe and uses it to point at my expensive silk dress. 'I do nothing but love you, Rose. Buy you beautiful things. I ask for very little in return.'

I go back to the dressing table and scrabble around in the back of the drawer for under-eye concealer and apply that before the rest of the make-up I'm in no mood to wear. 'I know you do a lot for me. And I am grateful. Really I am. But we're going to be late for the party, so let's just forget it, okay?'

'No. I want to get this sorted out now. I'm not going to enjoy the party until you explain why a stranger is more important to you than your own husband who takes care of you.'

'He's not more important. He's just a friend—'

'Oh, he's a friend now? I thought he was just Daisy's therapist?'

'I meant an acquaintance.'

'You just called him a friend. So is he a friend or an acquaintance?'

'An acquaintance.'

'How many times have you met?'

'Twice. One and a half times, since you cut the visit short today.'

'I'm not sure I believe you. You don't call someone you've only met twice a friend. Are you lying to me, Rose?'

'Of course I'm not lying to you. I barely know him.' I blot pale pink lipstick on a tissue. 'I just ran into him when he was visiting.'

'Well, that's exactly my point. Why is he visiting Daisy anyway? Don't you find it weird? He isn't being paid to see her. And you can't counsel a patient who's fucking unconscious. So what the hell is he *really* doing there? It's fishy if you ask me. He's clearly not there to see Daisy, he's there to see you.'

'Don't be silly, Nathan. Saeed's been seeing Daisy every week since she was brought in. He just changed days, that's all.'

66

'That's what he told you. But you don't *really* know that, do you? Have you ever seen him there before?'

'No. But he was there the last two Thursdays of our honeymoon, so I know he didn't switch days for me.'

'You're so naïve, Rose. You'd believe anything anyone told you. You don't understand how men work.'

I get up from the dressing table and reach around Nathan for my dress. 'He's not that sort of man.'

'Okay, so one minute you're telling me you you've only met him twice, and now you're saying you know what sort of man he is?'

Heaving in a shattered breath, I step into my dress and turn my back on him so he can zip it up, only he doesn't. 'Nathan, please. Can we just leave it? We're going to be late.'

'Well, that's hardly my fault, is it? You're the one who's delaying a resolution by evading simple questions. If the shoe were on the other foot, would you believe *me* if I was meeting another woman at the hospital? If you caught me holding hands with her? Would you believe *me* if I told you one thing one minute and something else the next?'

'I don't know, Nathan. Can you please just zip up my dress so we can go to the party?'

Finally he does as I ask, and as I turn away from him and go back to the wardrobe I catch him glaring at his watch. 'You've made us really late,' he says. 'And you've ruined the night for me. But I guess we have to go now we've said we would.'

I close my eyes, suck in another deep breath, and step into my cream leather shoes.

∼

For me, the argument lingers. It's our first, I think. We never disagree on anything. But, despite what he said, for Nathan it's all forgotten. As we step into Amelia's hallway, she takes our coats before running to the kitchen to fix us a drink, and it's as if, for him, it never happened. He exudes the buzz of a party mood. Even in the taxi here, he talked about his day as if what happened in Daisy's room and his grilling me about my relationship with Saeed weren't even part of it.

Relationship.

That's a funny way to think about Saeed; we don't have a relationship of any kind. We aren't even friends, not really. But, as I walk down the long, marble-tiled hallway with Nathan's arm around my waist, I fidget, prickled by an emotion I can't quite nail down.

Guilt?

That's silly, I know. There's nothing going on between me and Saeed, and talking to another man, even one I find attractive, isn't cheating. I find lots of men attractive; it doesn't mean I want to have an affair with them.

But I'd be lying to myself if I didn't admit to understanding some of Nathan's anger. I know why he's suspicious of Saeed.

When Nathan opened that door, he let something escape. We all felt it flee from the room.

After a sweep of the palatial lounge and a glance through the bi-folding French doors into the dining room at the back, Nathan turns to me and says, 'You look beautiful tonight. You're the hottest woman at this party by far. I'm a lucky man.'

'I'm the lucky one.' I reach up on tiptoes to kiss him on the cheek but he turns quickly, catching me full on the lips instead. Then he runs his hands through the short hair at the base of my neck.

'Get a room,' Amelia says, and we part company to accept our drinks as she breezes by.

'Will you be okay for a bit?' Nathan asks. 'If I go and talk to the boys?'

'Of course.' I make my voice light. By *boys*, he means the other heads of department who hang out in the dining room all night, ignoring their wives, drinking whisky and smoking cigars.

I scan the crowd for someone I recognise, someone other than Amelia, someone whose name I might remember. I do try to remember everyone's names but I only ever meet them in situations like this, when there's a house full of people. They group together in small circles according to their husband's department, forming tight cliques that socialise outside of these bigger gatherings.

I've never really noticed it at any of the other parties, but there's not a single man in the lounge. It's not as if there aren't female surgeons and heads of department at the hospital; I guess they just don't get invited. Which is why the spouses congregating in here are all women. They top up the food bowls and refill the glasses. And there's something fifties about it, as if feminism is running late (she's probably still at home arguing with her husband).

I don't have a clique; Nathan doesn't approve of them. He likes me to be sociable with everyone in every department. Which means I ricochet between groups like a pinball, bouncing out of conversations the moment they inevitably turn from small talk to a prior event I wasn't part of.

And the cliques don't mingle, which makes me the sole outsider in every one. And it's easy for them to remember the name of the leech who attaches herself to their clique, but by contrast I have to remember fifty or sixty names from one party to the next. So I flit about, blushing with the sense of my own discourtesy, and using my self-hypnosis techniques every time someone says my name and I don't say theirs in return. I've lost count of how many times someone has said, 'We met at the last head of department social, don't you remember?' Or, 'We met at the Christmas party, were you drunk?'

I usually recall their face. Janet, Jane, Joyce, Josie. It's often something beginning with J. And all I do is apologise and say, 'Jane! Of course! I'm terrible with names.'

And nine times out of ten they'll follow up with, 'Sorry, what do you do again? I can't remember.'

I swear they do remember that I don't work. And I don't think they mean to be condescending – it's really just an opportunity to fake whine about their comparatively frenetic lives with careers they're secretly smug about – but the condescension leaks out: *I can't understand why you don't want to work when it's not as if you have children to look after. I'd be bored out of my skull!*

But I don't have time to be bored. Keeping that enormous house clean and tidy is a full-time job on its own. And then there's the shopping, washing, ironing and cooking as well. A Möbius strip of things to do.

Just like here at the party, feminism has left the building.

Of course these women all have cleaners who strip the beds and do the laundry, but, as Nathan points out, that's a waste of money when we don't need the income from two jobs and my entire salary would go straight to a housekeeper.

Exhausted from another grilling – *but what on earth do you do all day?* – I escape to the kitchen and pour myself a large glass of white.

I've only had five minutes of peace before someone comes into the room. So I quickly turn my back and feign interest in the nibbles to avoid being dragged into another conversation that makes me feel as worthwhile as a shoe shop in the Shire.

'You're Rose, aren't you?'

I paste on a smile as I turn and try not to groan when I'm greeted by a formidable woman in a blue polka-dot vintage dress. It has a red collar and three-quarter-length sleeves and her hair's in a fifties roll.

She looks like a bloody film star.

The dress is slightly loose-fitting, comfortable and classic. And she's serene and relaxed in a pair of red Mary Janes with stack heels. In my stilettos and figure-hugging silk – which shows off every imperfection and makes you suck your stomach in all night – I feel like a Barbie doll by comparison.

'I am.' I reach out my hand and shake hers. 'Nathan's wife. I'm sorry, we've probably met before at one of these things but I'm terrible with names.'

'You're all right,' she says. 'I don't remember half of them either. I'm Penny.'

'Does your husband work at the hospital?'

'No, I do.'

I'm taken aback. 'I didn't think they invited female doctors to these things.'

'They don't. I'm a medical secretary, which is less intimidating for them. And I have the good sense not to try to mix with them. Dr Anderson usually invites me – he has since his wife died. He's one of the good ones. What about you? What do you do?'

'Nothing. I'm a housewife.'

Penny puts down her glass of red, hops up on to the counter and crosses her legs. My cheeks glow at the thought of Amelia coming in and finding someone's bottom on her marble worktop.

'And I can tell by your tone,' she says, 'that you hate every moment of it.'

I shrug.

'So, what's it like? Being married to the legend that is Nathan Winter?'

I laugh, not sure what to say.

'That good, huh?'

'He certainly keeps me on my toes. Are you married?'

'Hell, no! I had a husband once. Got sick of wiping his arse – so to speak – vowed I'd never have another. As far as I can tell, men stopped evolving in the twentieth century.'

'What about Denzel Washington? Barack Obama? Benedict Cumberbatch? Justin Trudeau?'

'Every rule has exceptions.' She takes a swig of wine. 'It doesn't mean it's not the rule. Evolution is a matter of need. Animals evolve when their present circumstances become untenable and change is beneficial. We're expecting men to do the opposite.'

'I've never thought about it that way.' I lean against the worktop, unwinding in her company. 'You're right: why would they evolve from centuries of free sex and slave labour?'

'Exactly. They still want rubber gloves in the kitchen and rubber panties in the bedroom. And I have far better things to do with my time than service some Neanderthal's needs. Suffrage was a hundred years ago! Move the fuck on!' Penny jumps down from the worktop and tops up her wine glass before delving in the fridge for a bottle of white and topping up mine.

'If you think about it that way,' I say, 'it's hardly surprising. Humans have been around, what, five million years? And we've only had a hundred years of equality.'

'Honey, we got the vote; we didn't get equality!' She hops back up on the worktop. 'We're fighting millions of years of male dominance. That history is in our genes as much as it is theirs: we're like salmon returning to spawn. It stains every relationship with an undertone of inequality on both sides. My husband wasn't all that bad, but he still had this instinctive superiority about everything – every decision, every task – it was only slight, but always just enough to tip the casting vote. He was always saying I was intelligent and capable, but three words always hung in the air—'

'For a woman.'

'Exactly. For a woman. Our battle to be acknowledged as equals is fought every day, even with men who claim to believe in equality. It's fought with needles and pins but so damn frequently we still sustain damage over time. I got tired of fighting for my opinion to be acknowledged, let alone heard. And now I'm just too damn old for that shit. Until men evolve or there's a drastic shift in attitude – which isn't likely to happen in my time – I'm much happier alone.' She pauses for a moment then adds, 'Sorry. I got carried away there for a bit. I'll get off my soapbox now.'

'No, it's fine. It's interesting. I've never been alone. I went from my mother's house to my first marriage, and when that ended I lived with my sister for a while before moving back in with my mother for four years. Then I met Nathan. I think being alone would frighten me.'

'Frighten you? What's there to be frightened of?'

I think about it for a moment. 'I don't know. Loneliness, I guess.'

'Honey, you can feel lonely in a room full of people and yet completely satisfied by a pizza, a big glass of wine and a damn good film.'

I laugh caustically. 'You're not wrong. I was lonely here until you came in.'

'They're a cliquey bunch.' She nods at the door. 'I doubt any of them actually enjoy these shindigs, not really. They're as insecure as we are, honey. These parties are like drugs for their insecurities. Don't be fooled by their Pradas and Guccis. They're just Band-Aids on fragility. Do you know those stockings Amelia's wearing cost a hundred pounds? I'm just waiting for her to ladder them.'

'I don't know how she does it, though. Work full-time and still manage to organise events like these.'

'She keeps a chain gang of slaves in the basement.'

I laugh, but it peters away. 'Whenever I come to these things, I go home feeling like a failure.'

'That's because you're being fooled by an illusion. Here...' She jumps down from the worktop again. 'Come on. Follow me.' Taking me by the hand, she drags me to the kitchen door, where she stops and opens it a crack. 'Coast is clear!'

'Where are we going?' I whisper.

'Shhh.' She puts her finger to her lips before dragging me along the hallway towards the stairs.

I pull back. 'We can't go up there.'

'Why not? We'll just say we were looking for the toilet.'

'She won't fall for that. We both know where the toilet is.'

73

'We'll pretend we're too drunk to remember. Come on.'
She drags me up the stairs, across the landing, and then throws
the door open on to Amelia's bedroom.

The sight takes my breath away.

The bed is unmade and there are clothes everywhere: dirty
knickers on the floor, washing basket overflowing, outfits cast
aside, worn and unworn. You can hardly see the carpet. And
the room smells of slept-in sheets that can't have been washed
for weeks. Then she drags me across the room to the en suite,
where the counter is strewn with make-up, the shower glass is
soiled by water marks, and the toilet has an orange rim above
the waterline.

'She's between cleaners,' Penny whispers. 'So...*not* coping
alongside a full-time job after all.'

Amelia's high-pitched voice rings out from behind us.
It trips up the stairwell and Penny grabs me again. 'Quick!
Run!'

And we do, laughing all the way to the landing, where
she leans over the banister to make sure Amelia isn't in the
hall. Then she drags me back downstairs and into the kitchen,
where we fall through the door in a fit of giggles.

'Oh, my God,' I say. 'I feel so much better now. The woman
is actually human!'

'Honey – ' she jumps back up on to the worktop ' – they're
all human. Some of them are just better at hiding it.'

'I thought I was the only one who struggled to keep it
together when I worked full time. I barely manage now.'

'What did you do?'

'I was a teacher.'

'I bet you don't miss that. Hard work! And Nathan runs
a tight ship at the hospital; I imagine it's the same at home.'

'He does like things ship-shape and Bristol-fashion.'

'Well, if you enjoy keeping house and you don't have to
work, don't let those snot-noses make you feel bad about it.'
She waves her wine glass at the door.

74

'That's the thing, though.' I climb up on to the counter opposite. 'I *don't* enjoy keeping house. I gave up work because it's a big place and I struggled to keep on top of it with a full-time job. I actually do miss teaching. I didn't find it hard work at all.'

'Hire a housekeeper, then.'

'But everything I earn would go straight to them. What would be the point?'

'Your sanity? Your sense of purpose?'

'Nathan doesn't see it that way. And he doesn't trust housekeepers to do things properly.'

'And there it is,' she says. 'The stain of inequality. He waves his penis in the air like a barometer, taking readings on what's best for you. And it's in your genes as much as his not to argue with the power of that apparatus. The penis always knows best.'

I laugh. 'He's not that bad. Not like my first husband.'

'As I said, mine wasn't *that bad* either. But honey, after five million years of inequality I think we deserve a bit more than *not that bad*.'

'No, I mean, he really is one of the good ones.' Then I laugh and add, 'That doesn't sound any better, does it?'

She shakes her head with a resigned smile and asks, 'So what was he like, your first husband?'

'Wonderful at first. But marriage was like a switch. The moment I was his wife, I was expected to "act like one".' I use air quotes. 'And that meant doing as I was told if I didn't want any trouble.'

'He hit you?'

'Rarely. Mostly, the threat of violence was enough. He'd get up in my face and I'd know I was standing on a line I couldn't cross without a fat lip or a black eye. So, more often than not, I did as I was told.'

'How did you get out?'

'My sister helped me. I lived with her until my mother had a stroke that left her with aphasia – she couldn't communicate at all at first – so I went back to help her. Then I met Nathan and within a month I'd moved in with him. I was lucky he came along when he did. Mum had already met someone new at stroke therapy and my presence was putting a strain on their new relationship. My husband had taken everything. He'd been hiding money for years, run our savings into the ground, remortgaged the house, and by the time we got divorced there was nothing left. I don't know what I'd have done without Nathan. He knew what a toll divorce takes on you; he'd had a terrible marriage himself. His first wife went out partying all night, leaving him alone in bed till the early hours. She spent all his money, never helped around the house, and whenever she was around she was cruel, apparently. So, when we met, we sort of clung to each other for support.'

'Claire? You're talking about Claire? Nathan's first wife?'

'You know her?'

'Yes.' Penny shifts on the worktop, avoiding eye-contact.

'What?'

'Nothing. It's just… It's just that doesn't sound like Claire, that's all. She's a really nice woman. She came out broken from that marriage, not the other way around.'

'Well, there are two sides to every story. Especially in a divorce. Ryan – my husband – contacted everyone we knew, even remote acquaintances, to tell them I was a controlling bitch who took him for everything he had, when in reality it was the other way round. But he was so good at playing the downtrodden victim, people believed him. It just wasn't in my nature to do the same: to contact every acquaintance and tell them my husband was a psychopath who hit me and took all our money. So because I wasn't the one doing all the talking, I guess they had no choice but to believe the person who was. Claire *would* have said Nathan was the bad seed in their relationship – and I'm sure she seems like a nice woman on the outside – but people rarely admit to bad behaviour. Especially when it leads to the breakdown of a marriage.'

76

'I suppose. It's just… Oh, I don't know. As you say, there are two sides to every story. You never know what goes on behind closed doors.'

And the moment she says that, the kitchen door flies open.

'There you are,' Nathan says, a hint of disdain in his eyes when he sees me sitting on Amelia's worktop. I jump down. 'What are you doing hiding back here?'

'Talking to Penny.' I point in her direction. 'You know Penny?'

'Penny,' he says.

'Nathan.'

'Would you mind if I stole my wife away?'

'Be my guest.' She raises her wine glass.

Nathan opens his arms for me and I curl into them as he guides me through the kitchen door, but then Penny calls out from behind us.

'You should pop round for a coffee some time, Rose.'

Nathan doesn't let go so I twist around awkwardly in his arms.

'Sure, I'd love to.'

'I'm by the cemetery near the hospital. Just past it on the right. The house with the yellow door. You can't miss it — there's a monkey puzzle tree in the garden. I'm home every Thursday. Pop round after you visit Daisy.'

I didn't realise Penny knew about Daisy but Nathan has already guided me into the hall before I can ask her about it. I guess everyone at the hospital knows Nathan's sister-in-law's in a coma.

'Sorry,' I say. 'I lost track of time.'

'It's no problem. But you need to do the rounds. You don't want people thinking my wife is rude and unsociable, do you?'

'No, of course not. It's just difficult when I don't know anyone that well. They talk about things I'm not a part of and I just end up lingering on the periphery like a floor lamp they barely notice.'

He pauses at the lounge door. 'Rose, I don't ask a lot from you. You have a great life and the primary reason for that is my career. It's not a lot to ask you to support it with a little polite conversation, is it?'

I look up at him and smile. 'No. Of course not.'

'Good.' He pushes open the door and points to a woman I vaguely recognise. 'Go and talk to Simon's wife, Emma. She's on the peer review team for Action Medical.'

'You mean, she decides whether or not you get your research grant?'

'Exactly. Which is why I can't have you hiding out in the kitchen. It wouldn't be right for *me* to go and schmooze her, but there's no reason my wife can't have a friendly conversation, now, is there?'

And, with his hand on the small of my back, he herds me in her direction.

⌇

'You should be careful of Penny.' Nathan watches himself in the wardrobe mirror while tugging one-handed at his tie.

'Why?' I unclip my earrings and lay them carefully in the velvet-lined jewellery drawer of my dressing table. 'She seemed nice.'

'People aren't always what they seem.'

I spin around on the seat and face him. 'I liked her. She's different from most of the women at the party. She talks about real things. Not jobs or money or holidays or clothes. She's interesting. She talks about feelings.'

Nathan attacks the buttons on his shirt. 'Yes, and she does that to get you to share yours. She's a gossip. Anything you told her tonight will spread like a virus around the hospital, and at the next party you'll realise everyone knows your personal business.'

'She didn't seem that way to me.'

78

'Well, she's very good at putting on a show that she likes people. Dr Anderson thinks she has narcissistic personality disorder.'

With no idea how to respond to that, I turn back to the mirror and remove my make-up. Dr Anderson's a sensible man, not prone to exaggeration; he wouldn't say something like that unless he had good reason to believe it was true. Penny *is* very confident, very focused on herself and her own wants and needs, so perhaps Dr Anderson is right. But turning on the only person I've ever felt a connection with at any of these parties feels traitorous, so I say, 'Well, she struck me as a really warm and genuine person.'

'Yes, but you're hardly a good judge of character, are you, Rose? You married a psychopath.'

My mouth falls open and, realising he's hit a nerve, Nathan comes over and rubs my shoulders. 'That came out wrong… Look, it's not your fault. People like Ryan and Penny are really good at hiding who they are. And you're so sweet – too sweet – you can't see it. You think everyone's just like you: good and kind. And that makes you exactly the kind of person Penny would target. I'm sure it felt like warmth and sincerity, but it's manufactured. She's manipulating you into a friendship that'll only serve her. And I don't want that happening to you.'

'She knows Claire.'

Nathan pulls away and turns his attention to his belt. 'What did she say about Claire?'

'That the divorce broke her.'

He laughs. 'See? I told you Penny was a liar. You know it was me who came out broken from that marriage. Broken and broke. That woman fleeced me for everything she could get. I'm not surprised Penny's friends with her; they're two heads of the same blood-sucking snake. Claire never loved me any more than Penny likes you. Why do you think they're friends?'

'I guess.' I get to my feet and turn my back to Nathan so he can unzip my dress, which he struggles with for a moment.

'Trust me, Rose. They're both bitches.' He takes a seat on the edge of the bed and pulls off his socks. 'I wasn't going to tell you this because I didn't want to hurt you. But I overheard Penny say something about you while you were talking to Emma. She called you dreary.'

My dress, still hanging off my shoulders, slips from my fingers and falls to the floor. I don't speak for a moment, then say, 'I suppose, to someone like Penny, I am dreary.'

Nathan darts to my side and pulls me into a hug. So I slide my arms around his bare chest and hold tight to his back muscles.

'Don't do that,' he says. 'Don't let her get to you. You're not dreary. You're perfect. You don't have to be gregarious or vivacious like them to be interesting to me.'

He lifts me up and carries me to the bed, where he lays me down before unbuttoning his trousers and letting them fall to the floor. His tight black briefs hug his slender frame and his bare stomach makes me tingle. Climbing on top of me, he kisses my neck, my breasts and my hipbones before going down on me until I can't bear it any longer.

'I want you,' I whisper, pulling him up towards me and guiding him inside.

He takes his time making love to me – he never comes until I do – but then the moment snaps and Penny pops into my mind. Nathan's spell is broken and I'm suddenly back where we started, unable to lose myself in our lovemaking. My mind is stamped with an image of myself in the kitchen downstairs, wearing nothing but rubber gloves. And then another of me here, naked in this bedroom, dancing for Nathan in a rubber G-string.

I shake my head to rattle Penny's words out and run my hands over Nathan's back, pulling him gently towards me, urging him to kiss me. But it's as if he's not here any more.

And I'm too much here.

I want to be where he is, and I can't get there in time.

'Nathan…'

He moans.

'Nathan…'

As if he can't even hear me, he doesn't open his eyes, just moves in and out of me.

'Nathan… Baby…'

And then he comes, groaning and shivering on top of me, which takes me by surprise because he always waits for me. Still, he's elsewhere, lost. So I say his name more firmly.

'What?' He groans.

'Why won't you look at me?'

He opens his eyes. 'I am looking at you.'

'I meant just then, while we were making love.'

'I didn't want to ruin the moment.'

'What?'

'What?' He pulls out of me and clambers over to his side of the bed.

'Seeing my face would ruin the moment?'

'Don't be silly, Rose. You know what I meant.' He flops down on his back in exasperation.

'No. I don't know what you meant.'

'Jesus. Why do you have to spoil everything?'

'I'm not trying to spoil anything. I just want to know what you meant.'

'You're too sensitive, Rose. It's cloying. I think Penny and that party have got under your skin. How can someone as beautiful as you be so insecure? All I meant was, I was in the zone. That's it, okay? Why do you have to turn everything into a personal attack?'

I let out a long breath and the arguments over Saeed, the party, Penny and Claire all seep out like a toxic fog. Nathan's right. I am too sensitive.

And now I just feel awful.

NINE

MAGGIE

I HOLD TIGHT to Alfie's hand as we take Cairo on our usual walk around the woods. Part of me is afraid of running into the strange man and part of me wants to. Then I'd know for sure he wasn't just a figment of my imagination and I could ask him what he thinks he's doing trespassing on private land.

The cabin and all the land surrounding it belong to John. We dreamed of buying it from the proceeds of Luc's first novel but his publisher cut deals with discount catalogues and supermarkets that left Luc with three to six pence per book. And even though he made the *Sunday Times* and *New York Times* bestseller lists, he barely scraped minimum wage. Once he's out of this two-book contract, if his second novel does well too, he'll be in a stronger position to negotiate a better contract with a new publisher. Maybe then we can buy the cabin. Hopefully before John sells it to someone else.

Luc is right about the unlikelihood of a stray hiker winding up in these woods; the land is fenced all around. But I know what I saw. Maybe he was just a hiker who took a short cut by scaling the fence and, when he saw us at the cabin, made a swift escape.

Maybe he's an axe murderer.

Maybe it's Ryan.

Ryan knows about the cabin; Rose brought him here to see us once. And he's certainly crazy enough to come here and terrorise us for helping Rose. In my head, I practise what I'll say to him if I run into him right here in the woods. *What do you think you're doing? You're trespassing on private land! I'm calling the police!*

Maybe I'd lose the nerve to say anything at all, and just run.

Or maybe I'd blow his brains out with my shotgun. I've often dreamed of doing that. When I first found out what he'd been doing to Rose, every clay pigeon had his face on it.

I scan the trees either side of us. It's trying to rain and we're exactly halfway around the gravel fire track that skirts the wood. We're going to get wet whether we turn back or press on, and I didn't bring my wax hat.

'Alfie, shall we go through the trees?' I lift the hood of his yellow rain mac. At least he'll stay dry.

'Twees.' He points to the overgrown path through the wood.

'Yes. It's going to rain. We won't get so wet if we stay underneath them. Does that sound like a plan?'

'Pwan.'

The moment we step off the path, the heavens open. So I guide us in a straight line through the trees in the direction of the cabin.

I check behind us to make sure Cairo is following but she's a few metres back, sniffing the ground where the trees line the fire track. Suddenly alert, she turns in circles, attempting to locate the source of whatever she can smell. She looks at us, then off to her left. And then she's gone.

'Cairo!' I call after her retreating form: a flash of chestnut and white and a flurry of dead leaves between the trunks. 'Cairo!'

We veer off the woodland path in her direction, calling her name as we go, Alfie lifting his head and shouting, 'Caiwow!' into the canopy. It doesn't usually bother me to leave her to her own devices; she can follow a scent for hours, and with no chance of keeping up with her we usually go home. She always finds her way back. But now, with a stranger on the loose, I'm uneasy. You hear sickening stories of dogs being killed on walks: stabbed, poisoned, thrown into fast-flowing rivers. And, until I know who this man is and what he's doing here, I don't want anyone in my family on their own in these woods.

Up ahead, leaves rustle and a twig snaps.

I follow the sound, lifting Alfie over a fallen tree and holding his hand as we negotiate waist-high saplings, brush, and broken branches. Between two trees in the distance there's a flash of white, so I speed up, pulling Alfie along. Still some distance away, Cairo's tail thrashes back and forth as if she's caught head-first in a trap, struggling to free herself.

I'm scared she's hurt, so I bend down and let Alfie climb on to my back. 'Jump up,' I say. 'Quickly.' And, once he's up, I jog.

Blood churning and heart slamming, more out of concern than effort, I leap rotten branches and skirt holly bushes, slipping in mud and wet leaves as I go. Then Cairo's white bottom comes into full view, her short legs tottering left and right as she fights against whatever she's caught in, grunting and whimpering.

Afraid Alfie will witness something that will scar him for life – his beloved dog caught in barbed wire, or torn and bloodied from a run-in with a badger – I lower him to the ground. 'Wait here,' I tell him. 'Don't move.' And I approach quickly but cautiously, gripping the bark of one of the trees as I negotiate the undergrowth.

It's not barbed wire; it's not a trap or a badger. Lying dead in the bracken is a huge stag, its eyes wide and black. And its neck is twisted so far back, it's as if its prodigious antlers have torn through its own skin. Its entrails tumble from the wide gash in its belly. And Cairo's snow-white face is buried inside it.

I've never seen her like this: growling and snarling in a frenzied attack, whimpering with excitement. Her body twists and jerks as she thrashes her head back and forth in an attempt to tear off pieces of the stag's flesh and skin.

'Mumma?'

'Stay back, Alfie.' I hold my hand up and he stops in his tracks, startled by the tension in my voice. 'Leave it!' I shout. 'Cairo, leave it!'

She doesn't hear me; she's as wild as the stag.

'Cairo!' I come up behind her, lean over and grab her collar. 'Leave it!'

But as I pull her away she jerks her head around, white snout bloody red, and snaps at me. I snatch my hand away in shock as she returns to her quarry.

Her teeth made contact but didn't pierce my skin: a warning to back off. My sweet little Cairo has never even growled at me, let alone snapped at me, and I'm as disappointed as I am stunned. It's a relief that, even in a wild frenzy, she still had the presence of mind not to bite. If she had actually bitten, drawn blood, I don't know what I would have done. The idea that I'd have to put her down to ensure Alfie's safety would be too much to bear.

I stare at her as she tears into the animal, too afraid to approach her again. It crosses my mind to leave her there, but she won't part with the carcass easily and is unlikely to come home before dark. If at all.

Her leash is around my waist, running like a belt through the back loop of my jeans, and I pull it out slowly, afraid to startle her again. Then, leaning over as quietly and cautiously as I can, I open the trigger clip and attach it to the loop on her collar, snatching my hand back before she has another chance to snap. She wrestles against her leash as I drag her away, twisting and yelping. And when she finally gives up the fight and turns away from the stag, Alfie takes one look at her blood-soaked face and screams.

Gripping the sideboard, the cabin swirls around me in a blur of colours; I'm going to pass out. It's as if I'm disappearing. Trapped in a maelstrom in the middle of the ocean as water swirls around me, dragging me down. I have an urge to spin in the opposite direction, as if spinning will ground me in my surroundings.

'Who was that?' Luc's voice permeates the darkness as he steps down into the lounge while I stare at the silent telephone, the black receiver strangled in my white knuckles.

'Maggie? Are you okay? Who was that?'

'Rose.' I cling to the handset as if it's a lifeline to her. 'I need to sit down.'

Luc eases the telephone from my grasp and drops it back on the cradle of the old-style rotary. Then he helps me to the sofa and, when I sit down, the world finally stops spinning.

'What's happened? Is Rose all right?'

'Yes. It's not Rose. Dr Anderson is pressuring her to remove life support.'

'What?! Maggie, no! When will you leave? Will you go straight away?'

'No.'

'What do you mean, no? You have to go back now.'

'I don't want to. I can't. I need to be here for you and Alfie.'

'Rose needs you!'

'She doesn't. She's got Nathan. And not only that, she has Dr Sharif now as well, it seems.'

'Dr Sharif? He's there with her?'

'Yeah. He's helping her. She'll be all right with him there. Actually, if I didn't know how much she loves Nathan, I'd say she has a crush on him.'

'What is it with this psychologist? Didn't you have a little crush on him too?'

'Don't be silly. There was only one man on my mind when I met Dr Sharif.'

'And that man would be me, would it?'

'You know the answer to that. This is good, though. Rose has all the support she needs.'

'Maggie...she needs her sister. That's who should be there for her.'

'She'll cope.'

'This is Rose we're talking about. She won't cope. You've always been the mother of the family – holding everyone together after your father died – she's always been the baby. You can't leave her to make a decision like this; she won't be able to live with it. You know what she's like. She's too fragile.'

'It won't be her decision, it'll be the hospital's. Nathan seems to be on board with it too.'

'Nathan? Why, what did she say?'

'Nothing. Just reading between the lines.'

'I know you've never warmed to the guy, but I don't think he'd do anything to deliberately hurt Rose.'

'I know, it's odd, isn't it? I think she was surprised by it too. But apparently he thinks it's been too long and the pressure is getting too much for her.'

'You can't stay here, Maggie. You have to go back. Not just for Rose's sake. You need her as much as she needs you.'

'I'll think about it. How is Alfie, is he okay?'

'He's fine. Asleep. Exhausted. I cleaned Cairo up and she's sleeping too. Big day for everyone, it seems. How's your hand?'

'It's fine, she barely touched me; it's not even bruised. I just startled her, that's all. But what could have done that? Killed a stag of that size?'

'Not Cairo,' he says, 'that's for sure.'

'They don't have any natural predators, do they? Other than humans? Do you think *he* did it?'

'Maggie...we aren't even sure it was a man you saw.'

'What else could have done it? Maybe he's a hunter, someone who lives nearby who's using the land.'

'Maybe.'

Luc wraps his arms around me and pulls me in close as if to protect me from the world outside and my imaginary man in the woods.

I didn't imagine him.

But I don't want to think about him right now. I don't want to think about anything that's happening outside of this cabin. So I bury my head in Luc's jumper, infused with the warmth of his body.

'Alfie and Cairo are sleeping,' I say. 'Why don't we take a break as well? We can go upstairs and steal an afternoon nap.'

'Do you actually mean a nap...or...'

'I mean...or.'

And when my legs are curled around his and he's deep inside me, filling me to the corners and warming my insides, his beard tingling my lips as we kiss, I push the world from my mind. But I can't stop it drifting to Rose. Rose and her brand-spanking-new husband.

I pull myself back to the moment but my mind continues to wander.

Luc is so different. Warm and fuzzy, compared to Nathan. I think the first time I met Nathan he was probably dressed in scrubs, but whenever I picture him, he's in a sharp grey suit and pressed white shirt. If you were to believe Rose, his attraction isn't a matter of taste or opinion: he's intrinsically handsome. And it's impossible not to be startled by his clean and chiselled looks. But taste aside — personally I prefer cute, furry, and funny — there's no arguing with his eloquence and charm. He has certainly swept Rose off her feet. And I'd be lying to myself if I didn't admit that, occasionally, I experience a pang of envy for my beautiful little sister with her wealthy surgeon-husband. It's always fleeting, though. Nathan rarely visits and, when he does, I find him difficult to warm to. Is it possible to warm to anything so flawless? It would be like curling up to an emerald-cut diamond.

Rose must see something I don't.

Wrapped in Luc's arms, my head pillowed by his thick chest hair, I wouldn't want to be anywhere else or with anyone else. He's my everything. My love. My life. Alfie's father – and a wonderful father – kind, gentle, funny. Finding a man like Luc is the stuff of dreams.

I cling to him, shut my eyes, and forget everything outside the cabin.

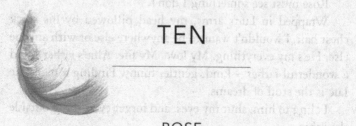

TEN

ROSE

SAEED AND I sit either side of Daisy's bed, looking at her instead of each other. I twirl the ginger curls that have grown past her shoulders over the three long years, down to her breasts. She'll kill me for not doing something with it, but I like it. I think it suits her wildness and strength.

Eventually I say, 'I'm sorry Nathan was so rude to you last week.'

'You do not need to do that.'

'Do what?'

'Apologise for other people. Not even your husband. You are not responsible for anyone's behaviour but your own.'

'I *feel* responsible.'

'Yes…well…marriage can do that…long-term relationships too. But apologising for a partner's behaviour can be habitual. It is not good for us.'

'How so?'

His forehead creases as he organises an explanation.

90

'Such apologies are prompted by our own discomfort. And that discomfort mimics the remorse we feel when we *are* responsible for something. It fosters a sense of culpability even when we are blameless. And it is circular. The more we apologise, the more often we experience that feeling of culpability and the more we apologise.'

'I see. That makes sense, I suppose.'

'Try to avoid it if you can, Rose. Because it could damage your other relationships too. People do it to be diplomatic, to defuse a situation, when in reality it excuses bad behaviour. When we say things like *he was just tired* or *she had a long day*, our justifications can be mistaken for approval and tar us with the same brush. It is especially important in a relationship like yours that you do not start down that road. It is a difficult one to come back from. Nathan will behave as he chooses. You have no control over it. And you should never apologise for it.'

'Why do you say that? A relationship like mine?'

Saeed shifts in his chair and looks down at Daisy's blanket. 'I am sorry. I forgot where I was for a moment, slipped into therapy mode. Forgive me.'

'Saeed...' I tilt my head to catch his eye and he finally looks at me. 'I don't believe you ever say anything without being sure of your meaning. But we've met three times. You've only met Nathan once. How can you have any idea of what kind of relationship mine is?'

He doesn't speak. He breaks eye-contact and turns his attention back to the blanket.

'Saeed... Please tell me what you meant.'

'It is not my place. I should not have said anything. I am sorry.'

I reach across the blanket and put my hand on his arm. 'I see you as a friend. I know that sounds strange when we've known each other for so short a time... But I think people are like magnets, don't you? Have you ever met someone and, no matter how much you wanted to like them, you just couldn't?

91

Often it's someone with a similar pole and you push each other apart. But then sometimes, with no effort or energy whatsoever, people snap together so tightly you can't tear them apart no matter how hard you try. I think we have opposite poles.'

He looks right at me and says, 'I feel that too.'

'Well, if you're really my friend, you'll tell me what you meant about my relationship with Nathan.'

'I cannot, Rose. Please. Do not ask me. As I said, it is not my place.'

'As my friend, it's very much your place. And I trust you. You've spent your life analysing people, understanding them. If *you* can't tell me, who can?'

He hesitates for a long while and I don't push him. I don't want him to retreat back into his shell, so I wait for him to speak. Finally, he says, 'Do you remember the day we met – two weeks ago – you told me about your first date with Nathan?'

'Of course.'

'You said your favourite song came on the stereo in his car. He ordered your favourite drink at the restaurant: pink champagne. He checked your work schedule and made plans for the next day, plans that must have taken a good deal of time and expense to organise. And yet, he had no idea whether you would even want to see him again.'

'So?'

He looks at Daisy as if she can help him. Then he says, 'It raised some red flags for me.'

'Red flags? What red flags? So what if I hadn't wanted to see him again? He could easily have cancelled everything. And as for us liking the same song, there are such things as coincidences.'

'There is something else too. When I met Nathan last week, I recognised him. It took a while for me to figure out from where, but I knew we had met before.'

'Where?'

92

'In Dr Anderson's office, the day you and I met for the first time. When I arrived, I found Daisy on the ventilator so I went to see Dr Anderson to find out what had happened. Nathan came in while I was there. Is he involved in Daisy's care? I thought you said his specialty was paediatrics?'

'It is. And no, he's not. Not as far as I know. Why?'

'He dropped a report on Dr Anderson's desk and said it was the one he had promised. I saw Daisy's name on it.'

'That's odd. Why would Nathan be giving Dr Anderson reports on Daisy?'

'I have no idea.'

I think about it. 'Well, he is a divisional director. Dr Anderson's boss. He oversees the whole department.'

'But then,' says Saeed, 'surely Dr Anderson would be sending reports to Nathan, not the other way around. And even then, I would be surprised at a divisional director being so closely involved with a patient outside of his area of specialty. Dr Anderson is extremely qualified and experienced.'

'She is his sister-in-law; he's bound to take an added interest in her.'

'I suppose,' he says. Then adds, 'Your phone is not pinging constantly today, has something happened?'

'Nathan's in a long surgery this afternoon.'

'I see.'

'Saeed... What is it? What aren't you telling me?'

He looks sheepish. 'Something else happened in Dr Anderson's office.'

Instinctively I reach out for my phone and turn it upside down, as if Nathan is watching us through the screen. 'What?'

'Dr Anderson had music playing on his computer when Nathan came in.'

'He often does. He says it helps him concentrate.'

'Well, on his way out Nathan said, "What is this shit? How can you concentrate with that caterwauling?"'

'So?'

93

'Dr Anderson was playing "Tawny Moon". It was my CD. I'd lent him *Before the Dawn* and we were discussing Bertie. What it must be like to live up to his mother.'

'That's odd. Maybe Nathan just doesn't like that track.'

'Then why not say as much? Why ask what it was?'

I lean back in my chair, unsure what to make of it. On our first date, Nathan told me he was just like me: one of those hardcore Kate Bush fans who took the day off work to get tickets the second they went on sale. Only fans with that kind of dedication got tickets – they sold out in minutes. And every Kate Bush fan knows Bertie – loves Bertie – because it was he who persuaded Kate to return to the stage for the first time in thirty-five years. If Nathan *had* been to the concert, he would have heard Bertie sing. He would know that song.

I say, 'You're saying Nathan lied about going to the concert?'

'Do you know "Tawny Moon"?'

'Of course.'

'And yet, you did *not* go to the concert.'

'But he... He was singing. He knew the words to "Sunset". We were both singing in the car.'

'"Sunset" is online, in many playlists. But the live recording is not licensed and you would have to *own* the album or have been to the concert to know that some tracks are missing. It is why Dr Anderson wanted to borrow my CD in the first place. Can you guess which track is missing?'

'This is silly. So what if he lied about liking an artist just to impress me? People do things like that all the time when they're first dating.'

'No, Rose, they do not. And he was prepared in advance, was he not? Therefore he must have *asked* people about you, found out your likes and dislikes. Looked up your Facebook profile and—'

'I looked at his profile too. People check each other out on Facebook all the time. It's hardly a crime.'

Saeed looks at Daisy again.

'She isn't going to help you.' My voice rises an octave, my defensiveness pouty and childish. But it's true, I *did* look Nathan up on Facebook; it doesn't make me a stalker. To be fair, there wasn't much to stalk, only three updates: him adding a profile picture where he's on holiday somewhere, tanned and wearing sunglasses; him adding a banner photo from one of those Ferrari experience days; and him changing his profile photo to one that looks as if it was taken in a studio rather than with someone's phone camera. He doesn't even use Facebook; he never posts.

'Rose,' Saeed says. 'I told you not to ask me. I said it was not my place.' And he won't look at me now.

'I'm sorry... I'm sorry.' I reach across for his arm and rub it. 'You're right. I did ask you to tell me. I *am* listening. And it's not you I'm angry at. I'm just confused, that's all. What were you going to say about Facebook?'

He draws in a breath, as if needing a moment to meditate over whether he should continue. Then he holds up a hand to me, saying, 'One minute,' while reaching into his trouser pocket with the other. He pulls out his phone, swipes at it a few times, and then turns the screen around for me to see. 'This is you, yes?'

My Facebook profile is on his screen. 'Yes.'

He's silent for a while as he looks through it, but we aren't friends so I'm not sure how much he can see.

He says, 'Just like apologising to a victim of our partner's behaviour, it is also common – out of love – to minimise their behaviour when *we* are the victim. And in such situations it is helpful to imagine yourself exhibiting their behaviour and noticing how it makes you feel.'

'Okaaay...' I drag the word out.

'I want you to imagine you know nothing about Rose Winter – so you cannot perform a specific search for anything in particular – and, from her profile, tell me her favourite drink and her favourite song.' He hands me his phone.

Raising my eyebrows, I take it and scroll through my profile. Kate Bush is in my music list, but so are twenty other bands, and there's nothing to indicate she's my favourite. Let alone which of hers is my favourite song. And there are photographs of me holding pink champagne, but there are far more of me drinking beer and wine. In the end, I give up and do a search for Kate Bush. I remember posting the tour announcement the day it hit the news and find that straight away.

It was four years ago.

Saeed is right. Specifics aren't easy to find. So either Nathan scrolled through four years of my Facebook posts or searched by keyword on every one of twenty artists to figure out which one I posted about most often. Either way, it crosses the line between curiosity and obsession. Glancing at bands I've liked on Facebook is one thing but interrogating my individual posts for explicit information in this way does make me feel uncomfortable. It's like stalking myself. And even then, I can't find any posts where I specifically mention 'Sunset'. Which means Saeed is right about that, too. Nathan must have gone one step further and asked people about me. Dr Anderson maybe. He and I have discussed our love of Kate over the years.

I thrust Saeed's phone at him. 'You could be wrong. Maybe Nathan was in the toilet when Bertie came on stage. And maybe he skips that song on the album because he doesn't like it and that's why he didn't recognise it.'

'Maybe.'

I remind myself that I made Saeed tell me these things and do my best to calm my anger. But my voice trembles when I say, 'Anyway, so what if he asked people what I like? Maybe he's just considerate and wanted me to have a nice evening.'

'Maybe.'

'Stop saying *maybe* and tell me what you think's going on here.'

'Do you actually want to hear what I think, Rose? You are obviously feeling very angry.'

'I'm not angry,' I snap, 'I'm upset. There's a difference. And yes, *actually*, I do want to hear what you're thinking. Because then I can put your mind at rest. Nathan isn't what you think he is. He's not a stalker.'

'I did not call him a stalker.' Saeed's voice is quiet, soft and calm. It's bloody infuriating.

'What, then?'

'I suspect – and I am only telling you this as a friend, I am not your therapist – that Nathan has narcissistic personality disorder.'

My mouth falls open and I glare at him. That's the second time in a week I've heard that term, when I've never heard it spoken before in my life. I mean, I've heard of it, of course, but it's not something anyone has ever *said* to me. Not even about Ryan.

'What on *earth* makes you say that? You don't even know him.'

Again, Saeed sucks in a breath, only this time there's nothing meditative about it. He runs his fingers through his hair as he blows out a long exhalation. Beneath his calm demeanour, he's struggling, I can see that. He would never be this blunt this quickly with a patient. So why is he walking such a fine line with me?

He says, 'I am concerned, that is all.'

'There's no need. Nathan's never been anything but wonderful to me.'

'Rose, you are right. I…I do not know Nathan well enough to offer any diagnosis. But from what little I have heard from you, and what little I have seen of him… Many traits of NPD overlap with sociopathy and psychopathy, and it can be hard to distinguish—'

'Sorry, did you just call Nathan a psychopath? Are you insane?! My first husband was a psychopath; I know what psychopaths look like. Are you saying this because he was rude to you last week?'

97

'Of course not; I would never let something like that affect my judgement. Rose...I am sorry...you say you were married before? And your first husband...he was a psychopath?' His voice quivers with concern.

'Yes. Ryan went to jail for beating up a man – a friend he assumed I was seeing – shortly after we got divorced. And Nathan is *nothing* like him. We're very happy. And he's a good man. Okay, maybe asking people about me before our first date is a little obsessive – if that even happened – but it *is* possible he just wanted to make a good impression.'

Saeed leans back in his chair. 'I am sorry. I have crossed a line. I should never have said anything.'

'It's all right, I made you.'

'Still, I should not be diagnosing someone I have only met once. Please try to forget I said anything.'

The silence stretches out until every sound around us – the whoosh of the ventilator, distant voices from the hallway, the rumble of stretcher wheels on lino – is deafening.

Eventually I speak. 'Can we forget this conversation ever happened?'

'Of course,' he says. But all the light has gone from his eyes and deep grooves line the bridge of his nose. Even if I could forget it, it's clear he's not going to.

I reach across for his arm again, touching it briefly, gently. 'Is there anything I can say that will reassure you you're wrong about Nathan?'

He shakes his head but then he looks at me and his eyes flash their dark grey metal.

'There is something you could do. Something small. Something very simple that would put my mind at rest.'

'Anything.'

'This may sound odd, but...on your way home this afternoon, can you take a detour? Not far, just deviate slightly from your usual route, pull into a side road and make a telephone call. Is there anyone you need to contact at the moment? It is best that the call be genuine.'

'I need to give measurements to our seamstress for the new curtains. I could call her.'

'That will work.'

'Why, though?'

'If I am wrong it will not matter. We can talk about it when we see each other next week. Is that all right?'

'Okay...' I struggle to hide the suspicion in my tone but it dissipates quickly. It's a relief that Saeed has asked for something so simple. Anything else and I would have said no. I won't play games with my husband and I won't lie. I feel disloyal for even entertaining this much, for allowing any shadow of doubt to enter my mind. Nathan loves me as much as I love him, I know it; nobody is *that* good an actor. I'm curious as to why Saeed wants me to stop and make a telephone call, but I already know him well enough not to press him. He'll tell me when he's ready. Next week.

Neither of us is willing to discuss Nathan any more, so I turn the subject to my sister. 'Have you spoken to Dr Anderson about Daisy? In the past couple of weeks, I mean?'

'I did. We discussed running further tests.'

'What tests?' I panic. 'Is Dr Anderson testing Daisy because he wants to remove life support?'

'He did not say so. Why would you think that?'

'Nathan said they discussed it. He thinks it's the best thing for me in the long run – with the stress of visiting all the time – but I don't find it stressful. I love visiting Daisy.'

'I think Nathan has his wires crossed. Dr Anderson and I have been discussing something else altogether.' He grins.

'What? You look like you're scheming.'

'You could say that. But I do not want to get your hopes up – Dr Anderson has not yet agreed and we need his referral – but I discussed with him the results of Daisy's EEG and the recent increases in her brain activity.'

'And?'

He's boyish with excitement. 'I have asked if we can get her over to the Clinical Neurosciences Division for an fMRI scan. And, depending on the results of that, we may be able to try vagus nerve stimulation.'

'You've lost me. I don't know what any of that is. Daisy's already had an MRI.'

'This is different. This is a *functional* MRI. It detects oxygenated blood in the brain: active areas stimulated by thoughts and feelings. We will be able to tell if Daisy is aware of her surroundings. And vagus nerve stimulation is an electronic pulse that stimulates consciousness.'

'Why haven't they tried this before? Why haven't you suggested it before?'

'It is very experimental. Even if the results are positive, it does not mean anything will change. People who have been in a vegetative state for more than a year do not normally recover consciousness. And, although there has been *some* success with vagus nerve stimulation, the research is limited. VNS is normally used to treat patients with epilepsy. With coma patients the studies are embryonic and it is likely that Dr Anderson will not be able to secure these tests and treatments. I did not want to mention it until I knew for sure. You must promise not to get your hopes up.'

'That won't be easy, but I will try.'

'There are other things we can do in the meantime. We can try more sensory stimulation.'

'Again, why has nobody suggested these things? They just say I should talk to her, hold her hand.'

'Because there is little evidence to suggest it works, Rose. When recommended, it is usually a means of comforting the loved ones, rather than effective therapy for the patient themselves. It is a Band-Aid on the uselessness families experience when their loved one is in a coma: it gives them something constructive to do.'

'Why should we bother, then? If it doesn't work?'

100

'Because, if Dr Anderson *is* considering removing life support, we will both cope better knowing we have done everything we could for Daisy.'

That's true. Once again I'm struck by Saeed's understanding of human nature.

'So tell me, what do we do?'

'We stimulate *all* of her senses: smell, touch, sound. Can you bring in some of Daisy's favourite things? Tactile things: soft pieces of clothing she liked to wear. Her favourite perfume. Her favourite music. Favourite films. It is important that the items you bring are things Daisy would have enjoyed before the accident.'

'Okay. Next week. I'll bring as much as I can.'

And, for the first time in a very long time, I'm hopeful.

ELEVEN

MAGGIE

'WHO WERE YOU talking to?' Luc walks out of his study with an empty coffee cup in his hand. Often it's the only time I get to see him during the day: when he comes out to make a fresh cup.

'Rose.'

'Any news?' Tension plucks his vocal cords, his voice breaking. He's been like this since I told him I wasn't going back. He doesn't realise Rose is stronger than he thinks. She may look like an ethereal wood nymph with her fragile features, but she's not the delicate thing people mistake her for.

That she often mistakes herself for.

Rose is a fighter; she just doesn't know it yet. She'll cope with this on her own. And anyway, she's not on her own, she has Nathan and Saeed by her side. She doesn't need me there as well. With that man hanging around the woods, I'm not leaving my family.

I say, 'Saeed has convinced Dr Anderson to do a functional MRI and something called vagus nerve stimulation.'

'Will it work?'

'I doubt it. It's probably a last-ditch effort to show they've done everything they could.'

Luc takes the steps down into the lounge area, puts his empty cup on the coffee table and pulls me into a hug. 'We'll be perfectly fine, you know. You can go.'

I kiss him. 'You won't be fine. Who'll recover all your data when your disk fails again?'

He laughs but then stops.

'But if this vagus thing works—'

'We'll cross that bridge when we come to it. But there's apparently little evidence it will. Saeed isn't confident. He's trying to keep Rose's hopes in check and not get her excited.' Then, caustically, I add, 'Good luck with that, Saeed.'

'What does that mean?'

'I'm not sure… At first I thought it was just a little crush. I mean, who doesn't crush on Saeed?'

'You! You said…'

I wrap my arms around him. 'Of course not me. But now I'm wondering if it's something deeper.'

'Why? Did Rose say something about him?'

'No, but there's something in her tone. Reading between the lines, I'd say she has feelings for him.'

'More than for Nathan?'

'I don't know whether *more* is the right word. But different. I think Saeed offers companionship. Someone on her wavelength.'

'And she doesn't get that from Nathan?'

'I don't know. Perhaps not. But she clearly likes him. And I think he likes her too. More than likes her. I think he's falling for her.'

'Did Rose actually say that?'

'No. As I said, I'm just reading between the lines.' Alfie wails from upstairs and I sigh. 'Looks like I'm on duty.' Pulling out of the embrace, I kiss him quickly on the lips. 'Mmmm.'

103

I kiss him again, longer this time. 'So cute. Far more crushable than Saeed.'

'Only he's handsome and I'm cute.'

'No. You're both. Which is what makes you so crushable.'

He laughs. 'I'm getting coffee. You want one?'

Alfie wails again, louder.

'No, thanks. I'll take him out to the lake.'

Alfie runs around the shore collecting stones for me while I struggle to get the conversation with Rose out of my head. I feel selfish for not going back, but at the same time I don't want to leave Luc and Alfie. I don't want to go back to real life, the busy city, my job, and that three-day commute. I'm sure Alfie will be okay; Luc's a better parent than I am. In truth, if it weren't for the money, I question whether he'd need me at all.

No, that's not fair. I know I'm not just a breadwinner to him. And, after work, I do try to give him a break from childcare so he can get more writing done. But, even with Alfie around, Luc works fairly well. Kids are like dogs with routines and Alfie knows that it's quiet time while Daddy is working. He does puzzles and drawings and keeps himself occupied. Even if he does talk to himself in bubble-speak the whole time. And Luc's a night owl; he works while Alfie is sleeping.

I know they'd be okay without me.

The thing is, I'm not okay without them.

I'm brought back to reality by a rumble of thunder and a shimmer of distant lightning on the horizon. Cairo starts at another thundercrack and runs to me, taking cover between my legs. The storm is coming this way, drawing closer, and her whole body shakes as I lift her into my arms.

We'll have to go in soon, but I want to keep Alfie outside for as long as possible, tire him out before we're stuck indoors for hours because of the rain. Alfie is clearly content in his own little world of pebble-hunting, so I trudge across the stones to the cabin with Cairo still in my arms. Luc looks up when I approach and I knock on his study window, which he opens.

'Can you take her? The thunder's scaring her.'

'Sure.'

He reaches over his computer screen and I pass her through the window. 'We'll be in in a bit. The rain'll be here soon.'

Luc looks at the horizon. 'Don't stay out too long. Looks like a bad one.'

'We won't.' I turn back to the lake and traipse back to Alfie, who's throwing stones with his usual ineffectual enthusiasm. Only he's not throwing them at the lake as he usually would. He's throwing them at something on the ground.

Something black.

'Alfie…? Honey? What are you doing?' He ignores me, his back turned. I draw closer, asking the same question in French, which he's often more responsive to after many visits to Luc's father who rarely speaks a word of English. '*Alfie? Qu'est-ce que tu fais?*'

I draw closer, barely able to see the black shape at his feet because he's blocking it with his body. And it's only when I'm right beside him that I see what it is.

A dead crow.

Its blue-black wings are spread out over the stones as if it fell from the sky in mid-flight. Its head is twisted to one side, its beak gleaming metal-black like shears, and its ice-blue eyes still glassy.

Alfie grunts, leaping a few centimetres into the air as he throws another stone at the dead bird, hitting it in the stomach where its midnight feathers are velvet-soft. The poor creature seems to flinch at the impact. And a second later, from one of the trees that surround the lake, there's a great squawk from another crow, as if it's been struck too.

Its cry chills my bones.

Alfie picks up another stone but I grab his hand before he's able to throw it. 'Don't do that, honey. Leave it alone.'

I try to work the stone from beneath his fingers but he grips it tightly, unwilling to let go. So I give up on the stone and grab his wrist instead, dragging him from his prize.

He whines.

'Don't fuss, Alfie! Do as Mumma says.'

He's surprisingly strong as he digs his heels in the shingle and leans back with his full body weight to prevent me from dragging him any further away from the dead bird. 'Nooooo.' He draws the word out into a wail.

'*Fais ce que Maman te dit.* Leave it alone.'

He bursts into tears and lets all his muscles relax, flopping to the ground like a rag doll, all the while twisting his wrist back and forth in an attempt to wrestle it from my grip. And now I'm afraid of hurting him so I have no choice but to let go.

I leave him there, belly-down on the stones, bawling and punching with both fists. Feigning uninterest, I saunter to the lakeshore, where I toe the pebbles for one that looks good enough to skim.

The thunder rumbles again, a little closer this time. In less than an hour the heavens will open and we'll be forced to play inside. Alfie will be no happier about that than being dragged away from the bird so, anxious to distract him, I grab any old stone and do my best to skim it.

The moment Alfie hears the fizz and plop of the pebble in the water he's on his feet, cheerful as the skipping stone, bird forgotten in seconds. And now I have his attention I find a flatter pebble, skim it fast and say, 'Wow! Look at that one, Alfie. Look at it go! Find Mumma another one.'

But, the moment he bends down, something in my peripheral vision catches my eye. Something dark. Standing on the path. I spin around.

The man.

The man is back.

TWELVE

ROSE

I TWIST MY wedding band and engagement ring, my strained and weary face staring back at me from the high-gloss surface of the white glass table top, a reflective lake in the middle of our kitchen.

Stress must age you; I look forty-eight not thirty-eight. Maybe Nathan's right – maybe Daisy's condition is taking more of a toll than I realise. And I don't think I can cope with anything else right now. Which is why my mind reels with anger. Not anger, that's too strong, but it's certainly something close that I feel for Saeed right now.

I did as he asked and took a detour on my way home, stopping to make a call. I don't know what he thought was going to happen or the purpose of the exercise, but nothing came of it. Whatever did he hope to gain by it?

I've never questioned my relationship with Nathan. And now this stranger, who knows nothing about either of us, steps into our lives making mountains out of molehills and psychoanalysing our marriage. So Nathan didn't recognise a song from a concert he went to – so what? He found out what I liked before taking me on a date – so what? These are hardly things you question your entire marriage over. But that's what Saeed is making me do. And how dare he? He doesn't even know Nathan. He doesn't know *either* of us.

In that room, in that hospital, he sees me as a patient, and I'm not his bloody patient. He wants something to be wrong so that he can play therapist. He said himself that he has no life outside of his work and has no idea how to talk to normal people…normal…I mean people who aren't his bloody patients. I haven't asked for his help or his advice with my marriage. And in fact, until he came along and started sowing seeds of doubt, I thought my marriage was perfect. It *is* perfect. And I know my marriage a hell of a lot better than Saeed does.

He's out of line. I'm beginning to suspect Nathan is right and Saeed has his own hidden agenda.

I jump at the touch of a hand on my shoulder and spin around in the chair. 'Nathan! Jesus!' I smile with relief at the sight of him, jump to my feet and wrap my arms around his neck.

'Sorry,' he says. 'Did I frighten you?'

'Just a bit.' I kiss him on the lips.

'Weren't expecting me?'

Pulling away, I check my watch. It's ten to five. 'No, I wasn't. How come you're so early?'

'I put a dentist appointment in the diary and left.'

'Playing hooky? That's not like you. What made you do that?' I go to the fridge and peer at the contents, wondering what to cook.

'I was worried about you.'

'Worried about me? Why?'

'I've been calling you for hours. Why didn't you answer?'

'Oh, sorry, my phone's upstairs. I haven't started dinner yet – is there anything you fancy?'

'What's it doing upstairs?'

'It's on charge. The battery died. I forgot to charge it last night. I can do crab cakes, chicken tagliatelle, or stuffed peppers. And since you're home early, you get to choose.'

'How come?'

'How come you get to choose?'

'No, how come you forgot to charge your phone?'

'How come I forgot? I don't know. I guess I forgot to remember. Crab?'

'You're funny.' He comes over and kisses me on the top of the head before grabbing a beer from the fridge. 'How was your day?'

'Okay, I guess.' I grab the crab and an orange pepper from the fridge. 'Saeed is trying to organise an fMRI for Daisy.'

'What good will that do?'

'If it's successful, he's going to try some kind of stimulation therapy.' Taking a knife from the block, I finely chop the pepper.

Nathan swigs his beer. 'He's not a doctor. Since when do we let random members of the public treat our patients?'

'He's not a random member of the public, he's Daisy's psychotherapist. And he does research for the Sleep and Circadian Neuroscience Institute. Did you know he used to be a neurosurgeon?'

'No. Why would I know that?'

'Look...I know you two didn't get off on the right foot, but you should give him a chance. He's a nice guy. He's very knowledgeable. You'd actually like him if you put your silly jealousy aside.'

'Silly jealousy? I'm not the silly one. I saw how he looks at you. You're so naïve about men.' He takes the knife from my hand, lays it on the chopping board and drags me away. 'Come. Keep me company while I get changed.'

'I have to cook dinner.'

'Leave it. We'll go out to dinner since I'm back early.'

I try to pull my hand from his but he doesn't let go. 'Well at least let me put these back in the fridge.'

*

In the bedroom, Nathan gets undressed while I relax on the bed. He loosens his tie and pulls it over his head still knotted, and while he's undoing it he asks, 'Where did you go today?'

'Dry-cleaners...hospital...home. Not exactly *The Incredible Journey* but somehow it felt like it.'

'Anywhere else?'

His tone is bland, his smile warm. And yet, in spite of it, I'm suddenly aware of my own heartbeat. 'No. Why?'

He tugs at the knot, not watching what he's doing but looking at me instead. 'Rose, you're blushing. Are you lying to me?'

I swallow. 'No. Of course not.'

'Did you go somewhere with Dr Sharif?'

'Saeed? Why would I go anywhere with Saeed?!'

'I don't know. Maybe he invited you to his house for a coffee or something.'

'Nathan? Where's this coming from? Are we going to have this same conversation every week now? I've told you there's nothing between us. We're not even friends.'

'Why lie, then?'

'About what?'

'About where you were.'

'I told you where I was.'

He throws his tie on the bed and I pick it up, massaging the knot while he tugs at his shirt buttons, staring at me. He's waiting for me to say something else and, when I don't, he reaches into his trouser pocket for his phone. After pressing a few buttons, he holds up the screen to my face. On it is a map – a screenshot I think – and, in its centre, there's a tiny photo of me. I'm sitting on the very street I pulled into to make the call.

'You went to Oxley Grove on your way home from the hospital. Is that where Saeed lives? Oxley Grove?'

'Where did you get that?'

'We activated Find My Friends before we lived together. Don't you remember? So I would know you'd got home safe.'

Did we do that? I don't remember. Perhaps we did.

'I just stopped to make a call, that's all.' My cheeks flush even more and he glares at me with suspicion. I'm just glad Saeed said to make sure the call was genuine.

'It couldn't wait till you got home?'

'I promised the curtain lady the window dimensions first thing this morning and forgot. I didn't want to forget again so I pulled over and called her.'

'Hands-free not working?'

'The dimensions were in my handbag. What's going on? Why are you grilling me like this?'

'Because you're lying. It's written all over your face. Trust is the cornerstone of every relationship, Rose. If I can't trust you, we have no relationship.'

My heart moves around inside my body. One moment it's in my ears, the next it's in my stomach, and then it's in my throat, making it hard to swallow. The problem is that Nathan isn't wrong. I *am* lying. I didn't need to stop and make that call. And now I have no idea whether his reaction is because it's painfully obvious I'm lying, or whether he'd have reacted the same way if I'd really had a genuine reason to stop somewhere.

I don't speak. He's only been home fifteen minutes and I was already tired before he got here. Now I'm exhausted.

He marches over to my phone that's charging on my bedside table, and yanks the cable out.

'Nathan, what are you doing?' I get up from the bed and go over to him, holding out my hand for my phone. 'It's not charged. Can you plug it back in, please.'

He ignores me, staring at the Apple icon blazing on the screen as it boots up.

'Nathan.' I hold out my hand. 'Can I have my phone back, please.'

Again he ignores me.

Before he realises my intention, I reach around him and pluck the phone from his hand. He turns on me, his bright blue eyes darkening, but then he lets his hands drop to his sides and flashes me a reassuring smile that suggests he's not that bothered anyway. But then, out of nowhere, he snatches for it, taking me by surprise. Just in time, I swipe it away and hide it behind my back. Then I step backwards until I collide with the mirrored wardrobe door. Nathan closes the gap between us and reaches around me for the phone. But I quickly transfer it to my other hand and hold it as far away from him as my arm will reach. We're like two toddlers fighting over a teddy bear. But I can't stop myself.

This isn't me.

Until the day I walked out, I never stood up to Ryan. And I've never challenged Nathan either, not once in our year-long relationship. Right up until this very afternoon, I wouldn't have batted an eyelid at him wanting to look at my phone. There's not even anything on it, but for some reason him wanting to check it is really bugging me.

This is Saeed's fault. He's got into my head. He's the cause of this discord. It started the day we met, with his raised eyebrows about how quickly Nathan and I moved in together. The undertone in his voice when he called Nathan 'attentive' with his frequent text messages. If it weren't for him, planting ideas in my head, I would never have stopped on the way home. I wouldn't have blushed when Nathan asked me where I'd been. And this wouldn't be happening right now.

All this is because of Saeed.

'Give me the phone, Rose.'

'No. Why? What do you want it for?'

'Because you're clearly hiding something. What's on your phone that you don't want me to see?'

112

'Nothing. I'm not hiding anything.'

'Then show it to me.'

'No!'

Nathan makes another grab for it, so I raise the phone high above my head, but he clocks my intention. And as he quickly changes direction, his elbow slams into my nose and the back of my head clunks the wardrobe door.

'Ow!' I rub my lip. My fingers smear blood.

'God, Rose...you're bleeding.'

'Funny that.' I cup my nose and push past him. 'That'll happen when someone elbows you in the face.'

Nathan follows me to the en suite, where I turn on the cold tap and lean over the sink. He says, 'I *didn't* elbow you in the face. You caught your nose on my elbow while we were messing around.'

'Messing around?'

'Of course. *I* was only messing around. Weren't *you*?'

Sliding my mobile into the back pocket of my jeans, I cup a handful of water over my nose before pinching it closed.

'Rose...'

I don't speak. I don't even look at him.

'Are you angry with me?'

I still don't answer.

'I was only messing about, honestly. Honey...'

I release my nostrils long enough to check the blood flow. It's subsiding, so I splash more water on my face before pulling a reel of tissue from the roll and mopping the bloody water on my lips. The end of my nose, rosy pink, glares against my pallid skin.

Nathan laughs. 'You look like Rudolf.'

'Ho ho ho.' I throw the tissue in the toilet, flush, and push past him into the bedroom.

'I don't understand why you're so upset; it was just an accident. Honestly, I was only messing about. Why are you taking it so seriously?'

113

Between my breasts there are scarlet splashes on my white T-shirt, so I yank it over my head and pull another one from the dresser drawer.

'Come on, Rose. Don't be silly. Don't be mad.'

I ignore him. Straightening the clean T-shirt, I grab my phone from my back pocket and throw it on the quilt. 'Go on, then. Look. If it's so important to you.'

Feet rooted to the spot, shirt still unbuttoned, his stomach muscles tense as his upper body strains to move towards the bed.

We're suspended in ice.

He looks at me.

I look at him.

But his curiosity blazes, furnace-hot. So he marches to the bed and snatches up the phone. I wonder if he even knows the passcode, but then he presses his thumb to the fingerprint scanner before opening my call log. I don't remember adding his fingerprint.

He bought me that phone for my birthday. Did we add his fingerprint then?

I catch sight of the fifteen or so missed calls from Nathan's mobile as he scrolls past them, stopping on a number that has no contact details associated with it.

He puts the phone to his ear.

'Nathan? What are you doing?' I reach out for the phone but he turns his back on me. 'What are you doing? You're not calling her! What are you going to say?'

A tiny voice tinkles through the speakers. 'Sweet Dreams Interiors?'

Nathan hangs up and turns to face me.

We stare at each other.

A smile so fleeting it's barely there, flashes across his lips.

Then my mobile rings.

'Jesus Christ!' I snatch the phone from him. 'What am I going to say?'

114

'Say you butt-dialled her.'

I accept the call.

'Hello?'

'Hi, Rose, it's Pippa. Did you just try to call me?'

'I did but it cut off for some reason, damn mobiles. Sorry to trouble you again, but I just wanted to double-check the drop I gave you for the snug curtains.'

'Just a minute…'

Papers rustle and remorse slaps my cheek, burning. I wish I'd done as Nathan suggested and said I'd butt-dialled her instead of wasting her time like this. But I'm too angry to do anything he suggests right now.

'Two hundred and twenty-three centimetres. For both the window and the patio doors. Is that right?'

'Yes, that's right. I just wanted to be sure. You know what they say: measure twice, cut once.'

'It's always worth a check,' Pippa says. 'You'd be amazed how many customers complain their curtains are the wrong length and then, when I get them to double-check the measurements, they realise they gave me the wrong drop.'

'Well, I wouldn't want to be *that* customer. You said three weeks, right?'

'Sooner if I can. But I don't like to make promises I might not keep.'

'Under-promise and over-deliver.' I cringe at my own fakeness. 'As sensible as measure twice, cut once.'

'Actually, I meant to ask earlier: do you want me to hang them for you?'

'No, I can do that, thanks.'

'Well, if you change your mind… I'll call you when they're done.'

'Thanks, Pippa.' I end the call and glare at Nathan.

'Don't look at me like that,' he says. 'You should have her number in your contacts; she makes enough ridiculously expensive curtains for us.'

'Ridiculously expensive? Curtain fabric *is* expensive, Nathan! You're the one who said the snug was looking ratty and tired and I should do something about it. And when I showed you the cheaper fabric samples you said they looked *cheap*. You expect me to find things that look like a million dollars but cost a hundred pounds. It's not how it works. Cheap looks cheap! That's why it's cheap!'

'Let's forget it.' He takes the mobile from me, drops it on the dressing table and pulls me into a hug. Then he lifts my chin and kisses me, the kiss intense, fuelled by the disagreement.

And before I know it, we're making love.

But my mind wanders.

What just happened?

And what will I say to Saeed?

THIRTEEN

MAGGIE

I WAS ABOUT to run after the man, chase him into the woods, when the heavens opened and I had to get Alfie inside. His gaze tracked me from the lakeshore to the cabin where I stopped and stared back for a long time, daring him to do something. Anything.

Just make a move! Show me why you're here, what you want from us. From me.

But he didn't. He just watched me for a while longer and then slunk away into the trees. I think he's waiting for his moment to strike.

Well, he's not the only hunter in these woods.

'You wanna watch something? Watch this! *Pull!*'

The voice-activated trap launches two clays simultaneously and I track them one after the other across a cold sky yellowed by my protective glasses.

John used to run a small gun club here. It's the perfect place: miles from civilisation with an open field behind that's

117

longer than the legal safety zone. He got me into clay pigeon shooting when we used to come and stay. I ended up getting my shotgun certificate and he leaves this gun at the cabin whenever he knows I'm coming.

It's the difficulty of the sport that's so appealing – shooting a target that's moving so quickly and away from you is very difficult because the shot gets harder the longer you take to aim. You have to be decisive and accurate with steely nerves. I'm easily bored by anything too simple to master, which is one of the reasons I usually enjoy my job, and why this sport is so perfect for me.

But it doesn't feel like sport today. I'm sending a message.

I hope he's watching; I rarely miss. But, even if he isn't, a shotgun's crack and fizz is unmistakable. Whatever language he speaks, he'll be able to understand *this* message.

Rain is on the way. Grey clouds swallow white as they advance, a lightning storm in their wake that casts bolt after bolt into the distant tree canopy. The resulting thunder is a constant, resonating rumble. But every now and then a piercing bolt of lightning strikes the trees and the thunder's comeback sounds as if God has his own shotgun. Even my ear defenders don't buffer the noise.

'I said STOP IT!'

Suddenly the defenders are ripped from my head. And before I even realise Luc's standing there, or can stop myself pulling the trigger, he's wrenching the gun from my hands. The shot flies off in a random direction, splitting the silver trunk of the eucalyptus on the far edge of the field. I stare at it in disbelief as a section of loose bark peels away and flutters to the ground. And even though it's just a tree – completely out of place in its surroundings as if it wandered in from some fantasy novel – the wound aggravates my temper.

I break the gun, barrels down, and take out the spent cartridges before turning on Luc. 'What the fuck is wrong with you?'

'What the fuck is wrong with me? Your child's asleep upstairs! What the fuck is wrong with you?'

'That was really dangerous, grabbing the gun like that! You could have got hurt. What the hell were you thinking?'

'What was *I* thinking?! *Bordel de merde!*'

'Why didn't you just ask me to stop?'

'I've been calling and calling you for ten minutes. I've had to leave Alfie on his own up there. You know this is his nap time. He's only been down twenty minutes and you're out here doing fuck knows what… Taking your shit out on little pieces of clay?'

'Actually they're not made of clay—'

'Maggie!'

'Fine. I didn't realise the time. I didn't know you'd put Alfie down, okay?' I switch off the trap and disconnect it from the battery.

Luc relaxes but I see his anger. His boiling point is everyone else's simmer. Anyone who didn't know him would think that small action – switching off the trap – would be enough to take him off the boil, but I know him. I know he's still ready to blow. He betrays it with the smallest of tics: a twitch in his bushy left eyebrow; the up-and-down motion of his Adam's apple; the tension in the hairs on his arms.

'I'm sorry. I've stopped. Look, I've turned it off.'

'You haven't used that thing in months. So why now?'

I look at the ground, toe the grass.

'Maggie. Why now? It's because of him, isn't it?' He points at the trees. 'I'm not stupid. This is target practice, isn't it? For Christ's sake, can't you see how crazy this is?'

'I'm not crazy!'

As if God is telling me otherwise, the sky flashes white and the thunder cracks so quickly it's clear the storm is right overhead. Then the heavens open.

Luc has to shout over the thunder that rumbles on and on. 'I didn't say *you* were crazy, I said *this*…this behaviour is crazy.

Something's happened to you, Maggie. You're not yourself. You've changed since that day in the woods…since you saw that man. Is there something you're not telling me? Do you know who he is? Why he's here? Why *is* he here?'

'I don't *know*!' And I say it with such vehemence that I spit rain at Luc as it runs down my face from my already soaked hair. 'If I knew, I would tell you. And you talk about me! You're not yourself either. Why aren't you *worried*? Why aren't you afraid for me and Alfie?'

He's calm again now. Too calm. And it's more annoying than his temper. 'Maggie, I've never even *see* him. The other day, when you were fixing my computer, you said he'd been watching us. But Alfie and I had been playing by the lake the whole time. We *never saw* him. I can't be worried about a figment I've never seen.'

'A figment? You mean a figment of my imagination, don't you? *I've* seen him! Just because you haven't doesn't mean he doesn't exist, and I don't appreciate you suggesting I've lost my mind. Someone's got to protect this family, and if you won't do it, I will.'

'This is mad.' What are you going to do? Blow his head off with a shotgun? Is that your idea of protecting this family? Going to jail for murder?' With one arm resting on his forehead, he walks in circles, mentally talking himself down. Finally, he quits turning and says, 'This has to stop. I know you don't want to hear it, and maybe you're already sick of me saying it, but you have to get out of here before this place really starts to get to you. You need your colleagues around you. You need that insanely cryptic and complicated job to keep your mind challenged and focused. That's who you are, Maggie. This place – just taking care of Alfie – it's too basic for you. You need challenges, deadlines. And you're due back to work soon enough anyway.'

'What are you saying? That I have to go back because one of us needs to put food on the table?'

'That's not fair! I've never pressured you into staying in that job. You used to like it. If anything, you pushed me to take care of Alfie so you could work.'

'I know. And I do like it. But I miss you and Alfie.'

He softens a little and says, 'We miss you too. But right now, I'm missing the *old* you. You need to go back. Right now.'

'The only way I'm going back is with you and Alfie.'

Luc closes his eyes, lifts his face to the rain and works a crick from his neck. 'You know we can't do that.'

'I know. Which is why I'm not leaving.'

'You can come back. You don't have to stay away forever. Just long enough to reconnect. Feel the buzz of the city. Spend time with your family. Your friends. Alfie and I will be okay. We'll be right here waiting for you.'

I look at him as if I'm thinking about it.

But I'm not.

FOURTEEN

ROSE

'LOOK AT THIS, Rose.' Saeed points at a computer screen when I walk into the viewing area, the door closing softly behind me. 'Look how bright these patches are.'

The MRI machine in the room behind the glass pounds like a persistent migraine. I've missed half of Daisy's scan and I'm frustrated with Nathan for making me late. Then again, I'm frustrated with myself, too, for putting a dampener on his spontaneous and romantic moment. 'Let's both be late,' he'd said, pulling me back into bed just as I was getting out of it. 'We can blame it on traffic. Come on, crawl back under the covers with me.'

I'd giggled as he'd wrestled me into his arms and pulled the sheet over our heads, but I was only playing along. Daisy was at the forefront of my mind. So I'd squeezed him tight and kissed him on the end of the nose, asking for a raincheck. 'It's Daisy's scan this morning. I have to go.'

'You can be a few minutes late.'

'Not today.'

I'd untangled myself from him and the sheets, but I only made it as far as the en suite door when he'd said, 'So much for spontaneity.'

Half an hour later, I finally made it through that door and into the shower. It wasn't the sex that slowed me down – that had only taken a few minutes – it was the twenty-five minutes beforehand spent reassuring him.

I wonder if Nathan's right: if after just eleven months of dating and seven weeks of marriage I've already turned into one of those wives who only cares about curtains, a tidy house and what's for dinner.

I think perhaps I have.

Or, more likely, I was never spontaneous in the first place.

Daisy's the impulsive one, not me. I've never been one of those women who throws caution to the wind. I always weigh up the potential consequences first, and it's hard to be spontaneous when your mind works that way. I've never been so drunk I threw up. I've never had a one-night stand. I never think of the fun; I think of the hangovers and unwanted pregnancies.

I do want to be more spontaneous with Nathan, show him I love him as much now as I did when we first met. Just not today.

That's the opposite of spontaneous isn't it? I will be spontaneous with you, baby, but is it okay if I do it tomorrow night at six o'clock?

Daisy's important to me – of course she is – but, at the same time, I don't want to put pressure on my brand-new marriage by neglecting my husband.

Nathan needs me.

Part of marriage is accepting your partner for who they are, loving them in sickness and in health, loving them in spite of anything and everything. I believe that. And even though, some days, I wonder if Nathan needs me a little too much, I'm okay with it. I would rather have a husband who needs me too much than one who couldn't care less whether I came or went. I'm grateful for his attention and I'm glad he requires all of mine. He may be a handsome, intelligent surgeon, but he's still human: as insecure as the rest of us.

I think all relationships go through phases like these. The masks you wear when you're first dating fall away and you begin to learn who your partner really is. They start to show you pieces of themselves you've never seen before.

Nathan's confidence is a mask.

Beneath it, he's insecure and jealous.

Saeed doesn't know that. He doesn't realise that on the inside Nathan is soft and vulnerable. Saeed sees the formidable surgeon, just as everyone else does. I see a frightened little boy who's afraid of losing me.

And, knowing that, I understand why he went to such lengths to impress me on those first dates. Maybe he did tell a few lies, but now I know why. A confident man wouldn't need the kind of reassurance he craved this morning.

Perhaps I'm the one with all the power.

His intense need gives me comfort that our relationship will stand the test of time. His jealousy is flattering. His attention unwavering. His love fierce.

We all want that, don't we?

Saeed's finger traces the bright patches of light as they dance around the screen, green, orange and red. 'Look,' he urges, as if it's inconceivable that I'm not dancing with them, twirling around the room with joy.

'What do they mean?'

'They are Daisy's neurons.' He turns from the screen to look at me, his hands gesticulating eagerly. 'Just like muscles, when they fire – when they are active – they expend metabolic energy which requires oxygenated blood.' He turns back to the monitor, chatting and pointing while I stare at the monstrous contraption behind the glass. Daisy, motionless on the sliding table, her upper body in the monster's gaping mouth, sends a chill down my spine.

I see a crematorium.

I imagine her just like this.

Coffinless.

And finally the curtains close around her as she's pushed by the feet along the rollers into the flames, consumed by the furnace.

I have to mentally shake myself to focus on Saeed's plush tones as he barely takes a breath between explanations about oxygenated haemoglobin. Periodically, he glances at the radiographer for reassurance that he's remembering everything correctly from his neuroscientific training.

'It has a magnetic signature that the fMRI can read. Each bang is a magnetic pulse that pings the brain's hydrogen atoms, and from the speed with which they return to equilibrium the machine can tell how much oxygenated blood is in that area of the brain. They call it bold activity: blood oxygen level dependent activity.'

I stare at the screen, at the three-dimensional image of my sister's brain, at the traffic-light flashes inside her head.

And then I burst into tears.

In a split second Saeed is at my side, easing my hands from my face and wrapping them around his waist. He pulls me close, weaving his fingers through my hair as he rests my cheek, wet with tears, in the crook between his neck and shoulder.

I cling tight to the thin cotton of his kurta and sob. And, as he holds me tight, I slide my arms up his back and over his shoulders, needing his strong frame to keep me upright. It's as if my bones have liquefied and, without him, I'll be unable to stand.

I have no idea why I'm crying.

Relief?

Is it the knowledge that there are still signs of life in Daisy's mind?

I've imagined this moment many times since Saeed suggested the fMRI, but I never saw myself sobbing. I'd pictured this as a moment of joy, throwing myself into Saeed's arms and laughing. Yes there were tears. But not like this.

Perhaps it's exhaustion.

I'm so tired, I can barely function. And yet, I have no reason to be exhausted. I don't work any more; all I do is keep house and visit Daisy. Yet motivating myself to do anything these days takes an unnatural amount of effort and I've felt this way for months.

'It is good news.' Saeed extricates himself from the embrace and brushes away the hair that's glued to my cheeks. 'It shows that Daisy's brain is responding to stimuli. And stimulating her brain further has a chance of success. A small one, granted, but a chance.'

'I know.' I suck in breaths between sobs like a child. 'It's not that.'

'What is it, then? Did something happen with Nathan?'

A chair squeaks and we both turn and look at the radiographer, who must have been watching us the whole time. None of us are able to make eye-contact as Saeed and I resume our places behind the technician, dutifully watching Daisy's brain on the computer screen. Neither of us speaks again but, as we stand so close to each other, arms by our sides, the space between us crackles with static.

FIFTEEN

MAGGIE

I SIT ON THE EDGE of the roll-top bath, hair dye doing its job under a plastic shower cap, my towelling dressing gown falling open as I lean over to check the temperature. There's something extravagant about having a bath fitted in a bedroom and I'm so glad they decided to do that when they built the cabin. They could have built a bigger en suite but this is the perfect place for a bath, right in front of the bedroom's wood-burning stove. Luc lit it for me. The flames lick the glass.

The water's too hot so I turn on the cold tap and resist the temptation to get in. I'm forty-three and still childlike when it comes to bath time. I light candles, add floral bath bombs that fizz into a liquid rainbow, and break open my best soaps and shampoos. And, once I've done all that, I can't wait to get in. I'm always impatient for the tub to fill and for the water to reach the right temperature. So I lower myself in gingerly, feeling stupid for burning myself, instead of waiting a few minutes for the cold tap to do its work.

I think back two and a half months to mid-December —
which feels more like three years — and remember lying in
this bath with the wood-burner roaring. It was surrounded
by candles. Christmas was creeping close, snow was on the
ground, and Luc had left the radio tuned to Radio 2. Stephen
Fry was singing 'Fifty Words For Snow', which made me think
of Rose.

Blackbird-Braille.

Shovelcrusted.

Zhivagodamarbletash.

She's obsessed by Kate Bush; she's an oddball like that. Give
me Radio 1 and a good pop song any day. I remember sinking
down in the water, closing my eyes, and picturing Omar Sharif
opposite me in the double-ended tub, snow melting from
his impressive *Zhivagodamarbletash*. Magnificently naked.
Well...apart from the Russian fur hat. I remember laughing to
myself. I remember the whole cabin quivering with happiness
at the excitement of Christmas.

It was beyond perfect.

I wonder if Rose still listens to Kate; I can't imagine it's
Nathan's cup of tea. If he's said he likes it, I'll bet my pension
he's lying.

I should go back.

I could, I suppose.

She thinks I don't listen, but I do. She's always saying she
wishes I would *hear* her. But I do hear her. I hear everything
she says. And it's not that I don't care. I care deeply. But my
priorities are here. Luc and Alfie – they are my priorities. They
will always come first. It's just how it has to be when you have
a family. Rose will understand when she has a child of her own.

I toss the idea of leaving to the back of my mind and think
about my family instead. I'm grateful to Luc for giving up
some of his writing time to look after Alfie while I have my
bath. Even though I've loved every second of this sabbatical
and being able to spend all this time with Alfie, I still need a

break from him sometimes. And it gives Luc some time alone with him, too. He loves every minute with Alfie as much as I do: playing Duplo or skimming stones. But at the same time he'll be mentally flogging himself for the impact it's having on today's word count. We've been here three months and he's only managed an outline and few thousand words. Finishing the draft by the first of April deadline – just eight weeks away – seems a daunting task. No wonder he's feeling the pressure. I should go and relieve him.

Just a few more minutes.

Sliding down deeper into the cast-iron tub, I shut out the world.

~

By the time I've shaved from ankles to armpits, scoured myself with my favourite sea salt scrub, washed out the dye and conditioned my hair with coconut oil, my skin has pruned. So, reluctantly, I get out. I slip back into my fluffy dressing gown and sit on the edge of the bath to pull on my felted bootie slippers. Then I roll the knitted cuffs high up my calves to trap in the bath's relaxing warmth.

Running a comb through my wet hair, I stare out of the window and watch Alfie play by the lakeshore. He picks up stones and tries to throw them into the water but they inevitably land at his feet. Filled with love, I laugh every time he nearly topples over with each throw. At eighteen months he's still unsteady on his legs, but I picture him as a young lad, able to skim stones as well as me.

Picking up another, Alfie places it on his palm and examines it carefully – the same way I do when I'm choosing the perfect one for skimming – then he lifts both arms and throws as hard as he can, only this time, instead of letting go too soon and the stone falling at his feet, he manages a good throw! I let out an involuntary cheer as it flies a surprising distance and splashes a few feet ahead of him. And, even though he can't hear me, I clap my hands while he jumps up and down with joy.

He's growing so fast.

Alfie doesn't move for a while. He just stares at the lake, at the ripples that stretch out across the water, emanating from the spot where his pebble went in. He appears to decide that it was the perfect stone and, determined to use it again, wades into the water to fetch it.

The shingled bank drops sharply a few feet in. Right where his stone would have sunk.

My heart leaps into my mouth.

I slam my palms against the window but that doesn't get Alfie's attention. He can't hear me. So I press my face to the glass and look left and right for Luc.

He's not out there.

Alfie wades into the water while I wait a lifetime in three seconds for Luc to come into view. He wouldn't have gone far. He wouldn't have turned his back for more than a moment or two.

But he doesn't come.

Alfie continues to wade, step by step, while I watch in horror as the water climbs the height of his wellingtons, centimetre by centimetre.

'Alfie!' I bang so hard on the window, I almost break the glass. 'Alfie!'

Like two tiny sinkholes, the water pours over the rims of his wellingtons. And still he keeps walking until his yellow boots, full to the brim, disappear beneath the surface.

He's heading straight for the drop-off and those wellies are so tight around his ankles, there's no way they'll slip off. Like diver's weights, they'll anchor him to the bottom.

'Luc!' I bang on the glass again. 'Luc! Where the fuck are you?'

There's still no sign of him, so I fight with the window catch, cursing John for painting over it, leaving it stiff and unworkable. Finally, I shove the window open and scream Alfie's name into the cold air.

He doesn't stop. He doesn't even turn around. The wind sweeps my voice away as he continues on his quest for the stone. And still Luc doesn't come.

My slippers slide on the oak floor as I bolt from the bedroom and fly across the landing. At the top of the stairs, I lift the skirt of my long gown to stop myself tripping over it, and leap the stairs two at a time.

'Luc!' I scream his name, hoping he'll hear me from outside and realise what's happening. 'Luc!'

Flying through the cabin door, I jump from the deck and, just as I round the corner, Alfie reaches the drop-off and his head disappears beneath the surface. Heels bruising on stones, pebbles kicking up beneath the thin soles of my slippers, I run across the shore, all the while keeping my eyes fixed on the patch of water where he went down.

'Alfie!'

I run into the lake, but the moment I'm up to my knees the resistance of water and the pull of my wet dressing gown slow me down until I'm forced to wade. And then suddenly, as if I had no idea the drop-off was there, the ground disappears beneath me. I topple backwards, flapping my arms as I slip down the bank. My head goes under, but my feet find the bottom and I kick hard, managing to flip myself forward on to my belly. Then I dive, the heavy gown dragging me down.

In the blurred darkness, I whip my arms around as I swim in circles, praying they'll collide with the flesh of my son, but they find nothing. My heart beats hard enough to burst from my chest and I can't breathe. I can't stay down any longer, my thrashing panic has drained all my oxygen. So I fight my way to the surface, desperate for air, but my gown and slippers drag me back down, stealing the last of my strength.

I can't breathe.

I can't see.

Feeling around my waist, I try to untie the belt, but the fluffy fabric has swollen and the knot is locked in place. I tug at it but it's useless, rock-hard.

I'm disorientated.

And yet I'm certain I'm sinking.

Down, down, I plummet. As if the lake is hundreds of metres deep, when I know it can't be more than fifteen or twenty.

I'm losing my mind.

Losing consciousness.

Everything turns black.

Alfie can't be far away. A strange thought strikes me: when Luc reports his wife and child missing, the police will drag the lake and find me and my son. Just a few feet from each other – but not close enough to touch – anchored to the bottom by a pair of felt slippers and brimful wellington boots.

SIXTEEN

ROSE

'I'M SORRY. Bursting into tears like that. I made a complete fool of myself. Heaven knows what the radiographer thought.'

Saeed pulls the chair from the door to the bed and I sit in it without really thinking. It's a routine we've slipped into in no time at all.

He takes the seat opposite, saying, 'He must see it a lot.'

I brush my hair from my face and rub my eyes, still sore from crying.

'I got overwhelmed.'

'It is a lot to take in, finding out Daisy's mind is still active and yet...'

'It's not just Daisy...'

'What?' He leans over the bed, his gaze fixed on me. 'What is it?'

I have an urge to lean forward too, but I don't. Instead I keep my distance. 'Why did you ask me to deviate from my usual route home? How did you know what would happen?'

133

'I did not know. I thought... What did happen? What did Nathan say?'

'He seemed concerned at first. Then jealous. He asked if I'd gone back to your house for a coffee.'

'My house?' His hand gravitates to his chest, his molten eyes wide.

'He thinks we're more than friends.'

'Does he know his wife at all? You do not strike me as a polyamorous woman, Rose.'

'I'm not. I would never.'

Saeed reaches for me and finally I lean forward, resting my arms on the blanket where he places warm hands over mine. 'I am sorry,' he says. 'It was not my intention to upset you.'

'Well, it did. It caused an argument.'

'I am sorry. I should never have asked. But I was worried. I let my personal feelings get in the way of my judgement. Only I was sceptical and...if I am truly honest...I wanted to prove myself right. It was selfish not to consider the situation it would put you in. Please forgive me. Are you all right?'

'I guess. I don't know. I think so. I don't want to make more of it than it is. And I don't want you making more of it than it is either.' I press the heel of my palm into my forehead and rub hard. 'You're getting inside my head, Saeed, making me question my marriage over the silliest of things.'

'Perhaps they are not silly. Perhaps that is why you are questioning—'

'You don't understand. I've *been* in an abusive relationship. I know what one looks like. And this isn't like that at all. Nathan isn't a narcissist, he's the very opposite. All *you* see is the man on the outside: handsome, cocky. But you don't see what he's like on the inside. He's insecure. Protective. Afraid I will leave. And I have no idea what makes you think you can pass judgement on someone else's intimate relationship. You barely know us!' My voice echoes around the room and the silence that follows takes up all the space.

I've shocked him.

And now he's too afraid to say another word.

So I speak. I keep my voice calm and even.

'So he has me on Find My Friends – so what? Lots of couples track each other on Find My Friends. It doesn't mean anything.'

Saeed nods in agreement.

'Don't do that.'

'Do what?'

'Pretend to agree with me when you clearly don't.'

'What do you want me to say, Rose? You are not my client and I should not be treating you like one. Setting an exercise like that…it is something I would do with a patient, not a friend. I have never stepped this far out of line in my career, neither personally nor professionally. Well…except once. But that was different and I had good reason.' He gets to his feet and turns his back on me, staring at the wall for a moment. Then he runs his fingers through his hair and says, 'I think I must visit Daisy on a different day.'

My heart stops.

And it only starts beating again when he faces me. 'I have to be honest, Rose. I have never felt like this before. We barely know each other and yet I have never had a friendship like yours. I have no idea how to do it. I spend every waking hour with patients and, even when I am not with them, I am still strategising ways to help them. I lack the skills to be your friend. I am always going to want to counsel you.'

'Saeed… Please sit down.'

He does as I ask.

'I don't want you to come on a different day. I want us to be friends. And, if your friendship sometimes feels like a counselling session, I would rather have that than nothing at all. So counsel me, if that's all you know how to do. I promise to be open to whatever you say. And I promise not to lose my temper if you say something I don't like. Deal?'

135

He puts a reassuring hand over mine but he still won't tell me what he's really thinking. And I can't bear it. I can't bear this estrangement. I've never felt this close to anyone in so short a time and I want things back the way they were. The air needs to be cleared. We need to talk this through, no matter how much I dislike the things he says about Nathan.

I say, 'You think I'm wrong, don't you? About Find My Friends?'

Still, he doesn't speak.

So I wait, my eyes boring into his until he's forced to.

'You have to accept that request, Rose. Did you?'

'I don't remember. He said I did. When we first met. So he would know I'd got home safe after a date.'

'But you do not remember that?'

I slide my hands out from under his and pull away, leaning back in my chair. And then Saeed pulls away too, leaving Daisy's blankets cold and bare.

It isn't as simple as slipping back into the way we were.

'What do you think's going on, Saeed? You clearly believe you know more about my marriage than I do.' My anger lingers, my tone still alien and hostile. I can't stop myself from defending Nathan, any more than I can stop myself apologising for him.

'Perhaps we should change the subject.' He leans down and picks up the reporter-style satchel he usually has with him. 'Did you bring anything for Daisy? I brought these to stimulate her sight.' He pulls out two small torches. 'She should see the light from behind her eyelids.'

I don't move or speak. I just look at him while he holds my gaze. I want to press him, ask him what he sees in Nathan that made him so confident he would react to the call the way he did.

I want to.

And I don't.

Because I know I won't like it.

136

Anger blights our companionship. Daisy brought us together, sparked our friendship, and now she lies between us, as if, rolled on to one side by the nurse, she's a wall. I think, if Saeed can't talk to me about Nathan, he can't talk to me at all. And I don't understand why he can't just leave my marriage out of it. He shouldn't be making assumptions. Nobody knows what really goes on behind closed doors and it's easy to jump to conclusions based on two brief encounters.

I don't know, but I suspect Saeed has feelings for me. Not in that way, not love. It may be that he feels the same way about me that I do about him – friendship based on an instant connection – but I think there may be more there, an infatuation perhaps. I'm not sure. But it makes me question how clear his judgement is when it comes to my marriage. Whether his feelings for me are leading him to pre-judge Nathan. He said it himself in so many words: he wanted to be right about Nathan; he *wants* there to be something wrong with my marriage.

I need to be careful with Saeed. I think, when he looks at me, he sees a sparrow in the snow, its wings broken. He wants to scoop me up, place me in a box of cotton wool and sit me by his fire where he'll tend to me every day until my bones set.

But I'm no bird.

And I don't trust his judgement.

I lean down, pick up my handbag and place it on the bed before rummaging inside. 'I brought her favourite perfume.' I lay that on the bed. 'And this.' I hand him a cube speaker. 'I've downloaded her favourite album to my phone but I'm hopeless with technology; I have no idea how to get it to work.'

Saeed doesn't say anything, but removes the speaker from its box and unwraps the protective cellophane. And when it's plugged into the wall by Daisy's bedside and switched on, I unlock my phone and hand it to him.

'I say favourite, but I'm not sure it really is. I'm not sure she had a favourite band. She liked anything and everything

137

really. She'd get attached to something for a while but quickly move on. This is what she was listening to right before…'

Saeed taps a few times on my phone and has the speaker working in moments. He makes everything seem so easy and soon the room is ringing with 'Tilted' by Christine and the Queens. And all three of us are breathing in Spellbound by Estée Lauder.

And, while we flash the torches back and forth across her eyelids, rubbing her arms to stimulate her sense of touch, we don't speak. And we barely look at each other.

It's as if Daisy is awake and right here with us.

An overbearing chaperone.

SEVENTEEN

MAGGIE

I HEAR MY NAME as if it's a familiar but long-forgotten sound and my mind sparks in the darkness.

What am I thinking?

What am I doing?

With the flick of a switch, I could let go of this world. If Alfie weren't in it. If Luc weren't in it. But they are in it. Alfie is right here, just a few feet away. I can almost feel him. My nostrils swim with lake water but I swear it's the sweet scent of my baby's skin.

Alfie!

If I die, he dies.

And suddenly my eyes are open.

My mind teeters on the brink of consciousness. I have no strength left, no air in my lungs, yet somehow I find the wherewithal to reach down and rip my slippers from my feet. Then, wriggling my shoulders, I yank at the lapels of my dressing gown and manage to release my arms. Once my upper

139

body is free, I grip the gown by its belt and tug it down over my hips. The wet towelling fabric clings to my skin and I have to fight my way out but, eventually, I slip through. The gown claws at my legs as I kick it away like a writhing jellyfish. But it's only when I break the surface that it finally slips from my toes.

Sucking in one great breath, I take a split second to orientate myself before flipping over and diving beneath the surface again. Released from wet fabric, I'm able to navigate the water quickly, and I search it with my fingertips, clawing the darkness in every direction.

Then, finally, my hand connects with something solid.

Alfie!

I wrap my fingers around his peach-soft flesh but in the black water I have no idea what I'm holding. A wrist? An ankle? I think it's his wrist and, holding on tight, I claw and kick my way through the darkness as if my life depends on it.

Because *his* life depends on it.

Sunlight dilutes the water as I pull Alfie up from the depths and break the surface for a second time. But, as I lift him on to my waist, I'm gripped by exhaustion and slip back under. Getting him this far took all the strength I had and now, no matter how hard I kick, slowly, slowly, we still fall. Wrapped in my arms, Alfie's tiny body convulses and the sensation of his torso pulsing against mine is more than I can bear.

My little boy is dying in my arms.

I pull him close and he struggles against me.

And I realise I was wrong. This is no involuntary seizure of a boy taking water into his lungs and drowning. Alfie is fighting. Coughing and spluttering, he beats the surface with his fists in his determination to keep his head above water.

And that's all I need.

Adrenaline surges through my body and my muscles spark with life. My legs find their rhythm and my free arm claws the water, pushing us to the surface. Alfie inhales with lake-soaked lungs, and I stare into his eyes while he breathes in bubbles as if he's drowning in air. His legs are wrapped tightly around my waist so I let go and pinch his tiny nose, forcing what little breath I have left into his lungs. And then we're both gasping, hacking up lake water.

But he's alive.

Alfie is alive.

Once I'm sure he's breathing, I tuck him under one arm and swim on my side to the shore. He must be too exhausted to cry because he barely makes a sound, just shivers and breathes heavily. And when I finally reach the drop-off and wade the final few metres, Luc is standing at the shoreline. He stares in confusion as his naked wife strides from the lake carrying his half-drowned son, wellies still full to the brim.

'Where the fuck were you?' I spit.

'In my study.' He barely gets the words out as he points lamely at the cabin.

'In your study? You left your son to drown so you could swan off and write a fucking story?'

'I thought he was with you.' Stunned shock punctuates his words as he reaches out for Alfie with trembling hands.

But I pull him closer. 'Why would you think he was with me?'

'Why wouldn't I?'

'You said you'd look after him while I had a bath!'

'No, I didn't.'

'Luc. Don't play fucking games with me.'

'I'm not, I swear. I didn't say I'd look after Alfie.'

I glare at him. Is this some kind of sick prank? 'Alfie was playing in the lounge and, on my way upstairs, I popped my head round your door and asked you if you'd keep an eye on him.'

He thick eyebrows curl over the bridge of his nose and his eyes widen. Concern? Fear? I can't tell. But his voice trembles. 'Mags... You didn't ask me.'

141

My eyes narrow. 'You mean you didn't hear me. You weren't even listening, were you? You were so engrossed in that fucking book, you weren't paying attention.'

'I'm never *that* engrossed, Maggie. If you'd come into my study and asked me to look after Alfie, I would have stopped writing and listened to you.'

'Are you saying I just left my son by the lake and went inside to take a bath? He was playing in the lounge. How did he get outside? You're doing it again...making out like I'm some kind of crazy person!'

'I'm not saying that.'

'Then what are you saying?'

'Nothing,' he says. 'I'm not saying anything. I'm just as confused as you are. I don't know what happened here.' He moves in to hold us both but I take a step back, restraining myself from slapping him around the face. 'He's all right,' he says. 'That's all that matters.'

'Take him,' I hand him Alfie and turn on my heels.

'What are you doing?'

I ignore him and stride into the cold water, this time prepared for the drop-off. And before my feet have a chance to slip out from beneath me, I reach out in a long breast stroke. With air trapped in the fabric, my dressing gown and slippers have floated to the surface and I swim out to them. And, by the time I've dragged them back to the shore Luc's carried Alfie to the deck where, perching him on his lap, he tugs off his waterlogged wellies.

Naked, cold to the bone and shivering, I stumble over the stones towards the cabin, the bundle of wet fabric in my arms. But then I stop. The sight of Luc on the brink of tears, holding his son so tight to his chest he could break him, breaks me. How could either of us have made such a stupid mistake?

Then movement to my left catches my eye and I turn.

Standing at the head of the path is the man. And this time, nothing Luc has said about the distance between the trees and

142

the cabin can make me doubt that he is watching us. I can't see his face but I can feel his eyes. They scour my naked skin like fingernails.

Stock still, I stare back.

Then he turns and walks away into the forest.

It takes another bath to warm me. But, although the wood-burner is still lava-red from the last log, nothing can soothe me. Not candles. Not glasses of wine. And certainly not Stephen Fry reciting fifty different words for snow.

Luc bathed Alfie first and now they're in his room. He's reading him a story and Alfie's managing to stay awake, probably because he's too afraid to close his eyes. He must have been terrified. It sickens me to think of it. The dull throb of their voices is absorbed by the wooden walls but my ears prick at every sound. I can't relax. I'm on edge. As if I need to be ready to leap out of this bath at any second and run across the hall to protect Alfie from Luc's neglect.

I know I asked him.

I know it.

It wouldn't be the first time Luc's been too engrossed in his writing to hear me. Sometimes I ask him something and get no response at all. Sometimes he responds on autopilot, not really registering what I've said, saying yes when he means no or vice versa. But it's never been over anything this serious, just whether he wants a cup of tea or whether he's remembered to call his mum on her birthday. When it comes to Alfie, the mere mention of his son's name is enough to snap Luc to attention. Because, for him, Alfie's needs come before anything, even his work. It's one of the things I love about Luc: his dependability.

He's never let either of us down.

Sickening doubt clouds the bathwater.

143

It seeps in through my pores.

I replay the events of earlier in my mind. Alfie and I had walked Cairo through the woods. She'd seen a rabbit and run off. I'd known she'd be gone for hours, so we'd come back to the lake to skim stones while we waited for her to give up the chase.

The wind was biting and, although I'd wrapped Alfie up warm, I had stupidly not taken my jacket, thinking I'd be okay in my thick cardigan. By the time Cairo returned from her escapade, I was cold through and tired. The events of the past couple of weeks – the stranger in the woods, the pressure to go back and support Rose – were starting to take their toll. I'd wanted some time alone. I'd needed some time to think. So, I'd taken Alfie and Cairo inside and left them playing on the rug in the lounge while I went to ask Luc if he would keep an eye on them while I had a bath.

Something had distracted me then.

The phone.

Rose.

She'd made a fool of herself at the hospital, apparently, bursting into tears in front of Saeed and the radiographer. And I don't know why exactly, but the fact that he'd been there to comfort her – perhaps even overstepping the line in that regard – had given me a thrill. I don't know Nathan, not really, but there's something about him that puts me on edge. I'm not sure he's the right man for Rose. It's not as if I really know Saeed either, not in a personal capacity, but I can't help thinking he's a better man for my sister.

But then Rose became defensive, angry almost, which isn't like her.

I'd hung up but my mind had remained on the call. I was thinking of her, not Alfie. Is it possible that the intention to ask Luc to keep an eye on him was so fixed in my mind that I'd convinced myself I'd actually done it? Had I gone upstairs to take a bath without even thinking?

But how did Alfie get outside?

I know I didn't leave him by the lake. I'm not *that* crazy.

But it is possible I didn't close the cabin door properly when we came inside? It's not like me to do something like that, I'm usually so careful.

But then again, it's not like Luc either.

If either one of us isn't behaving like ourselves these days, it's definitely me and not him.

Fuck.

Did I get distracted by a phone call and almost kill my son? Or is Luc lying and he knows I asked him but he's too afraid to admit he got distracted by his book?

Or was it neither of us?

That man is still out there, watching us. He was standing right there, staring at me when I came out of the lake. Could he have crept into the house and taken Alfie outside? Did he take Alfie down to the lake then go back into the woods and watch it all unfold from his hiding place?

I have to know who he is.

Why he's here.

Why he's watching us.

EIGHTEEN

ROSE

'Don't move.' Nathan spins in excited circles. 'Wait right there. Sleep, rest, read, whatever. I'll be back in bit.'

'Where are you going?'

'It's a surprise. Promise you won't move?'

'I promise.'

Still gripping the test stick, I crawl back into bed. Cold light bleeds through the white curtains, far too bright for a February morning, as if it snowed overnight. The sun reflects off every mirrored surface.

I pull the covers over my head, breathe in fabric conditioner on crisp sheets, and stare at the letters on the grey screen. It's not as if I don't want a child. I do. It's just that I wanted some time alone first, for us to get to know each other a little better and form a deeper bond. Everything with Nathan has happened so quickly. I'm still reeling from the honeymoon and now I'm pregnant.

I haven't had a moment to catch my breath.

I know I'm more than two months gone because I skipped my last period. But I didn't think much of it at the time because I missed a period in August as well when I lost two stone in a month. It's common to skip periods when you lose that much weight so quickly. And I'm scrupulous with my cap, applying soup ladles of spermicide every time, so I didn't even think to do a pregnancy test.

I've never been this thin in my life. Nathan has been so supportive, paying for personal trainers, fitness trackers, nutritionists. I haven't had a moment to enjoy this new body, and now I'm going to get fat all over again.

Stop it, Rose! You've wanted a child your entire life. Desperately. You've missed being around the kids at school and now you're finally getting one of your own. Who cares about the timing? And who cares about getting fat?

Truth be told, I do miss my boobs. I had great boobs before I lost all the weight. No more padded bras. For seven months anyway, then I'll need maternity bras.

I'm not prepared for this.

I'm not ready.

I wake up when the bedroom door opens with a kick and pull back the sheets to find Nathan standing in the doorway. Ceremoniously, he stands there with a tray, a single red rose across a breakfast plate.

'I should get pregnant more often.' I lift myself up and plump up the pillow behind me.

'You can get pregnant as often as you like!' He places the bed tray carefully over my lap, taking care not to spill the coffee and orange juice over the plate of poached eggs, kale and tomatoes.

'What's that?' I point at a blue velvet box resting next to the cutlery.

147

'Open it.'

Picking up the delicate case, I crank it open and inside, resting on a bed of pale silk, sits a diamond eternity ring. The platinum setting is a subtle trellis that's barely visible from the surface – almost identical to my engagement ring – so all you can see is a circle of large, brilliant-cut diamonds.

'Nathan!' I look up at him and he's grinning. 'It's beautiful.'

'Put it on.'

I do and it fits perfectly. 'How long was I asleep?'

He laughs.

'Seriously, I know you didn't just rush out and buy this. When did you get it?'

He shrugs.

'Nathan? When did you buy it?'

'What difference does it make? Do you like it?'

'I love it. And it doesn't make any difference, I'm just curious, that's all.'

He shakes his head, 'I don't know, a month ago.'

We've only been married two, but I don't say that. I don't want to say, *You bought me an eternity ring two weeks after we got back from our honeymoon?* I'd sound like an ungrateful cow. But, like the pregnancy, everything is moving so fast. It's a little too soon for eternity.

'You enjoy that – ' Nathan points at my breakfast ' – while I jump in the shower. Then I'll crawl back in there with you and we can make love to celebrate… Carefully!' He chuckles to himself, almost dancing across the room before disappearing into the en suite.

I stare at the plate of food.

I can't face it.

So I slump down and stare at the ceiling, which sparkles when I twist the three heavy rings on my wedding finger.

Refreshed from a shower, I come downstairs in my robe and the moment I open the kitchen door I'm taunted by the smell of freshly toasted bagels. Like burning too much incense in a small room, it overwhelms my senses. I swear I feel its crisp top on the roof of my mouth, its soft dough giving way beneath my fingers, its crust crunching in my ears. The butter-toast smell twists my stomach with a delicious muscle memory.

It's ridiculous that so small a thing can have such an impact on your body. It's just a bagel. But I haven't eaten one in seven months. I used to eat them all the time, loaded with cream cheese and bacon sprinkles.

I want to slap myself. And I want to slap Nathan, too, for tormenting me with them.

'Fucking... Fucking...' Nathan struggles with a jar of honey. 'Cunting... Fuck!'

'Easy.' I flinch at the C-word. 'What's up?'

'Fucking lid is jammed on. I've told you to wipe the fucking jar.' Nathan can't tolerate inanimate objects behaving badly. He expects me to behave irrationally, but objects should be predictable.

I say, 'I don't eat honey.'

By the look on his face, I swear he's going to throw it across the room. But instead he raises his elbow high as he fights to twist the lid.

I rush over to him, hold out my hand and speak softly. 'Leave it, baby. I'll do it for you.'

'If I can't open it, how are you going to?'

'Just give it to me.'

Reluctantly he hands me the jar, and I take it to the sink. I run the lid under the hot tap and then use a rubber glove for grip. It opens easily, and I hold it out to him.

He doesn't take it. He just stares at me, hands on hips.

'What?' I ask. 'In the absence of strength, us girls use our noggins. The heat expands the metal.'

'I know that, Rose. Don't talk to me like I'm stupid.'

149

'I wasn't, I—'

He snatches the jar. 'Are you going to the hospital today?'

'Of course. Daisy's surgery is today, did you forget?'

I put the portafilter in the grinder, fill it with fresh grounds and tamp them down. The coffee machine whirs while an unasked question curdles the air. I wait for it.

'And is the ubiquitous *Dr Sharif* going to be there?'

'Of course. The surgery was his idea.'

'After today, you should start visiting on a different day.'

'Why?'

'For me. To make me happy. I don't trust that guy.'

'You don't trust him to do what?'

'Don't be obtuse, Rose. I don't trust him to leave you alone.'

'Don't be silly. I've told you, he's not that sort of man.'

'Jesus. All men are *that sort of man*.'

'I can't go on a different day. Between taking care of this house, the personal trainer, the nutritionist, doctor's appointments, hairdressers and beauticians, I barely fit everything in as it is.'

'Reorganise it.'

'No.' I keep my voice light. 'You can't just change appointments willy-nilly; these are busy people. Besides, I've always seen Daisy on a Thursday and I'm not changing it because you have a funny feeling about someone who's perfectly nice.' I take my coffee and kiss him on the cheek before turning to leave. 'You'll just have to trust that your wife loves you as much today as the first day she laid eyes on you. And she wouldn't want another man. Besides, we have a baby on the way and it's for eternity, right?' I wave the ring at him as I back out of the room.

'Rose!' Saeed is on his feet and walking towards me the moment I step through Daisy's door. He's fidgety, out of sorts, not his

150

usual calm and collected self. 'I was hoping you would come early. I wanted the opportunity to talk to you before we go down.' He reaches for my hand but doesn't take it and then his own drops to his side. 'You have been on my mind constantly and I wanted to apologise again. I should never have interfered in your personal life. It was unforgivable and—'

'Please don't apologise. You were just looking out for me. I was on edge and upset. Let's just forget it ever happened. Okay?'

'Okay.'

He reaches out again and, this time, I do the same. Unsure whether to hold hands or shake them in agreement, we do a little of both. But then he doesn't let go. He holds me as if my bones are spun sugar.

Those little orbs light up my cheeks as I slide my hand from his. 'I didn't expect you to be here already. Don't you have patients?'

'I cleared the whole day. I thought you might need support.'

'You have no idea. I'm still not sure I've made the right decision. When Dr Anderson talked me through exactly what would happen, I didn't understand a word.'

'Oh, no, it is actually very simple...' He stops speaking and looks at me as if I'm a stranger. 'You look well today. Much...more yourself.' Then he studies me for a while longer.

I don't know whether to say anything. It's too early to be telling people. But this is Saeed; he's different somehow. 'I'm pregnant.'

His smile falters – I think – I'm not sure, because now he's bright, eyes shining. 'Congratulations. I can see you are very happy.'

'I am. I've always wanted a child. Maybe not quite this soon... But now, giving up teaching – saying goodbye to the children – doesn't hurt quite so much. I'll have a child of my own to take care of.'

'I am over the moon for you. You will be a wonderful mother.' Saeed raises his voice as he turns to the bed. 'Do you hear that, Daisy? Rose is pregnant. Now you have to wake up so you can babysit your niece or nephew. She is going to need you.'

I laugh, but then a thought strikes me. 'Daisy always wanted to be an aunt. But after everything that happened I'm not she'll be happy for me.'

Saeed turns to me, deep lines creasing his drawn eyebrows. 'Do not think that. You must not think that. Daisy *will* be happy for you. Having a niece or nephew to fuss over will be just what she needs. You know your sister – far better than I do, of course – and she would never resent your happiness. I am sure you know that, deep down.'

'I hope so. It's just so unfair. I never dreamed her life would turn out this way. That she would end up here, like this. I always saw her as this formidable, unbreakable woman. But now I wonder if we knew her as well as we thought.'

'We do not know she did this to herself. Let us believe the best rather than the worst. Especially at a time like this.' His eyes drift to my stomach and my hand gravitates to it. And then the sun streams through the window and catches my finger. The ceiling sparkles. 'That is very beautiful. It is new?'

'Nathan gave it to me this morning.'

'Eternity.'

'Yes.' I clear my throat, the word stuck in it.

'You deserve to be happy.'

We turn at the sucking swoosh of the door and, as Zesiro greets us, I wonder if Saeed's heart stopped beating at the same time as mine.

'*Jambo*, Miss Rose.'

'*Jambo*, Zesiro.'

'I've come to take Daisy down. Is she ready?'

His bright, cheerful face reassures me and I'm glad that, of all the porters who could have come for Daisy, it's him. I step aside to make room for the transport stretcher.

'This is Dr Sharif, Zesiro. He treated Daisy before the coma.'

'Saeed, please.' He shakes the porter's hand with both of his.

While Zesiro is loading Daisy on to the stretcher, I turn back to Saeed and grab the sleeve of his kurta. 'I'm scared. Are you sure this is the right thing to do?'

'No need for nerves. As I said, the surgery is simple and we have nothing to lose.'

'Don't worry, Miss Rose,' Zesiro says. 'Daisy is in good hands. Dr Anderson will look after her. You can see her in recovery.' But, as he wheels her through the door, I have to suppress the urge to grab the other end of the stretcher and fight him for her.

Saeed and I are the only two people in the recovery room. Daisy hasn't been in that long but the whole day could have gone by while we've sat next to each other on hard plastic chairs. She's my older sister but, right now, I feel like her mother. The decision to put her through this was the hardest I've ever made, and I wonder how I'll cope with making tough choices for my child when it comes. When Dr Anderson explained the procedure to me, I had been too preoccupied with the weight of the decision and the potential side effects and complications to listen properly. And then Zesiro had come for Daisy before Saeed had a chance to explain.

'Should it be taking this long?' I ask. 'I'm going crazy in here.'

'I promise you it is very straightforward. It is unlikely that there will be any complications. I would not have suggested it if I thought it would put Daisy in any danger.'

'Dr Anderson made it sound quite frightening, what I remember of it anyway.'

'Not at all.' Saeed slides around in his chair to face me and the space between us narrows. 'Dr Anderson will implant the vagus nerve stimulator here.' He places his palm on the upper left side of his chest. 'It is a small device with wires that travel beneath her skin, and Dr Anderson will wrap them around her vagus nerve, here.' Tilting his head to the right reveals the prominent muscles in the left side of his neck. Then he pulls apart the V of his kurta to reveal a river of dark hair down the centre of his chest. 'She will have two five-centimetre scars, one here...' He draws a line with his index finger from the left side of his throat to his Adam's apple. 'And one here...' And then another on the left side of his chest just below his clavicle. 'Because she is slim, you may just be able to see the implant in her chest here...' He runs his fingertips back and forth over his upper pectoral muscle where his chest hair recedes to taut, bare skin. 'But it will not be too noticeable.'

'How big is it?'

'About the size of a pill box.' Still using his body as a model, he traces a line from his chest to the back of his head and says, 'Every five minutes the device will send a thirty-second electrical pulse to the vagus nerve, which projects to several regions in the brainstem.'

'And what will that do?'

'Without boring you with the science, the device stimulates the hypothalamus, which excretes a peptide that regulates our nervous system, energy levels, hunger levels and sleep duration. In other words, it should stimulate wakefulness in Daisy.'

'Is it going to work?'

'It would not be right to get your hopes up, Rose. As I said before, VNS with coma patients is very experimental. But the fMRI was positive, and if we continue our stimulation exercises... who knows.'

Without thinking, I cross my fingers.

Saeed adds, 'The VNS device comes with a magnet, and when we swipe that across the device it produces a sixty-second period of deeper stimulation. We can combine that with our existing therapy when we visit Daisy.'

'When can we start?'

'Straight away.'

'This afternoon?' I can't hide my excitement.

'You do not have to get home?'

'I'm not going anywhere. Not today.'

NINETEEN

MAGGIE

'Wake up!'

Still half-asleep, I open my eyes a slit. A hazy Luc sits on the edge of the bed leaning over me, so I close my eyes and turn over. 'I don't want to.'

'You do. Come on. Wake up.' He grabs my shoulder beneath the winter quilt and rocks it.

'It's too cold. I don't want to.'

'You do. You really do. Come on, get up! Get dressed!'

He pulls the quilt down, but I snatch it back and yank it over my head. 'You're gonna have to sell me on it. Otherwise I'm not moving.'

'It's snowing.'

I throw off the quilt and sit up. 'Does Alfie know?'

'Not yet. He's still asleep.'

Kicking the discarded covers into a ball at the bottom of the mattress, I lean on Luc's shoulder, leap out of bed and rush to the window. It must have been snowing all night because there's a thick blanket on the ground. Like a dark grey iris, the lake is surrounded by a sclera of pure white, and it stares at the clouds overhead. I half expect it to blink at the snow falling on its surface.

I turn from the window back to Luc, almost bouncing on the spot with childlike delight. 'I'll get dressed. You get Alfie.'

'Deal!' He hotfoots it from the room.

'Don't tell him,' I shout after him.

And he leans back around the door and says, 'And spoil it? As if!'

The four of us stand at the closed cabin door, me keeping it pushed to but with the handle cranked open and ready. Cairo scratches at the base, desperate to be set free; she can smell the snow.

'Are you ready, buddy?' Luc asks.

Alfie nods, excitement and confusion on his sweet little face while Luc and I grin at each other. Then I throw open the door and a whoosh of frigid air, clean and crisp, hits us all in the face. We can't help but laugh.

Cairo is gone in a flash of orange and white, closely followed by Alfie, who squeals and runs out, almost tripping over the threshold. Only Luc is right there before he has a chance to fall. '*Attention, mon petit!*' He grabs Alfie by the hood. 'Slow down.'

But our boy doesn't even break his stride, his legs kick the air as he's momentarily scooped off the ground, and the second his feet touch the deck he's running again. At the steps, it's clear he thinks he can jump them, but Luc's there again, lifting him up by the underarms this time and taking the leap with him into the snow.

A soft silence has fallen over the lake and forest: the water's too cold to move, frozen at the shoreline, and the trees are too

157

weighed down to quiver their leaves and branches. It feels as though nature has stepped in and insisted we be left in peace.

Luc makes snowballs and tosses them for Cairo, who leaps into the air to catch them. When she misses, she searches the ground, confused by their mysterious disappearance. Then, if Luc doesn't make another snowball right away, she barks at him until he does, shuffling her white bottom backwards as she readies herself for another catch.

Meanwhile, Alfie and I make a snowman. Unlike the ones we make back home, which are always dirty brown from the muddy lawn, this one is pure white, magical in its perfection. But when I realise we've made his tummy much bigger than his bottom I suggest we build him upside down, and it warms my heart to see Alfie so delighted. Especially when we upturn a pair of Luc's old wellingtons on top and dig some twiggy arms into the ground so it really looks as if he's doing a headstand.

When the snowman is finished, Alfie takes over the job of throwing Cairo snowballs. And, with a moment to ourselves, Luc and I both steal a glimpse at the wide patch of untouched snow by the side of the cabin.

'Shall we?' Luc holds out his hand.

'I'd be delighted.'

'One second.' He lets my hand drop before dashing back into the cabin. And a few moments later his study window opens a crack and 'A Beautiful Mess' by Jason Mraz spills through the gap. It's the perfect choice for a waltz in the snow, and before I know it Luc's by my side again, taking me in his arms.

We laugh as we dance, constantly checking the floor to see where our feet are landing. The rule is that every footprint must land in fresh snow until there's nowhere left to step. We've got pretty good at it over the years; the secret is to make sure you cover the whole area from the start of the dance and take wide strides so there's plenty of room between footsteps. But the dance gets harder and harder and funnier and funnier until we're more leaping than dancing. And when we're surrounded by flattened snow with nowhere left in jumping distance, we fall to the ground, exhausted. Then Alfie and Cairo come running over and climb on top of us.

Only once, maybe twice, do I even glance at the forest path.

The man doesn't come.

And for the rest of the day he's forgotten. If he was camping out in the woods, the snow will have driven him away. If he's on a journey, perhaps he's moved on. Perhaps he's moved on so far that there's no reason for him ever to return.

Perhaps our lives will go back to normal.

We'll be the happy family we were before he arrived to unsettle us all.

Unsettle me.

I follow Luc, Alfie and Cairo as they make their way back to the cabin, stopping and turning only one last time to check the break in the trees.

He's not there.

I smile at the empty path with a contentment I had long forgotten.

TWENTY

ROSE

WHEN ZESIRO wheels Daisy into the recovery room, the relief is so overwhelming I feel physically sick. I have to check my tears as I rush to her bedside, anxious to assess the damage. Because I signed the consent forms. I did this to her.

I damaged her.

Just as Saeed explained, she has a bandage on the left side of her neck and another on her upper left chest. They're much smaller than I'd thought they'd be. Below the chest bandage, beneath her skin, I can just make out the implant. It looks like an oval pill box inside her and because Saeed explained it so well, because everything looks exactly as he said it would, I'm less afraid of it.

The sickness subsides.

I want to touch it but I'm scared of hurting her. 'Will it be working already?'

Saeed smiles and nods.

'You mean she could wake up at any moment?'

'Rose...' Saeed is serious. 'You said you would not get your hopes up. I could not bear to see you broken by disappointment if this comes to nothing. Remember, it is only experimental.'

'I won't.' I'm barely able to keep still. 'I promise.'

A deep line forms between his eyebrows and his mouth draws down.

'What? I said I promise!'

Saeed shakes his head but his eyes are bright.

'Dr Anderson asked me to give you these.' Zesiro hands Saeed two small black boxes, one of which has a fabric strap attached to it. 'He said you'd know what to do with them.'

'I do. Thank you, Zesiro.'

Having made Daisy comfortable, Zesiro says, 'I'll be back in a little while to take Daisy to her room.'

And as soon as he's gone, I turn to Saeed. 'Can we try it now? You said straight away.'

'We should let Daisy rest, but we can try one pass just so you know what to do when I am not here.'

'Can I do it?'

'Of course. It is better if you do.' Saeed hands me one of the magnets.

'What's the one with the strap for?'

He glances at the magnet in his palm. 'This one is designed for epilepsy patients, so they can wear it on their wrist or ankle for ease of access in case of a seizure. Daisy will not need it.' He points to the one I'm holding. 'We can keep that one by her bedside.'

'What do I do?'

'You swipe it across the device in Daisy's chest. But it should be a quick pass, two seconds, no longer. If you hold it over her chest for too long it will disable the device rather than boost its function.'

And, in the same way we do when we're in Daisy's room, we take our places on either side of her: Saeed on her right, me on her left. We're like an old married couple who chose which side of the bed to sleep on fifty years ago and have stuck to it ever since, regardless of whether we're home or away.

'Ready?' he asks.

'Ready.' I hold the magnet between my fingers, hovering it high above Daisy's chest, but my hands tremble. 'I'm scared.'

'No need.' He places his hand over mine. 'Shall we do it together?'

I nod. And quickly and decisively, he swipes my hand across the VNS device.

Nothing happens.

'Did it work?'

'Yes.'

'How do you know?'

'I saw it.' He points at Daisy. 'When you know what to look for you will see a slight contraction in Daisy's throat, here. The vocal cords contract when you stimulate the vagus nerve.'

'I didn't see it – can we do it again?'

'Later, when Daisy is back in her room. We should leave her for now. Let her rest. Remember the VNS will stimulate her vagus nerve at regular intervals, all day, every day. The magnet is just to boost it now and then.'

And, with perfect timing, Zesiro knocks on the door and comes inside. 'I will take Daisy down now. You can join her in her room in about fifteen minutes.'

Reluctantly, I drag myself away, only realising when we get to the door that Saeed's as reluctant as I am. Leaving her, even for a matter of minutes, is too hard for either of us right now.

'Come on,' Saeed says. 'We can get a coffee while we wait.'

I nod, but we both stay glued to the spot, staring at her while Zesiro preps the equipment for transport.

And then Daisy moves.

Her arm flies up and her hand flicks back and forth as if she's pestered by a fly.

162

'Did you see that!' I point, almost shouting.

'I did!' Saeed's face lights up with wide eyes and a smile so broad he looks like a different man. I've never seen him so animated, so excited. He wouldn't react this way if this weren't a huge milestone. And his excitement thrills me. Laughing with joy, we stumble out of the recovery room into the corridor, where I leap into his arms and he spins me around.

TWENTY-ONE

MAGGIE

Immersed in the wonder of him, I watch Alfie whack an old oak tree with a long, thin branch. His hands are too small to grip it tightly so it keeps slipping through his fingers. He's trying to break it into small enough pieces to fit in the log-burner, only his arms aren't strong enough. He can't swing it with enough force to snap it against the trunk.

I don't intervene.

He's so curious, so enamoured by his father and so reliant on and attached to me, that he mimics everything we do. That has its advantages and disadvantages: he learns quickly by copying, but we have to be so careful what we say and do around him.

I pick up a tree branch. For its heft and length it's very light, which tells me it's seasoned long enough for firewood. As if I'm swinging a baseball bat, I whack it hard against the trunk of another oak and its end ricochets off into the undergrowth. Cairo chases after it as it rustles like prey through the dead leaves, and then she drags it away to chew in a moment of quiet contentment that lasts as long as it takes me to snap off another piece. I rotate around the tree trunk before whacking the branch again to make sure it doesn't ricochet in the same direction. And when it goes flying, she abandons her quarry for this new prey.

Collecting firewood keeps Alfie and Cairo entertained for hours and it doesn't feel like a chore. Back home in Oxford, we'd have firewood delivered. This is a luxury that time affords, and I don't want to give it up and go back.

My father-in-law taught me this trick when we were visiting him in France. After the divorce, he kept the vine-yard in Val-du-Layon and Luc's mother kept her house in London. Despite marrying Gabriel, she hated the remote location, the isolation. Luc's a lot like his father: earthy and grounded. Over the years of visiting, Gabriel has taught me so many things about plants – growing flowers and vegetables – along with this technique of breaking branches without the effort of chopping. It's a good test of the wood's viability too: if it's seasoned enough to burn, it'll be light and snap easily.

Usually I get Alfie to break twigs into kindling, but he soon tires of that and wants to be like me and his dad: able to break down big branches. I dream of the day he'll be able to. Maybe, if Luc and I buy the cabin, he'll come up for weekends as a grown man and we'll walk through this forest together, talking about his job or his latest love affair, gathering branches as we go. I feel sorry for his future wife already; Luc's always saying I'll terrify the living daylights out of any girl Alfie brings home. That I'll be an imposing and formidable mother-in-law and no woman would ever be good enough for my beautiful boy.

It's not true.

I'd love a daughter-in-law.

So long as she loves him the way I do.

165

The three of us move through the forest, me carrying the backpack that's almost full, stopping occasionally to break another good-sized branch that feels seasoned, or to snap kindling from a fallen bough that's been on the ground for years, its bark peeling and dry.

Up ahead, the sun shines bright through the trees, light relief after the previous week of snow and rain, so I chase it, Alfie and Cairo in tow. But when we break the treeline and step into a clearing I'm taken by surprise. I was expecting to come out on to the track. We must have got turned around and taken off in the wrong direction. The large clearing is carpeted with leaf litter, airy and light, and in its centre six fallen tree trunks are arranged in a circle around a fire pit.

Alfie runs to the circle and I follow him while Cairo sniffs about, uneasy. She can smell my apprehension. The trunks look freshly cut and it would have taken a very strong man to drag them here.

Alfie darts around them, oblivious, as I step between them into the centre. The blackened pit is surrounded by large grey stones which are so smooth, they must have been carried here from the lake.

It's possible John did this years ago, for barbecues on a sunny day; it's a beautiful clearing. But it all looks too new, too fresh.

I bend down by the stones and scan the ashes. They're cold, but there's nothing else among them, no leaves, no debris. Nothing has blown into the pit in spite of last week's storms, which means the ashes are as fresh as the newly cut trees.

Luc keeps telling me that nobody comes through these woods, but he's wrong. This is proof. Not that I needed it; I'm well past believing I'm imagining things.

There is someone here.

The snow didn't move him on. He's still camping, sleeping in the woods. But why? To watch us?

Whenever I catch him staring, I feel something.

Malice.

It emanates from him.

I've never even seen his face and I know it's crazy — how can you detect malice from someone's posture dozens of metres away? — but I do. And somehow, I know he's not just passing through.

He's here for us.

After all, who stands and glares at people in that menacing way? An innocent stranger would come up and say hello, introduce himself, apologise for trespassing on private land, ask if it's okay to hike through.

I think it's Ryan. It's too coincidental that the moment Rose's ex-husband is released from jail, we're terrorised by a man in the woods.

Behind me, Alfie screams.

I look up from the fire pit and he's running away from the circle across the clearing. But I can't see what he's running from. His little legs won't go as fast as he wants them to and his upper body leans so far forward he's bound to stumble at any moment.

'Alfie!'

He can't hear me over his own screams.

I stand up and cup my hands around my mouth, shouting, 'Alfie! Wait! Alfie!'

Then I see what he's running from.

From high in the trees, four huge black crows swoop down, each of them closing in on Alfie from a different direction. Diving at his face and the back of his head, they take him to the ground.

'Alfie!'

I break into a run, leaping first across the fire pit and then over the furthest log. Behind me, Cairo barks but I can't tell if she's following or retreating. Half of me hopes she'll run to help Alfie and the other half hopes she'll run for the trees and be safe.

167

Alfie's face down on the ground but he doesn't even lift his arms to protect himself; he just lies there while the crows peck the back of his head. Then they arc upward into the sky and Alfie's back on his feet and running. In my peripheral vision the birds return to their perches in the canopy, but I sense they're readying themselves to dive again.

I've never seen Alfie run so fast, and I'm shocked by the distance he's managed to put between us when his legs are so tiny. And before I can reach him, the birds come again.

'The trees, Alfie! Run to the trees!'

But instead of heading for cover he gets himself turned about and heads left across the clearing, the distance to shelter now even greater. I switch direction and follow as, in unison, the four crows dive again. Desperate to frighten them off, I scream at the top of my lungs, 'No! Get away!' But they aren't afraid of me.

They attack.

Pecking at his face and hair, they take Alfie to the ground again. And this time only three of them retreat, swooping away and returning to the canopy. The fourth continues its assault. Its claws grip the hood of Alfie's coat while its black beak, shining hard, drives like a blade through his baby-soft skin. I run faster than I ever have in my life, but the gap between me and my son seems to grow rather than shrink. And I can do nothing but watch the scene play out like some grotesque horror in bright sunlight.

Finally the gap closes, but then I step on a large stone and the hard sole of my boot rocks forward, throwing me off balance. My legs give way and I fall to the ground a few metres from Alfie, who's still under attack. Scrabbling quickly to my knees, I reach behind me for the offending stone, snatch it up and, with as much force as I can muster, skim it through the air at the bird. 'Get away! Get away from my baby, you fucker!'

Beating blue-black wings, the crow lifts off into the air, and makes for the safety of the canopy while I stagger to my feet and run to Alfie. He's face down in the grass and I rub my hand over the back of his head. 'Alfie! I'm here, baby. Mumma's here.'

Warm blood seeps through his golden-brown hair and, when I pull my hand away, my palm is red and wet. I'm about to cry out when, from behind me, there's the crack and swoop of wings.

I scoop Alfie into my arms and run.

Up ahead, not far, is the clearing's edge, and I make for the safety of the tree canopy. Cairo barks – she's right behind us, frantic. And then I realise why: wings beat the air around me and I scream as I'm whacked in the face by hard quills. My hair's a sudden tangle before my eyes, like a forest of twigs I can't see through. And then comes pain. Claws or beaks – I don't know which – stab like knives through my skull.

But I don't stop.

I just run.

The treeline retreats; it seems the closer I get to it, the further away it moves. And then the crows come again. Their claws tear my hair from its roots, their black wings smack my face, and their razor-sharp beaks drive through my flesh as I stumble forward, unable to see where I'm going. But it isn't me they're attacking, not really; they're trying to get to Alfie. So I wrap my arms around him tightly, holding my chin over his head to protect it as their wings beat each other in a squabble over my child.

'Get off!' I scream at the top of my lungs. And, shifting Alfie on to my hip and gripping him one-handed, I beat them off with my free arm.

Finally, we make it to the treeline.

Deep in the wood, under the shelter of the canopy, I kneel down on the floor and set Alfie on his feet. Cupping his face in my hands, I check his wounds. Blood oozes from nicks and cuts all over his cheeks, forehead, and the bridge of his nose. Snot trickles down his lip, and tears run down his face over the cuts, diluting the blood, which pools in the corner of his mouth. Another trickle of blood runs from his rosy lips down his chin, and his little body shudders with terror.

Cairo stands guard, staring at the clearing in the distance, and, before I have a chance to clean Alfie up, she's barking again.

The crows are coming.

I'm on my feet, scooping my boy into my arms. He wraps his legs so tightly around my waist it's hard to breathe. But I don't care, I'm running. Negotiating the forest, heart pounding, legs quivering from exertion, I snake around the trees, keeping as close to the trunks as I can. Cairo follows. But so do the birds. They're on the wing, just beneath the canopy, but it's not easy for them to attack at this pace, this close to the trees. My throat burns, and I'm desperate to stop for a breath but I can't.

I won't.

After what feels like hours, I finally break through the opening on to the lakeshore and, as quickly as they attacked, the crows retreat. I spin around, searching back along the path and through the trees, but the only evidence they were ever here is the blood trickling through my hair and slowly drying on Alfie's face. Heaving breaths and shaking, I only now realise I've sprained an ankle. This new pain hits and suddenly I'm limping, struggling across the gravelly shore towards the cabin.

Through his study window, over the top of his computer screen, Luc greets me with a cheeky grin which collapses the moment he sees the state of us. In less than a second he's on his feet and running for the door. He stumbles over the stones in his eagerness to reach us and, as soon as he does, he lifts the sobbing Alfie from my arms and wraps him in his own. 'What the fuck happened?'

Barely able to catch my breath, let alone speak, I puff out the words, 'Get inside first.' And, as I hold open the cabin door for Luc to carry Alfie inside, I take a long look back at the path through the trees.

'Is he asleep?' I ask.

'All cleaned up and sleeping like a night monkey.' Luc flops down on the sofa next to me.

I've lit a fire, though it's not that cold, and have a blanket over my curled-up knees. 'How's his face?'

'Sliced up pretty bad. But they aren't deep. Are you hurt?'

'A few cuts, but I've cleaned them up, I'll be okay.' I run my fingers through my hair, where the scabs are already forming.

'What the hell happened out there?'

'We were attacked by crows.'

'What?!' Luc half-laughs.

'I'm not joking. Crows.'

'Not really?'

'Yes, really. We stumbled on a clearing in the forest where someone's been camping. I was trying to figure when the fire pit was last used, and Alfie started screaming. He was running across the clearing and they were swooping down on him from the trees. By the time I got to him they'd attacked him twice, three times maybe, I'm not sure. And when I got him in my arms, they started attacking me just to get to him.'

'Jesus Christ.' He pulls me into his arms and I bury my face in his woolly jumper. 'Are you all right?'

'I'm fine. Just a bit shaken up, that's all.'

'When did you last have a tetanus jab? And when did Alfie?'

'Tetanus! I didn't even think of that. Alfie's was at sixteen weeks. He's not due for the next one until he's gone three. But I don't remember the last time I had one.'

'Well, you'd better drive him into town in the morning. Get the doctor to look him over and get a booster yourself.'

'Can't you drive him?'

'What? I can drive Alfie but I can hardly get a tetanus shot for you, can I?! You'll have to go.'

'No, of course... I'll drive him.'

We're quiet for a while then Luc asks, 'Did you do something to piss them off?'

'Who?'

'The crows.'

I sit up. 'What?'

'They remember faces.'

'What on earth are you talking about?'

'Crows. They're really smart; they recognise familiar faces. Did you chase them away from some prey or something?'

'Don't be ridiculous.'

'I'm not. I'm serious. They take revenge if someone wrongs them. Like, if one of their clan does something out of line, they place it a circle and pace around it, chattering away while they decide its fate. They call it a crow court.'

I picture this ritual: black birds with tucked wings circling a defendant, like barristers in gowns and powdered wigs pacing a courtroom. 'And what do they do to it?'

'If the crow is found not guilty it's set free, but if they find it guilty they peck it to death.'

'You're not serious?'

'Google it. They're smart little beasts.'

'Little bastards more like. How do you know all this shit, anyway?'

'Research for the novel.'

'You have crows in your novel? Tell me they don't attack people?'

Luc looks sheepish.

'Oh, Luc. Please tell me you haven't written some silly blonde going into a bedroom, opening the door inwards, and still managing to shut herself inside?'

He laughs at the reference.

'No, I ended up cutting the scene.'

'Thank heaven for small mercies.'

We're both thoughtful for a while, until I say, 'Don't you find the fire pit odd?'

Luc shrugs. 'Could be old. One of the previous renters camping out or having a BBQ. We've talked about camping with Alfie lots of times.'

'It didn't look old. I think it's the man's camp.'

'Your heavy breather, you mean?'

I scowl at him.

'Well, I've never seen this guy. And I spend all day at my study window.' Then, after a long silence, he asks, 'When are you going back, Maggie? You know things aren't right here.'

'What do you mean?'

'You know exactly what I mean.'

He's trying to rile me by bringing this up now but I won't let him. 'I'm not having this conversation. Don't you think I've been through enough today?'

'You're right.' He pulls me back into a hug and kisses me on the top of the head. 'I'm sorry. Forget I said anything.'

We stare into the fire for a while. The glass has a black stain down the front, and with the vents closed there's no flame, just an ashen log lying over the embers. It still holds the remnants of its tubular form, but I know if I were to prod it with the poker it would crumble to dust.

TWENTY-TWO

ROSE

'FOR HEAVEN'S SAKE, Nathan. Can you even hear yourself? So I hugged him. Should I have asked him to put on a condom first?'

'It's not just that you hugged him, it's the way you hugged him, the way you look at him.'

In yellow Marigolds, carrying my cleaning caddy of sprays, scouring creams and sponges, I barge past him into the main bathroom at the top of the stairs. 'That's quite a talent. You could tell how I was looking at him from the back of my head?'

'I could tell from the way he was looking at you.'

'That's called empathy, Nathan.' I get down on my hands and knees, squeeze a zigzag of Cif along the inside of the bathtub and scrub frantically with the scouring sponge. 'It's when someone is able to experience the feelings of another person.'

'Yeah, you share your feelings, all right. Everyone in that corridor saw you throw yourself at him. It was embarrassing. You humiliated me in front of my colleagues.'

I snatch the shower from the mixer tap and rinse the bath, trying not to splash water on myself. Cleaning in a pink dress and cardigan isn't exactly sensible but Nathan hates me wearing sweatpants and hoodies. He says they look 'pikey', whatever that means.

I use Nathan's own words, employ his talent for dancing around every apology, and say, 'I'm sorry you felt humiliated. But Saeed and I do share the same feelings: for Daisy. We both want her to wake up.'

'For Daisy, and for each other.'

'Oh, for heaven's sake, Nathan. I can't keep having this same conversation. I am allowed to talk to other men. I am allowed to shake hands, hug them, be friends with them.'

I chamois down the tub, grab my caddy and get to my feet. But when I try to leave the bathroom Nathan stands firm in the doorway, blocking my exit.

'Excuse me!' I say.

'You're pretending there's nothing going on between you, but everyone in that corridor saw. It's so blindingly obvious. You were fawning all over him like a filthy little whore.'

Wide-eyed, I step back, slapped by his words.

This afternoon, seeing Daisy move, was the most joyful moment I've had since finding her unconscious in her lounge and having to put a brick through her patio window. I laughed. I cried. Heartsick and euphoric at the same time, I was sure my chest would burst open and a rainbow of butterflies would flutter into the corridor, as if they'd been cocooned inside me for three long years. And now, just two hours later, Nathan's stamping them to death.

I'm so disappointed, hurt and angry I want to scream. I want to flail his chest with my fists for taking that joy from me, for giving me so little time to relish it.

I try to push past him but he won't move.

'Will you let me through?'

Reluctantly he steps aside.

175

I circle around him, put the caddy on the floor outside our bedroom door and take out the glass cleaner and kitchen roll before going in. Nathan follows me.

'How come he's always there, anyway? He says he's there to see Daisy, but we both know that's not true. He may as well be visiting a corpse. He's there to see you.'

I spray glass cleaner on the mirrored wardrobe doors and wipe, wishing I could crawl inside and shut him out. 'I told you. He's been visiting Daisy every week since she went into the coma. He checks her charts, talks to her, tries stimulation techniques; he even tells her jokes. She's still his patient as far as he's concerned, and he cares about her. I know you can't possibly understand that, Nathan. It seems to me you think relationships between men and women are all about fucking. But for some people, feelings run a lot deeper.'

'He probably is fucking her.'

'Jesus Christ.' I stop wiping and stare at him.

'What?'

I don't speak.

Finally, I tear my eyes from his and move to the dressing table, where I sit on the stool and spray down its polished surface. If the choice of decor had been mine, I would never have this many mirrored surfaces; they show every speck of dust and you have to dry them thoroughly with kitchen roll to prevent them smearing. It's an endless, mindless task. One I've never seen Nathan do.

I rub out my anger and frustration.

'It just seems awfully convenient to me,' he says, backtracking from his outrageous statement as if he hadn't said it. 'That, after running into you, he's suddenly there every Thursday when he never used to be.'

'It's not *convenient*. One of his patients didn't need that time slot any more, so he visits on his way home. He's the one who suggested the surgery. There's a chance it could wake Daisy up and, if that happens, he'll never see me again.'

Nathan snorts and I glare at him.

'You're not going on a Thursday any more.'

'Yes, I am!'

'You can go on Fridays instead.'

I get up and go to the dressing screen – another bloody mirrored surface – and wipe it as if I bear it a grudge. 'I can't go on a Friday. I do the weekend shop, take a few things down to your mother so she has everything she needs for the weekend, and then I have my session with Sarah.'

'Move Sarah to Thursday.'

'Sarah's fully booked, Nathan. I *can* move the gym to Thursday but I'll have to change trainers.'

'Fine. Change, then.'

'All the other trainers are men.' Gripping the kitchen roll in my fist, I'm tempted to pick up the glass cleaner with my free hand and throw it at him. 'You chose Sarah because you said you didn't want me "in tight gym gear, getting close and sweaty with a fit male personal trainer".'

'I never said that.'

'Yes, you did. And I'm not reshuffling my entire life around your paranoias. There's nothing going on between me and Saeed. You'll just have to trust me.'

After flitting around the rest of the bedroom furniture, I go to leave, but again Nathan blocks the doorway. And when I try to push past him he grabs the architrave on both sides, gating me in.

'Let me out.'

'No. Not until we settle this.'

'It is settled. I'm still going to the hospital on a Thursday and you're going to stop behaving like a child.'

'You say I have to trust you, but how can I? If you were telling the truth, if you cared about my feelings at all, you'd visit Daisy on a different day. But no! You have to go when he's there because you want to see him.'

That strikes a nerve and I blush.

177

'Look at you.' He points at each of my cheeks in turn. 'You're lying. It's written all over your fucking face!'

I tell him I'm not lying, but there is an element of truth in his accusations. I don't want to change days. Not because I can't be trusted not to cheat on him – I would never do that; I love him. But because I enjoy Saeed's company so much. He's transformed my difficult and depressing visits with Daisy and given me hope for her future, a hope I had long forgotten. He's become a friend and I enjoy being with him. Is that so wrong? I like the way he looks at me, not with lust or anything as superficial as that, but with his full attention. As if he's on edge with anticipation over what I might say next. He listens to me with his whole body. And when he speaks, even the harshest truths – like the possibility of Daisy not waking up – are delivered with cotton-softness.

I never feel like *this* around him. I never feel these knives between my ribs, cutting nerves and tipping bone.

I say, 'I'm not having this conversation any more.' And again I try to get past him. But Nathan stays firm.

'Let me through!'

'I bet if I called Sarah she'd be able to change days, switch a client around. But you don't want me to do that, do you, Rose? You want to keep seeing that *Paki*. I didn't see it before but you're just like Claire: a lying, cheating bitch.'

Holding tight to the kitchen roll and the bottle of glass cleaner, I shove him as hard as I can and his right hand slips from the architrave, sending him backwards. He tries to force me back into the bedroom with his body, but I'm already part-way out and he barges into my shoulder instead. I'm caught off balance and drop the cleaning supplies as I reach for the door frame to steady myself. But Nathan's blocking it and I grab nothing but air. I step sideways and my foot lands in the cleaning caddy. When I'd put the caddy down, outside the bedroom door, it was half-hanging over the top stair, and it's that edge I step on. My whole body weight bears down on empty space.

178

My world is in slow motion.

Nathan, stock-still on the landing, watches me as I fall backwards, arms outstretched, fingertips reaching out to him. Time slows. And then my back strikes the edges of the stair treads so hard that my legs scissor forward towards my face and send me into a roll. Halfway down, my feet career into the banister and twist me sideways, slamming my head into the side wall. Finally I hit the winders at the bottom, crash into the base wall and everything goes black.

≈

There are footsteps in the darkness.

I hear my name.

'Rose! Are you all right, baby?' Nathan's arms are beneath me, lifting me, but my body's twisted at an angle and I cry out in pain.

I open my eyes and his face is pressed to mine so I push him away. 'I'm all right. I'm all right. Don't touch me.'

Slowly, carefully, I untangle my body and arrange myself in a sitting position on the top winder step. But it's a lot longer before I can get to my feet.

Nathan leads me like an invalid into the lounge, supporting my weight as I sit down on the sofa. But the moment I'm seated, I pull away from him. 'Leave it, Nathan. I'm all right.'

'Are you sure? Maybe we should get you to the hospital?'

'No. I just need a minute. I'm okay.'

He sits down next to me and we stay there in silence for a while. But I can't bear to sit next to him for a second longer, so I struggle to my feet. He springs up to help me.

'Leave me alone.' I push his hands away. 'I don't want your help.'

'Rose…' Nathan's voice is grave so I turn. He's not looking at me. He's looking behind me. I follow his gaze to the sofa cushion where I'd been sitting.

There's a small, dark patch.

With Nathan following closely behind, I stumble out of the lounge and up the stairs, clawing the wall and banister not only for support but to propel myself away from him as quickly as possible. In the bedroom, I grab a clean pair of panties from the chest of drawers and a skirt and jumper from the wardrobe. Finally, I snatch up my mobile from the bedside table and hurry to the en suite, yanking the door closed behind me and locking it.

A few seconds later, Nathan knocks. 'Baby? Are you okay?'

I ignore him.

Fingers shaking, I pull my GP from my list of contacts and dial. But she's with a patient so the receptionist tells me she'll call me back as soon as she can.

Lifting the skirt of my dress, I pull down my bloodied panties and sit on the toilet, fighting the urge to burst into tears. Once I've tidied myself up, I put a panty liner in my clean knickers and put on the skirt and jumper. As I'm filling the sink with cold water to soak my soiled clothes, my mobile rings.

'The receptionist explained what happened,' says Dr Francis. 'I've already called ahead to the hospital and they can fit you in for an emergency ultrasound. You may have to wait, but they'll get to you eventually. Now I don't want you to worry, Rose. The chances of a fall – even down an entire flight of stairs – causing a miscarriage at this early stage in the pregnancy is incredibly low. So try to stay calm. And get them to look you over while you're there, make sure you haven't broken anything.'

'Shall I go now?'

'Yes. Go now.'

'Thank you, Dr Francis.'

'No problem. I hope everything's okay. Call me, will you?'

'I will. Bye.'

I hang up, unlock the door and barge past Nathan, straight through the bedroom and down the stairs, ignoring the pain in my stomach and legs.

'What's happening? Was that the doctor? Rose? What did she say?'

I take my coat, handbag and sports shoes from the under-stairs cupboard and sit on the bottom step to tie the laces.

'Where are you going?' Nathan asks.

'Where do you think I'm going?'

'To the hospital?' He grabs his coat from the cupboard.

'I'll drive myself.'

'Don't be stupid. What if something happens on the way? What if they have to keep you in overnight? I'll drive you.'

I picture myself leaning over the steering wheel in acute pain, almost colliding with another car, and reluctantly agree to let him drive.

But I don't speak to him for the whole journey.

Nathan and I sit next to each other on the hospital's hard plastic chairs. Ahead of us, off the main waiting area, is a small room filled with toys and books, and I watch a young boy push a toy car around a parking garage. He looks just like Alfie and my hand gravitates to my stomach.

It doesn't hold me together.

A silent tear falls from my cheek on to my skirt.

'Mrs Winter?'

I look away from the boy to a young nurse who's standing at the edge of the seating area holding a clipboard. She has blonde hair and a smile too bright for the circumstances. Nathan helps me to my feet and I have to hold myself back from shoving his hands away and yelling at him to leave me alone. I don't want him in the room for the ultrasound, but don't want to cause a scene by insisting he wait here; he'd make a fuss I don't have the energy for.

The nurse leads us through a small office into a dimly lit examining room and asks me to remove my skirt and panties.

181

'There's a sheet there,' she says, her smile so conspicuous it's as if this whole thing is an inside joke. 'You can put that over yourself while you wait for the sonographer. We'll be with you in a moment.'

Nathan sits quietly while I do as I'm told and, a few minutes later, the bright-smile nurse returns with the sonographer in tow.

'Hello, I'm Nessa Wylie. How are you feeling? Any abdominal pain?'

'A little,' I minimise. After all, if I don't admit to it, it isn't really there, is it?

In a matter of seconds the sonographer has donned gloves, put a probe cover over the ultrasound wand, smothered it in gel and deftly inserted it inside me. Then she twists the monitor so both she and I can see the image while she moves the wand around.

I quickly realise that, before calling me in, the sonographer had been telling the nurse about an embarrassing email she'd sent without proofreading it, because the nurse continues their conversation as if Nathan and I are not here. She chatters away, relaying her own experience of an unprofessional email. And I can't decide whether she's trying to lighten the mood or whether she's too inexperienced to recognise the fine line between putting a patient at ease and completely disregarding the gravity of their circumstances. And, as the sonographer concentrates on the screen, the nurse tells her about the email she sent to her very handsome and charismatic estate agent which she accidentally signed off with kisses. Nathan sniggers in awkward politeness, but the nurse laughs enthusiastically at her own story while speculating over whether he might think she'd done it on purpose.

Then the sonographer says, 'I'm sorry. There's no heartbeat.'

And the laughter stops.

TWENTY-THREE

MAGGIE

I SIT IN THE car with the engine running and the driver's side window wound down. Alfie kicks his car seat with the bored impatience that only a child can muster in less than a minute of sitting still.

Luc leans in through the window and kisses me goodbye, the kiss long and lingering as if I won't be returning for months rather than hours.

'I love you,' he says.

'I love you too.'

He pats the roof a few times, as if slapping a horse on the rump. But I just sit there, knuckles white on the steering wheel.

'You have to go,' he says.

In the rear-view mirror, Alfie's face is a mess of cuts and dried blood. I close my eyes and grip the steering wheel harder.

'Maggie.'

'I know, I know. I'm going.'

I put the car into drive and roll out of the garage, barely touching the accelerator until the crunch of gravel dissipates as we roll on to the track that leads to the main road.

It's an overcast morning. Bursts of lightning fleck the clouds on the horizon. More rain is on its way. Over the years, storms have bent the trees that line the track inward and their thick canopies form a tunnel. It exacerbates the darkness. A gust of wind blows raindrops on to the screen, and I turn on the wipers. It must have rained while we were tucked up in front of the fire last night.

I have no idea why I'm so reluctant to drive into town. I'm aware that the feeling is completely irrational, but that awareness doesn't make it go away. I never used to be this way. I've always been a firm, decisive person. I've always had my wits about me. And, if I'm honest with myself, I know Luc's right: I've been spending far too much time alone, or in the company of Alfie. It's not healthy for an adult. The Maggie I used to be is getting lost back there at that cabin. Stone by stone, I'm skimming myself across that lake, sinking to the bottom and disappearing in the sand.

The track through the woods is long, and at this speed we'll take an hour to reach its end. I accelerate. Luc will start to worry if we're gone too long. Won't he?

The car bumps along the track, the bonnet bucking occasionally when I hit a pothole, but I don't slow down. I have to face this irrational fear. I have to go into town; I have no choice. The doctor may decide Alfie needs his tetanus booster early, to be on the safe side, and him not getting it is a risk I cannot take. He's chatting to himself on the back seat, speaking in bubble-talk.

At the T-junction where the track meets the tarmacked main road, I stop. The road is empty. I switch on the indicator.

But I don't turn.

Instead, I lean forward and tap my forehead on the steering wheel in frustration. 'Come on, Maggie. Come on!'

My pep talk dies in the footwell.

'Mumma!'

I spring upright at the sensation of Alfie's little hand on my shoulder and spin around. He's wriggled his arms free of the shoulder straps of his car seat and has shuffled forward, barely held in by the lap belt.

'What on earth do you think you're doing?!' I undo my own seatbelt and crawl on to the centre console. Alfie bursts into tears as I grab him by the armpits and lift him back into the seat, shouting, 'You never...' and my face is right up in his as I shove him backwards with a flat palm against his fragile chest '...climb out of your car seat! Do you hear me?'

And then he's sobbing, his cheeks as ruddy as his lips.

I twist his arms awkwardly, forcing them back under the restraining straps one by one. I pull the tightening belt as far down as it will go, and his sobs turn into wails. But I ignore his cries, climb back into the front seat and take a few deep breaths before collapsing on to the steering wheel in tears, sobbing as uncontrollably as my son.

After a few minutes of crying I manage to compose myself, but Alfie's still bawling, so I twist in my seat and reach out to him.

'I'm sorry, sweetheart.' I rub his knee. 'I didn't mean to shout at you, but you frightened Mumma. You must always, always stay in your seat, okay?' Alfie nods and his tears finally subside. So I tickle his tummy and sing, 'What's It All About, Alfie?' until he's laughing.

And then everything's all right again.

I place a hand on his forehead and he doesn't feel too warm. He's bright as a button – just as he always is – as if the cuts on his face aren't even there. They're already scabbing over, healing. If there were anything seriously wrong after the crow attack he'd be showing symptoms by now, surely? And he's not due for that tetanus for ages. I count the months on my fingers: twenty-two. The doctor's not going to give him an extra dose so soon. I can just keep a very close eye on him over the next week, and if he shows any signs of being unwell I can rush him straight to the doctor then.

I turn off the engine, put Alfie's favourite MP3 compilation on the car stereo and relax in my seat, singing along with him until he nods off. Then I switch to Radio 2 and listen to Ken Bruce play 'This Time I Know It's for Real' by Donna Summer and 'Everybody Wants to Rule the World' by Tears for Fears. Then Ken plays a couple of tracks I don't recognise, an Abba song, and then 'Stop Me from Falling' by Kylie. A few tracks later, 'Stairway to Heaven' comes on and I check my watch to see if I've been gone long enough.

Just about.

I put my seatbelt back on, put the car in drive and do a three-point turn at the junction.

'That didn't take long,' Luc says.

'No. The doctor said he didn't need another tetanus, that his baby jab will see him through till the next one.'

'Oh, that's good. Poor little man's been through enough without being stabbed with needles as well. What about you?'

'It turned out I'd had one in the last ten years and forgotten about it, so neither of us needed it.'

'Good news all round then,' Luc says.

Alfie's a ragdoll over my shoulder, head buried in my neck, arms dangling down my back. 'I'm gonna put him down. It's early for his nap but it's been one hell of week; he must be exhausted.'

'I'll come up with you.'

We climb the cabin stairs together and I say, 'I think I'll have a bath while Alfie's sleeping. I'm chilled to the bone.'

'A quick bone in the bath, did you say? I'm up for that.'

'Is my Frenchman deliberately mistranslating my English?'

186

'Well, he's not very sophisticated, what can I tell you? A bit of a wild man, actually. I have absolutely no control over him.' Luc gets down on all fours, crawling the last few steps and biting my bottom as I reach the top of the stairs.

'We'd better get that dirty wild man in the bath, then, hadn't we?'

'I'll go and run it,' he says.

~

In our bedroom, Luc has filled the bath to the rim with bubbles, lit candles on the surround, and even gone downstairs to get us each a glass of malbec.

'This is romantic,' I say. 'Not what you expect from your average wild man. But it's a little early for wine.'

'It's wine o'clock somewhere.' He pulls me into his arms and kisses me deeply, gently, his tongue lightly brushing mine. 'Besides, wild men need to relax sometimes too. Especially when they have their work cut out for them in the bedroom.'

He lifts my sweater over my head and even though he can't take his eyes off my breasts, bulging out of a bra that's a little too small, he asks, 'How's your head? Did the doctor look you over?'

I drive my fingers through my hair and rub my scalp, tentatively tracing the outline of each scab. 'Mm…nothing to worry about. Just a little sore.'

Luc slides a hand over my breast and down my belly. 'I think I have a cure for that.' He drops to his knees and kisses my stomach before unbuttoning my jeans. As he pulls down my zipper, he follows the slider with his tongue and, when it reaches the end, he stays there for a while.

I moan.

In the bath, I rest between his legs with my back against his chest while he gently squeezes spongefuls of warm water

187

through my hair. It stings at first, but the pain eventually dissipates.

The memory of the birds doesn't scab over so readily.

'Is it really true?' I ask. 'That crows deal out punishment and remember human faces? Or were you just making that up?'

'It's true. Why?'

'I just remembered something... Alfie was throwing stones at a dead crow by the lake. Maybe they thought he'd killed it.'

'Don't think about it any more. Just maybe don't go in his bedroom and close the door on yourself without checking the rafters first.'

I laugh, and Luc nibbles my ear.

Moments later, he's soaping me all over and then sponging me off before lifting me out of the bath and towelling me down.

'I think they're dry,' I say, when he gets carried away towelling my breasts. 'Come on, let's light the fire and crawl into bed.'

'I'll light your fire in a minute.'

He shows off some Cuban hip action while flossing his undercarriage with the towel, which I grab and pull him along by to the wood-burner. 'Come on, wild man, show me your fire skills.' And then I leave him to it and crawl under the quilt to stay warm.

Even after all these years of marriage and having a child together, I still love making love with Luc. He never rushes me, despite the potential for interruption from a crying child. He kisses me all over, and goes down on me until I have to stop him for fear of coming too soon. And when he finally makes love to me, he straddles my legs and pushes them together while shifting his body forward, making sure that every inch of him touches every inch of me. And I have to hold back, delaying the inevitable for as long possible before crying out.

And this time, like most times, Luc puts his hand over my mouth, 'Ssssh, you'll wake Alfie!'

So I stick my tongue through his fingers.

'Eeeww!' Luc pulls his wet hand away and wipes it down my cheek.

'Eeeww!' I wipe my cheek and then twist sideways, forcing Luc on to his back and climbing on top of him. I know, in this position, he won't last. So, I throw my head back, thrust out my breasts and ride him to a rapid finish before falling into his arms.

And then, for a while at least, everything's quietly perfect.

TWENTY-FOUR

ROSE

ONCE I'D PULLED myself together, got dressed and come out of the examining room into the sonographer's office, she told me that the fall down the stairs had caused a placental abruption which had starved the baby of oxygen. And that, since I was still in my first trimester and already bleeding, it would be best to allow the miscarriage to continue naturally. But if the bleeding doesn't stop in two weeks, she said, I can take medication to open my cervix and hurry the process along. She offered me a D&C and, looking back, I wish I had taken her up on it. Now, every time I go to the toilet and find blood on a panty liner, I break down in tears all over again. But at the time, sitting in that tiny office with her, Nathan and the giggling nurse, I couldn't have made a decision between tea and coffee.

I was pregnant for eight weeks, but I only knew for a day.

One day. That's all the time I had to adjust to it.

At the hospital, after seeing Daisy move, I had pictured a new start. It had felt right. A chance to put all the unhappiness of the last few years behind me and look towards a future filled with love and laughter. I'd pictured Daisy back with us, holding my baby in her arms.

I have never felt as happy as I did in that moment in the corridor.

And now it's gone.

I hadn't been at all prepared for what I saw during the scan. At only eight weeks, I'd expected to see nothing more than a dark smudge on the screen, perhaps in the shape of a kidney bean, but it hadn't looked like a kidney bean at all. It had eyes, a swollen tummy, little arms and legs, and you could even make out its tiny toes.

I didn't see a smudge.

I saw my dead baby.

Now, pushing a trolley around Tesco, I try to focus on the boxes in the cereal aisle and, as I've done every day since the scan, try to un-see what I saw. I've been in pain all morning and now I'm hot and sweaty. I just want to go home. But I've been resting for three days, there's no food in the house, and Nathan won't eat take-away during the week. It was a push to convince him to relax his stringent rules over the weekend, but I couldn't face cooking. I couldn't face doing anything.

I pull a box of muesli from the shelf and then, as I lean over the trolley handle to put it in the basket, a sharp pain stabs through my belly. At the same moment, the pad in my panties fills up, telling me I need to get to a toilet as soon as possible. Discreetly holding my crotch while covering the front of my skirt with my handbag, I abandon the trolley and totter to the end of the aisle.

Desperate, I scan the signs that hang from the ceiling for one that will direct me to the ladies'. It's at the far end of the store, past all the checkouts, and I half-run, half-waddle past the queues of customers.

It's a relief that all three stalls are empty. I take the middle one. In a series of swift manoeuvres I lock the door, hang my bag on the door hook, lift my skirt, and pull down my tights and panties together in one. But, before I have a chance to sit on the toilet, what seems like the entire contents of my womb empty out on to the floor. My shoes, tights, panties and the entire stall floor are covered with blood. Staring down at the massacre beneath me, I let out a shriek.

Stumbling backwards, I burst into tears, grabbing the partition for support as I sink down on to the toilet. Sobbing, I spread my legs and watch more blood pour into the bowl.

I have no idea how I'm going to get out of this stall.

I have no idea what to do.

Looking up at my handbag on the back of the door, I consider using my mobile to call for help, but blood still runs into the toilet bowl and I don't have the strength to get up. I lift my head and direct my voice to the ceiling.

'Help!'

At first my calls are tentative, probing. But when nobody comes, they get louder and more desperate. 'Help!!'

Nobody comes.

I have no idea how much time has passed, twenty minutes perhaps, when I hear the swoosh of the ladies' room door. I sit up from my stooped slump and call out, 'Hello? Can you please go and get help? I think I'm having a miscarriage.'

It takes a moment for the stranger to respond but they must see the blood seeping out from beneath the stall door, because I hear a disjointed, 'Oh, God! Yes. I'll be right back.'

While waiting for help to arrive, I ruminate over what an odd thing that was for me to say to the stranger. I don't *think* I'm having a miscarriage. I know I had a miscarriage. I know exactly what's happening to me.

At the swoosh of the outer door, I press my palms into the partition walls either side of me and force myself on to my feet. Shuffling through the blood, I unlock the door and then shuffle backwards again so I can open it inwards. Standing with my blood-soaked tights and panties around my ankles, sick with humiliation and grief, I'm confronted by two people dressed in staff uniforms – one male, one female – and presumably the woman who brought them to my aid.

'An ambulance is on its way,' the man says.

And the relief is so overwhelming that my embarrassment fades along with any strength I have left. The staff reach out their hands to help me, but the moment I lift my arms, my last drop of energy vanishes and I collapse on the floor in the puddle of my own blood.

～～～

Nathan sits beside the hospital bed, his face a picture of sympathy, and strokes the back of my hand as if everything I've been through over the past four days has nothing to do with him. I stare blankly ahead, silent tears running down my cheek, the white hospital room a blur. I barely register Nathan's touch but, when I do, I pull my hand away.

I've been here all day, unable to eat or drink in case I need surgery later this evening. I'm still waiting for the doctor to come and assess me; the hospital is busier than usual and I'm not an urgent case.

After all, the patient's already dead.

The nurses administer morphine every four hours: short, sharp injections of fluid into my mouth.

It doesn't numb the real pain.

I wish they would give me something stronger, something to shut down my brain. I want to think about something other than where my baby is now. I want to stop wondering whether he or she went down the toilet, or was mopped off the floor and sloshed down a sink with a bucket of dirty red water.

I laid my baby to rest in Tesco.

And other than all the blood, other than my tiny baby floating in a bucket or in a toilet bowl, there's one more thing I can't unsee: Nathan.

I'm falling backwards…stretching out my arms to him…grappling thin air with my fingertips. He's stock-still on the landing. Watching. He doesn't lift a hand. He doesn't reach out. He doesn't even flinch.

'Is there anything I can do?' he asks.

I shake my head.

We sit like that in silence. But in my head a different scene plays out. In my head, I say what I really want to say right now: *Go home.*

What? The Nathan in my head looks at me with wide eyes.

I said, go home.

Do you think you'll be able to sleep?

No.

Then I'll stay until the doctor comes, until we know whether you're going into surgery.

No. I don't want you to stay.

I'm not leaving you.

And the Rose in my head says, *Nathan. If you don't go, right now, I'll leave you for good. So unless you want a divorce I suggest you do as I ask for once, and go home.*

What are you talking about? What did I do? This wasn't my fault. You fell!

Do not. Ever. Talk to me again about what happened. If you ever bring the subject up again, I will leave you. If you don't stop talking this minute, I will leave you. And if you don't get away from me, right now, I will leave you. I can't look at you. I can't stand being in the same room as you. You need to leave because, if you don't, I'm going to start screaming and I won't stop until they strap me in restraints and sedate me. Do you understand me, Nathan? You have ten seconds to get out of here.

And the Nathan in my head says, *Rose? This is crazy talk!*

Ten.

Rose!

Nine.

You're not serious. You're behaving like a crazy person.

194

Eight.

He doesn't move. His eyes glaze over and his face turns to stone.

Seven... Six... Five.

He gets out of his chair but doesn't move away from the bed.

Four... Three...

And then, almost ripping the curtain from its hooks as he pulls it aside, he storms from the cubicle.

But that doesn't really happen. I know because, if it had, I'd be able to breathe again. Finally, with him gone, I'd be able to picture my baby as it's flushed down a toilet or washed down a sink and know that, either way, it ended up in the sea. I'd be able to picture my tiny little girl playing with My Little Pony, or my tiny little boy playing cowboys and Indians, riding a seahorse through a kelp forest.

Instead, Nathan's still here.

195

TWENTY-FIVE

MAGGIE

'IS EVERYTHING all right, baby?' Luc comes out of his study, empty coffee cup in hand, on his way to the kitchen and stops when he sees me in tears. 'What's happened?'

I put the phone back in its cradle and wipe my face on the hem of my shirt.

'Rose lost the baby.' More tears fall and I brush those away with my palm, rubbing it dry on the thigh of my trousers. 'She was having an argument with Nathan and she fell down the stairs.'

Luc hurries down the steps into the living room and takes me in his arms. 'Jesus, no. Poor Rose.'

'Nathan pushed her.'

'What?!' He steps back, holding me at arm's length. 'You aren't serious?'

'He didn't push her down the stairs, but he pushed her on the landing and she fell. She said he just watched her. Didn't even reach out to save her.'

'My God.' It takes a while for that to sink in, then he says, 'That sounds a bit odd, doesn't it? I can't imagine pushing you for any reason, let alone when you're standing at the top of a flight of stairs…and pregnant. I don't even want to say it about Nathan, but that sounds like borderline physical abuse.'

'I know.'

Luc hugs me for a little longer, then appears to need space to appraise the situation, so perches on the arm of the sofa. 'What's she going to do? Leave him?'

'I don't know. I hope so. The bastard doesn't deserve her.'

'Will you go back *now*?'

'I don't know.' I twiddle a piece of plastic I'd been rotating around my fingers the whole time I was talking to Rose and then ask Luc, 'What's this?'

He leans in to take a closer look. 'I don't know. It looks like a syringe.'

'I can see that. What's it doing in the sideboard drawer?'

'I don't know,' he says. 'Don't you know?'

'No. And why say it like that? As if I should know?'

'Because this place is your hideaway, Maggie. Everything in this cabin is where you decided it should go.'

'Well, I didn't put it there.'

'I didn't put it there either.'

I look past him, out of the window and into the woods.

'Oh, come on,' he says, 'let's not start that again. You don't seriously think your heavy-breathing stalker broke in here in some drugged-up stupor and left his used syringe in the sideboard?'

'Well, I didn't put it there. You say you didn't put it there. And Alfie can't reach – thank God! Heaven forbid he get his hands on a used syringe.'

'I can't keep having these conversations, Maggie. You're starting to drive *me* crazy as well. The whole point of coming here is for a little peace and quiet, but that's the last thing it's giving you. Meanwhile, you're neglecting your responsibilities back there – your family, your job – only to go out of your mind over a hallucination!'

Through the squares in the leadlight window I stare at the trees beyond the lake. 'It's not a hallucination.'

And then I run.

'Maggie!'

Luc calls after me as I reach above the fireplace for the shotgun, but I barely register him because I'm already through the door.

The man is right there!

I run across the shore towards him at such a pace my feet hardly sink into the shingle. But the whole time I'm running, my mind is split in two. And the parts are not equal. A tiny part screams at me: *What the hell are you going to do when you get within range, shoot him? Luc is right, that's something only a crazy person would do.* Only that tiny part is overwhelmed by the greater part that's consumed by rage. This man is dangerous – here to hurt me and my family!

Here to kill me.

I know it.

He won't stop until he's taken everything. And, as certain as I am about that, I know beyond any doubt that I won't let him. He won't take my family from me. Or me from my family.

The man watches me as the gap between us closes, and even though I'm carrying a shotgun he just waits there, leaning up against the tree at the head of the path.

It's as if he's giving me the chance to catch up.

As if he wants to make this easier for me.

And that just makes me even wilder.

The moment I'm sure I'm in range, I stop running and mount the gun to my cheek. But the moment I look down the rib, he spins around the tree trunk and disappears.

I don't pause. I'm at the head of the path in seconds and follow him into the wood.

He's up ahead, darting between the trees, his dark green coat buffeted by pumping arms as he jumps fallen logs, and flies at speed through the forest. But I fly just as fast. My resolve is so strong, my courage so steadfast, that the gun feels weightless in my hand and the forest barely exists. A twig scratches my cheek, leaving a small cut I barely register. Tall bracken and broken branches tear my trousers, stinging my legs like knives, but I don't care. Startled crows caw as they take to the sky, but I pay them no attention. The trees close in all around, but I don't look at them. I keep my eyes trained on that green rain mac as the chase goes on.

All I know is him.

All I see is him.

And then I get my chance to close the gap. The man loses his footing, twists as he reaches out for a tree to steady himself, but his hand slips from the bark and he falls hard on his side before rolling along the forest floor.

I stop.

I take aim.

And, as he's scrabbling to his feet, I fire.

The bullet ricochets off a tree to his right, tearing shards of bark from the trunk. He pauses for a second, glances at the damaged timber and then back at me. Though he's too far away for me to see the expression on his face, I read the surprise in his body language.

I smile. He didn't think I had it in me. But I do.

He runs.

I keep up.

The trees thin out ahead and the forest opens up for another clean shot. Mounting the gun, I take a deep, steadying breath to calm my irregular heartbeat and take aim. He's fast, darting left and right, but there's a pattern to his movements, a dance. Predicting his trajectory, I aim to the right of a large oak and, the split-second that green mac appears, I fire.

The man stops dead.

Time stretches out as I wait for him to fall.

Only he doesn't. He turns. His face, buried in the hood of his raincoat, is nothing but an empty black space which stares back at me.

I missed!

The gun is empty now. Both shots fired. It's what he was waiting for. And I didn't hang around the cabin long enough to collect any shells.

From his side – from the pocket of his mac perhaps, I can't tell – he pulls out a knife and brandishes it at me. The belly of the blade is deep, with a pronounced grind line and rip teeth, curving to a sharp point. Its face shines silver-blue in the light between the trees. And, though he's still too far away to be sure, somehow I know he's grinning.

Everything turned on the fall of that empty cartridge.

I'm no longer his hunter. I'm his prey.

I drop the gun and run.

Now, instead of coursing with adrenaline, the muscles in my arms and legs weaken with fear as I trip and stumble through the undergrowth and small trees as if wading through a quagmire. From somewhere in the forest, the startled caw of a crow disrupts my heart, and I look up as if it might bring someone to help me.

Then I stop dead.

The treeline ends suddenly and I'm standing at the edge of the clearing where the crows attacked Alfie. I recognise the fire pit circled by fallen trunks.

And in its centre stands the man.

Shaking my head in confusion, I look behind me. There's no one there. He's no longer chasing me. He's standing right there with his back to me, the hood of his mac pulled low over his downbent head. Rooted to the spot, I'm as afraid to move forward as I am to run back.

The man turns, his hood falls away, and right there in the light of the clearing I see his face.

'Luc?'

'Maggie!' He comes running towards me. Behind him, no longer obscured from view, Alfie's on his haunches in the fire pit, poking the cold cinders with a stick. And Cairo wanders from spot to spot, sniffing the charred ground.

Luc wraps me in his arms. 'We were so worried. We've been searching the woods for ages. Why did you run off like that?'

'I saw him again. I wanted to find him. Where did you get that coat?'

'This?' Luc tugs at the collar, looking down at the mac as if he's never seen it before. 'I don't know. I just grabbed it from the rack. It must be John's. Are you all right?'

'Yes... No... He...' I point back at the trees. 'He was chasing me. He had a knife.'

'I thought you took the gun? Where is it?'

'I dropped it, back there.'

'*Putain, Maggie! Ça va pas, non?* What were you thinking? You could have got yourself killed.'

'I thought you didn't believe he existed. You said he was a hallucination.'

'When you chase a man with a gun I'm going to start taking you seriously. You obviously believe he exists.'

'That's not the same thing.'

'Does it matter if I believe it? You do.'

'It matters to me. You think I'm crazy.'

'I don't think you're crazy.' He tucks a chestnut lock behind my ear, my straightened hair curling in the misty rain. '*Ma beauté, mon amour.* You are the strongest woman I know. The most together woman I know. I believe you. But it's gone too far. Surely you see that? I need you to do this one thing for me. I need you to go back. You're not safe here.'

'And you and Alfie are?! He's still out there!' Again, I point at the trees.

'It's not us he's after. We've never even seen him.'

'Alfie may have.'

'Alfie!' Luc calls out to him and he looks up from the fire pit. *'Est-ce qu'il y a un homme dans la forêt?'*

Alfie shakes his head and then turns his attention back to his stick.

'See? Just you. I'm afraid for you, Maggie.' He tries to pull me into a hug but my arms remain stiff by my sides, so he rubs them instead. 'You need to go back. Even if it's just for a while. We'll be all right, I promise. And so will you once you see Rose. I suspect, with a little distance, everything will fall back into place.'

And, as if I'm held up by nothing but the adrenaline and cortisol that finally drains from my muscles, I collapse into his arms.

TWENTY-SIX

ROSE

AFTER EXAMINING me, the doctor concluded that I didn't need surgery; the bleeding had subsided but they wanted to keep me in for observation for a few days. And, for two days I did nothing but stare at the ceiling, unable to eat or sleep.

But it's Thursday now.

With a little persuasion the nurse agreed to get me a wheelchair, and now I wheel myself as quickly as I can along the corridors, stopping only when I reach Daisy's door.

The moment I see her strong face and wild red hair I burst into tears again, sobbing through my explanation of what happened as if she's still awake, listening to me and comforting me. And when she's finally up to date, exhaustion takes over. So I bury my head in her blankets and cry myself to sleep where I sit.

203

I wake to the brush of fingertips and, haunted by the memory of Nathan stroking the back of my hand, I flinch and snatch my arm away. But then I look up into Saeed's soft, expressive face.

'I am sorry. I did not mean to wake you.'

I brush the hair from my cheeks and rub my eyes. 'Sorry. You took me by surprise.'

'What happened, Rose? Why are you in a wheelchair?'

'I fell down the stairs.' My face crumples. 'I lost the baby.'

Saeed kneels down beside my wheelchair but he doesn't say anything while I bury my face in my hands and sob. When he leans into me, I rest my arms over his shoulders and bury my face in his neck. But even after I've stopped crying, he still doesn't let me go.

When we finally do separate, we do it at exactly the same time. My cheek grazes his and our lips are so close our breath mingles. We pause there, each of us teetering on the moment...

But then Saeed leaps to his feet and I wonder...if he had lingered a moment longer...

'How did you fall?'

I explain about the argument, the tussle at the door and the cleaning caddy.

'He pushed you?'

'Not like that. He didn't actually push me down the stairs.'

Saeed paces back and forth until it makes me antsy and I insist he sits down. Only he doesn't sit down, he flings himself down, props his elbows on the bed and scrubs his forehead with his fingertips.

'You're desperate to therapise me, aren't you?'

He looks up but doesn't speak.

'It's okay. I said it was all right. I said I'd take therapy over nothing. So just say whatever it is you're dying to say. Judging by the look on your face, if you don't you'll have an embolism.'

Still he doesn't speak, so I wait.

204

Eventually he leans down, picks up his satchel and pulls out a mobile phone, which he lays on the bed.

'What's that for?'

'It is for you.'

'I already have a phone.'

'This one Nathan cannot track. But you should be aware that he probably has a tracker on your car as well. This phone is programmed with my home, mobile and office numbers. And several books I hope you will read.'

'About what?'

He looks at me as if it's obvious.

'I don't need to read books about my husband. I already know him.'

He lays his arms across Daisy's bed, his hands reaching out to me, but at the same time he maintains his distance by leaning back slightly in the chair. When he finally speaks, only one sentence comes out before he's silent again. 'You know the husband Nathan wants you to know.'

This time it's me who's silent.

'This is so hard, Rose. What makes a man like Nathan so dangerous is the covert nature of his behaviour. These books—'

'Covert? Dangerous? You make him sound like a spy!'

'He is. After a fashion. A double agent who pretends he is on your side when he will only ever work for himself.'

'This is getting laughable. And yet, it's not funny at all.'

'Please, Rose. I am deadly serious. I believe...I believe you are a victim of domestic abuse without even being aware of it.'

'Domestic abuse! Now you really are joking.'

He looks right at me. 'I am not. Pushing you like that...that is domestic abuse.'

'He didn't mean to push me that hard. It was a tussle in a doorway. Nathan wanted this baby – he was more excited about it than I was at first. He would never have intentionally harmed it – or me.'

205

I picture Nathan at the top of the stairs, not even reaching out to save me, and yet for reasons I can't explain – not even to myself – I continue to defend him.

'Rose…you do not understand. Nathan is a doctor. He would have known how unlikely it was for you to lose the baby from a fall so early in your pregnancy. And cornering you during an argument, standing in a doorway and blocking your escape – that is domestic abuse.'

'That's ridiculous.'

'No. It is not ridiculous. I know you do not want to hear this but these are recognised signs of abuse. They are recognised because they are common early indicators of the behaviour that inevitably follows. Abusers first test the limits of their partner with these small transgressions. If they are tolerated, they escalate with further, more serious violations.'

'Well, you weren't there. And you don't really know Nathan, so you aren't in a place to judge.'

'I know that, Rose.' He looks right at me again. His nickel-grey eyes don't bore into me, they're too gentle for that, but they hold me. I can't turn away from them. 'Do you remember what you said about a month ago? About people being like magnets and, when their polarities are right, they snap together?'

'Yes.' And I remember looking straight at him when I said that. But now my cheeks warm and I turn away. Because now, I can't look at him when I know exactly what he's going to say.

'I feel that connection too. I have never felt this way about anyone. And I cannot bear this. I am afraid for you.'

'There's no need to be.'

I pick a piece of fluff off Daisy's blanket and Saeed leans forward, sliding his hands closer to mine. 'There is, Rose.'

'You're scaring me. I feel like I know you well enough by now to think… I mean, you wouldn't say these things unless you really believed them, would you?'

He shakes his head but it's barely noticeable; even his actions are cautious. And how can I blame him when I was so defensive before?

I say, 'You don't strike me as the kind of man who would make these accusations lightly. So, what is it? What makes you so certain, when you know so little of Nathan?'

'Everything you have ever told me.'

'Like what?'

'Everything.'

'Like *what*?'

He thinks for a moment, orders his thoughts.

'That first day, you said you met Nathan here at the hospital when you were visiting Daisy. But you had seen him around and did not believe the handsome doctor would look twice at you.'

'That's right.'

'How many times had you run into each other before he asked you out on an official date?'

I shake my head as I tot up the numbers. 'A lot. Ten, maybe twelve times, why?'

'And did you run into him in bars and restaurants around town, or was it always at the hospital?'

I'd almost forgotten about that. 'No. Not always here. We kept running into each other in all sorts of places. Why, what are you saying? Are you saying those meetings weren't a coincidence? That Nathan engineered them?'

'Yes.'

'Why on earth would he—?'

'Kismet. It is a romantic notion. People want to believe that the universe pulls them together, that they are meant to be. And people with narcissistic personality disorder use that to their advantage. So, when they finally ask you out on a date, to say no would be to deny fate. It engenders trust. When he asked you out, you felt as though you already knew him, yes? Already trusted him?'

207

'I suppose.' I slide my arms forward, resting them on the blanket right next to his but not close enough to touch.

'And during one of those coincidental meetings, did you tell Nathan about your previous marriage?'

'I think so. We ran into each other at a party and got talking.'

'And you told him your first husband was abusive?'

'Probably. Why?'

'Men like Nathan seek out empathetic women who are more likely to tolerate abuse, especially ones who have tolerated it in the past.'

'I didn't tolerate it. I left.'

'Yes, but he will be convinced that you left because your previous partner was not clever enough to manage you. He will see himself as a superior being, one who does not make such mistakes.'

'You can't possibly know these things.'

'I knew the first day I met him. I even suspected the first day you and I met.'

'How?'

'Your expensive clothes, for one thing. You are always immaculately dressed, your make-up and hair perfect, as if you are going somewhere special rather than visiting your sister in the hospital.'

'Plenty of women take care of themselves and like expensive clothes.'

'True. But not you.'

'What makes you say that?'

'Your Christian Dior handbag is always cast aside on the floor, your cashmere coat discarded over the chair. And there is a mirror above the washbasin right there – ' he points at it ' – but I have never once seen you look in it. Clothes usually reflect the woman, but not you.'

'And that tells you what exactly?'

'That someone else cares about your appearance far more than you do.'

I turn away from him and look up at the ceiling.

'Does Nathan buy you clothes?'

'Of course. Sometimes.'

'And has he ever thrown away any of your clothes without asking?'

I don't speak.

'You do not have to answer, Rose.'

I can't. I don't want to tell him that a few weeks before we got married, while I was out for the evening, Nathan went through my wardrobe and sorted out two black bin liners of my clothes. I'd come home early, before he'd had a chance to throw them away, and asked what he thought he was doing. He'd said they were old, things I never wore any more. And he was telling the truth when he'd pointed out that I'd been meaning to clean out my wardrobe for months; he was just trying to help. But he wouldn't let me open the bags. He'd said it would confuse me. That I'd hold on to things because of an emotional attachment rather than because they fitted me any more.

I'd believed him.

'What else?' I ask. 'What else did you see that first day we met?'

'His text messages. I caught glimpses. I did not mean to read them, honestly, but you showed me the screen. I could not help noticing the content, their greeting-card artificiality. It is not how people speak to each other, Rose. Especially intimate partners.'

'Maybe he's romantic. You said yourself you've never been in a romantic relationship. Maybe you don't know what one looks like.'

'I have seen more romantic relationships in my profession than most people encounter in a lifetime.'

'It's not enough. These things aren't enough.'

'No. You are right, but the signs kept coming. The dates, they worried me too, everything on the fourteenth – your first

209

date, moving in together, getting married.'

'Why?'

'Because it is a sign of control. Relationships run at an emotional pace, not by a clock or calendar. People move in together when they have reached that place emotionally. The same with marriage and children.'

'You're saying my relationship is manufactured?'

He doesn't answer that. Instead, he asks, 'Who first suggested that teaching full-time was putting too much strain on you? You, or Nathan?'

'Nathan.'

'Because he was worried about you?'

'Yes.'

'And were you worried about yourself? Did you feel under pressure from your job?'

'Yes. It was a lot to handle.'

'And were you finding your job a lot to handle before you met Nathan?'

'Yes.'

The moment that word is out of my mouth, my mind flies back in time. It's so long ago now. When you don't work, days bleed into each other, weekends lose all meaning. Time expands. Months stretch out. 'No... No, actually, I didn't. Teaching is hard, of course it is, but I handled it fine.'

'So, what changed?'

'Nathan's house, I suppose. I couldn't keep up with it and all the other chores.'

I'd loved Nathan's beautiful home the first time I saw it, and the first few times I'd stayed there. But when I'd moved in I had realised what it meant to own a home of that size.

'Did you suggest a cleaner? Between the two of you, you could have afforded that.'

I nod. 'I did. But Nathan said he'd had cleaners before and they were hopeless. They broke things. Didn't turn up when they were supposed to. One of them even stole from him. Some diamond-studded cufflinks, I think he said.'

'And your friendships? Have they drifted away over the past year?'

I nod again, slowly, remembering what Nathan said at the picnic: that if my friend at the hospital had cared about me, she would have called. And then Penny comes to mind as well. Nathan told me she'd said I was dreary at the party. But we'd had such a laugh together, sneaking upstairs in Amelia's house. I hadn't felt at all dreary that night. My mind spirals. Have any of my friends called without me knowing? Has Nathan picked up the house phone or my mobile and said something to them?

Saeed says, 'That day he came in here and found us talking, did you not find his reaction disproportionate?'

'He was jealous, that was obvious.'

'Finding your wife's hand on another man's arm is enough to give any man pause – we are all capable of jealousy – but Nathan's response felt like ownership. As if I was playing with a toy that belonged to him. I have held back from saying too much, but Rose, you are in a wheelchair. To say nothing now would be irresponsible.'

'I'm not your responsibility.'

'I know that. But you are my friend. And you are Daisy's younger sister; I feel a responsibility to you on her behalf and I believe you are in danger.'

'Danger?!' I grip the armrests of my wheelchair, about to spring to my feet, only realising then how exhausted I am, and that I can't. So I wheel away from the bed instead, ready to leave. 'You're crazy! Nathan may not be perfect and maybe he is a narcissist, but now I'm beginning to think you're as crazy as each other. You're grossly overexaggerating what he's capable of.'

'Rose...please.'

I let go of the wheels.

'Please hear me out.'

Reluctantly, I wheel back to the bed, but fold my arms

across my chest.'

'I wish I were exaggerating. I hope I am. But your pregnancy...'

'What about it?'

'You told me you wanted children but perhaps a little further down the line. You were not trying for a baby?'

'No. Our contraception failed.'

'The pill?'

'Diaphragm.'

'You should check it.'

'That's ridiculous!' I snap.

'Is it? You should check your phone too. Find My Friends will tell him your location but he probably has spyware installed to monitor your calls and texts as well.'

I shake my head and Saeed leans far back in his chair; the distance between us is now as wide as it can be without one of us getting up.

This would be easier if he weren't so gentle. My outbursts make me feel as though I'm the aggressor in this relationship and I'm not used to that. It's not me. And if I continue to snap at him, he will shut down. I know that from before. He may even leave, visit Daisy on a different day. And, even though I don't want to hear these things, I don't want that. He said he has no idea how to be my friend without counselling me, and I agreed to it. But I feel under attack, and he's making me retaliate. Even though he's not attacking me, he's attacking Nathan. And he isn't even doing that really; he's just asking questions. For all he knew, I might have said no to every one of them.

He knew I wouldn't, though.

Which is why he's asking.

I'm beginning to think he knows Nathan better than I do, as if he's a third party in our relationship. As if he's lived with us over the past year. He seems to know everything. And how is that even possible? It's not. It's as if he's some kind of private detective, hired to tear me and Nathan apart. And yet, I can't deny that his intentions have never seemed malicious. On the contrary, Saeed seems to genuinely care about me.

I uncross my arms, lean forward, and lay them across Daisy's bed in a gesture of peace. Saeed reciprocates.

I say, 'I don't understand how you know all these things.'

'I know because not only are men like Nathan all turned out from the same mould, they all use exactly the same techniques. As if every coercive controller was given an abusers' handbook as a child – and in some cases they were: they follow examples set by their parents. And they follow the handbook to the letter, using the same methods and often even the same language.'

'Why? What purpose can it possibly serve?'

'Every purpose. And yet one sole purpose: his. Look at you, Rose. You are a beautiful woman, intelligent, easy to talk to. You look good on his arm, bolster his status with his peers, and at the same time you cater to his every need. You cook, you clean, run errands for him. And…'

'And?' I see it – that barely discernible blush on his warm olive skin. So I say what he's not prepared to. 'I have sex with him whenever he wants.'

He bows his head.

'But now it makes even less sense. You say that Nathan is exhibiting behaviours that are precursors to abuse. But I left my last husband for that, so he must know I would leave him too. And if he's getting everything he needs, what purpose does abusing me serve? Why do it?'

'Because it is not sustainable. People with NPD are often charming and successful but they lack emotion and empathy; they cannot make deep emotional connections. In the beginning, Nathan kept the spotlight of your attention trained on him by buying you gifts, booking expensive holidays and sending romantic platitudes. You fell in love with the kind, generous man, but he knows these things wear thin for an

213

emotionally intelligent woman like yourself. You will begin to search for a deeper connection, one he is unable to give you, and the spotlight will inevitably wane.'

Saeed is right; I have already felt that first glow fading. I say, 'But that still doesn't explain the abuse. The nicer he is to me – the more he shows how much he loves me – the more likely I am to stay.'

'Yes. But pretence takes energy. It is not sustainable on his side. Narcissists know this. Nathan knows this. He is preparing for it. The positive nature of the spotlight matters little to him because *attention* is his fuel: positive or negative, it is all the same to him. He will take as much pleasure – more, perhaps – from hurting you. From seeing you in pain. From watching you cry. But, to keep the supply of narcissistic fuel, he must prevent you from leaving.'

'And how will he do that?'

'Rose ... he has already begun.'

'This is too much. I really have no idea what you're talking about – what has he already begun?'

He cups his hands over mine, as if I will need comfort and support for what he's about to tell me. 'The texts, Rose. Not just their frequency and artificiality, but think about how he refers to you: dainty, delicate, pale, fragile.'

'Perhaps that's how he sees me.'

'Then he does not see you. But when you are told you are fragile a dozen times a day you will begin to believe it.'

'You're saying he's brainwashing me?'

'It is a form of brainwashing, yes. And I promise you, it will worsen. He will begin to laugh derisively when you make innocent observations, strip your confidence with insults which he will disguise as advice designed to help you become a better person. As if you are not good enough to begin with.'

'He calls me naïve.' As soon as I've said it, I want to bite it back.

214

'You have only been together a year, but time is of the essence. Nathan must crush your self-esteem and undermine your strength to leave before you figure out who he is. But, at the same time, he must do it so gradually that you do not even notice it happening. This is why relationships with narcissists are so confusing: because you are bombarded with love and broken at the same time. At first you are delicate, fragile and naïve. But, eventually, when he is confident your spirit is broken, you will be oversensitive, paranoid, crazy, useless and stupid. And you will hear these things many, many times, every day, until you begin to believe it. You will find yourself in circular arguments that make no sense and leave you exhausted. You will walk constantly on eggshells, wondering what you will face when he next walks in the door. You will blame yourself for everything that goes wrong because he will *teach* you to take the blame. And in the midst of all that, even if you were not too physically exhausted, too emotionally drained, and stripped of self-worth to believe yourself capable of leaving him...'

'What?'

'You will find yourself married, financially dependent, and with a child to support.'

TWENTY-SEVEN

MAGGIE

I STARE at the man.

He's here every day now, standing by the path at the edge of the treeline, staring back.

He always watches us from the same place, partially obscured by the oak tree. And in his olive-green mac, hood pulled low over his head, he blends into the bushes at its base.

He never comes any closer. He's waiting for something but I don't know what. And I know I'm not going crazy. I know my own mind. I know he's been in the cabin when it's empty. He closed the curtains that day. He left that syringe behind. And sometimes, things move from places I know I left them.

Life here was perfect before he showed up. And his presence isn't just putting me under strain, it's putting Luc under strain too. This man does not want to be seen by anyone but me; he makes sure Luc and Alfie never see him. And that's convincing Luc that the solitude is playing on my sanity. He's putting even

216

more pressure on me to leave, even if it's only for a short while. Luc thinks that if I go back to Oxford I'll find myself there. As if my mental health is in a trinket box on the sideboard in our apartment and I just need to open it and take it out.

I think that's what the man wants.

To drive me away.

He wants to frighten me into leaving. And when I do, if I do, he'll come for Luc and Alfie. But his presence here every day ratchets up the tension, and somehow I know that if I don't leave he'll force my hand. He'll come for me first.

But I'm not abandoning my husband and son.

Not even to save my own life.

Whatever he has planned for me, bring it on. He won't get to my husband and son without going through me first. I'll do whatever it takes to bring equilibrium back to our peaceful cabin. And I know now, the only way to do that is to eradicate him.

I wasn't prepared last time.

I am now.

The man and I stare at each other for a long time.

'Alfie.' I hurry him along by his little bottom, padded with a nappy. 'Go in and see Daddy.' When we reach the deck, I haul him up by the wrist, step by step, until he's at the top. And then I push the cabin door open and shout across the lounge to Luc's study.

'Yeah?'

'Look after Alfie for a while?'

'Sure.'

'And you really hear me this time?'

'I really hear you.' He leans around the door, smiles at me and winks. '*Viens, mon petit gars.* Come on, buddy.'

'Go on. You can sit on Daddy's lap for a bit while he writes.'

Alfie runs into Luc's legs, burying his face between his knees, and I don't take my eyes off either of them until the door falls closed. Then I replay that moment in my mind a

217

few times – my sweet boy, running to his daddy with that ungainly waddle as if his legs are too short for his body – and my heart brims.

One second later, it turns to stone.

I run down the porch steps and from the pebbly beach, look to the treeline. He knows I'm coming for him. I expect him to set off into the woods and I'm half surprised, half afraid when he doesn't.

He's waiting for me.

I don't run this time. I stride across the shore, feet sinking in the gravel and slowing me down, but I never take my eyes off him.

Is that because I'm starting to believe Luc?

Is that because I think he's going to disappear?

No. I said I know my own mind, and I do.

When I'm about twenty metres away, he turns slowly and saunters into the forest. And, as he slinks between the trees, I notice something I hadn't before: a large hunch on his back as if, beneath his raincoat, he's carrying a rucksack.

Keeping my eyes trained on the gap through which he disappeared, I follow.

The last golden leaf fell months ago and the forest floor is now a brown carpet of dead leaves. Above me, the trees hold their gnarled fingers to the sky to catch what little light there is from a weak February sun. The trees are sorrowful in late winter, as if they've dropped their dead children and hold up their hands in grief.

I crunch their babies beneath my feet.

There's a low-lying mist on the forest floor, plunging the wood into hazy shadow, and when I skim the smoke between the trees I realise I've lost sight of him.

He's gone.

Something bright beneath the leaves at my feet catches the lowering sunlight and I kneel down to pick it up.

His knife.

I recognise the blue-tinted blade, the rip teeth along its spine. Did he drop it by accident? I can't shake the feeling that I was supposed to find it. And there's another feeling I can't shake. Something I just know.

I'm going to use it.

Movement in my peripheral vision catches my attention and I look up. In the middle distance, the man strides slowly, deliberately, across my path.

I grip the handle of the blade and run.

The chase is hard; I don't have the strength or speed I had last time. Whenever I lose sight of him my stomach plunges with disappointment, but then he reappears and my heart sparks. His pace is relaxed and yet, after twenty minutes or more, I'm no closer to reaching him.

A shooting pain in my right sole forces me to stop, sit down on a tree stump and remove my trainer and sock. Resting my foot on my knee, I twist it over to look for an injury. The pain is knife-sharp only there's nothing there. No cut. Not even a bruise. I tip my trainer upside down and shake it but nothing falls out. Bending forward, I put my sock and trainer back on and then hold my knees while I get my breath back.

He's still there.

In the trees.

Watching me.

His dark trousers root him to the forest floor while his shapeless mac forms a canopy over his body. If the trees were in leaf, he could disappear before my eyes. But, like the ghost of him, his malice would remain.

Still bent over my knees, I suck in a few more breaths and feign exhaustion, as if I've lost the will to give chase any more. He turns away, looks back in my direction one more time, and then disappears.

And I'm on my feet and running.

I bolt across the forest floor, faster than I've ever run in my life. Nothing will stop me from catching up with him this

219

time. I curve around the tree he disappeared behind and stop dead.

In front of me, the forest opens up. Ahead, the fog has dissipated, the trees are sparse and there's a view to the horizon where the sun has just dipped beneath the tallest trees. It spills red and gold across the leaf litter like a forest fire, burning the trunks orange.

He's gone.

I scan the wood right and left, left and right, but he's nowhere to be seen. I slam my palm against the rough bark as if the tree's to blame for allowing him to slip away without a trace.

He's out there somewhere, hiding no doubt, playing with me. If only I knew why.

I turn and retrace my steps back to the cabin.

TWENTY-EIGHT

ROSE

WITH THE BLINDS up and all the lights on in the main bathroom, I examine my diaphragm. It looks fine, so I hold it up to the window but still can't see any holes. Not knowing whether I want Saeed to be right about Nathan or not, I flop down on the toilet seat, pulling at the diaphragm as if the answers lie cupped inside.

I have no idea what to believe any more. Nathan tells me he loves me, that I'm the only woman for him, and that he wants to spend the rest of our lives together. And in my heart I still believe that. I remember his face when I told him I was pregnant: he was beside himself with joy. Now Saeed is telling me the whole thing is a lie. But why should I believe Saeed over Nathan? Especially when I know Saeed has feelings for me; he said himself that he's never behaved so unprofessionally in either his personal or professional life.

I've been reading since Nathan left for work. It's hard to admit but there is a ring of truth to the books Saeed loaded on the phone, about coercive control and red flags. I do see some of Nathan's behaviour between their pages. But everyone has their faults. It doesn't make them narcissistic sociopaths. I'm sure these books help women who live with genuine abusers, but I'm not going to read them like a horoscope of my marriage, seeking similarities, desperate for echoes of my own life. There's no more truth in Saeed's concerns than there is in a horoscope.

But Saeed's words pick at me as if I'm a different Rose, the old one beneath a scab that's not quite ready to come off.

The two books I've got through so far have both mentioned spyware, just as Saeed did. And Saeed was right about Find My Friends: I don't remember enabling that. I pull my phone from my skirt pocket and search Google. One of the top results is for a mobile security app, which I download and run. The search takes an interminable amount of time, but when the results come back they don't really surprise me, not as much as I thought they would. Nathan has installed an application called mSpy.

I Google that. It's supposed to be for parents monitoring their children's phones, for safety, not to spy on your wife without her knowledge.

I feel sick.

My phone convinces me that Saeed is right about the tracker on my car as well. And then I wonder again about my diaphragm. He's been right about everything else. I just don't want him to be. Because, if he is, I'll be facing another divorce.

Across the stark, grey-marbled space, something catches my eye: a drip of water from the basin tap. I've been meaning to call the plumber but too much has been going on. I hurry across the room, turn on the tap and fill the diaphragm. Lifting it up, I brush excess water from the bottom and wait.

Nothing.

There's another drip of water so I brush that away too.

But then another drip forms.

And another.

I squeeze the rim together, putting pressure on the water inside. It seeps through a dozen tiny holes. I drop the diaphragm, lean on the sink and stare at my stupid face in the mirror.

Then something else occurs to me.

Bent down on my haunches, I open the cabinet beneath the washbasin and pull out my tube of spermicide. I unscrew the cap, squeeze some out on the back of my hand and then rub it in with my fingers. It feels thin, watery. And it doesn't smell of anything.

When Nathan and I were first dating, he'd complained that my spermicide stung a little. He'd said I shouldn't bother with it, play a little Russian roulette, but pregnancy wasn't some idiotic game with a bullet to me. I'd switched brands. Then he'd complained that my punani had a medicinal smell. We'd laughed about it. He'd squeezed it on the back of my hand, rubbed it in and made me smell it and then lick it. He'd said if he had to taste it, I had to as well. We were in stitches, practically rolling about on the bathroom floor with laughter.

It's not so funny now.

I inspect the end of the tube, digging my fingernails beneath the folded metal, but it's sealed shut. And the ribbing on the seal is flawless; it doesn't look as if it's been tampered with.

But if Nathan is capable of fooling me into believing he loves me, what else is he capable of?

The garage is as immaculate as the rest of the house, but I rarely come in here. I have no idea what I'm looking for really – some kind of vice or clamp, I suppose. There are several tools on the worktops: circular saws, cordless drills and screwdrivers. Everything yellow and black. Everything DeWalt. Everything clean and new-looking. I walk past them, running my fingers over their surfaces. There's a sturdy clamp attached to the middle of the worktop and I run my finger through its jaw. It's smooth.

One by one, I go through the drawers and cupboards. Everything is well organised: clear plastic cabinets of nails and screws are mounted on the wall above the worktop, smaller tools are ordered by size and function in the bench drawers, and the larger tools are arranged in the cabinets beneath. Some of the contraptions are alien to me; I have no clue as to their purpose. But they clearly don't perform the function I have in mind. I find a sturdy pair of scissors in one of the drawers and hold on to them.

I've never seen Nathan do any DIY so I'm not sure what he needs all this for. Nothing has a speck of dust or dirt on it, as if the cupboards are rarely opened. This isn't a workshop, it's a shrine to manhood.

In the final bottom cupboard, pushed back into the shadows as far as it will go, I find what I'm looking for. I lift the metal contraption up on to the worktop. It has a sturdy label on the front – 'PackAbility Packaging' – and a lever handle on the right. Lifting the lever up and down causes two sets of jaws in the machine to open and close simultaneously.

Cutting the base off the tube of spermicide, I keep the detached metal strip, laying it carefully on the workbench. Then I place the end of the tube inside the top set of jaws. They have no teeth, so when I pull the lever down they create a clean fold along the aluminium, and repeating the process causes the tube's end to fold over again. Logic tells me to next insert the tube in the bottom set of jaws, which do have teeth: a fine line along the top and bottom. I pull the lever again and the teeth crimp the tube perfectly, sealing it closed. And finally, I compare the teeth marks to those in the cut-off end.

They're identical.

I swallow a surge of bile as realisation clamps down as hard as the jaws in that machine.

TWENTY-NINE

ROSE

I DRIVE THROUGH Oxford's back streets as if my car is submerged and I'm underwater. I'm floating around in a life that looks a little like mine, only blurred, the horizon vague and unfocused.

I have no idea what's true any more. Can it really be possible that I've married another man I don't know? Only, this time, a man who abuses with emotions instead of fists? A man who sought me out because, damaged by my previous marriage, I'm a suitable target?

I can't believe it. And yet, it's becoming harder and harder not to.

I pull the car to the side of the road and park. If I'm going to get to the truth, I need to speak to someone who has nothing to lose or gain from it.

Nathan said his ex-wife, Claire, was a narcissistic, adulterous bitch. But, according to the books, your partner telling you that is in itself a red flag. They place the culpability for the breakdown of their previous relationships entirely on the other person so nobody looks to them for blame.

Penny didn't agree with Nathan's account. She said Claire, not he, came out of the marriage broken. And I got the feeling she was holding a lot more back, protecting me from the truth.

Halfway up Penny's drive, I stop. My feet, reluctant to take another step forward, want to protect me from the truth as well. They know I don't want to hear it.

'Come on, Rose. Come on.' I force myself to walk, taking the bend in the drive and, finally, the two steps to the yellow front door. It has an old-fashioned lion's head knocker, which I rap.

A few moments later, a shadow appears behind the glass some distance away. I suck in a deep breath and blow it out in a tremulous exhalation.

The door opens.

It's not Penny.

It's a woman of a similar age and she's so relaxed in the doorway, this must be her house. I look behind me to make sure I wasn't imagining things. I wasn't. There is a monkey puzzle tree at the bottom of the garden, just as Penny described. I turn back and check the bright yellow paint on the door. Did I remember it wrong?

'Can I help you?'

'I'm sorry. I must have the wrong house.'

But, before the woman has time to reply, Penny's voice rings out from one of the rooms inside. 'Hurry up, Claire! Amelia's having a meltdown.'

Everything falls into place.

This would have been the mother of all coincidences if Penny and Claire weren't really good friends and Claire wasn't here on a regular basis. And Penny's obviously not only really good friends with Claire, she's really good friends with Amelia too. Nathan was right: that whole thing at the party was a

226

sham. Probably to find out more about Nathan's new wife and report back to the narcissistic, adulterous bitch.

I look her up and down, trying to figure out from one brief encounter whether she fits that description. I'd imagined her a redhead, dressed in risqué clothes with red lipstick and high heels. In my head, she'd always been standing outside a bar or a nightclub, a half-smoked cigarette between the fingers of one hand and a sloshing glass of white wine in the other. And always, in a brash and high-pitched voice, she'd be flirting with the bouncer, barely able to stand.

But, poised and demure in Penny's doorway, Claire doesn't fit that description at all. Her shoulder-length blonde hair frames a sweet, pretty face which is only lightly made-up. Her plain linen trousers and long shirt are neither tight-fitting nor revealing. And she's wearing flat, comfortable shoes. She looks nothing like the type of woman who goes out partying every night and comes home drunk to her poor, lonely husband.

She looks like me.

'I'm sorry.' I turn away and dart down the steps. 'I've got the wrong house.'

I'm halfway down the driveway when Penny calls my name. 'Rose! Wait! Where are you going?'

Cheeks burning, I turn back with no idea what to say. They both stare at me, waiting for me to speak. 'Sorry. I popped by for a chat but I can see you have company.'

'Nonsense.' She beckons me up the drive. 'Come in.'

'No. I can't. I don't want to intrude.'

'Don't be silly, you're not intruding. Come on.'

I look down the drive to my car, parked on the street, then back up to the front door, with no idea which way to turn.

Feigning exasperation, Penny strides out, grabs me by the arm and drags me up the driveway.

'I'm not letting you leave, so there's no point fighting it. Claire, this is Rose, Nathan's wife. Rose, this is Claire, Nathan's ex-wife.'

'Yes, I think she's figured that out already, Penny. Come inside, Rose. We could use the help. We're plying Amelia with wine.' And when I step into the hall, she whispers in my ear, 'Her husband's been cheating on her for years, and we're bolstering her courage to leave. We've made it through one bottle already, and we've only just got started.'

I manage a smile but only make it as far as the open lounge door. I feel so out of place in this house. Half of my body is too bewildered to leave and the other half is on the starting blocks, ready to bolt back down the driveway. I would, too, if it weren't for one of Saeed's red flags waving from the monkey puzzle tree at the bottom.

I came here for the truth, and I won't leave without it.

Claire asks, 'Can I get you a glass of wine, Rose?'

'No, thanks. I have to drive.'

'Nonsense,' Penny says. 'Leave your car here and get a cab home. You can pick it up tomorrow. Go on, have a glass of wine with us. White?'

Before I can answer, Penny has disappeared into the kitchen. So I step into the lounge, where Amelia is sitting on the rug with an enormous glass in one hand and what looks like a twisted cheese breadstick in the other. Mascara runs down her cheeks and her hair is all over the place. I stare at her. On the outside, she looks exactly how I feel on the inside.

'Rose!' She looks up at me as if she's been caught stealing then tries to rise, but struggles with her hands full.

'Please,' I say. 'Don't get up.'

Claire joins Amelia on the rug, saying, 'Yeah, Amelia, stay down, darling. If you don't, you'll only fall down.'

Then Penny comes up behind me with two glasses of white and hands one to me before joining Claire and Amelia on the rug.

I stand there awkwardly but it isn't long before I feel like a fool and have no choice but to join them on the floor. After a few moments of shuffling around, I'm still ill at ease but suspect I would feel even more so perched on the edge of one of the sofas. Catching up seems the wisest course of action, so I chink their glasses, saying, 'Cheers,' and down half the glass in one.

Amelia laughs, caustically. 'Not just me, then?'

My voice breaks on the lemony tartness of the wine. 'Not just you.'

'Well, at least you're not a cliché.' Amelia's head droops over her glass. 'My husband's been fucking his fucking medical secretary for two whole years. And I've known about it for six...six months! And still I can't pluck up the courage to leave!' She starts sobbing but her mascara tells me that's been going on for some time. 'And it's not even him I don't want to leave! I hate him! I don't want to leave my beautiful home and live in some flophouse I can barely afford.'

'Fuck them all!' Claire chinks glasses with the three of us.

'Ladies,' Penny says, 'I've told you time and time again, they aren't bloody worth it. Getting out was the best thing I ever did. I mean, honestly, what do you actually need them for anyway?'

We all look at each other blankly and then Amelia says, 'Opening jars?'

'Hot tap and a rubber glove,' I say. 'Works every time.'

'For opening jars or something else?' Claire says. 'Because I have a vibrator for that.'

We all burst out laughing.

But, seconds later, Amelia is sobbing again. 'I don't like vibrators. They're so noisy. It's distracting. And you have to do all the work yourself.' She rocks her breadstick back and forth.

I say, 'I used to be pretty good at DIY before I met Nathan.'

Amelia laughs through her tears.

'Get one of these...' Penny jumps to her feet '...and I promise you you'll never need a man again.' She leaves the room and comes back a few minutes later holding a giant pink rubber sperm.

229

'What the hell is that?' Claire asks.

'It's called a Lovense.' Penny holds it out to Amelia, who turns her nose up as she puts her breadstick down on the coffee table. 'It's all right. I washed it.'

Reluctantly, Amelia takes it and turns it over and over in her hands. Meanwhile, Penny gets out her mobile and presses a few buttons. Then Amelia shrieks and drops the giant sperm on the floor, where it vibrates in a series of changing patterns.

We all stare at it on the rug.

But then curiosity gets the better of Amelia and she picks it up again, resting it on her palm.

'Quiet as a mouse,' Penny says. 'And depending on whether you like it rough, you can program it to any pattern you like.'

And we all laugh again, passing the vibrator between us as if it's a bomb that's about to go off.

God, I've missed this. Just hanging out with other women and laughing over a glass of wine. I used to do this all the time with my girlfriends. I glance out of Penny's lounge window as if Nathan's house is right there on the other side of the street. And it's only now that I realise how much time I've spent in that house over the past ten months: cleaning, cooking, washing, ironing. I only go out to run errands for Nathan or visit Daisy at the hospital. Never for fun.

How did I become this person so quickly? This slave to his needs?

Where did Rose go?

While Penny talks Amelia through flophouse-avoidance tactics – spousal maintenance, trading his pension for the house, letting him have her Jaguar – I curl up on the sofa.

Claire comes over, tops up my wine and then sits down next to me. 'Are you okay?'

'Honestly? I have no idea.'

'You've been with Nathan just over a year now, haven't you?'

I nod.

'And...things are starting to get confusing?'

'How do you know?'

She raises her eyebrows as if that's obvious.

Half wanting to know and half in pain at the idea of having to hear it, I ask, 'What was he like when you first met?'

'Too good to be true. Romantic. Attentive. He'd do anything for me. Which is no doubt what it's been like for you, right?'

I nod.

'You moved in together probably after, what? Three months?'

I hold up one finger and waggle it.

'Wow, he's getting efficient. And I'll bet, before you moved in, he cooked for you and wouldn't even let you help clean up afterwards. And you saw him as this incredibly capable man who cured sick children during the day and kept an enormous but immaculate house by night. And all single-handedly, without even breaking a sweat?'

I nod again, remembering how impressed I was.

'But then, one day, not long after you moved in, he ruined one of your favourite things in the washing machine?'

I open my mouth to speak.

'No, don't tell me! A roll-neck jumper – something comfortable that you loved but he didn't like you wearing – and he put it in a ninety-degree whites wash and shrank it. Then he played innocent afterwards, saying, "Well, it was white."'

'Pretty close.'

'That's how it starts. He plays the *I can't possibly be trusted to do the XYZ* card, closely followed by the *But you're so much better at it* card. And before you know it he has a straight flush and you're doing all the washing, ironing, cooking and

231

cleaning because you're so damn good at them all. I mean, how difficult is it to put a wash on, really? Clearly too difficult for a paediatric surgeon to figure out.'

'I think his penis prevents him from getting too close to the machine.' I stretch out my arms trying to reach past my imaginary penis and Claire laughs.

But then the laughter stops.

I feel stupid for falling for it.

She says, 'It became a struggle, didn't it? Holding down a full-time job while running his enormous house to his five-star standards. Being his full-time cook and bottle-washer?'

I nod.

'So, you asked for his help. At which point, he chided you for being unable to cope with something he'd managed perfectly well himself for years. But if you needed help, he was going to give it to you because that's how kind and generous he is. So he gave you the ultimate solution: quit your job. After all, you'd be a stay-at-home mum soon enough anyway.'

I swallow a large gulp of wine.

'What did you do before?' she asks.

'Teacher.'

'I was a nurse. Now I'm a single mum with a young child to support.'

My mouth falls open.

Claire stares at me. 'He didn't tell you he had a child?'

'No.' I bite back tears.

'Well, Emma's not his child anyway, not as far as I'm concerned, she's mine. And if you ask him about her he'll tell you I don't allow him to see her. That's what he told everyone when we separated.'

'Would you have?'

'He's her father. But I'll admit I was relieved when he wanted nothing to do with her. I was glad he reserved the vitriol for me and left her out of it.'

'Vitriol?'

232

'Come on, Rose. I'm sure you've heard it. What did he tell you about me?'

I clear my throat and look down. 'That you were a narcissistic, adulterous bitch who stayed out every night leaving him alone to fend for himself.'

'Narcissistic? Oh, the irony. And who was caring for our child while I was sleeping with every man in Oxford, then? Where was Emma in his fictitious scenario?'

I can't look at her.

'No.' She shakes her head. 'I promised myself, if I ever met you, I wouldn't start down that road: slagging him off the way he did me. I mean, I refused to listen to anyone who tried to warn me about Nathan in those early days. Not even my friends. And you're probably no more ready to hear any of this than I was.'

'Your friends noticed something was wrong?'

She nods. 'They saw a change in me, started to make comments, ask questions. But he managed to separate me from anyone who saw through his charade by saying they were just jealous of us and trying to split us up. He used to say my girlfriends had hit on him behind my back and I couldn't trust them. I had to open my own eyes, Rose. You do too.'

'I think they're opening already. He did that to me too. After Amelia's party, when I met Penny, he said she'd called me dreary.'

'What the fu...? Hey, Penny?'

Penny looks up and I put my hand on Claire's arm. 'No, don't—'

'Nathan told Rose you called her dreary, at the party.'

She barely registers the remark, turning back to Amelia, saying, 'Of course he did.'

Claire tops up my wine again and I gulp it down. 'God. I don't know what to believe any more.'

'It's exhausting, isn't it? You spend your life on eggshells trying to please him, wondering whether he loves you, playing his sideways remarks over and over in your head.'

And, when she says that, I think back to Nathan saying he *didn't want to ruin the moment* by looking at me when we were making love. 'Discards,' I say.

Claire looks at me, surprised. 'You've been reading?'

'A friend... He...he gave me some books.'

'He?! How does Nathan feel about "he"? I'll bet he's tried to put a stop to that friendship real fast!'

I nod.

'Don't let him. You need friends around you right now. They're the ones who'll keep you sane in the midst of his madness.'

'Can I ask you something?'

'Anything,' she says.

'On your first date, when Nathan picked you up, did he happen to be playing your favourite song on the stereo?'

She shakes her head, almost laughing in despair. 'Hozier. "Take Me to Church".'

'He hates Hozier.'

'I know that now,' she says. 'There's a name for that too: they call it mirroring. It makes you think you've met someone who's just like you – your soulmate.'

'It really is a handbook, isn't it? That's what my friend told me.'

'Yes, and it works. It worked on me. It worked on you. It'll already be working on the next one.'

'The next one?'

'There's always a next one, Rose. Nathan had two other women on the go while we were married. He plays the victim card, tells them his wife doesn't understand him or won't give him sex. Whatever it takes. And he's so charming they fall for it every time. Men like Nathan leave nothing but ruin in their wake: financial ruin, broken careers, destroyed friendships, emotional damage. I'm sorry, Rose, you seem like a nice person. And I'm sorry you've ended up where I was.'

Claire pulls her mobile from her pocket, unlocks it, then opens an app called Decipher before handing me the phone. It holds a log of text messages from Nathan. 'You have no reason to believe me,' she says, 'but I had to log these for the divorce.'

I scroll through dozens and dozens of messages which are full of the vitriol Claire mentioned. Those I can barely read; they don't sound like Nathan at all. But, eventually, I reach the earliest messages and their familiarity sours the wine in my stomach. One in particular catches my eye and I stop scrolling.

> My captivating Claire, I love you more than I did this morning, as much as is possible right now, but still less than I will tonight. Your Doctor of Love. Xxx

I say, 'He sent this exact message to me. About a month ago.' I pull my phone from my trouser pocket, find the text, and show it to Claire. 'He just switched our names.'

'Why waste time when you've got a formula that works?'

'We're nothing but appliances, are we?'

'Huh?'

'That's what one of the books said: that men with narcissistic personality disorder don't see women as people but appliances. And what works on one appliance will work just as well on the second or third.'

'Sounds about right,' she says. 'And when the appliance stops working properly, they dump it and buy another one.'

'I thought he loved me. I thought he wanted me to move in with him, get married so quickly because I'd swept him off his feet. Just as he had me. But really he just wanted to make sure I'd stay put and give him everything he needed.' I put my third glass of wine down on the coffee table and get up. 'I'm sorry. I have to go.'

'No!' Penny says. 'Stay for dinner. Claire's bought enough pizza to feed the neighbourhood.'

'I'd love to. But I really have to go. Nathan will be home in a couple of hours and I have to get dinner ready.'

'Of course you do,' Penny raises her eyes to the ceiling.

'Leave her alone, Penny. You may not know what it's like being where Rose is, but Amelia and I do.'

'You're right, I'm sorry.' Penny gets to her feet and pulls me into a tight hug. 'I'll call you a cab.'

'No, it's okay. I want to walk for a while, clear my head. I'll get one outside the hospital; there are always a few there.'

'If you're sure. Come back soon, though, you hear?' She hugs me again and I nod, my head bobbing against her shoulder, close to tears but grateful for this sudden friendship.

'Wait a second.' Claire disappears into the kitchen and comes out holding a large pizza box. 'Take this. It'll save you having to cook dinner with a wine-head.'

I stare at it as if it's something she dumpster-dived. 'I can't give that to Nathan.'

'Yes, you can,' she says. 'Have a bit of fun. See how he reacts to you eating pizza. I bet my fat ass he loses his shit over it.'

I laugh. 'You don't have a fat ass.'

'No,' she says. 'And neither do you. Remember that, Rose. You're allowed to eat pizza. Wear flat shoes. Wear sweatpants around the house. And nobody needs Sarah flogging them at the gym three times a week until they puke.'

My mouth falls open.

'He sends all his girls to Sarah.'

I take the pizza. 'Thanks. It's been really great. It was...just what I needed...sort of.' And then, to Amelia, I say, 'You're better than him, okay?'

Still sitting on the carpet, she lifts her wine glass and nods. 'Thanks.'

Claire sees me to the front door, and when she opens it for me I hug her hard but then have no idea what else to say. She doesn't say anything either, but as I'm walking down the drive she calls out to me.

'Rose!'

I turn to face her.

'Nathan isn't just a narcissist. He's a psychopath. Be careful.'

Dumbly holding the pizza box, I stand there for a moment. And then I turn and walk away.

~

I know Nathan will be angry the moment he walks in the door, because he'll know where I've been. I should have left my phone at home so he couldn't locate me on Find My Friends. But, if Saeed is right about the tracker on the car, it wouldn't have mattered anyway. He'll know I've left it at Penny's.

I lay the cream cloth over the dining table and picture one word written across it like a billboard.

Psychopath.

I see it everywhere I look.

Is it true?

Have I married another psychopath?

If anyone would know, surely Claire would.

I catch my reflection in the mirrored splashback of the drinks cabinet. There's even a mirror in our dining room.

Saeed said that many traits of narcissism overlap with sociopathy and psychopathy. And in one of the books it said that it isn't so much that narcissists like to look at themselves, but when their personality borders on sociopathy or psychopathy they need mirrors to practise and monitor their expressions. They learn to show emotions they can't possibly feel by mimicking the facial expressions of others. I picture Nathan standing in front of the drinks cabinet practising the compassion, happiness and love he's always shown me.

Then I remember him at the top of the stairs: the blank expression on his face as his pregnant wife fell. The instinct to reach out and catch her not even registering on his emotional radar.

My mind reels like one of those hamster wheels, spinning so fast and so constantly that it sucks every morsel of energy I have. I can't stop analysing every aspect of my life with Nathan, like the way he closely guards his phone and laptop. No doubt because he's grooming some other woman as well, maybe many women: back-up sources for his narcissistic supply. The latest iPhone and MacBook were two of the earliest presents he gave me, so I would never have an excuse to use his.

I check my phone.

Nathan is only a minute away, so I put a song on the sound system and pause it just before it starts. Then I sit down at the table and wait.

The front door clicks shut and the moment his shoes tap the hall floorboards I press play on the sound system remote before slipping it in my pocket.

Moments later, Nathan comes into the dining room holding a dozen red roses wrapped in blood-red tissue paper and crinkly plastic.

Yesterday I might have swooned.

Today, they're a dozen red flags.

The air fizzes with tension when he kisses me on the lips and hands me the flowers. In the background, Lily Cornford recites the Gayatri prayer. I was going to play 'Tawny Moon', but after the saga in Dr Anderson's office it seemed too obvious, so I went for 'Lily' instead. The song opened *Before the Dawn*. I may not have been at the concert, but I'm enough of a fan to know that. And the thing with 'Lily' is, because it opens with this prayer, it isn't immediately obvious it's a Kate Bush song. You'd have to know it.

Stepping back, Nathan waits for me to shower him with praise for the flowers but instead I say, 'What's the occasion?'

'No occasion. I just adore you, that's all. Does there have to be an occasion for a man to buy his wife flowers?'

'No. Of course not. They're lovely, thank you.'

'Well, don't strain yourself.'

'I won't.' I look up at him and smile, and in the flash of a second – before he has time to modify his expression – I catch a glimmer of hate.

'How was your day?' His eyes dart around the room as if he's under attack by Lily Cornford, who's talking over him at a volume that's borderline annoying. 'Where did you go this afternoon?'

He knows exactly where I went.

'Penny's.'

'What did you go there for?' His tone is clipped, simmering.

'No reason. Just to be friendly.' I go to the sideboard, pull out the silver placemats and cutlery and start setting the table. 'She told me to pop in if I was in the area – at the party, remember?'

'I told you what she said about you. Why would you go and see her after that?'

I shrug.

'What's going on, Rose?' His words blend with Lily's as she speaks about truth, until finally his irritation boils over. 'What *is* this shit?' He jabs his finger at one of the surround-sound speakers mounted in the corner at ceiling height.

I don't answer.

I look him right in the eye for the four long seconds it takes for Kate's unmistakable voice to burst through the speakers. Nathan's expression flicks from anger to recognition. Then a whiff of panic. Then back to anger again.

Saeed was telling the truth. Nathan didn't go to the concert. If he had, this song would be branded on his memory. Because apparently, the moment the audience heard her sing – most of them for the first time – they burst into tears. A concert hall of complete strangers crying, hugging and high-fiving each other.

He doesn't like Kate Bush. It's just another manufactured

239

lie like all the rest, told to make me believe we were mirrored souls who loved and hated all the same things.

A trick.

The same one he played on Claire.

The same one he plays on all his women.

And I see him now.

His skin writhes over his bones as if Kate is nothing but fingernails down a blackboard. 'It's too bloody loud!' He scans the room for the remote control and when he can't find it he gets down on his hands and knees and fiddles with the catch on the sideboard to get to the amp.

'Leave it, baby.' I slip the remote from my pocket. 'I'll do it for you.' And I turn down the volume.

'Thank you. You know I love Kate, but not at that volume.'

'Sorry.'

'No problem.' He pulls me into a hug and kisses me again. But it's as if the curtains have lifted. His trickery is exposed and I can see the revolving stage, the video projections and his floating props. Returning the kiss feels staged too. Only I'm no actress and my performance falls short.

'Is everything all right?' he asks. 'You seem off.'

I smile. 'I'm fine.'

'Good. But in case you do need cheering up after an afternoon with Penny, I bought you something else too. Close your eyes.' He takes my hand, uncurls my fingers and places something on my palm.

I open my eyes. 'What is it?'

'Open it.'

Inside the small jewellery box, sitting in familiar pale silk, rests a pair of earrings, each with a subtle trellis holding a large diamond. Scepticism prickles. He bought these at the same time as the eternity ring. No doubt when he bought my engagement ring and wedding ring too. Efficient. He probably got a good deal on a bulk purchase. I wonder what's next: a matching necklace?

If the authors of these books are right about Nathan, he's brought the earrings home tonight because he's angry. They're the advance guard for the argument he's pre-prepared. Something to use against me in an hour or two when any complaints about his behaviour will be met with: *after everything I do for you!*

I'm ready for it.

'They're beautiful,' I say. 'You shouldn't have.'

'Of course I should. My lovely wife deserves lovely things.'

'Well, your lovely wife is about to serve dinner.' I close the box, pull away from him and make a show of finishing the table settings. 'Why don't you go and get changed while I serve?' And I have to hold myself back from adding: *because that's what I do, isn't it, Nathan? I serve.*

~

'Pizza?' He stares at the plate in front of him. 'What's going on, Rose? Did you waste so much time at Penny's house, you didn't have time to cook a proper dinner?'

'Not at all,' I say sweetly. 'I thought it would be a nice change.' And I think of Claire while I stare at his white knuckles on the edge of the table.

'It's not exactly healthy, is it?'

'We don't always have to be healthy, do we?' I take a seat at the opposite end of the table, using it as a shield. 'We can treat ourselves once in a while.'

'*I* can.'

'What does that mean?'

'Nothing. Just that I have a fast metabolism. You don't. You're going to regret eating this when Sarah weighs you at the gym tomorrow morning.'

'I've cancelled Sarah.'

'Why? Aren't you well enough to go?'

'No, I mean I've cancelled her altogether.'

241

'What the hell, Rose? She's paid up three months in advance.'

'She said I could transfer to another class.'

'I don't understand. What's going on? One afternoon at Penny's and you're throwing away a year of hard work? I told you she was a bitch. She's just jealous that you're slim. She wants everyone to be as fat as she is.'

'Penny isn't fat.'

'Well, she's not thin either. What did she say to you?'

'Nothing. We didn't even talk about the gym. But I'm not going any more. I don't enjoy it. I've signed up for yoga classes instead.'

'Yoga?'

'Yes.' I pick up a slice of pizza and take a mouthful. I can't remember the last time I ate pizza or a burger and it tastes amazing. Not because it's the best pizza I've ever eaten, but because it's like meeting an old friend after a long time apart.

Nathan stands up. 'I don't know what's going on with you today, but we aren't eating this and I'm not paying for fucking yoga classes. Sarah's a good trainer and she's made real progress with you.'

'You don't have to eat the pizza if you don't want to. There's chicken and salad in the fridge.' I take another bite.

'You... You sit at home all day while I work my ass off to support you and I'm expected to eat shit or cook my own dinner?'

'It's pizza, Nathan, not shit.'

'It's not about the pizza. It's you. There's something going on with you and I don't like it. It seems to me that Penny's been filling your head with poison.'

I glare at him and say, 'No, actually. She gave me the antidote.'

And then I duck, face down in my pizza, as Nathan picks up his plate and hurls it. It smashes into the wall behind me and I sit there shaken to the core as he strides from the room.

242

THIRTY

MAGGIE

ACHING AND TIRED, I haul my broken body up the decking steps to the door. But, as I press my thumb down on the lever, the door swings towards me. I'm sure I closed it on the way out. After the incident in the lake, I haven't left the cabin without checking and double checking the front door is closed and properly latched with Alfie safe inside.

'Luc?' My voice echoes around the cabin's high ceilings, making the place feel worryingly empty. 'Luc?! Alfie?!'

Not bothering to remove my trainers, still muddy from my run through the forest, I cross the rug in front of the wood-burner and then stop. Up ahead, on the split-level floor, there are footprints. Hesitant, I take a few steps closer. They're far too big to be Alfie's. Luc's? No, they're a little too small for Luc.

Watching my step, I glance at my trainers as I take the two steps to the raised floor. Dark mud skirts their soles, which roughly match the footprints on the floor. I have big feet – size

243

seven – but these footprints aren't mine. When I brought Alfie inside, I didn't come through the lounge, and my feet weren't muddy then anyway.

I hunker down on my haunches for a closer look. Each footprint is surrounded by a rim of water, as if snow has been dragged inside and then melted. But it hasn't snowed for days. I run a finger through the mud and it isn't thick and gritty, it's fluid and viscous.

I rub my finger against my thumb.

The mud is red. Mixed with…

Blood.

In a split-second I'm running, tracking the footprints across the floor towards Luc's study, screaming his name.

'Luc?!'

'Luc?!'

At the door, I slip on another bloody footprint and just manage to grab the handle before I go down. Then I throw back the door, and my whole world freezes on this one frame.

I can't move.

I can't think.

I can't breathe.

My fingers clamp around the knife, squeezing it hard enough to break the hilt; and then, as if I've been punched in the chest, I fall to my knees. I want to close my eyes and pretend this isn't real, pretend it's just a nightmare, but I can't. My petrified brain ceases to function and my whole body shuts down.

The study curtains blow in the breeze where both windows behind Luc's desk have been smashed into tiny shards. Only a few fragments remain, trapped in the frame. Luc's desk, keyboard and chair are littered with splinters of glass and Luc is lying on the floor, his face covered in blood. And just a few feet away, face down and unmoving, lies Alfie.

A cry lodges in my throat.

When my senses return, I scrabble across the floor on my hands and knees to my little boy. But when I turn him over he just stares at me with blue-brown eyes.

Still.

Dead.

A trickle of blood runs from his rosy lips down his chin and his round, soft face is covered in cuts. Tiny shards of glass stick out from his broken skin.

One word plays on repeat in my mind:

No.

No.

No.

Clutching his body to mine, I grope my way across the rug to Luc. Like Alfie, his near-black eyes are wide and still, and his face is lacerated from hairline to beard with shards of glass.

Leaning forward over his body, with Alfie trapped between us, I bury my face in his jumper and ceaselessly, silently scream.

245

THIRTY-ONE

ROSE

'PLEASE WAKE UP,' I run my palm over Daisy's forehead and down her hair, twirling her red curls between my fingers. 'I need you. More than I ever have in my life. Nathan hasn't spoken to me for days and I need to talk to you. I'm going to have to leave him. He's not the man I thought he was and I'm going to be alone again. Please come back to me. I know you probably don't want to be here. I'm sure that the life inside your head is much nicer than this one. But I'm going to be selfish now and beg you. I'm begging you to wake up. I need your help, Daisy. Please.'

Swallowing tears, I run my hand down her arm to her hand and squeeze her fingers a little too tightly, as if the discomfort might reach her on the other side. Then I rest my forehead on the back of her hand, as if my thoughts can pass through her skin and be carried like molecules of oxygen along her bloodstream to her brain.

I thought Nathan loved me.

And perhaps he does, in the only way he knows how. But I'm not a real person to him, I'm a possession that reflects his status, just like everything else he owns.

It's not love. It's coveting.

That's why he cares so much about me. I'm the Mercedes on our driveway. He chose the colour, the alloys, the interior leather, and he makes sure it's always washed, waxed and shining. No one's allowed to drive it but him. Nobody can even sit in it without his permission. And he must know where it is at all times: either safe in the garage or in the hospital car park.

And, in the same way that he loses his temper if his palatial house is untidy, or his Mercedes doesn't start the moment he presses the button, he gets angry if my paintwork isn't up to scratch, if I'm not upholstered in the right fabric, or I put pizza in the engine instead of chicken salad. After all, he's spent a lot of money on this model; he expects it to come with the features he's paid for.

The door opens behind me and I sit up.

'Rose.'

'Dr Anderson. Hi.' I wipe away my tears.

'I didn't expect to see you today.'

'I wanted to spend some time with Daisy.'

'I understand.' His voice is grave and he takes her chart from the end of the bed, lifting up pages and running his finger along the results. 'You'll want to spend as much time as you can with her before tomorrow.'

'Tomorrow?'

He doesn't look up from the chart. 'Yes, the young man is being transferred first thing in the morning.'

'Young man?'

'The patient.' He hangs the chart back on the bed, moves to my side and perches on the edge of the mattress. 'I know I'm not supposed to say anything and I promised Nathan I wouldn't. I know it's difficult and you don't like to talk about

247

it. I swore I wouldn't even bring the subject up. But someone has to thank you for your sacrifice. He's only thirteen and he has a good chance of recovery. You've saved this boy's life, Rose.'

'I'm sorry, Dr Anderson, I don't understand. How have I saved a young boy's life?'

He's confused. 'By removing Daisy's life support.'

The blood drains from my face as my mouth falls open.

Dr Anderson gets up, clearly uncomfortable. 'I'm sorry. I thought... I mean... I underestimated...' He moves quickly to the door.

I spring to my feet. 'Dr Anderson, wait! We aren't removing Daisy's life support. I haven't consented.'

He turns back to me, his startled expression a mirror of my own. 'Nathan authorised it. He said it was what you wanted. And Daisy has consented to organ donation. She's on the register.'

'Well, it's not what I want. And you can't.'

He looks at me with an expression of regret for bringing up a subject he was asked not to discuss and is now expected to dance around. 'I shouldn't have said anything, I'm sorry. I understand the pressure this puts you under and why you wouldn't want your consent to be explicit.'

'I *don't* consent!'

'But, Rose, donation is what Daisy wanted. And legally, a court ruling is no longer required. Provided it's in accordance with good medical practice, withdrawal is down to the clinical judgement of the doctors responsible for a patient's care. In Daisy's case, that's Nathan and myself. And we are in agreement. It's in Daisy's best interest. Also... Rose...we have already allocated the organ to the other patient.'

'You will have to reallocate it.'

'I can't. This is the only one available.' He puts a firm hand on my shoulder. 'Daisy is declining, Rose. I thought you knew that. They did another scan yesterday and the results were not good. The VNS hasn't yielded the success we'd hoped for and there's really nothing left for us to try. It's been three years. Even if Nathan wasn't on Daisy's team and the divisional director, I would have been encouraging you to let her go. I know this is terribly upsetting for you but I also know that you wouldn't deprive a young man of his life when Daisy is declining. Take as much time as you need today, but you need to prepare yourself. Say your goodbyes.' He rubs my arm up and down, as if that will make everything better, and then leaves the room.

A small cry sticks in my throat as the door closes behind him.

It's as if the door has closed on my life.

Everything I ever wanted is out there, out of reach.

I walk back to the bed with tears flowing so fast it would be pointless to wipe them away, so I leave them to fall on my blouse. And with narrowed eyes I stare at my sister's face with a hatred that only someone who loves can understand. I hate her for not being more careful with her insulin. I hate her for doing this to herself. For not fighting harder. For not forgiving herself. For wanting to die. And for leaving me.

'Wake up!' My fury spills out. 'Do you hear me, Daisy? Wake up!'

And then I'm screaming.

'Wake up, you selfish bitch!'

And I slap her.

'Wake up!'

I slap her so hard her head snaps sideways and her face hits the pillow before slowly turning back again. But she doesn't open her eyes. It's as if I haven't even touched her. So I collapse on the chair, slump over her sleeping body and sob.

THIRTY-TWO

MAGGIE

I SIT ON THE floor next to Luc, rocking Alfie in my arms.

He did this.

The man.

He lured me away from my husband and child so he could skirt the wood, double back to the cabin, and kill them both.

Why?

Why didn't he kill me first?

And then, clutching my dead son and staring at my husband's body, the answer comes.

Because this is worse than death.

He wanted me left alive so I could suffer the torment of life without them. But now I am dead. My life ended the moment I stepped through that door. And now I can't move. Can't go on. Can't live another day.

I have no idea how long I've been here like this, covered in Alfie's blood. Hours? Days? I don't remember it getting dark so it can only be hours. My breath smokes in the ice-cold room which smells of the clean outdoors, like freshly fallen snow. But, in it, there's a hint of metal and chemicals.

Blood and petrol.

Did I disturb the man when I came back?

Was he going to burn the cabin to the ground?

A stray thought of calling the police flits momentarily through my mind but the man will be long gone before they make it all the way out here. And prison is too good for him anyway. I don't want the police here.

He may be gone already. He's done what he came here to do. But, if he's still out there, he'll pay for taking my life from me.

He'll pay with his.

I lay Alfie in the crook of Luc's arm, his head so small on the pillow of his father's shoulder, and, somehow, I find the strength to stand. And the moment I'm on my feet, hate and adrenaline charge through me like a bolt.

Without missing a beat, I pick up the knife and fly out of the study. I leap the steps from the split-level floor, run through the lounge, and throw open the cabin door with such force that it almost splinters when it hits the wall.

My brain is empty of all thought except him. And, once again, I run across the stony beach towards the wood.

THIRTY-THREE

ROSE

SAEED STEPS through the door twenty minutes after I called him using the phone he gave me.

'Did you explain that you did not give consent?' He rushes to my side, as if he's going to hold me, but then stops himself.

'I did, but he said Daisy hasn't responded to the VNS and the latest scans were bad. He said we've given her three years to wake up and if I don't let her go now, this kid is going to die. And then Daisy still won't wake up anyway. What am I supposed to do?'

I burst into tears and he hesitates for just a second before pulling me into his arms. When we finally let go, he lifts Daisy's chart from the end of the bed, sits down in his usual chair and scans her test results line by line. I take the seat opposite and stare at the deep grooves between his eyebrows as if hope lies in those small crevices.

'She is declining,' he says. 'And rapidly.'

He looks up from the chart.

'I am so sorry, Rose, but these results are not good. It looks as if they did another fMRI yesterday—'

'Nobody told me she was having another fMRI.'

'No. Nobody told me either. Dr Anderson must have ordered it before agreeing to the organ transfer. Although her brain still shows some activity, it is no longer responding to stimuli. A very different result from the one we saw before she had the VNS implant. In just two weeks, her GCS has dropped to three. The scale does not go any lower. She is now showing abnormal *extension* to pain, a sign of traumatic injury to the brainstem.' Saeed looks right at me, deep pain in his eyes, and says, 'Rose, even if she did wake up – and according to these new tests that is highly unlikely – Daisy would have significant and permanent brain damage. That is why Nathan and Dr Anderson have made this decision for you.'

Tears roll down my face. 'But if the damage is that bad, why doesn't it show on her scans?'

'I am not sure. I would have expected it to, given the severity of her motor response. But a standard MRI only picks up significant tissue damage. A more sophisticated MRI with contrast dyes would probably show it. But Dr Anderson is right: Daisy has slipped deeper into the coma.'

I can't speak. I just bury my head in the blanket and cry.

Saeed holds my hand but he doesn't say anything. What is there to say?

When there are no tears left and I'm finally able to speak, I say, 'I can't believe all this is happening. I'm not sure I can take any more.'

'All this? Has something else happened?'

I brush the damp hair from my cheeks and rub my eyes. 'I met Nathan's ex-wife. Everything you said about him is true. Every romantic thing he's ever said to me, he said to her first,

253

word for word. He lied to her, cheated on her, and finally left her with a child.'

'A child? Nathan has a child?'

I nod.

'My God, Rose, I am so sorry.'

'I challenged him – not directly, I was too afraid to do that and Claire told me to be careful, she said he wasn't a narcissist, he was a psychopath – so I just behaved differently, did a few things I knew he wouldn't like.'

'Like what?'

'I went to see a friend he didn't want me to see. And then I gave him pizza.'

'What did he do?'

'He threw the plate at me.'

Saeed launches himself to his feet as if he's about to storm from the room and search the hospital corridors for Nathan.

'It's all right, I'm all right. I ducked. He missed.'

Saeed sits down with some urging and placating from me.

'But what am I supposed to do now? How am I supposed to go on? He hasn't spoken to me for days and I don't know that things weren't better before, when I just thought his outbursts were isolated incidents. Things he could blame on stress or too much to drink. Now I know it's not stress, it's not drink. This is who he is. He's always going to behave this way. And if there's nothing to trigger an outburst he'll create one, to keep me on edge and unsettled. He wants me afraid, insecure, too scared to leave, and he'll never stop exerting his control.'

'I am sorry. But ignorance is not bliss, it is just ignorance. The truth is hard, but without it we have nothing. Nothing that is real, anyway.'

'But I was happy. Now I'm going to lose Daisy, and if I leave Nathan I'll be completely alone.'

'You will not be alone. You have me. But you should not rush into leaving Nathan. If he throws plates when you give him pizza, what will he do if you tell him you are leaving? If

Claire is right, it is not safe. Do not underestimate a psychopath, Rose. These men can go from zero to homicidal in a heartbeat.'

'Homicidal? You aren't serious?'

'Very. There was a study done on victims whose abusive partners had attempted to kill them. Only half of them believed their partners capable of that kind of violence because they had never been violent before. But Nathan has already shown he is capable, on more than one occasion. So you must make a plan to leave, and execute it on a single day while he is at work. Do you have someone you can stay with?'

'I can go to my mum's.'

'Does she live far? You need to get as far away as possible.'

'Yes, she lives in Yorkshire.' A single tear rolls down my cheek. I must look a complete wreck, so I tell Saeed I need a minute and go to Daisy's en suite, where I splash cold water on my face before sitting on the toilet seat for a while. I need to pull myself together but I have no idea how to do that. I'm feather-light, as if I'm not inside my own body any more but somewhere else. As if this is all happening to someone else.

Saeed knocks gently on the door. 'Rose? Are you all right?'

I open the door and linger there, holding myself up by the surround. 'No. Not really. I never imagined my life would turn out like this. I thought I'd be happy and settled by this age, not divorced twice and losing my sister at the same time. How will I get through this without her? And how will I start again when I'm nearly forty?' I burst into tears.

Gently, Saeed takes my hands from my face and wraps them around his middle, pulling me in close, where I cling to the back of his kurta and sob into his shoulder just as I did in front of the radiographer. And, already, it feels habitual.

'You will be all right, Rose.' His words whisper through my hair. 'You are a lot stronger than you realise.'

I pull back and look up at him, at those deep creases between his brows, at his soft, strong features. 'I wish I were as sure as you are.'

My eyes are puffy from crying, the skin around my nostrils red and sore, and my lips chafed and swollen. Two tears rest beneath my chin, waiting to fall, but I'm not willing to let go of Saeed long enough to wipe them away.

I must look exhausted.

Broken.

But Saeed doesn't look at me as if I'm broken.

He looks at me in a way no man has ever looked at me in my life, his grey eyes filled with confusion and uncertainty. I know why. Because I feel it too. I'm a married woman. And I have no doubt that the notion of having any kind of relationship with a married woman is as inconceivable to Saeed as it is to me.

But I'm not really married, am I? Not if my vows were a lie, a sham. Marriage is a union of love, loyalty, respect, kindness and trust. Mine has none of those things.

I feel small and fragile in his arms but, although I know I'm safe in them, his anger burns into me. It's caught in the narrowness of his pupils and it bristles between the hairs on his skin. I'm sure I'm by no means the first woman he's met who's in an abusive relationship, but I may be the first one he hasn't been able to separate his anger from.

He wants to break Nathan.

In the same way Nathan broke me on that staircase.

In the same way he has broken me down, day by day, taking everything from me so gradually that I didn't even notice I was losing anything.

As I look up at him, still wrapped in his arms, one of the tears falls from my chin on to my sheer blouse. And he looks down at me with as much uncertainty as I feel, my chest heaving against his as I struggle to breathe. There's not enough air in the space between us, and what remains is charged with static.

I sense his hesitation.

He's trying to figure out which side of his professional line I stand on. He has counselled me, supported me, guided me to the truth. Does that make me his patient?

No.

Daisy is his patient, not me.

His heart, beating fast and in time with mine, tells us both that no matter how professional he has tried to be, he has failed. I could never be his patient. We may not have crossed the line physically, but we have certainly crossed it emotionally.

And in the same moment that he leans into me, I raise myself up on my tiptoes and our lips meet.

At first, that's all it is: a kiss. A moment of recklessness we can both put an end to as quickly as it started. But then the kiss deepens, no longer tentative and unsure but charged with hunger and longing. And I'm as struck by the shock that it's happening as I am by the need for it to happen – needing it more than I've ever needed anything.

Neither of us is able to pull away.

His mouth opens on mine, our tongues meet and he wraps his arms around my middle and lifts me gently off the floor. I wrap myself around him and drape my arms over his shoulders, which flex with the tension of the moment. As we press our bodies into each other, there's heat in our mouths, and our need for each other is as violent as the kiss is slow and tender.

Then the door swings open.

Hurriedly we disentangle ourselves, both of us sure beyond doubt that Nathan is standing there. And both of us let out the breaths we're holding when we realise it's just the nurse who comes in twice a day to swipe Daisy's VNS.

'Oh, excuse me…' She blushes and backs out of the room. And, in spite of everything, we almost laugh at the profound awkwardness that should be ours instead of hers, and relief and amazement that it simply isn't there.

Determined not to let the interruption mar the significance of the moment or what that kiss meant to me, I dive back into Saeed's arms and bury my face in his neck as he rests his chin on top of my head.

'I am sorry,' he says. 'I should not have done that.' But he doesn't pull away. He doesn't let me go.

'You didn't do it. We both did. And I don't regret it.'

'You are not ready, Rose. And I am too ready, too eager.'

'I know.' I hold him tight.

'This cannot happen again. I cannot let it, not yet. If I were to kiss you again, even once, I would not be able to stand back and watch you return to Nathan, not even for an hour. And the last thing you need from me is coercion and confusion. I know what kind of man Nathan is, and if you leave him he will pressure you to return with the same intense love and romance that made you fall in love with him in the first place. Most women in controlling relationships return at least once, because the abuser's apologies, explanations and remorse are so convincing. And I will not be able to help myself. I will be an equal force in the opposite direction, pressuring you to stay away. Between the two of us we would tear you apart. I could not bear that.'

I bury my face under his chin, my cheeks still damp with tears, and then I press my lips to his neck in a slow, gentle kiss. He shivers beneath my touch. Then he kisses the top of my head, inhaling the smell of orange blossom in my hair. And although neither of us is able to let go, between us we make a silent agreement that we will never discuss what just happened, never reveal our feelings to anyone. Not until I'm ready to entwine my life with his.

And, to do that, I have to disentangle it from Nathan's.

THIRTY-FOUR

MAGGIE

DARTING BETWEEN the trees feels different this time. My movements are so free and agile, I could be running on the road. My heart pulses in a powerful rhythm and my breath blasts through my cheeks in perfect time with my footfall. I grip the knife and my arms swing back and forth, propelling me forward as I skim each tree, turning swiftly this way and that. Instinctively, as if guided by muscle memory, I know which direction to take, and I'm unhindered by decision-making.

He's there.

Up ahead in the trees.

He's not as agile as he was. He's ungainly. The rucksack beneath his mac weighs him down and he stumbles over fallen branches. Maybe Luc injured him in the attack. Luc would have done anything to protect Alfie, would even have given his own life. And unless the man caught them by surprise there is no way this killer wouldn't have met resistance.

At the sight of him, weak and vulnerable, a burst of energy surges through me and I charge between the trees with the mastery of a trained sprinter. My body has no weight. It barely crushes the undergrowth beneath my feet. No roots or branches trip or hinder me. And I run with the speed and intent of a predator.

Because I am.

I grip the knife even tighter, pump my arms even faster. And, as my legs power me through the forest, I close the gap between us.

Five metres.

Four.

Three.

THIRTY-FIVE

ROSE

AT ANOTHER swoosh of the door, we disentangle from each other again and let out another breath at the sight of Dionne struggling with the tea trolley. Saeed rushes to help her and the heat in the room evaporates when I'm left standing alone. Suddenly cold.

'Rose,' Dionne says, 'I heard about Daisy. I'm so sorry, my love. But you've been here for hours, sweetheart, and you need to keep your strength up. I brought you some dinner. There were a few meals left over. Do you like chicken?'

I nod. 'Thanks, Dionne, that was very sweet of you.'

She puts the tray down on Daisy's over-bed table, which she repositions in the centre of the bed as if eating is an instruction not open to negotiation.

'Can I get you a plate, Dr Sharif?'

'No. Thank you, Dionne.'

Then she leaves quickly, quietly, sensitive to the weight of the air in the room. Saeed takes his usual place on the chair opposite while I sit at the foot of Daisy's bed and stare at the tray. Eating right now would take as much effort as running a marathon and, even though I'm grateful to Dionne, I want to move the table aside.

I want to push aside every barrier between me and Saeed. Instead, I push slices of honeyed chicken around the plate while we sit in silence for a long time.

Finally, I break it.

'How will I ever get through this? I might just manage it if Daisy were here.'

'You are not fragile. You are not delicate. And you will manage just fine.'

'I feel like a fool. I never imagined I'd end up like this: an abused woman. Twice. What is it about me? Am I not very bright? Am I a poor judge of character? Gullible? Is there something about me that attracts men like Ryan and Nathan?'

'No. And do not say such things.' His voice is stern. 'It hurts me to hear you say them. Do not even think them. After suffering at the hands of abuse, you are now falling prey to the language of victim-blaming – something so pervasive we barely notice it. And victims even use it on themselves.'

'What did I say?' I've already forgotten; the words just slipped out.

'You searched for fault and blame in your own character, called yourself an abused woman.'

'Aren't I?'

'One of the many reasons victims of rape, domestic violence…emotional abuse…coercive control…look to themselves for blame instead of placing it squarely where it belongs is because of a language construct propagated by our male-dominated society: a form of victim-blaming as covert as the abuse itself. It suggests, very furtively, that the issue is with the victim – part of their identity – rather than a crime that has nothing whatsoever to do with the victim but is solely a violation on the part of the perpetrator.'

'A language construct? I'm not sure I understand.'

Saeed looks past me to the whiteboard on the wall behind Daisy's bed and gets up. The board lists her name, room number, physicians and nurses, allergies and medications, care level, and a colour and number chart from one to five based on a score calculated from her pulse, temperature and blood pressure. Beside it is a large space for notes but, with Daisy in a coma, there's little to say. The space has remained blank for years. Saeed picks up a marker pen from the tray at its base and writes on the board:

NATHAN ABUSED ROSE

'This is a basic English sentence,' he says. '*Nathan* is the subject, *abused* is the verb, and *Rose* is the object. But the moment women report abuse – domestic violence, rape – they become the *subject* of that report. The interest turns from the person performing the action to the person experiencing the action.' He writes on the board:

ROSE WAS ABUSED BY NATHAN

'Now Rose is the subject of the sentence. And through this language construct – the passive voice – the perpetrator is distanced from his actions.'

I eat a little of the chicken but don't take my eyes off Saeed. He's unlike any man I've ever met. Most people float through life, but Saeed is truly in it, always looking around him, always paying attention, always listening and analysing. The world would be a better place with more people like him in it. I watch him intently as he goes on.

'And, because rape and abuse are such everyday occurrences in our society, the analysis – the focus – is often turned to the crime itself: why is it so prevalent? What can be done to prevent it? And the language construct changes again. Just

263

like one in every three women in our society…' He writes on the board:

ROSE IS ABUSED

'The perpetrator drops off the end of the sentence. Without realising it, our whole cognitive structure is skewed by language to exclude the perpetrator and throw light on the victim. And, with no one else to focus on but the victim when trying to answer why the crime is so prevalent, we see the final subtle change in phrasing you yourself used. Why is it that, like so many women in our society…' And he writes:

ROSE IS AN ABUSED WOMAN

'Now, not only is the perpetrator entirely out of the picture, but the crime itself is not even a verb. It's an adjective. Through language, violent crimes are transformed into descriptions of the victim. And this construct forces us to focus completely on her. Who is Rose? Why does she keep putting herself in these situations? Why is she attracted to these kinds of men? What should she be doing differently? Why does she put up with it? What does Rose do to make him abuse her?'

Taken aback, unable to eat anything else, I lay the knife and fork across the plate and get up from the bed to take my usual chair where I'm most at home. I say, 'I've never even noticed that.'

'People rarely do.' He puts down the marker and comes back to the bed. And when he takes the seat opposite, everything feels right. If I could just stay in this chair, sit across from him, listen to him talk, I think I could face anything. But I can't stay here forever. At some point I will have to face Nathan alone.

'Language is very powerful,' Saeed says. 'Abusers themselves use this very tool to turn blame on their victims. *Look what you made me do* is a very common phrase for abusers. Fortunately the media is recognising the power of language, and far more reports these days use active language that places the blame where it belongs. Things are changing. Society is finally starting to ask the right questions: why do men rape women? Why do men physically and emotionally abuse the women they are supposed to love? So when you look back on your own abuse, when you remember being pushed and falling down the stairs, always ask yourself: why does Nathan abuse Rose?'

'I'll try.' And when I reach across the bed for him, he places his hand over mine and holds it tight.

I want to say something to him. Three words. But I can't. They'd be true, but it's too soon.

Then suddenly Daisy's hand flies out. She grabs Saeed's wrist and we both spring to our feet. Across the bed, we stare at each other, shock mirrored in the whites of our eyes. Saeed still has hold of my hand and Daisy still has hold of his wrist. So I pull away slowly, carefully, as if any quick movements will make this disappear and Daisy will return to her motionless state.

But she doesn't let go. She holds Saeed's wrist so tightly, her knuckles are white. His face contorts with pain and he winces, twisting his hand in an attempt to release it from her vicelike grip. I'm about to run for help but I don't want to leave him. Daisy's clearly hurting him, her strength beyond anything she would be capable of if she were awake. I vacillate. I have no idea what to do. But then, prepared to try anything, I rub her forearm vigorously back and forth, saying, 'Let go, Daisy! Let go!'

And finally, she does.

Saeed and I look at each other, our breath hanging in the air between us, but then we both glance at Daisy and laugh.

He says, 'There was nothing abnormal about *that* motor response. It is not just me, is it? And not just today... No matter what those scans say, there is a change in Daisy. Have you felt it?'

'She's never grabbed me before.' I point at her frantically moving eyes, as if she's immersed in an exhilarating dream. 'And she's never done that before, either.'

'Perhaps she has but we have not been here to see it.'

'Patients in a persistent vegetative state don't dream, do they?'

'No,' he says. 'Rapid eye movement does suggest a state of minimal consciousness. And it does not tie in with her latest scans and tests.'

'I've noticed a change too, but thought it was my imagination: getting my hopes up after the VNS was implanted. But you're right, she *is* different. She has a different energy. That sounds crazy when most of the time she's just lying there.'

'No. Not crazy. Not to me. When I used to visit her in those early months, I was convinced she was going to wake up at any moment. I felt she was...present. But the longer the coma went on, the less convinced I became. Not because of its longevity but because, sitting next to her, her body felt empty. As if she was elsewhere. But over the past few weeks I have felt her presence again.'

'Dr Anderson isn't going to listen to a feeling,' I say. 'Telling him we can feel Daisy's presence sounds like science fiction.'

'You are not wrong. Doctors pay attention to test results, not intuition.' Saeed gets up and looks at her chart again. 'Considering the success we saw initially with the VNS, these scans are surprising. There should not be this rapid decline. Hand me that spoon.'

He tugs Daisy's blankets and sheets from the bottom of the mattress while, confused, I take the spoon from the dinner tray and hand it to him. He runs the point of its handle up the sole of her foot and her toes clench forward.

'What are you doing?'

'When Daisy was first brought in, what was her GCS score?'

'Eight.' I count up her scores on my fingers, listing them one by one. 'Three for opening her eyes to sound. Three for flexing to pain – though that was abnormal, Dr Anderson said, because of her brain injury – and two for moaning and groaning.'

'Eight,' he says. 'I thought so. Anything lower is considered a severe brain injury and Daisy was borderline.'

'But she declined when she stopped breathing. She stopped opening her eyes to sound and only opened them to pain – when Dr Anderson pressed a pen into her fingernail. Her score dropped to five, which is really bad.'

'Not as bad as you think,' he says.

Taking Daisy's right hand, he presses the neck of the spoon into the nail bed of her middle finger. Her eyes open and I stare into them. Before she stopped breathing, it wasn't unusual for her eyes to open, even for no reason. The first few times it happened, it freaked me out. But I've got used to it over the years.

I take Daisy's other hand, and say, 'It sounds bad to me. If you drop three points on a scale of one hundred, that's not bad. Drop three points on a scale of fifteen, that's a lot. And you said yourself, the scale doesn't go below three.'

'But that physical decline left her intubated. Being unable to speak or make sounds does not make her zero on the verbal scale, it makes her non-testable. Yes, she stopped opening her eyes in response to sound, but her motor score remained unchanged. And, when the VNS was put in, we saw improvement there. Do you remember that afternoon when Zesiro was preparing to move her and she lifted her arm? There was nothing abnormal about that response. And look...' Saeed points to her endotracheal tube. 'Look at her lips.'

Beneath the plastic fastener that holds the tube in place, Daisy's lips are moving.

'I don't understand. What does it mean?'

'Watch my lips, Rose.'

I do as he says and watch his mouth as Saeed lets out a series of moans and groans. His lips barely move. Not like Daisy's at all.

'She's trying to talk!'

Saeed nods enthusiastically with a bright smile.

I fidget on the spot, stirred by excitement. 'Are you saying if we assume the VNS has improved Daisy's speech as much as her motor responses, she could be back at the level she was when she first came in? An eight?'

'No. I am saying if she were not intubated, and if her lips are moving like that because she is uttering discernible words, she is now a ten.'

'Ten!? You're kidding? How ...?' I try to count the numbers in my head but everything's a muddle.

'Let us assume that, without the tube, Daisy would utter words – not moans and groans as she did when she first came in, but *words* – that in itself scores three. There are two *abnormal* motor responses to pain: decorticate and decerebrate posturing. Decorticate posturing or abnormal *flexion* suggests damage to the cerebral hemispheres—'

'The swelling from her head injury,' I say. 'Dr Anderson showed me. He would press his thumb into Daisy's eye socket and she would curl her hands into her chest and stretch out her legs in a strange, erratic movement. It frightened me.'

'Well, according to her chart, that motor response has declined further to decerebrate posturing or abnormal *extension*, which is where both her arms and legs extend outwards and away from the source of the pain. That is the worst motor response beyond paralysis, and indicates damage to the brainstem itself.'

Saeed catches a look of horror I can't conceal.

'No.' He shakes his head emphatically. 'Her chart is wrong. There is *nothing at all* abnormal about her response to pain; she

268

is localising it. Look…' He moves to the top of the bed and pinches Daisy's right shoulder at the base of her neck. When he does, her left arm swings across her chest. At first she only touches his hand but, as he continues to press, she grabs it, just as she did before, only with less force. 'That is a five. And this…is a two…' Once again, Saeed presses the spoon into her nailbed and once again, her eyes open – her beautiful hawk-brown eyes – but then he releases the pressure and they close again.

'Daisy!' I shout at her. 'Wake up!' And her eyes open again.

'I take it back,' Saeed says. 'She is not a three. She is not even a ten. She is an eleven.'

I bolt for the door. 'We have to go and tell Dr Anderson.'

'Rose.' Saeed's voice is stern. It stops me in my tracks and I turn to face him. He's holding Daisy's chart again.

'What?'

'You said you confronted Nathan on Friday and he has barely spoken to you since.'

'Yes, why? What does that have to do with Daisy?'

'These tests with a GCS of three were taken on Monday. That is when Dr Anderson accepted Nathan's decision. Based on Daisy's decline, and the severity of the incoming patient, it no doubt seemed the only fair and ethical one to make. Daisy is an organ donor, and the incoming patient has a far higher chance of survival.'

'But Daisy's GCS isn't three!'

'No. The chart is wrong. As are the fMRI results from Monday. With the level of improvement that we are seeing now, I doubt these scans are even Daisy's.' Saeed pauses, as if the next thing he's going to say is difficult. 'Nathan became medically involved in her care some time ago, did he not? I saw him handing progress reports to Dr Anderson. Have you ever read them?'

'No. And I don't understand what you're saying. That he falsified the reports? Why would he do that?'

'Rose…you know what Daisy is like. She has had more than her share of trauma, but I would bet my practice that if she saw you in trouble she would put her own pain aside for you. If she saw what Nathan was capable of, she would not rest until she freed you from his grip. And so, the absolute last thing Nathan will want is for Daisy to wake up.'

'But Nathan has no idea what Daisy's like. They've never met.'

'No. But no doubt you have mentioned that Daisy helped you flee the abuse of your first marriage? He will look at the mistakes your first husband made and make sure to do things differently. Starting with removing your support systems. He will want to separate you from your family so you have nowhere to go. And who knows the lengths he will go to, to achieve that. The lengths he has already gone to. I knew something was amiss with Daisy's chart that day we first met. The increases in brain activity, her energy – we both felt it – they did not tie in with the results. So yes, I *am* saying he falsified them.'

'He wouldn't. That's insane. That's…murder!'

'That is not going to happen.' Saeed tucks the chart under his arm and marches past me to the door.

'Where are you going?'

'To see Dr Anderson. To give him the results myself.'

'What about the boy? The recipient.'

'He will have to find another donor. You cannot ethically remove life support from a patient whose GCS has leapt to eleven!'

THIRTY-SIX

MAGGIE

TWO METRES.

One.

I leap on to the man's back, wrap my legs around his waist and plunge the knife in.

I miss.

The blade slices through his coat, then the backpack, where its tip hits something solid. Something metal. From the faint tinny clink, I think it's the backpack's frame. So, gripping tightly with my thighs, I lift the knife out with both hands, raise it to the sky and then drive it diagonally into the soft gap where his neck meets his shoulder blade.

This time, the steel slices through his flesh with ease.

The man thrashes around, trying to shake me off, but I grip the knife handle as if it's a saddle horn and cling on even tighter with both legs.

He weakens.

His thrashing subsides.

271

Then he's still for a moment. And, when I find my balance, I withdraw the knife. Blood gushes from the open wound, his rapid heart pumping it through the deep cut, and within seconds we're both covered in it. The man reaches back to stem the flow but he's barely able to lift his arm; he's already too weak.

He stumbles.

Trips.

And finally falls, face down, taking me with him. The force of his body slamming into the ground throws me forward and I roll across the forest floor, tumbling through the dead leaves.

But it takes only a split second for me to recover, and I'm back on my feet.

Still gripping the knife, I run back to him and, with both hands, wield the weapon high. Standing astride him, I'm ready to plunge the blade into his back the moment he moves or tries to get to his feet. And if he flips over and tries to grab me, I will drive it straight through his chest. But he doesn't move. He just lies there.

Still.

Dead.

THIRTY-SEVEN

ROSE

SAEED HAS BEEN gone a long time, so I try calling from the mobile he gave me. But the moment I lift it to my ear, the door opens.

It's not Saeed.

It's Nathan.

He's still wearing his surgical scrub cap. He's supposed to remove that before leaving the theatre, which means he rushed over here without thinking. Something's riled him. Maybe he saw Saeed on his way to Dr Anderson's office.

I pull the phone away from my ear and press the end call button. Aware that my mouth is slightly agape, I close it, preparing myself for what's about to come.

There's rage in his eyes. 'Whose phone is that?'

'Nobody's. Mine.'

'Where did you get it?'

'I bought it.' My fingers, clasped around the handset, tremble.

273

'You're blushing, Rose. You always blush when you lie. Plus... that's an expensive phone. If you'd put it on your credit card, I'd know. If you'd taken cash out, I'd know. So, where did you get it?'

'A friend lent it to me.'

'What friend? Why?'

'Just a friend. I was having problems with mine.'

'What problems?'

I don't answer.

'Rose... What's wrong with your phone?'

We both know this conversation is pointless. I'm lying through my teeth and Nathan knows it. So what's the point in continuing with neither of us saying outright what's really going on here?

Saeed is right about the power of language. It doesn't just add to the societal problems of victim-blaming, it makes it difficult for victims to recognise their own situation. Every time Saeed says the word *abuse* I flinch. I've always equated abuse with a black eye. I've read all the books he gave me and yet, still, I find it hard to associate that word with Nathan.

Instead, I imagine myself in conversations where people ask why I left him. And my imaginary self says things like: because he liked me to eat well; because he liked me to dress nicely; because he booked a personal trainer so I could lose weight; because he liked to know where I was all the time.

And then I imagine their responses: I wish my husband looked after me like that; if you didn't like the personal trainer, why didn't you just cancel it; my husband has me on Find My Friends, so what; this is why you're divorcing the man of your dreams? Are you insane?

None of his behaviour is severe enough to justify divorce, and none of these behaviours *really* sound like abuse to me. I begin to question myself, think I'm overreacting. And then I think I am oversensitive, paranoid, crazy, useless, and stupid.

I haven't even really tried to sit down with Nathan and talk to him about my concerns over his behaviour. The books tell me it's a waste of time. Nathan won't change because he doesn't want to. His life, his wife, they're exactly how he wants them to be: they serve him well. And if I did try to talk to him, we'd have a circular conversation that ended up right where it started, with him reminding me of all the wonderful things he does for me, telling me how ungrateful I am, pointing out that he's just trying to help me be a better person. That these concerns are of my making, and ultimately my fault. And then I'm back to questioning myself again.

The problem with coercive control is that it *is* coercive. You're never absolutely certain that anything really bad is even happening to you. Everything is small. And there's never one thing you can put your finger on as being so intolerable you have to leave.

It's like opening the front door in the morning and finding that a cat's taken a dump on your lawn. You huff and you puff and you clean it up. But then you forget all about it and go on with your day. But a day or two later you find another parcel on your freshly mown grass. You curse and you swear, maybe look up and down the street for the little blighter, but then you clean up the mess again and forget all about it. And you could continue like that for years, decades even, dealing with these tiny parcels. But if someone dumped ten years' worth of crap on your doorstep, you wouldn't be able to go on with your day. You wouldn't rest until you'd found the owner and dealt with them. One of the books described coercive control as being like fine rain. You don't notice the drops when they fall one at a time. And it takes years to realise you're soaked to the skin.

If it weren't for Saeed, it would have taken me years.

But I know this isn't right. I feel it. And when I add up all the things Nathan's said and done over the past year, pile up the little parcels of crap, stare at the evidence, I just know this isn't love.

275

Maybe it's time I used the power of language to my own advantage.

Abuse doesn't only mean a black eye.

Abuse means: to use to bad effect; to treat in a way that causes harm; to speak in an insulting way. And, by struggling to label Nathan's behaviour as abuse, I am no better than anyone else who uses language to conceal it.

I'm not doing that any more.

It's time.

I stand up straight, push my shoulders back and say, 'What's wrong with my phone, Nathan? Nothing. Nothing's wrong with my phone.'

The sweet placatory tone that has become habitual over the last year is gone. And the moment I speak without it – the moment I remember my old voice – I realise how many times I've clung to it to keep the peace. I've walked on eggshells for a whole year without even knowing it.

I hold up Saeed's mobile as if it's a weapon.

'I'm using *this* phone because *this* phone doesn't have mSpy installed on it, and I can have conversations without you listening in.'

A storm blows across Nathan's eyes and yet he's smiling. 'How long have you had it?'

'Weeks!' I lie. And my hands tremble as I glare at him with defiance. 'That's right, Nathan, for weeks your wife has had telephone conversations with other people that you haven't heard. Do you know that in *normal* marriages women telephone other people without their husbands listening in? In *normal* marriages, women go to the supermarket without their husbands tracking their every move? They send texts and emails to friends that their husbands don't read? Do you know that, Nathan? Do you know what a normal marriage looks like?'

'A normal marriage?' He spits bile. 'Whose fault is it if we don't have a normal marriage? If you didn't lie and go sneaking around behind my back, I wouldn't have to check up on you. The only reason I do those things is because you can't be trusted. All you've done is prove me right.'

His twisted logic catches in my throat and a confounded breath escapes. I say, 'When I asked you about Find My Friends, you said you put it on my phone when we first started dating so you could make sure I got home safe. Now you're saying you turned it on because you suspect I'm a liar. But if you'd suspected that when we first started dating, why date me at all? You're saying that if you can't track my phone in order to prove I'm a liar, I must be a liar for not allowing you to track my phone. That's called a double bind. Either way, I'm in the wrong. Either way, I can't win. But these tricks won't work any more. My eyes are open.'

He lowers his head, shaking it in despair as if I'm a naughty child. And, when he looks up, his eyes dart away to something behind me. I turn and follow his gaze.

The writing on the whiteboard.

My heart stops. And when it restarts, it beats so loudly I swear Nathan can hear it.

'What the fuck?' He points at the words. 'What the fuck is that? Abuse? Abuse! I've never done *anything* but love you. I've given you everything! And you accuse me of *abuse*? Jesus Christ, Rose. You really are fucking unbelievable. You've lost your fucking mind. When have I ever abused you? When have I ever laid so much as a finger on you?'

'I lost the baby because of you.'

He stands there for a moment, jaw clenched, fists balled, and then takes a step in my direction. 'Is that what you've been telling people? You trip, and you're going around telling everyone I pushed you down the stairs? Is that what you've been saying? That you lost the baby because of your abusive, wife-beating husband?!'

'I wouldn't have fallen if you hadn't pushed me. And not all abuse leaves bruises, Nathan. Coercive control is just

277

as damaging as physical abuse. At least when you've been punched you know what's happened to you.'

'"Coercive control"? Did you read that in some feminist self-help book? Poor hard-done-by Rose. Poor wilting Rose. All I've ever done is love you, try to help you become a better person, the best version of yourself.'

'You don't know what love is, Nathan. Love isn't control. It isn't trying to mould someone into your idea of the perfect woman. It's loving them for who they are already. What you've been doing to me is emotional abuse.'

'Emotional abuse. This is a fucking joke! That's a snowflake's get-out clause for blubbering over a tiny bit of constructive criticism. And you're making me out to be a monster who beats his wife!'

'So, you're saying there's no such thing as emotional abuse? Only physical abuse?'

'Everyone's in control of their own emotions. How you feel is up to you.'

'So it doesn't exist?'

'No.'

'Oh, good, because I was going to admit to having an emotional affair, but I guess if there's no such thing as emotional abuse, there's no such thing as an emotional affair either.'

He takes another step in my direction. 'You filthy, cheating little whore!'

'Ah, but I've only cheated emotionally. And that doesn't count, does it, Nathan? It's only the physical stuff that counts. If there aren't bruises, it didn't happen.'

'You want bruises?'

'Is that a threat?'

He looks down at the floor again, laughing. And seeing it reminds me of all the times he's done it before: laughed derisively over something I've said, put me down and humiliated me. I always thought it was because he was so

278

intelligent and I'd said something stupid. But now I realise I'm not stupid. And if I question something, or don't know something, that's normal. Nobody knows everything about everything. And good people don't make others feel inferior for not being omniscient.

The curtains fell when I met Claire. This isn't love; it's an illusion. Nathan looks like the great magician, robes flowing while he saws the woman in half. But her legs are fake. Lift the lid and her real ones are curled up inside. With a trick of the eye, stalking looks like attraction from afar. Constant surveillance is cloaked in concern. Gifts come with strings attached. And cruel comments are curtained behind constructive criticism. On and on the magic show plays, blinding its audience to the gradual undermining, humiliation and isolation, the subtle tone of violence beneath veiled threats. But now I see it all: the hidden wires, the concealed compartments.

Getting up in my face when we have an argument: that's abuse. Trapping me in rooms is abuse. Kicking doors and punching walls: that's abuse. And throwing plates is abuse. It's abuse because what he is telling you in those moments is that, if you don't toe the line, next time the door will be you. The wall will be you. The plate will be you.

'I knew you were a lying bitch,' he spits. 'I knew you couldn't be trusted.'

'It's a self-fulfilling prophecy, Nathan. I *could* be trusted, up until a month ago. But that didn't stop you listening in on my phone calls, reading my emails and texts or tracking my every move, did it? Tell me, what did you find in all that information that led you to believe I was a lying bitch? Come on: you heard everything, you read every word. What did you find?'

He doesn't answer because he can't.

I say, 'It was only when I found out who you were, what you'd been doing, that I started hiding things from you, doing things behind your back. And now you're right. I can't be trusted. Now, I do lie to you.'

279

His lip curls and his eyes narrow.

But I've opened the gates and everything's flowing out too fast for me to close them now. I say, 'All those things I never dreamed I'd do, not even once in our entire relationship – I'm doing them now. And I'm doing them because I don't love you any more. You've stripped it from me with your need to control everything. Everything I do, everywhere I go, everyone I see; what I eat, what I weigh, what I wear. You have beaten love out of me with a year of backhanded compliments and derisive laughter. And you've scared it out of me with your subtle threats and intimidation. It's gone, Nathan. I don't love you any more. I want a divorce.'

'A divorce? You don't mean that. We've only been married two months!'

He looks at the floor for a long moment, then looks up, brushing his fingers through his hair. The movement is akin to donning a mask: his muscles relax and his demeanour completely alters. He takes the last few steps towards me, closing the gap between us. 'Look, Rose…all marriages have difficulties. If you felt my comments were anything other than constructive, you should have said something. If you thought my outbursts were meant to intimidate you, you should've told me. If you were having problems, you should have come to me. I could have fixed them. But how can I fix problems I don't know about? I love you. And you love me. And you aren't going to throw away our marriage when you've barely given it a chance.'

Saeed said that all men like Nathan are turned out of the same mould. And he's right. Nathan's using every tactic in the handbook. He's even using the same words. It's like standing in that final scene in *The Matrix* when Neo's false reality disappears and he sees the computer code that's generating the illusion. I almost laugh.

'Can you even hear yourself? As I said, Nathan, I see you now. These tactics won't work any more: if *I* felt; if *I* thought;

if *I'm* having problems. You're saying that if our marriage is failing, the solution is to fix *me*. These things you say and do, these strategies and techniques, they have names. You're playing games. But, once your opponent knows all your moves, you've lost. You have no power over me any more. I have *one* problem, Nathan: you. Your behaviour is a problem. And what you're doing is called projection. You are projecting your problems on to me so you can blame me for the breakdown of our marriage instead of accepting responsibility for your own behaviour.'

'Honestly, Rose, I'm completely confused. You're making up nonsense. None of this is true. Someone's filled your head with a load of New Age crap and it's coming between us. I promise you, there aren't any conspiracy theories at work here. I don't understand what you think I'm doing to you, but I'm really not doing anything at all. You make it sound like I'm deliberately trying to hurt you when you know I love you. I've only *ever* loved you. And if you can't see that, I think you need to look inside yourself. Clearly that Paki psychologist has been putting ideas in your head because he's got a thing for you. He's trying to pull us apart and you're so naïve, you're actually letting him.'

'Not that it matters, but Saeed isn't from Pakistan. He's from India.'

'So what?'

'So, it's a different country. And so, I'd appreciate it if you kept your racist bullshit to yourself. It just makes you uglier to me.'

He jabs me above the ear. 'He really has got into your head, hasn't he?'

I shove his hand away. 'Who *are* you? What kind of person behaves this way? Instead of asking yourself why your wife's so unhappy, you wonder why your puppet strings aren't working as well as they did. And you assume that if you aren't pulling them, someone else must be instead. It doesn't even occur to you that I have an independent mind and can think for myself, make decisions for myself. Well, I can! And I'm not doing this any more.'

'You say he's not pulling your strings, but everything was fine until he showed up.'

'By that, you mean everything was fine for *you*. Your little wife was behaving herself. She gave up her career and her friends to be at your beck and call. She did your shopping, your cooking, your washing, your ironing, your cleaning. And on top of that, she spread her legs the moment you clicked your fingers. It was perfect for *you*, wasn't it? A slave and a hooker rolled into one. And you didn't even have to pay for her services.'

He smiles, just for a second, and then it's gone. And, like everything else Nathan does, I can put a name to that now too. Because it's also in the handbook. Psychologists call that 'duping delight' – a flash of a smile that betrays what they're thinking – the self-satisfaction of getting away with murder right under your nose.

'Look at you,' I say.

'What?' He shrugs.

'I see you.'

'Do you?'

I smile too. 'I do. And it's over, Nathan. I'm leaving you.'

I brush past him, but when I touch the door handle he rushes after me, pushes past me. Then he slams his palm against the door, preventing me from opening it.

'You aren't leaving, Rose. I don't know what's got into you or why you're behaving this way. But you're being unreasonable.' He grabs my arm, squeezing it tightly as he spins me around to face him. Then, gripping both my arms, he presses me up against the door, saying, 'How can you be so unfeeling? How can you even think about leaving like this? Out of the blue! You haven't even given our marriage a chance. Given *me* a chance.'

I twist out of his grip. Determined not to show how much he's scaring me, I look him right in the eye. 'It's not out of the blue, and our marriage isn't a game of chance. You don't get to pick a card and have another try at behaving like a decent person. That's not how it works. I'm not responsible for your behaviour, you are. And I don't have to like it or lump it. I get to choose whether or not I want to stay. Whether I will put up with it. And I won't. I can't.'

In the limited space between him and the door, I turn my back on him and pull the handle, but he pushes it shut again. 'We can talk about this, can't we? We can work through it. If you have trouble with constructive criticism, we can work on that. If you have issues with trust, we can work on that too. If you feel like your only job is to make me happy, we can sort that out. We can get counselling.'

I rest my forehead on the door in exasperated despair.

'What?' he asks, easing my hand from the handle and urging me to turn around.

So I do. I say, 'You're doing it again. If *I* have trouble with constructive criticism. If *I* have trust issues. If *I* feel like making you happy is my only job. *We* can get counselling to fix *me*! Even now, as I'm walking out the door, you still can't acknowledge which of us needs fixing. I don't have trouble with constructive criticism: I have trouble with abusive comments. I don't have trust issues: you have spyware installed on my phone. And I don't *feel like* making you happy is my only job: you've made damn sure it is! And if I don't do it exactly to your liking, you'll lose your temper. The only way this marriage can be saved is by you having a personality transplant. Becoming a kind, loving and emotional man instead of a narcissistic bully.'

'Narcissistic bully? Rose, this is crazy. You've clearly lost your mind.'

'Have I?' I glare at him and then point at my sister. 'What about Daisy?'

'What about Daisy?'

'I know you faked her tests. I know you've been feeding false reports to Dr Anderson. And I know you signed the consent forms without my permission.'

'Rose...' He puts his hand on my arm again and this time, I shove it away. 'Rose...come on.' His words ooze out like sickly treacle. 'I only did that for you. It was clearly getting too much for you. Daisy isn't going to wake up. She's been in a coma for three years. And she probably put herself in it. You need to accept the fact that your sister doesn't want to be here. She never did. You can't throw away our marriage over something I've done with your best interests at heart.'

'You always know what's best for everyone, don't you, Nathan? Well, I'm doing what's best for me now. I'm leaving.'

'You're not, Rose.'

Like all our conversations, we're going in circles. And it doesn't matter what I say, he'll keep the circle spinning. Dozens of studies on men like Nathan all say the same thing: they know exactly what they're doing. Any excuses they make for their behaviour are just that: excuses. Any promises to change are empty. Suggestions for counselling are delay tactics. They won't change because they like things just as they are. And they know exactly how to keep things just as they are.

Men who beat their wives often say they'd had too much to drink and just *lost it*, as if a red mist came over them. As if their behaviour was attributable to something outside their control: if only they had been able to keep their wits about them, the beating would never have happened. And yet, when questioned as to why, in the middle of this attack of red mist, they punched her in the stomach, bruised her upper arms, kicked her in the thighs while she was on the floor, they slip up and say: *Well, I wasn't going to punch her in the face, was I?* They still had the presence of mind to give her a beating that couldn't be seen.

Men like to say that women love cruel men, that the bad boys always get the girl. But it's not true. We like strength, confidence, someone to take care of us and protect us. But cruel men are very good at pretending they have all those attributes when they don't. And then women end up with a reputation for liking cruel men.

I could keep talking to Nathan until I'm blue in the face. I could keep trying to explain why his behaviour is wrong and why coercive control is a recognised form of abuse. But, for us to have any chance of an equal marriage, for him to change, he'd first have to admit to his behaviour.

I know what Nathan is doing.

Nathan knows what he is doing.

But he cannot – must not – confess. Because, if he does, everyone will know, and his perfect life will be over. Word will spread, and that will make it impossible for him to get another puppet because, knowing him to be a narcissistic coercive controller, no woman would ever get close enough for him to attach the strings.

Because women *don't* like cruel men.

And no matter how many times I tell him black is black, he'll say it's blue. He'll defend his actions with lies until I feel like I've circled the earth a thousand times or more. And I'm already exhausted.

'It's over, Nathan.'

I reach out for the handle again, but it's torn from my grasp when he slams his hand against the door and holds it firmly shut. Then his voice turns to stone.

'I said, you aren't leaving.'

THIRTY-EIGHT

MAGGIE

TAKING THE KNIFE in one hand, I reach out cautiously with the other, sure he's faking, waiting for his opportunity to catch me off guard. But when I shove him he doesn't move. His hood still covers the back of his head and blood seeps out from beneath it, turning the mud red.

I step over his legs and kick him hard in the ribs before quickly backing away, convinced he's about to grab my ankle and take me down. But still, he doesn't move.

I wait.

I've seen too many films where women go back to their attacker, certain he's dead, and it's always their undoing. I need to be absolutely sure. So I watch the pool of blood swell across the mud, knowing that when the river stops, his heart will have stopped too.

Time swells like that pool of blood.

For months, hour by hour, day after day, I have been plagued by this man's presence. He's hounded my thoughts, been forever at my side, just waiting for his moment to strike. Waiting to take my whole life from me.

He succeeded.

He ripped Luc and Alfie from it.

And now I have taken his.

A strange thought enters my mind: a medieval myth that you could verify the identity of a murderer if blood oozed from the dead person's corpse in their presence. Cruentation, they called it: proof of guilt.

His blood oozes in my presence.

I have spent weeks searching him out, desperate to know who he is. And, now that moment is here, I can't move. I stare at his back – at the hunch beneath his rain mac – hands still trembling, breath still catching, waiting for my presence of mind to return.

Finally, with the sole of my boot pressed against the hunch, I kick forward with all my might. I expect the force to roll him over but instead, under the mac, the rucksack slips from his back. I must have cut through its straps when I stabbed him.

I pull hard on the coat's hood and peel it back with surprising ease, as if it was only wrapped around him or buttoned loosely at the neck. But, underneath, it isn't a rucksack. At first I'm not sure what it is; the grey and green ripstop fabric is muddy. But as I lean over him I recognise the pale blue koala logo with the word AiryBear embroidered beneath.

It's a baby carrier.

And inside, there's a child with honey brown hair.

Dropping the knife, I fall to my knees. I know that mop of hair as well as I know my own. This can't be happening. Trembling, I slide both hands into the carrier and gently lift the child out. He slips out with ease, not properly strapped in. I'm too terrified to turn him over and look at his face. But I have to.

When I lay him on the ground, his head flops sideways and his hair falls away from his sweet little face, which is covered in cuts and shards of glass. And when I pull my hand from under his back, my palm is covered with blood.

That's where the knife went in.

I plunged a hunting knife into my own son.

I scream, and a flock of crows lifts from the trees above my head, carrying their cries into the forest along with mine. Wailing, I turn on the man and pummel his lifeless back with my bloodied fists. Not only did he kill my husband and child, he doubled back to claim my son's body.

Why?!

Why would anyone do something like this?

I have to know.

But now the man is dead. What answers will I ever get?

At the very least, I have to know who he is. I have to look into the face of the stranger who took my entire life from me in one mindless act of violence.

And with what little strength I have left I drive my hands between his stomach and the forest floor, lift him, and roll him on to his back. A mess of bloodied leaf litter is stuck to his hair, face and beard and I wipe it away, even though I don't need to.

I know his face as well as Alfie's.

It's Luc.

THIRTY-NINE

ROSE

'YOU CAN'T FORCE me to stay, Nathan. Don't you get it? This isn't how relationships work. You just have to love someone and hope they love you back. But people are free to come and go as they choose.'

'This is different. We're married. You made vows to me. We're going home together and we're going to sit down and talk about this.'

'No. We're not. I'm leaving.'

'You really think I'm going to stand by and watch you run off with that Paki?'

I can't look at him any more. Closing my eyes, I shake my head in despair and disbelief. All he's doing is making it worse.

Seeing him like this, listening to him speak with that vague threat of violence in his refusal to let me leave, I know that this hollow loss in my stomach hasn't cracked open because I don't love him any more, but because I never loved him to begin with. This man standing in front of me isn't the one I fell in love with. That man never existed. And the way *this man* talks about Saeed makes me hate him.

'Look at me!' he says. 'Tell me the truth. Is that what you were planning?'

Exasperated, and more to hurt him back than anything, I look him dead in the eye and say, 'Yes.'

And then I'm on the floor.

It happened in a blink. Nathan lifted his hand high in the air and brought it down so hard on my cheek it was more of a punch than a slap, the force of it slamming me to the ground where my tooth cut through my bottom lip.

Grasping the side of my face, tears filling my eyes, I look up at him, wide-eyed.

His blocking the door didn't come as a surprise, but I never imagined him capable of hitting me. He looks almost as shocked as I do that, finally, he's exposed himself. But for me it's almost a relief. If I'd had the smallest doubt in my mind about leaving, I don't now.

Nathan kneels down beside me, his face twisted with remorse as he reaches out a hand to help me up.

'Don't!' I hold up a palm to him. 'Don't!' I reach out for the rail at the end of Daisy's bed and haul myself to my feet. Then, still grasping my burning cheek with one hand and wiping the blood from my lip with the other, I say quietly and calmly, 'I'm leaving now, Nathan.'

Tears fill his eyes and he reaches out to me in a gesture of apology, but I ignore it. The realisation that apologising won't do any good this time, that his actions are irrevocable, and that he's destroyed whatever was left of our marriage, seems to have finally sunk in.

I walk past him to the door.

And he turns and watches me go.

FORTY

MAGGIE

LUC'S FACE is covered with dried blood and shards of glass, just as it had been back at the cabin, just like Alfie's.

With the dead bodies of my husband and son lying in front of me, my world spins, the trees a circling blur around me as if I'm in the eye of a tornado. How is this possible? How can they be here in the woods, covered in blood and leaf litter, when less than an hour ago their bodies were in Luc's study?

Did I hit my head when I fell from the man's back? Knock myself out? And did he survive the attack, leave me here unconscious, and go back to the cabin? Did he collect their bodies and drag them out here to torture me? Is he trying to make it look as if I killed them?

No! I didn't hit my head. I didn't lose consciousness, not even for a second. I stare at the olive-green rain mac lying in the mud next to Luc. He was wearing it when I ran into him in the clearing. He said he'd just pulled it from the rack and it must be John's.

Am I going mad?

Was the man a hallucination after all?

Luc thought he was.

Was what I saw in Luc's study a hallucination too?

Did I chase down my husband and son and plunge a knife through them both?

I turn my palms face up, stare at the blood, then lean forward and retch. The solitude, the self-indulgent inactivity, the maniacal obsessiveness with the stranger in the woods... it all makes sense now. Luc was right all along: I lost my grip months ago and, since then, it's been nothing but a slow and steady descent into madness.

This can't be real.

Maybe it isn't. Maybe it's a dream and I'm back at the cabin still, holding the bodies of my husband and son in my arms, insane with grief. And soon, I'll wake up.

I bring my knees to my chest and bury my face in them while I wait.

Only I don't wake up.

And every time I open my eyes, their bodies are still there.

The sun is going down; I can't stay here much longer. Part of me wants to take Alfie with me but I can neither bring myself to lift his dead body nor leave him here.

What's the point in doing either?

What's the point in doing anything at all?

What's the point in living?

I pick up the knife, lying in the pool of blood next to Luc, and, gripping it with both hands, point it at my chest. Its tip rips through my jumper and shirt and pierces my skin. It stings like a hot blade, my body catastrophising the pain in some sick attempt at self-preservation I have no interest in or control over.

I can't do it.

I can't because there's one small thing left to live for: truth.

I have to know what's going on.

I don't feel crazy; I feel perfectly sane. A few months in a cabin doesn't turn a normal person into a lunatic. And I *was* sane. I fix computers, for Christ's sake. I fixed Luc's just a few weeks ago. That isn't the behaviour of a crazy person. I stare at Luc's and Alfie's bodies and wonder if they're real or whether I'm hallucinating. And then I remember something else.

The used syringe in the sideboard drawer.

And in one swift motion I'm off the ground and running. Darting between the trees, I make my way back to the woodland path. In spite of everything, I neither tire nor run out of breath. I run as if the nightmare I left in the trees is chasing me, and I don't stop even when I reach the lake. I don't stop when the shingle hampers my speed. I don't stop until I reach the cabin.

Pressing the latch, I pull open the door and step inside.

With dusk falling, the lounge is in shadow, the wood-burner cold. The cabin is empty and dead, as if no one has lived here for years. My measured steps on the wooden floorboards echo up the stairway to the floor above, and I move as slowly as I can. I delay the inescapable necessity of opening Luc's study door.

Standing on the mezzanine floor for an eternity, I grip the knob without turning it. I'm terrified of what I will find inside, sick at the thought that behind this door I will find the bodies of my husband and son, and at the same time terrified that Luc's study will be in perfect order, the window panes intact, no shards of glass, no blood on the floor, no bodies. That that was a figment of my fragmented mind: an abhorrent illusion manufactured by a diseased consciousness. And that the real truth is that I killed my husband and son in the woods.

I don't know which is worse.

I turn the handle.

293

The last light of the setting sun burns through the window, blinding me, and I'm forced to shield my eyes to bring the room into focus.

'Hey, babe.' Luc spins around in his chair.

'Mumma!' Alfie runs over and wraps his arms around my legs, squeezing his face between my knees.

I freeze, unable to speak, unable to lift my son, despite his upraised, pleading arms.

'Mags? Honey? Are you all right? You look like you've seen a ghost.'

I don't speak.

Luc leaps to his feet and rushes to my side, saying, 'What's wrong, baby? Are you sick? You look sick.' He ushers me into his chair. 'Sit down, I'll get you a glass of water.'

'No!' I reach out and grab his arm. I need the warmth of his skin. I need to know he's really here. Only I have no idea what's real any more. I don't know whether my husband and son are even here, or whether they, too, are ghosts of my lost sanity.

I ran back here in the hope of learning the truth and now I'm more confused than ever.

Are their material bodies really lying cold on this very floor?

Or are they lying out there in the forest, bleeding from knife wounds I inflicted?

Luc's face is grave. His arm twists beneath my grip, and when I let go he rubs it. 'What's going on, Mags?'

'I don't know. I'm not sure… I'm not sure… I'm…'

'You're what?'

'I think I'm losing my mind.'

'Maggie? You're scaring me.'

I'm scaring myself. I see one thing here, then another in the forest, and then something else here. Clearly something is wrong with my mind. Perhaps the man did break into the house as I suspected. Perhaps he drugged me in my sleep, injected me with something. The only way to know whether what I'm seeing is real or a drug-induced illusion is to have someone with me: a witness.

'We need to go out to the woods,' I say. 'Right now, all three of us, together.'

'It's almost dark. It's Alfie's bedtime.'

'I don't care. We'll take torches, but we need to go now.'

FORTY-ONE

ROSE

THE MOMENT I take hold of the handle for the fourth time, Nathan takes two long strides in my direction, grabs me by the hair and drags me from the door. I howl in pain but my cry is stifled when he throws me to the ground and kicks me hard in the belly.

With all the air knocked out of me, I can't even breathe, let alone scream. And then he grabs me by the hair again, lifts me a little way off the floor and slaps me so hard across the face that my head slams into the linoleum.

Everything goes black.

The moment I come to, I wish for the blackness again as Nathan kicks me in the ribs. I cough, retch and spit on the floor, as I shield my body with my slender arms. But he doesn't kick me again. Instead, he turns his back on me, grabbing the roots of his hair, which he tugs in fury. While his back is turned, I drag my limp body across the floor and crawl under Daisy's bed for protection.

All I can see are his feet. Still facing the wall, he paces left and right. Then he stops and a metronomic thud reverberates along the wall. I think he's banging his head against it. He repeats to himself, 'Look what you made me do, Rose. I didn't want to do that. But look what you made me do.' And his voice, racked with frustration, could be coming from someone else entirely. The calm, professional surgeon I've known for a year has disappeared, and this stranger has taken his place.

His words are wretched, as if he's having a tantrum over a toy that he broke himself. Then, finally, his composure returns and he turns around.

I feel his eyes on me and tuck myself further under the bed, curled up and foetal.

Nathan laughs, 'What are you doing under there, Rose?' And he peers underneath, laughing again, as if this is nothing but a game.

I watch his feet as he walks over to the right-hand side of the bed, where he drags the chair out of the way and reaches underneath to grab me. The metal structure that supports the wheels obstructs him and I scrabble away, but, with barely enough space to squeeze through, the mechanism slices through my ribcage. I ignore the pain.

For less than a second, it crosses my mind to make a run for the door; but I won't make it. He's closer to it than I am.

He laughs again. 'All right, Rose, that's enough playing silly buggers. You can come out now.'

I don't say anything. I just stare at his shoes, ready to scramble in the opposite direction if he comes around to my side. If I stay here long enough, Saeed will come back. I just have to wait it out.

We remain in this stalemate for what feels like forever.

Gingerly, I press my cheek and then my eye. They're both swollen and my lip is split. Blood seeps through the back of my hair where I hit my head on the floor that second time. And I'm fairly certain that at least one of my ribs is broken. The bones

297

grind when I move and the pain is like nothing I've ever felt. I'm afraid to even touch my side to seek out the wounds.

Surely Nathan can't possibly imagine he'll get away with this? Unless he has a cover story he turns to each time he beats a woman. Is it as well rehearsed as his texts? Does he threaten women into sticking to his story? Did he beat Claire? And, if he did, why didn't she warn me?

To be fair, she did warn me. She said he was a psychopath. I should have listened. I should have left then and there.

Nathan takes a deep breath and says, 'Come out, Rose.'

I lie there, frozen.

He's silent for a while. Waiting. Then he says, 'If you don't come out, I'm pulling the plug.'

I stare at his green scrub trousers. And a moment later they lean to one side as he reaches over Daisy's life support machine. My heart beats so fast I'm convinced it will fail. He can't mean it. Nathan may be capable of many things, but murder? He's bluffing to get me to come out.

But then I hear the click of the plug's safety cover.

'I'll count to five…' he says. 'One… Two… Three…'

If I come out, he'll beat me again. I could shout for help, scream at the top of my lungs but I'm sure, if I do, Nathan will be under this bed in seconds with his hand over my mouth. I imagine his meaty palm pressing down until the life drains out of me.

'Four…'

If he pulls the plug, I'm fairly sure the alarm will go off on Daisy's machine. Will that bring the nurses running? No. Nathan knows how to silence Daisy's various alarms as well as I do. I've done it hundreds of times: when her IV has run out, when the battery is low.

The battery!

Pulling the plug won't do anything at all. If the machine loses power, it continues on the back-up. Nathan must think I'm too stupid to know that.

298

'Five.'

I don't move.

There's a grinding of metal as Nathan pulls the plug. The ventilator beeps just once before he disables the alarm, and the split second of silence before the battery kicks in and the ventilator hisses and pumps feels like a full minute.

I breathe out.

But then another alarm sounds, silenced the moment it speaks. And then come more beeps, marking the pressing of buttons.

He's turning it off!

There's a quiet click and the ventilator stops.

Searing pain cuts through my ribs as I shuffle across the floor, yelling, 'Turn it back on! Turn it back on! I'm coming out!'

Crawling out on the opposite side of the bed from Nathan, I grab the metal frame for support, and haul myself to my feet. My broken ribs crunch and I double over when hot pain leaks from their exposed marrow. It drowns out the pain in every other part of my body.

'Turn it back on!' I pant through the agony. 'Right now! Or every person in this hospital will hear me scream.'

Nathan smiles.

He waits.

The absence of the ventilator's clunking wheeze is ear-splitting. I glance at the door, about to scream, but the moment my lips part, Nathan pushes the plug back into the wall. And, while my heart's finding its rhythm, he presses a few buttons on the machine until both Daisy and I can breathe again.

'That's better,' he says. 'Now, we're going to walk out of here quietly and calmly. I'll act surprised at Daisy's remarkable recovery and convince Dr Anderson to find another donor. But, just so we're clear, if you *ever* so much as mention leaving me again, I'll come back here while you're sleeping and switch this fucking cabbage off. Do you understand me, Rose?'

Silent tears well up and run down my cheeks. I can't bring myself to say yes to him, to agree to return to that life. And now I've admitted to an emotional affair, now he has Daisy's life to hold over me and has learned the efficacy of violence, what remains of our sham of a marriage will be unbearable.

But what else can I do?

With the demand for organ donors, Daisy's days were already numbered. And if her recovery doesn't continue, if her scores decline again, Dr Anderson will be forced to remove life support anyway. But going back to Nathan changes all that: he has influence here. And, now that he knows I've seen through him, if he wants to keep his power over me, he needs Daisy alive. She's the perfect sword to hold above my head and he'll safeguard that weapon. No doubt he would even pay for private care just to keep her alive and me by his side.

Going back is my opportunity to keep Daisy alive indefinitely.

Yet, still, I can't say yes.

Suddenly, Nathan reaches across the bed. His elbow catches the over-bed table and knocks it with such force that the cutlery clatters off the plate on to the blankets. On its wheels, the table careens to the end of the bed, where it crashes into the frame; the plate flies on to the linoleum and smashes.

He grabs me by the neck so hard I swear it will snap. And my throat, delicate in his powerful fingers, closes. Leaning over the bed, he pulls me towards him, squeezing. And, pressing his face to mine, he sprays my lips with spittle as he snarls, 'Do you understand me, Rose?'

Desperate to breathe, I try to prise his fingers from my throat but can't get any purchase. My scream is caught in his fist as I gouge my fingernails into the back of his hand. But still his grip doesn't ease, not even a millimetre.

I can't breathe.

I can't move.

All I know is, if I don't submit, Nathan will kill me. So I nod, but the action is awkward and unrecognisable above his taut grip, so I squeeze out words instead. 'Yes… I'll do whatever you want.' But it's as if he can't hear me. As if something has snapped inside him. His eyes are glazed and blank and there's no sign of Nathan behind them.

If he was ever there at all.

His face turns dim, loses focus, as if he's walking backwards into a grey fog. And the last thing I see, before the blackness closes in completely, is his terrified expression.

His hand leaves my throat.

But if what I see is regret, it's too late.

Because he's gone.

Everything's gone.

FORTY-TWO

MAGGIE

'WHO IS HE?' The beam of Luc's Petzl headlight shines on the dead man.

'I don't know.' I glance back at Alfie. He's breaking twigs by torchlight, making piles of kindling, while Cairo chews on a broken branch. We didn't want to bring either of them any closer to the body.

I look back at the man.

What I thought I saw from a distance, all those times he watched me from the trees, doesn't match the detail of what's in front of me now. He isn't wearing a rain mac, he's wearing a long-sleeved cotton tunic that reaches his knees over matching green trousers. The tunic's tied at the neck and waist, loose-fitting, like a hospital gown. And it crosses my mind that he may have escaped from some psychiatric hospital. What I thought was a hood isn't a hood at all, it's a cap that's tied at the base of his skull, and what my disturbed mind had thought was a baby carrier really is just a rucksack after all.

302

Every time I saw him in the trees, it crossed my mind he might be Rose's ex-husband. But, now I see him up close with a clear mind, I realise he's too tall to be Ryan, his frame too broad. I always thought part of Ryan's problem was small-man syndrome, like those toy dogs that are aggressive to breeds three times their size. Toy dogs are braver than men like Ryan, though – he would never have picked on a man three times his size. He picked on women instead.

He picked on my baby sister.

I thought I'd turned the body over earlier, but now I'm not sure because he's face down. But my mind is finally clearing and things are starting to make sense. Part of what happened was my mind playing tricks on me. But part of it was real too: I did kill a man. Only it wasn't Luc.

Perhaps I did hit my head when I fell. It would explain all the hallucinations – just a dream – when in reality I was unconscious. But now Luc is here, grounding me in reality, and I know what's real. This is real. This man is really here. Luc has finally seen him.

And I've really killed him.

I kneel down next to the body and, just as I did when I was dreaming, I insert my hands between his stomach and the forest floor, lifting and rolling him on to his back. Luc doesn't help. I don't think he wants to touch the body.

I brush away dead leaves, stuck to the man's forehead and eyes. The bottom part of his face is covered by a dark green surgical mask and, with trembling fingers, I pull it down to his neck, where the blood has coagulated around the open knife wound.

His eyes are open.

'Do you know him?' Luc asks.

I shake my head. He's not even vaguely familiar. He's strikingly attractive with bright blue eyes and well-kept stubble. Pulling the skull cap from his head reveals a mass of thick, golden-blonde hair. It's styled, well-kept and shiny.

He looks more like a catwalk model than a psychiatric ward escapee.

I thought seeing his face would finally give me answers. That he would know us. That I would know him. But I don't. So, what does this stranger have to do with any of us?

Something blue around his neck catches my eye: a lanyard. I tug at it, but it's snagged on something. So I yank it and a plastic identity card flicks out from beneath his body. It's covered in red mud. I look up at Luc, wondering if his heart is beating as fast as mine. Finally, after all these weeks of torture, I hold the answer in my hand.

I wipe the card on the man's tunic and turn it over. The company logo in the top left corner is familiar: my local hospital. But there's still dirt smeared across his name and I have to wipe it again.

I turn it back over and stare at it, my mind swimming. Then Luc's voice breaks through.

'What the fuck is he doing here?'

FORTY-THREE

MAGGIE

BACK AT THE cabin, we put Alfie to bed in a strange kind of trance, disconnected from real life as if there isn't a body in the woods and this cabin exists on a different plane. I see everything around me but don't feel part of it any more, as if my fingers might slip through anything I touch, like smoke.

I'm a ghost in my own reality.

I sit on the sofa next to Luc with my knees tucked into my chest and confess everything: what I saw in his study, what I saw in the woods. And when I finally finish speaking I expect him to pull me into his arms, rest my head in the warm wool of his jumper and pull my cold feet under his thigh. That way, everything will be okay again.

But he doesn't do any of those things.

He laughs, cruelly.

'Well, what did you expect? I've been telling you this for weeks but you wouldn't listen, and now someone's dead.'

'Luc...? I...'

The distance between us on the couch opens up like the lake outside.

'You've been stuck out here all this time – me working all hours – with only a baby for conversation. I told you the solitude was taking its toll. It's not normal for a person to have so little contact with the outside world. If I've told you once, I've told you a hundred times: you need to go back!'

It makes no sense, even to me, but I don't feel guilty of murder. It's as if someone else did that, not me. I feel nothing at all. But, even if it was imaginary, after seeing Luc's and Alfie's bodies, first in his study and then out there in the woods, the thought of leaving them now is too much to bear. 'No,' I say. 'I'll be all right. Everything'll be all right. I'm not going back, I can't.'

Luc grabs a fistful of his own hair and drops his head in frustration and despair. And when he eventually looks up, his voice and demeanour alter beyond recognition.

'He's dead, Maggie! Dead! You killed him!'

'I know that, Luc! But what was he doing here? Why has he been watching us, stalking us?'

'Given the hallucinations you've been having, how can you even be sure he *was* stalking us? Maybe he came out here to talk to us about Rose and you attacked him!'

'No... That's not... I...'

'We're out of time, Maggie. This isn't a game any more. You're playing with your life. Rose's life. The truth is right there in that fucked-up head of yours –' he jabs his finger at my forehead '– and I need you to admit it. Right now.'

'I don't know what you're talking about.' My words come out quiet, stilted. This isn't Luc. He's never lost his temper with me, not properly. I've never seen him like this.

I'm afraid.

'All right,' he says. 'I've tried the softly-softly approach and it's clearly not working. Enough is enough. I'm not going to sit back and watch you throw away your life away for me and Alfie. You're going back and that's final.'

He leaps to his feet and the force of his outrage takes my breath away. I stare at his back as he flies away from me, up the steps to the split-level floor and then up the stairs.

'What are you doing?'

He doesn't answer.

'Luc! What are you doing?'

I stay where I am, one foot on the floor, one on the sofa, hugging one knee to my chest. Half of me wants to stay here and wait for Luc to come back and comfort me; the other half wants to run up the stairs and find out what he's doing.

Grating sounds like moving furniture travel down the staircase from our bedroom and curiosity gets the better of me. I run upstairs. Breathless, I throw back the bedroom door. Luc is striding from wardrobe to dresser, piling clothes into my suitcase, which he's dragged from beneath the bed.

'Stop it, Luc. I've told you, I'm not going.'

'This isn't up for discussion, Maggie. I love you. It's time you started loving yourself. It's time you forgave yourself. I've allowed you to wallow in this self-berating bullshit long enough. It's run its course. It's done. And I'm not going to be a party to it any more.'

'What self-berating bullshit?'

Gripping one of my dresses in his fist, Luc throws me a look that says I know exactly what he means.

I go over to the bed and shut the suitcase. 'I don't know what's got into you, Luc, but you can't force me to leave.'

'Can't I? Who's my grandmother, Maggie?'

'Luc, give me the dress.'

He shakes it at me, still balled in his fist. 'I want to hear you say her name.'

I turn away from him, defiantly.

He throws the dress on the floor and snaps the suitcase shut in spite of its meagre contents. 'You think being deliberately obtuse is going to work?' Then he snatches it up, grabs me by the arm and drags me from the room. 'Come on. Wake Alfie. You're leaving.'

'Stop it, Luc!' I pull away but his grip is too strong. And when we reach Alfie's door he throws me inside, and I fall on my knees.

With none of the anger he's reserved for me, Luc combs Alfie's hair from his eyes with his fingers, and my little boy stirs and rubs his eyes. *'Viens, mon fiston, on va faire un petit tour.'* Then he puts Alfie's duffel coat over his pyjamas and lifts him into his yellow wellingtons. 'We need the car. So we'll drive with you to the station, and there you can say goodbye.'

I don't get up. I stay rooted to the floor, my palms pressed into the floorboards as if that will keep me here, ground me here, and prevent Luc from sending me away. But, suitcase in hand, he grabs me by the arm again and yanks me to my feet before dragging me across the landing and down the stairs. I glance behind me and watch Alfie turn around, lie down on his belly and slide down the stairs after us.

Across the lounge, the cabin door looms like a dark figure and I don't want to go there, so I jerk my arm away. 'Stop it, Luc! Stop it!'

He drops my suitcase on the floor, jabs a finger at my belly and says, 'Lift up your shirt.'

'What?!'

'Lift up your shirt! Look at your stomach.'

With no idea what he's talking about, wondering whether he's the one who has really lost his mind, I do as he asks, bending over to look. Either side of my belly there are patches of small, pale bruises. I don't remember how I got them. I look up at him in confusion, expecting him to explain what they are, but he doesn't. He's waiting for me to confess something, as if I've been hurting myself and won't admit it.

'Shall we go on?' He grabs me by the arm again, this time manhandling me towards the sideboard. 'You talk to Rose every week, isn't that right, Maggie?'

'You know I do.'

'On the phone?'

'Of course.'

Pressing a palm into the middle of my back, he shoves me hard. 'Pick it up.'

'No. Why?'

'Pick up the phone!'

I shudder as his voice goes right through me and reach out for the telephone. I've answered it dozens of times, spoken to Rose dozens of times, but now I can't bring myself to lift the receiver. I step back. But then Luc barges past me, knocking me off balance as he snatches it up.

'Listen!' He thrusts the receiver at me and, when I refuse to take it, presses it violently to my ear.

There's no dialling tone.

Luc drops the receiver, yanks the cable out from behind the sideboard and waves it in my face. 'Look!' The wires are bare and exposed. 'You don't speak to Rose, Maggie. You talk to yourself!' Then he seizes me by the arm again, snatches up the suitcase and manhandles me across the room. He lets go of me just long enough to throw open the cabin door, but then he's dragging me down the steps, where I drop to the ground like a dead weight.

Cairo races from the cabin, closely followed by Alfie, who totters down the steps behind me. Bending down on his haunches, he takes my hand. '*Viens, Maman.*' And he pulls as hard as he can to haul me to my feet.

I burst into tears. 'Please, Luc. Don't do this, I'm begging you.'

He ignores me and Alfie says again, '*Viens, Maman.*'

Luc grabs me by the collar and drags me towards the garage on my backside. I kick at the stones, trying to get to my feet, but, before I can, I'm at the garage door and he lets me go. He drops the suitcase and slides back the wooden doors. The moment his back's turned, I'm on my feet and running. But I don't even make it to the cabin steps before he's on me again and dragging me back. He opens the driver's door, but I refuse to get in. So he tries to force me, but every time he grabs my arms I beat his hands away.

The he slaps me.

He slaps me so hard my head snaps sideways.

I stop fighting and we stare at each other in shock. Luc has never hit me. Never. He's never even so much as spoken a threatening word. His face falls for a moment, but then his remorse evaporates and he grabs me again, throwing me into the car before slamming the door. I twist around and watch him toss the suitcase through the rear passenger door, strap Alfie into his car seat and lift Cairo into the hatchback.

By the time he sits next to me I'm sobbing, head down on the steering wheel.

'Drive!'

This isn't Luc. I'm actually afraid he's going to hurt me, even though an hour ago the mere thought of that would have seemed impossible. But, scared as I am of what he will do to me if I don't, I still can't bring myself to drive away.

'Goddammit, Maggie! Drive!'

I lift my head from the wheel and turn to face him. He looks like a different man, a hard man, not Luc at all. His kindness, his gentleness, has turned to stone.

'Drive!'

I turn the key and the engine sparks into life. Then I close my eyes, squeeze tears on to my cheeks and put the car into drive. Slowly, it rolls out of the garage. And only when the wheels stop crunching gravel, only when I know we've rolled on to the woodland track, do I open them again.

Alfie's sleeping like the dead by the time we reach the T-junction, where I come to a stop and put the car into park.

'The road is clear,' Luc says.

'I can't.'

'You can. And you will.'

I slam the gearstick into reverse, but Luc puts his hand over mine and forces it back into park.

'This place is killing you, Maggie. You have to leave.'

'I don't care. I'm not leaving you and Alfie.'

'Then I'll make you.'

Luc tries to force the gearstick into drive but I push it forward. 'Stop it! Stop it!'

Finally he gives up and throws himself back in the seat. Neither of us speak, we just stare at the trees opposite the junction. I can't look left or right. I can't look at the open road.

Suddenly, between the trees, caught in the car's headlights, a stag appears. Its great antlers soar like branches and its breath smokes in the cool night. The striking beauty of the animal warms the air between us, breaking the tension, and then it saunters away, disappearing into the forest.

Something moves in my peripheral vision and I jump.

Alfie's little hand reaches out from the back seat and in his fist he holds a flower by its stem, its centre sunshine-yellow, its petals stark white.

'*Pour toi, Maman.*'

'Where did you get that, baby?'

Alfie doesn't answer. He just waves the flower in my face.

'I didn't think they grew around the cabin.'

'They don't,' Luc says. And then asks Alfie, '*Est-ce que tu sais comment elle s'appelle?*'

'*Mawgwite,*' Alfie says.

'That's right, buddy,' Luc says. '*C'est une marguerite.* Like your grandmother. Like your *maman. Et en anglais?*'

Alfie screws up his little face as he searches his mind for the English translation. It's the sweetest thing I've ever seen

311

– at least it would be on any normal day – an exaggerated expression that lets us know he's really thinking hard. And it's so adorable and funny, it's as if there's a hand inside my chest squeezing droplets of love from my heart.

But not today.

Today, it fills me with sickening dread. Because he knows the name of that flower. Luc has always called me Maggie, but Alfie's heard it a thousand times on Rose's lips.

And the moment he says it, my whole world will crumble.

I put my fingers in my ears as if I'm Alfie's age. I won't listen. I don't care if I'm going to die here. I don't care. I'll sacrifice my life before I abandon my husband and child.

'Maggie...' Luc pulls my hands away from my ears, so gently, so tenderly. And all the cruelty and anger has gone from him when he says, '*Ma belle Marguerite*. It's time to go.'

And then the worst thing happens.

The translation slips from Alfie's lips in triumphant bubble-talk.

'It's a daisy!'

And my whole world crumbles.

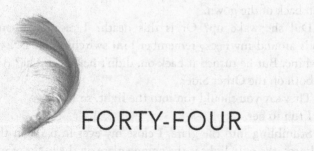

FORTY-FOUR

ROSE

'DAISY!'

She's far away. Her bed, her hospital room, are just a circle of light at the far end of this dark tunnel.

It's hard to breathe in here, the air thin and stale.

I reach out but she's too far away and my arms are heavy and weak. It's a struggle to drag myself forward but somehow I have to get back to her. So I claw my way through the darkness.

Is this a dream?

If it is, it must be one of Saeed's lucid dreams; he said they feel as real as life. And it must be a dream, because Daisy isn't lying in her bed any more, she's sitting up. No, not sitting. Her body is straight, in an upright kneel on the bed, feet on the pillow. She's still in her hospital gown, red curls tumbling to her breasts.

I draw closer.

Her eyes are still closed, but her arms are lifted, her back slightly turned to me so I can see her bare bottom through the open back of the gown.

Did she wake up? Or is this death? I recall Nathan's hands around my neck, remember him switching off Daisy's machine. But he turned it back on, didn't he? Or did he? Are we both on the Other Side?

They say you should run into the light, so I do.

I run to her.

Stumbling into the glare, I close my eyes in pain. In the darkness, the only light is the orange glare on the backs of my eyelids as I fumble around and grab cold metal. Daisy's bed frame. Barely holding myself up by it, I choke, cough and suck in breaths.

When the pain subsides, the first thing I hear is the suck and whoosh of Daisy's life support system. It's still on. Thank God, it's still on. I open my eyes, just a crack at first. But then the yellow weave of her hospital blanket sharpens and for a moment that's all I can see. Contracted at first in the bright fluorescent lights, my pupils slowly dilate until my eyes finally focus.

And then, mouth open, I stagger back.

This can't be happening.

What I saw in the darkness wasn't death. And it was no dream. It was real.

Knees pressed into the mattress, Daisy's bolt upright, breathing tube hanging from her mouth, cables wrapped around her. I stumble to the corner of the bed, blink a few more times and Nathan comes into view. His face is contorted in an expression I don't recognise and there's blood on his surgical scrubs.

Oh, God... Oh, God... What's he done?

What has he done to Daisy?

His eyes – glossy, wet – aren't looking at me. They're looking through me.

The last traces of darkness recede, the strip lights penetrate my peripheral vision, and finally the whole room comes into sharp focus.

In a tangle of bloodied fingers, both Nathan and Daisy have their hands pressed to his neck, grasping the flesh between his ear and shoulder blade. Nathan's eyes are wide but hers are still closed, her expression blank.

Daisy yanks her hands away and I scream as blood spurts from Nathan's neck and sprays the wall, her hospital gown and her blankets. Gripped tightly in both of her hands is the dinner knife that fell from the over-bed table when Nathan attacked me. Blood runs from its handle all the way to the tip of the blade.

Nathan lets go of his neck, glances down at his bloody hands and wobbles, as if he's faint at the sight of them. Then Daisy lifts the knife again, high above her head, and brings it down hard, but the blade strikes thin air as Nathan staggers back and collapses on the floor.

Then Daisy sways. Without thinking, I hold out my arms and dart over as she flops sideways, bloody weapon still in her grasp, and falls from the bed, taking me to the floor with her. And I cry out as the dead weight of my sister collapses on top of me and the alarm sounds on her life support machine.

I scrabble out from beneath her, crying in pain.

Her lifeless body is covered with Nathan's blood; the tracheal tube has been ripped from her throat, and the telemetry leads yanked from her chest. Only her IV remains in place on the back of her hand, but it's torn the skin; the needle hangs half out.

I have no idea what just happened but there's no time to think. I need to get Daisy back on the bed and intubated. Dismissing the voice at the back of my mind yelling that I have neither the capability or knowledge to do that, I try to lift her.

It takes only a moment or two for the futility of my efforts to sink in. So I ignore the pain searing through my broken ribs and scream loud enough to push my lungs through them.

'Help me!! Somebody help me!!'

316

FORTY-FIVE

ROSE

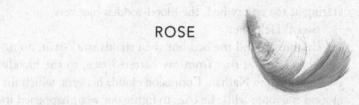

NOBODY COMES.

'Daisy!'

'Daisy!'

Clasping my sister's face, desperate for some sign of life, I press my ear to her lips to listen for a breath. I can't hear anything. If she is breathing without the ventilator, it's very shallow. So I press my ear to her chest instead and listen for a heartbeat.

Nothing.

'Help!' On my knees, I scream at the door. 'Help!'

Still nobody comes.

I reach up for the bed frame, but pain sears through my ribs and I snatch my hand away. Unable to stand, I consider crawling to the door. But if there were anyone in the corridor they would have heard me scream. Dragging myself along on my stomach, how long will it take me to find help?

Too long.

Somewhere at the back of my brain I understand that the blood she's covered in isn't hers, but there's so much of it that it's blinding my reason. Panicking won't help her. I need to think straight. Even if I could stand, even if I could lift her back on to the bed, I wouldn't know how to intubate her anyway. I can't get her back on the ventilator. She's going to die in my arms, right here on the floor, if I don't do something right now.

I have to keep her alive until help comes.

I'm about to press my lips to hers when the door flies open and Saeed steps into the room. Though I can only see his feet from my position on the floor, I know it's him by his cotton trousers and sandals. But he can't see me and I picture his face, staring at the empty bed, the blood-sodden blankets.

'Saeed! Help me!'

He runs around the bed but then stands stock-still, doing nothing. His eyes dart from my battered face, to the bloody bed, and then to Nathan. Confusion clouds his eyes, which flit around the room while he tries to figure out what happened in the half-hour since he walked out of the door.

'Saeed!! For fuck's sake! Help me!'

Finally the empty bed and the alarm of the life support machine break through the chaos and he bends down to my side. 'My God, Rose. What happened in here?'

'There's no time to explain. Daisy's not breathing. We need to get her intubated.'

'All right... Okay... First, we must get her back on the bed. You lift her legs. I will lift her torso.'

Grateful for someone to take control, I don't waste time and grab Daisy by the ankles, but the moment I take the weight of her legs I cry out in pain again. It's as if my ribs have cut through my flesh and are breaking out through the skin.

'Rose? What is it? You are hurt! What the hell happened?'

'I'm fine. Don't worry about me. Worry about Daisy.' In my desperation to help her, I fight through the agony and struggle to my feet while holding tight to her ankles.

But Saeed takes the bulk of her weight with ease, asking, 'How long has she been extubated?'

'I don't know. Not long. A minute, maybe less.'

The moment we have Daisy back on the bed, Saeed presses the call button, but I'm stunned when he turns away from her to tend to Nathan.

'What are you doing?' I grip the bed frame and limp to his side. 'We need to get Daisy back on the machine first!'

'It has been years since I have intubated anyone. We need a trained nurse or physician. I have sounded the alarm; someone will be here soon. He has lost a lot of blood.' He kneels down to assess Nathan's wounds.

Slumped on the floor, Nathan has managed to prop himself against the bathroom door, where he presses his neck wound closed. But then, sapped by blood loss, the last of his strength evaporates and his grip slips. I flinch as blood spurts between his fingers to the rhythm of his heartbeat.

'Come here.' Saeed eases him down on to his back and beckons me to my husband's side, but I don't move.

'Daisy will die if we don't help her!'

'Daisy still has time! If we do not help Nathan – right now – he will die! You help him and I will get help for Daisy.'

I glance at my sister, lifeless on the bed. I don't know if she's breathing. If her heart's beating.

'Rose!'

I snap out of it and kneel on the floor. 'All right. What do you want me to do?'

'Put your palm flat over the wound, like this.' Saeed pulls Nathan's limp hand away and presses mine in its place. 'Create a seal and keep the pressure on, yes?'

I nod and press down on Nathan's neck, just above his shoulder blade, while Saeed springs to his feet to check on Daisy. I can't look at my husband without remembering the hatred in his eyes – I can still feel his hands around my throat – so I stare up at the clock instead, aware of the minutes ticking by.

How long has Daisy gone without oxygen? How many minutes until brain damage sets in? Three? It must have been that long by now.

Saeed checks her airway, then her pulse. But then a gasp leaves his lips. I twist around to look at him.

'She is breathing, Rose! She is breathing on her own!'

And the relief is so overwhelming that, for a second, I relax the pressure on Nathan's neck and blood seeps beneath my palm.

'Keep the pressure on! I will get help.'

Saeed bolts from the room, leaving me to take care of Nathan. I'm exhausted from his beating and my arms are already tired, so I quickly switch hands from left to right and rest my elbow on his chest. His face is clammy and pale, and beneath my arm his chest barely moves, his breathing rapid and shallow. His eyes, anxious with fear and longing, bore into mine.

I know that fear. I felt it just moments ago as I cowered on this very floor staring up at the man who claimed he loved me. I remember the agony of his shoe in my stomach, then its hard toe snapping my ribs. His eyes mirror the horror in mine as I fell backwards down the stairs. Those endless seconds of nothing but air beneath me, waiting for the crack of a step against my spine.

I picture his hands, limp by his sides.

He stood by while my unborn child died inside me.

He stood by while it was mopped up in a bucket of dirty water and tipped down a drain.

My hand goes limp, just enough for a spurt of blood to gush between my fingers. And the fear in his eyes turns to cold terror. Desperate to stem the bleeding, he gropes and scratches at my fingers, hands fumbling in the same way mine did when he had his hands around my throat.

I thought he loved me.

Only a clever man like Nathan – a man who knows exactly what he's doing and how to do it – could make a woman believe one end of the spectrum of truth while concealing what's furthest from it. And he won't let me go. Even now.

Not because he loves me. He's not capable of that. But because he *owns* me. I'm his possession. Another one of his belongings. And, after today, I won't only live in dread of what he might do to Daisy if I tell the truth about what happened in here. I won't only live in fear of what he might do to me if I step out of line.

I'll be subjugated by it.

Slipping on warm blood, Nathan's fingers wrestle with mine. But, just as I lacked the strength to tear his hands from my throat, he now lacks the strength to tear mine from his. Instead of pressing down, I make a cage over the wound with my fingers and let his life gush through them, pulsing in time with his waning heartbeat. And with my free hand I push Nathan's away and say, 'Leave it, baby. I'll do it for you.'

FORTY-SIX

MAGGIE

LUC'S RIGHT, it is time to go.

The weather forecast said snow was on its way but we didn't expect it to come so soon or so heavily.

As I take the T-junction on to the main road, 'The Wheels on the Bus' tinkles through the speakers and Luc and I sing along while Alfie makes bubble noises from the back seat, convinced he's word-perfect.

Although it's dark, the snow's already settling on the road, sparkling in the headlights. It won't be long before the moon is up and, with its reflection on the white roads, the journey home shouldn't be too bad. I adore the snow. Not just because Alfie loves it, but because everything smells so pure, looks so clean, and sounds so quiet. It's like pulling a white flannel sheet, fresh from the dryer, and laying it over the landscape.

This sabbatical was just what I needed – five months at the cabin has felt like a decade and I still have another month off – but I still don't want to go back. To our home or to work.

I want to turn this car around.

With the exception of a short maternity break, I went straight back to working from home with a hungry Alfie on my breast. And I hadn't had a holiday in six years, which was why I was able to take the sabbatical without losing any pay. It gave me the chance to spend time with Alfie, have quiet evenings with Luc where I wasn't stressed over something that had happened during the day, or interrupted by an urgent call. And it gave Luc the peace he needed to finish the draft. Which is really good. I know I'm biased but I think it's better than the first.

And Alfie and Cairo have loved every minute, too. Walking in the woods, skimming stones by the lake, falling asleep in front of the fire in the evenings. I could have stayed there forever, making love in the quiet darkness, having barbecues on the deck, exploring the forest with my whole family whenever Luc took a break.

It was heaven.

I sing along to 'The Wheels on the Bus' with a bright smile but a small pain in my chest over having to leave. It crosses my mind that we *really* could turn around, say to hell with the world, sell our house in the city and live there permanently. And before I know it, I've said it out loud.

'What?' Luc is flabbergasted.

'I mean it. We've often talked about buying the place and John's been talking about selling it for years. If we sold our house, we could buy it twice over and still have no mortgage. You could write, and I could home-school Alfie.'

'You're crazy!'

'I'm not saying it wouldn't be hard – the winters especially – but it could be fun too, couldn't it?'

Luc stares at me with wild eyes. 'You're serious?'

'Deadly!'

He bursts out laughing, as if he'd been singing along with the same small pain caged in his chest and, just like for me, the relief of setting it free is breathtaking. We glance at each other and then we're both laughing.

From the back seat, Alfie lets out a chuckle. 'Mumma!' he says, his burbling voice so close it's as if his lips are pressed to my ear. And a moment later he's crawling over the centre console and into my lap.

I stop laughing. 'Alfie!'

The gap between my belly and the steering wheel isn't big enough for him to squeeze into so he stands up instead, feet on the edge of my seat, hands wrapped around my neck, squeezing tight.

'What are you doing out of your seat?!' I shout in his face as I let go of the steering wheel with one hand to grab him under the armpit before he falls. 'You never, never climb out of your seat! Do you hear me?'

He bursts into tears.

'How the hell did he do that?' Luc unbuckles his seat belt and leans over to grab Alfie by the underarms.

And he's about to clamber between the seats and put Alfie back when I say, 'No, don't. Not in the snow. Put your seatbelt back on; I'll pull over.'

Luc settles Alfie on his lap before reaching behind him for his seatbelt while I scan the road for a passing place to pull into. But the snow is coming down more heavily now and it's hard to see more than a few metres ahead.

Then something black slams into the windscreen.

'Jesus!' I scream, swerving momentarily.

Instinctively Luc lets go of the seatbelt and wraps his arms around Alfie, leaning over him to protect him from the projectile. 'What the hell was that?'

'I don't know.' I pat my chest with my palm to still my beating heart when Alfie senses the tension in the car and bursts into tears all over again. 'It's all right, baby.' I reach over the console and grasp his knee. 'It was just a bird. Mumma didn't mean to frighten you. And she didn't mean to shout at you either.' Then I say to Luc, 'At least I think it was a bird; I didn't really see it, did you? I hope I didn't kill it. I hate killing things.'

'I'd be surprised if it survived that.' Luc bounces the bawling Alfie on his lap while, once again, reaching behind him for the seatbelt. 'Are you all right?'

'I'm fine. Bloody well scared me half to death, though.'

I give Alfie's knee another squeeze and glance over to make sure he's okay.

Then Luc screams, 'Maggie!'

Lying across our path is the body of a huge stag, hit by another motorist and left for dead on the road. I slam on the brakes and twist the wheel.

Luc braces himself against the dashboard with one hand and cradles Alfie with the other as we slide across the snow, swerving around the dead animal.

Only we don't quite make it.

We collide with the rump of the carcass, the passenger-side wheels lift off the road and, with the steering fully locked into the turn, the car flips on its side. None of us even manages a scream as Luc and Alfie are thrown on top of me. And with all three of us piled together on the driver's side, the car skates across the road as if there's black ice beneath us.

At full speed, we slide off the tarmac, bump over the stony embankment and slam, bonnet-first, into a huge tree. The last thing I see is a chaos of arms, bellies, chests and flowing locks of hair as we fly forward with such force that none of us can lift a hand to prevent it.

Then a sharp pain sears through my chest as the seatbelt cuts into my body and my face slams into the airbag.

FORTY-SEVEN

MAGGIE

I LIFT A HAND to my forehead and it's sticky with blood. There's a swollen lump, as if I've been hit with a baseball bat. Pushing my fingertips into the flesh, I wince at the bruised bone. It's hard to move, my body stiff and cold.

How long have I been here?

Luc and Alfie aren't in the car. They must have gone for help.

What happened?

I remember singing. I remember talking with Luc about buying the cabin. A bird? I think a bird hit the windscreen. I don't remember. The windscreen is shattered, almost completely gone apart from a few fragments still trapped in the frame, and everything's covered in glass. Me included.

Cairo cries, wolf-like, from the boot of the hatchback. She must have hit the rear seatback frame quite hard. I wonder if Luc checked on her before he went for help.

Clicking the release button of my seatbelt, I crawl over the broken glass of the side window, clamber over the steering wheel and fight my way through the windscreen. Glass slices my hands and knees as I crawl, but finally I make it on to the verge and get to my feet. But the moment I do, I regret it. Tottering on the spot, I'm in the eye of the tornado as my world spins around me, the trees a circling blur. So I grab the tyre for support and wait for my vision to clear.

On its side, the car is lodged in the wide trunk of a large oak, the front bonnet concertinaed. My breath smokes on the ice-cold air, which smells of freshly fallen snow. But in it, there's a hint of metal and chemicals.

Blood and petrol.

Cairo's still wailing, so I glance up and down the road for Luc and Alfie. They must have left several minutes ago as there's no sign of them, so I gingerly make my way to the hatchback, holding on to the roof as I go.

I tug at the boot catch but it won't open; with the car on its side, it's jammed. And Cairo's now howling so loudly, so painfully, it twists my heart. I can't leave her like that, so I scan the roadside for a rock.

When I break the rear screen, the glass clings to itself, tinged with green, and I have to hit it quite a few times to make a hole big enough to lean through. 'It's all right, sweetheart, Mummy's here. She'll get you out.'

But when I grab her collar to pull her towards me she jerks her head around, white snout bloody red, and snaps at me. Just in time, I snatch my hand away in shock while she curls herself against the back seat, whimpering in pain. She must have hit her face, broken her jaw maybe. Her teeth made contact but didn't pierce the skin: a warning to back off.

My sweet little Cairo has never even growled at me, let alone snapped at me. She must be badly injured, letting me know she's in too much pain to be moved. So I leave her there; I'll need Luc's help to get her out.

'It's all right, sweetheart, Mummy'll get you out soon. Shush-shush. You wait.'

I glance up the empty road.

They must have walked back to the cabin.

About ten metres away, a stag lies on the tarmac. Its neck is twisted so far back it's as if its prodigious antlers have torn through its own flesh. Its entrails tumble from the wide gash in its belly, and flakes of snow melt in its blood.

Did we hit it? I can't remember.

There are tyre tracks but no footprints in the snow. If Luc went to get help, they didn't go back to the cabin. Which is odd because that's the closest place; there's nowhere else for miles. Maybe Alfie was hurt and Luc thought it would be quicker to get him to the nearest village than walk to the cabin and wait for an ambulance.

I stumble around the boot, grabbing the rear tyre to stop myself falling, and have to pause a few seconds when my world starts spinning again.

I didn't think I'd seen footprints in the other direction either, but my mind is so fuzzy, my head pounding. I was right. The road is pristine white.

'Luc? Alfie? Luc?!'

The snow deadens my calls.

Struggling forward, almost falling when I reach the front tyre, I stagger past the crushed front bonnet and around the tree.

'Luc!!'

He's lying face down in the snow a few metres away.

The muscles in my arms and legs weaken with fear as I trip and stumble through the undergrowth as if wading through a quagmire. From somewhere in the forest, the startled caw of a crow disrupts my heart, and I look up as if it might bring someone to help me. But then I step on a large stone and the hard sole of my boot rocks forward, throwing me off balance. My legs give way and I fall, having to scrabble through the last few feet of snow to get to my husband.

'Luc?!'

He doesn't move.

He just lies there.

And when I shake him, he still doesn't move.

With what little strength I have left, I drive my hands between his stomach and the forest floor and lift, rolling him on to his back. A mess of bloodied leaf litter is stuck to his hair, face and beard and I wipe it away before shaking him and screaming his name. 'Luc?! Luc!!'

His near-black eyes are still and wide, his face lacerated from hairline to beard by shards of glass, and a pool of blood melts the snow beside his head where he's bled from a neck wound. Hands trembling, I pull back the hood of his rain mac and retch. A large shard of glass is wedged between his neck and shoulder blade. I can't bear the sight of it – he must be in agonising pain – so I pull it out, its sharp edges cutting my fingers.

Blood gushes from the wound and I realise my mistake. I should have left it in there to keep the wound closed. I'm about to seal it with my palm when I see that blood isn't spurting: it's barely seeping.

Luc's heart is no longer pumping.

I take hold of his wrist and it's cold, yet still I feel for a pulse.

Nothing.

I stare at the pool of my husband's blood with no sense of where I am. I've even forgotten my own name. Instead, my mind loops with three repeated words: I did this. I did this. But then my little boy breaks through my locked thoughts.

'Alfie.' I shout his name as I twist on my knees, my head spinning this way and that as I scan the forest for him. 'Alfie?!!'

He's there!

His yellow wellingtons gleam against the bright snow just a few metres away, but I can barely make out his blue toggle coat. And his head is obscured by something... Something black.

It moves.

A bird!

A crow!

Spread across Alfie's body, its wings flap as it pecks and claws at the soft skin on the back of my baby's head. Its eyes are ice-blue, glassy, and its beak gleams like metal-black shears. He doesn't even lift his arms to swat it away; he just lies there.

Reaching behind me, I scrabble around in the undergrowth for the stone that tripped me and snatch it up, skimming it through the air with as much force as I can muster, screaming, 'Get away! Get away from my baby, you fucker!'

Beating blue-black wings, the crow lifts off into the air, and makes for the safety of the canopy while I stagger to my feet and run to Alfie.

He's not moving.

He's face-down in the snow.

I collapse over his little body, dig my hands between him and the ground, and scoop him into my arms. Just like Luc's, Alfie's face is cut with shards of glass; protruding from his soft cheeks, they glint in the moonlight through the trees. His legs dangle, doll-like, over my crooked elbow, and his yellow wellingtons are filled with snow from being thrown across the ground.

His socks have holes in them.

I didn't bring enough for the trip.

His poor little toes must be freezing.

One-handed, I tug at one of the boots, but it's packed with snow, too tight around his ankles, and I don't have the strength to pull it off. So I leave it, brimful, and rub the back of his head where the crow had been pecking.

'I'm here, baby. Mumma's here.'

His golden hair is warm, wet, and when I pull my hand away it's red. Blood-soaked from a gash in his skull much deeper than a crow's beak. I scream.

My brain ceases, to function, petrified, frozen on this one frame.

I can't move.

I can't think.

I can't breathe.

A trickle of blood runs from Alfie's rosy lips down his chin. And then his little body shudders as he lets out a cough.

He's alive! Alfie's alive!

He inhales with blood-soaked lungs, and I stare into his eyes while he breathes bubbles as if he's drowning in a lake of his own blood.

Then he coughs again and is still.

'Alfie!'

'Alfie?!'

I shake his ragdoll body before pressing my ear to his mouth but I can't feel his breath. So I press my ear to his chest instead. There's no heartbeat. Then I lay him gently in the snow and start CPR. Only I have no idea how much pressure to use on his dainty ribs and I'm afraid to push too hard, afraid to hurt him.

But I can't hurt him.

Because he's not breathing.

So I shove my panic deep down and focus my mind just enough to remember the rhythm of 'Staying Alive'. And I say the song out loud as I pump his chest.

I don't stop after three minutes.

I don't stop after ten.

I don't stop even when the moon has dropped below the treeline.

∽

Hunkered down on my haunches, clutching my baby boy, I stare into his wide eyes until I can't bear it any longer. The light has gone from them. So I close them gently with my finger and thumb, then glance across the expanse between us and Luc's body.

There's a line of muddy red footprints between us where I stepped in his blood in my panic to reach Alfie. He's all alone over there. Cold. So I clutch my son to my chest and grope my way through my footprints back to my husband. There, I lay Alfie in the crook of Luc's arm, his head so small on the pillow of his father's shoulder. It's only then that I notice Luc's not wearing his own mac, he's wearing John's. He must have picked it up by accident in his hurry to get on the road before the snow really came down. He's always doing that, picking up the nearest coat on the rack without paying attention. I pull it close around him and Alfie to keep them warm.

Then I pick up the shard of glass lying in the pool of blood next to Luc and, gripping it with both hands, point it at my chest. Its tip rips through my jumper and shirt and pierces my skin, stinging like a hot blade, my body catastrophising the pain in some sick attempt at self-preservation I have no interest in.

I can't do it.

I can't fucking do it.

With Alfie nestled between us, I lean over Luc's body, bury my face in the soft wool of his jumper, and ceaselessly, silently scream.

Caws like cries of pain sound from the canopy and wings flap overhead. The crows take flight, leaving empty air in their wake, as I kneel on the forest floor waiting for death to take me too.

And it will.

If I get cold enough.

If I wish hard enough.

FORTY-EIGHT

ROSE

THE ROOM is quiet.

The linoleum floor is still a wash of red.

And, high on painkillers with bandaged ribs, I find myself once again sitting on the chair next to Daisy's bed with Saeed on the opposite side.

Back where we started.

The details of earlier today slip through my fingers like Nathan's blood. I remember a flurry of nurses, being lifted off the floor and dragged away from Nathan so they could tend to his wounds. He'd lost consciousness by then and they wheeled him away on a stretcher while two other nurses poked and prodded me.

One nurse put an oxygen mask over Daisy's nose and mouth while another reinserted the cannula that was torn from the back of her hand when she fell from the bed. Then they hooked her back up to the infusion pump while Dr Anderson checked her vitals. But they didn't intubate her.

Daisy's breathing on her own, albeit shallowly.

I have no idea whether Nathan is dead or alive.

Tentatively, softly, Saeed asks, 'What happened, Rose?'

And I hardly know where to start or how much to tell him. I'm no fool. If Nathan dies, I could be charged with his murder. And Saeed is the kind of man who would be torn between his feelings for me and lying to the police when they come.

I won't put him in that position.

'I tried to leave,' I mumble. 'But Nathan stopped me... Beat me.'

Saeed reaches over Daisy's bed to take my hand. 'I should never have left you alone in here.'

'You couldn't have known. Even I didn't think he'd go that far.'

'And you...? Did you...?'

'Stab him? No, of course not. I crawled away, hid under the bed. But when I wouldn't come out, he turned off Daisy's life support.'

'What?!' He turns to Daisy then, his concern redirected. And I love that he cares about her so much. Cares that someone would try to hurt her.

I tell him about Nathan forcing me to come out and my hand gravitates to my neck. 'He knocked the knife off the table on to Daisy's blanket. She picked it up and stabbed him.'

'Daisy? Daisy stabbed Nathan?'

'Yes.'

He looks at her again. 'But she is still in a coma.' His words are tinged with doubt. Naturally. Who would believe it?

'I know,' I say. 'Her eyes weren't even open. It was like a reflex. As if she was stabbing thin air and Nathan just happened to be in the way. She still had the knife in her hand when she fell from the bed. That's when you came in.'

'Thank God for Daisy.' He leans over the bed and brushes my cheek. 'Those are some nasty cuts and bruises. He must have hit you very hard.'

'I've never seen him like that. I had no idea that man even existed.'

'I am sorry I was not here to protect you.'

'Please, don't say sorry. It's over now. Have you heard anything? About Nathan?'

Saeed is grave, his eyebrows knit together. 'He is dead, Rose. And I am not sorry for that.'

I suck in a breath and close my eyes. Tears form in the corners but they don't fall.

I won't cry for him.

Saeed doesn't speak for a long time. But then he asks the question I prayed he wouldn't. 'Rose... How did Nathan die?'

I look him right in the eye. 'I told you. Daisy stabbed him.'

'He was alive when I left the room. His heartbeat and pulse were still quite strong. It was only a few minutes until help arrived.'

He knows.

I hold his gaze for as long as I can, but it's too penetrating and my face burns.

'You can tell me anything,' he says. 'You know that.'

If I tell him, he'll have to tell the police. But he knows anyway, so what difference does it make? 'All right. It's true. Daisy did stab him. But she didn't kill him. I did. I didn't keep pressure on when you told me to. I let him bleed to death.'

Saeed just stares at me. And I can't tell if it's disappointment, whether he sees me differently now: a woman he had no idea even existed. And how could he not? Whenever he looks at me now, he'll see a murderer.

I say, 'I know you'll have to tell the police. I don't need you to lie for me.'

He grabs my hand. 'No more than I need you to lie *to* me.'

'I didn't want to put you in that position.'

'It would not be the first time I have been in this position. And it may not be the last. But it can be a difficult choice: what is right is not always what is legal. But I could never live with myself if anything happened to you. I would die to protect you. And I will lie to protect you as well.'

I lose myself in his eyes for a moment, forget the nightmare of my reality.

'Rose... I want to say something to you but I... The last thing you need is another man...someone you have known for so little time, telling you... You trusted Nathan. Loved him. And yet—'

I put my free hand over his and say, 'I know. I want to say it too.'

'Will you stay here?'

'No. I'll go to my mum's as I planned. I need time. After two marriages, I can't—'

'I know.' And he puts his free hand over mine: a pile of fingers, warm flesh and comfort. 'May I write to you there?'

'Of course. I'll give you my email—'

'Not email. The address.'

And I smile. Of course a man like Saeed would write letters. We squeeze each other's hands and although his grip is gentle, I'm suddenly aware of his physical strength, his powerful fists, his muscular arms. But I don't flinch. He thinks I'll struggle to trust another man so soon. But he's wrong. I thought I knew Nathan and that error in judgement nearly cost me my life. It cost me my child's life. But now I know how it really feels to trust, to truly love, I know I never felt this way about my husband.

Never.

Suddenly, our hands are snatched from each other as Daisy sits bolt upright, eyes wide, her empty arms open and her mouth twisted in a ceaseless, silent scream.

FORTY-NINE

ROSE

'DAISY!' I take her outstretched hands in mine but her expression doesn't alter. Though her eyes are open, it's as if she's still back there, stuck in the darkness of that coma.

'Daisy!?'

She has no idea I'm here. So I let go of her hands and climb on to the bed, inserting myself into her empty arms. Then I wrap myself around her and whisper in her ear, 'I'm here, Daisy. I've got you. I'm here.'

And I hold her as tight as I can, rocking her back and forth like a child, until her silent scream turns to sobs so wrenching she can barely catch her breath.

And then, for the first time in three long years, my sister speaks.

'They're dead.'

She says it over and over.

'They're dead.'
And I know she means Luc and Alfie.
'I know, Daisy. I know.'

FIFTY

DAISY

One month later

'YOU DYED your hair.' Saeed comes out from behind his desk to greet me.

'Well, I wasn't going to leave it like that. I don't know what the fuck Rose was thinking. I looked like someone who dances around Stonehenge naked on the summer solstice.'

'Perhaps that is what she was hoping for.' He scratches Cairo behind the ears. She's getting heavy in my arms, but she hasn't been able to walk very far since the accident.

I raise my eyebrows at him. 'No doubt she was.'

Saeed takes his usual seat in his high-backed chair, saying, 'You think she should have dyed it for you every eight weeks for three years?'

'And cut it. And straightened it. What are sisters for?'

I put Cairo down and she totters over to sniff Maggie, who's sleeping under Saeed's desk. I wish he hadn't called his dog Maggie. Without Luc – the only person who ever called me that – it's hard to hear it spoken on anyone else's lips. Even

Saeed's. My heart fractures a little every time I hear it. Soon there will be nothing left but tattered tissue.

Cairo muscles in on Maggie's giant pillow and they cuddle up together while I take a seat on Saeed's couch, leaning forward and gripping the ox-blood leather like an old memory beneath my palms.

'How are you holding up?' he asks.

'I have good days and bad. The physiotherapy's a bitch.'

'Should I be worried?'

'About a repeat performance?'

He nods.

I smile but there's nothing behind it. 'Not just yet. Rose needs me.'

'Not just yet? Are you teasing me, Daisy?'

'A little.'

'Good. I would rather you stayed out of hospitals for a while. Three years is long enough to spend in one. The last thing I want is for you to become a suicide risk and force my hand.'

'I wouldn't do that. I'd miss our talks. Besides, I didn't intend to do it the first time. It was an accident, I promise.'

'Accident or not,' he says, 'I feel responsible.'

'Well, you're not.' I get to my feet, needing to move after so long lying down, so long sleeping, dreaming. I go and stare out of the window at Magdalen Street. Nothing's changed. People still meander past the graveyard railings, the road as busy as ever with cars and bicycles. It seems so long since I've watched them.

'I taught you lucid dreaming to help with the nightmares, not as a means of escape.'

I stare down at the graves, saying, 'It did help. You know what it was like before: waking up screaming every night. I couldn't close my eyes without seeing their faces in the snow.' I brush my cheek with my fingertips, touching the memory of broken glass. 'You taught me to control it, showed me how to walk away from the accident, back to the cabin where Luc and Alfie were always waiting. If you hadn't done that, I think I would have died. If I hadn't wasted away from lack of food and sleep, I would have taken my own life.'

'You underdosed on your insulin, Daisy. I am struggling to believe that was an accident.'

'Oh, no, that part was intentional. What I meant was, I didn't intend for it to land me in a coma.'

'What did you intend?'

'To sleep. To dream.'

'But you must have known the risk you were taking. You played with your life so you could dream?'

'I don't think I cared. I meant what I said when I told you I'd found a way to be happy again. You gave me that with lucid dreaming. I practised and practised. And by the end I'd become a master. I didn't even need to relive the accident. The car would be on its side, the bonnet crushed into the tree, but I wouldn't be in it. And Luc and Alfie wouldn't be in the woods. Their footprints would be in the snow on the road where they'd gone to get help. And I would follow them back to the cabin. I was able to construct that world with such precision, it was as real as real life. Of course, the more time I spent there, the harder it was to distinguish between that and reality.'

'Then why take risks with insulin?'

'Well, that's the problem with dreams, isn't it? Eventually, you have to wake up. I'd been taking powerful sleeping pills for months so I could sleep from the afternoon right through to the next morning, spending every hour I could at the cabin. I'd get up for our sessions, or to eat, and then I'd go back to bed again. But the sleeping pills were wearing off. I needed more and more of them.'

'Tolerance,' Saeed says. 'Continued exposure renders many drugs useless.'

'I know that now.'

'So, the sleeping pills stopped working and you under-dosed on your insulin to cause diabetic fatigue?'

I nod, but I don't turn away from the window. The shame burns. How could I have put Rose through that? And, to a lesser extent, Saeed. His gaze exacerbates my shame, not because his expression is in any way judgemental – Saeed has a way of silently compelling you to forgive yourself regardless of how foolish you are; it's like confession and therapy rolled into one. He's not chastising me like an irresponsible child; I'm doing that to myself.

He says, 'For someone who did not intend to take their own life, you took one hell of a risk.'

'Ah, but that's an entirely different question, isn't it? I said I didn't want to take my own life because I'd found a way to be happy. But take Luc and Alfie away…' I touch my fingers to the glass, to the memory of the broken window in Luc's study.

I'm tired.

Exhausted by the grief of reliving the accident when I hadn't done it for so long. So long, I'd almost forgotten it entirely.

Almost.

Wishing for sleep, I return to the sofa and sink down into the leather, saying, 'You know what lucid dreams are like, Saeed. They aren't the dreams of the subconscious. They don't slip through your fingers the moment you wake up. Their memories are as real as the ones we make every day. To me, they were alive again.'

'But we agreed that through lucid dreaming you would construct new realities, not return to the old ones. We knew that would not be healthy. You said you would imagine time with Rose. Prepare yourself for returning to work. Travel perhaps. Once we had control of your nightmares, you were supposed to dream of the life you were too afraid to face: experience it first from the safety of your dreams before confronting it in reality. I believed that was what we were working towards.'

342

'Sorry. I lied.'

'But you did that here in our sessions: imagined returning to work, facing the reactions of your colleagues.'

'Yes, and then I went home and went back to the cabin.'

His voice is calm but I know he's frustrated. Saeed has a tic. You'd never notice it if you didn't know what to look for. He doesn't narrow his lips or glare, but for a split second the groove in his right eyebrow deepens. Only the right, not the left. And then it's gone. He acknowledges his anger, deals with it internally, adjusts, and then presents himself to his patients in a way that's supportive. But he still feels those emotions, deeply, because he cares. He cares about everyone.

I say, 'When Luc and Alfie were alive, I would barely see them all week. I'd be at the office or in the study at home. Always too busy to spend time with them. All I had were stolen hours in the evenings and the rare weekends I didn't have to work. That Christmas at the cabin made me see what I was missing: how meaningless my job was compared to my family. On the way home, Luc and I talked about buying it, making a life there. I think we would have done it, too. You made that a reality: the sabbatical never ended.'

'Daisy. I thought you trusted me. You could have told me what you were doing. Why did you keep that from me?'

I half smile – because talking about Luc and Alfie brings them to life for a moment – and say, 'Because… Saeed…you would have made me stop.'

'I thought you were getting your strength back, sleeping again, eating again. I thought we were making progress when we were making none at all.'

'We were! I was! But not because I was learning to live without Luc and Alfie.'

Saeed closes his eyes. 'Because I had taught you how to live *with* them.'

'Exactly. What is it you always say about lucid dreaming?'

343

'That the oneironaut is the master of her dreams. Conquer lucid dreaming and your world is limited only by your imagination.'

'Well, I conquered it. Every day I'd get up and go through the motions of dressing, brushing my teeth, eating. And I was content because I knew, once I'd done all that, I could go back to sleep again. It became a drug. And, like any drug, it was never enough.'

'I should never have taught you.'

'Don't say that. Don't ever say that. It saved my life. You saved my life.'

'You almost died!'

'I never meant to, I swear. You did make me want to live. Only not for the reasons you thought. It's not your fault. You couldn't possibly have known the lengths I would go to, to be with them. Especially when I was coming here and lying to your face.'

'Rose found you, Daisy. Do you know that? She came to your house and saw you through the window. She thought you were dead. Thought you had finally taken your own life. She put a rock through your patio door to get to you.'

'Poor Rose. She's been through so much.'

Saeed's right eyebrow creases again and then softens but he's still careworn. For me. For Rose.

I say, 'I heard her, you know? In my dreams. We'd have these long conversations on the phone and she'd tell me all about you.'

He smiles then. Briefly. He can't help himself.

'Of course, now, I realise I was just overhearing you both in my room.'

'How did you find your way back?'

'Luc, I guess. He kept pressuring me to leave. Kept bringing it up over and over. He wouldn't stop going on about it. And finally he dragged me the hell out of there. But I think it started a couple of months before that. I was out in the woods

344

with Alfie, standing on the forest path. Only I don't remember how we got there. I have no memory of us walking there. We were just there. I heard something…in the trees…someone breathing. Rasping. Drowning out every other sound.'

'The ventilator.'

'What?'

'You said you heard things in your dreams…things that were taking place in your hospital room. Rose and I talking. Two months ago, you stopped breathing.'

'I did?'

'They put you on a ventilator. You were on it until the day you woke up.'

I think about that moment, how the path between the trees narrowed on the horizon. 'It felt like a tunnel, and we were being propelled along it. I remember the sickening sense of dread, as if death was waiting at the end.'

'It was. You nearly died. If the nurse had not been there, changing your feeding tube and catheter, you would have.'

Whenever anyone mentions death, like a reflex action my mind snaps to that moment in the snow, holding that piece of glass. I was so angry at myself for not having the strength to take my life that I could have stabbed myself with it over and over. That's what I see every time I remember that moment: driving that shard into my chest until every part of me is red.

I force my mind back to Saeed's office, saying, 'There was a man there… Nathan.'

'Nathan was in your dream? You saw him? But you had never met in real life.'

'I'd never *seen* him. So I didn't recognise his face – he was just a man, always there, always in the trees – but *we'd met*. I know that now. He'd been in my room, done tests, checked my responses. No doubt to make sure I wasn't about to wake up.'

'He had been falsifying your tests, did Rose tell you? He was the one who persuaded Dr Anderson to remove life support.'

'She did. But somehow I already knew. I knew he was there to kill me. To take Luc and Alfie from me. So I killed him. In my dream. It was only after he was dead that I saw the lanyard on his body, his hospital ID card.'

'Dreams are always part real, part fantasy. With all that was going on in your room, reality will have been shaping your dreams while your dreams shaped your reality.'

'It did. I felt his malice when he was in the room with me. He would pull back my blankets, lift my gown and look at me. And in the depths of my consciousness I knew it was happening.'

I think back to the man in the woods – Nathan – watching me all the time and recall the day I stepped out of the lake naked, his eyes scouring my skin like fingernails.

'Have you heard from the police?' Saeed asks, and I come back to reality.

'The CPS aren't pressing charges. Even if the doctors hadn't confirmed that I was still in a comatose state, they felt it was reasonable force. Claire came forward too, Nathan's ex-wife. She gave a statement about his psychopathic behaviour when they were married. Apparently he beat her too, when she tried to leave him.'

Our eyes meet then, our expressions knowing, both of us thinking of Rose and what she did, but neither of us prepared to speak of it. As if speaking of it, even here in this closed room, might somehow expose her. And we both protect her with equal and violent force.

Saeed changes the subject. 'You said Luc made you leave...?'

'Yes. But my world was already crumbling – not just the man in the woods. Even inside the cabin I couldn't sustain it.'

'How so? You said you were the master of your dreams. That you were able to construct the cabin with such precision, it was impossible to distinguish between it and reality.'

'It wasn't the cabin. That was simple. And to a certain extent so was Alfie. He was such an easy child, so happy, he came alive in my mind exactly as he had been. It was Luc. I couldn't capture his nuances, his depth, his perfections and imperfections. When bad things started happening, like when the man showed up and when Alfie was attacked by a flock of crows...'

My mind wanders to the accident, to his little body face-down in the snow.

'And when he nearly drowned...'

I picture his wellingtons full to the brim with lake water, just as they'd been full to the brim with snow. Alfie unable to breathe through punctured lungs, drowning in his own blood...

'Daisy? Are you all right?'

'Sorry...yes...I'm all right... What was I saying?'

'Something about Alfie nearly drowning.'

'Oh...yes... I was going to say that Luc didn't respond the way he would have in real life. I couldn't capture...I couldn't reimagine the intensity of his love, the depth of his pain, or the affection he felt for us. He would never have reacted that way to either of us being in danger. I was always the logical one; he was the one with all the emotional intelligence and creativity. So his responses were a mirror of me: too rational, too stolid. And the more the dream-Luc failed me, the harder it became to maintain that reality. And the more it fell apart, like a circle of action-reaction, until it collapsed entirely.'

'Which was when Luc finally forced you to go?'

'Yes. He showed me the phone wires – they weren't connected. He was trying to get me to admit that I was lying to myself, force me back to reality. Make me see that I couldn't have been talking to Rose. I never needed insulin in lucid dreams, but then I found a syringe in the drawer. Luc made me look at my stomach; it was covered in needle marks the way it always is in real life. And yet still I couldn't let it go.'

'Because the moment reality slips in through the cracks, the moment you are aware it is only a dream, the harder it becomes to maintain, to remain there, to not wake up.'

'Exactly. I'm sure that somewhere very deep down I knew it wasn't real. Because all the things that were happening to us didn't feel quite real. There were elements of the fantastical about them.'

'That is how dreams are: part reflections of our real lives, part imagination and fantasy, part hope, part despair.'

'Yes…that's precisely what it was. Even before the coma, I'd been at the dream cabin for so long, it was already real in my mind. And when I first went into the coma I couldn't have got out, even if I'd wanted to. And I desperately didn't want to. My mind constructed the world – part fantasy, part real – where that woman in the hospital wasn't even me. It was as if we had a third sister and it was her who was going to die, not me. If it hadn't been for Luc forcing me to leave…'

Saeed grins. It's barely noticeable, but it's there.

'What?'

'Would you mind waiting, just two minutes while I make a quick call?' Saeed gets to his feet and picks up his mobile from the desk, but then he pauses, waiting for my permission.

'Um – okay, sure.' I've never known Saeed to interrupt one of our sessions to make a call. Whatever it is must be very important.

'Sorry.' He comes back into the room and takes his chair again, still with that hint of a smile behind his eyes. 'Where were we…? Of course, yes – reality slipping through the cracks. There is something you said that does not quite make sense to me. You said that long before Nathan arrived in your dreams you had been at the cabin many times without these strange events – attacks by crows, near-drownings – these moments you describe as fantastical, not real.'

'That's right.'

348

'And that your inability to reimagine Luc as the man he was in real life created cracks in your reality.'

I nod.

'But that is not quite accurate, is it? If the problem *really* was your inability to recreate Luc — if that was to blame for reality slipping through the cracks — that would have happened years ago. You were in the coma for three years, contentedly trapped in the lucid dream. So what changed two months ago? What happened to manifest Nathan?'

'You said it yourself — I stopped breathing.'

'That is true. But you were immediately put on a ventilator. A minor disturbance in your world. And an oneironaut of your skill would have quickly returned to normal.'

I half nod, half shake my head, not sure whether I agree with him or not. Or what he's trying to suggest. 'What do you think it was, then? You clearly have a theory.'

'My theory is that your world began to crumble when you started running back towards life.'

'I'm not sure my conscious mind agrees with you. What makes you say that?'

'You heard Nathan tell Dr Anderson it was time to remove life support. That he — Nathan, I mean — would do some tests to confirm your condition had deteriorated, and he would prepare Rose for what was to come.'

'How do you know that?'

'I just asked Dr Anderson.' He points at his mobile on the desk. 'Whether he had ever discussed the removal of life support in front of you. He had. Twice. Once the day you woke up. And two months ago: the day after you were put on the ventilator.'

It takes a moment for that to sink in. That's the day I first saw the man in the woods. The day after I stopped breathing.

'Your conscious mind knew that Nathan was going to take your life. And at that point, whether your subconscious knew it or not, you had to choose: in order to live, you had to abandon

Luc and Alfie. Maybe you did not want to live for your own sake. But you said it yourself: deep down, you knew what kind of man Nathan was. And you would not abandon Rose for your husband and child who were already gone. But your conscious mind had three years of illusions to break through. A dream so deeply entrenched in your subconscious, it had become your reality. It was not Luc trying to get you to admit what was real. Luc did not exist. It was your own mind trying to break through the walls of your subconscious.'

I remember Luc dragging me from the cabin, kicking and screaming to the car. Forcing me to drive back down the road to where the accident happened. Forcing me to relive it. To remember reality. It wasn't Luc.

'It was me.'

'It was *you*. You truly are the master of your dreams. Your conscious mind exerted control over your dream even in the depths of a coma that had lasted three years. You brought yourself back because you wanted to live.'

I'm still not sure that's true.

Not yet.

But Saeed believes it. And there's that smile again. But it's not just a smile. It's something I've never seen in Saeed before – contented happiness – and it makes me think of Rose. Our conversations felt so real. I loved talking to her. I've missed it. I say, 'I wish it hadn't been Rose who found me. She's so fragile. Finding me like that must have broken her.'

'She is stronger than you think.'

'Are you in love with her?'

Saeed blushes. On his olive skin it's barely there, but I know his face too well.

'Daisy.' His tone is uncompromising.

'I know, I know, it's not professional for you to talk about her with me. Just tell me if you're planning on visiting her in Yorkshire and I swear I'll never mention your relationship again.'

'We have no relationship, Daisy. If we did, I would not be able to continue treating you. And right now you are my priority.'

'You sent her away?'

'No. She was leaving anyway. I did not try to stop her. That is not the same thing.'

'It is for Rose! She's delicate, easily bruised. You only had to say "stay" and she would have stayed.'

'Exactly! Rose is not a dog, Daisy. She needs to be her own master, find her rudder. She has been tossed in a storm – in her first marriage, and then with Nathan – and until she learns to steer the course of her own life – with certainty and with confidence – she will always be vulnerable.'

'Not with you. You could have taken care of her!'

'When it comes to Rose, I want neither the role of therapist nor father. A lover – a partner – is someone you trust to share your life's journey with, not someone you rely on to carry you on it. Relationships where one person leans too heavily on the other – to be held up, mothered, cared for – will inevitably lead to pain or failure. Either the carer suffers under the weight of the burden or the caree feels they are not supported enough. True love – lasting love – requires balance. And for Rose to have a balanced relationship she must come to it with the same strength as the person she is meeting, otherwise she will be crushed beneath its weight.'

I know he's right. But I don't like it. I want him for Rose.

Did I crush Luc sometimes? I wonder about that. He was gentle, too. Sweet, kind. I wonder if I took advantage of that on occasion: used my strength to get what I wanted, even if that meant he was worse off as a result. I put my career first. When Luc had first toyed with the idea of giving up work to write, I'd encouraged it – because I knew it would be good for *me*. I wanted everything: a career and a child too. I knew, if he stayed at home to write, he would be my permanent childminder. I didn't consider how challenging that would be for him: to take

351

care of a child while forging his own career as a full-time writer. If I'm really honest with myself I hadn't expected him to throw himself into the writing the way he had, have the passion for it he had. I hadn't anticipated his success either. And when the time came for me to support him – to take the sabbatical and go to the cabin, to take care of Alfie so he had time to write – I'd resented that at first: the sudden importance his career had over his role as a father. It was only a quiet resentment but it was still there. I wonder if he noticed.

I think part of the reason I kept going back – other than to spend time with Luc and Alfie – was to do everything differently. Be a more supportive wife and mother. Less selfish. Less hard. More like Luc.

Saeed's voice brings me back to the room.

'It is not only Rose,' he says. 'I am not ready either. I have feelings I need to reconcile within myself before I can move forward.'

'Feelings? You mean regrets?'

'Yes.'

'You freed her from that marriage. What regrets can you possibly have? If you hadn't done what you did, she might never have found out what Nathan was doing. His true nature.'

'It is not that simple… I should not be speaking of this with you.'

'Explain it to me…just once…and I swear we'll never speak of this again. Because I need to know. I won't settle here, settle back into our sessions together until I understand why you've done what you've done. Or why you have these regrets. If I had been there, I would have done exactly what you did.'

My words flip a switch in Saeed. The control knob between therapist and man. And suddenly he's no longer regulating every sentence that leaves his lips. Suddenly he's passionate, angry.

'No. You would not! You would have let Rose guide you. You would have listened to her, steered her carefully in the right direction. I *wanted* something to be wrong with Nathan. I wanted it the moment she told me she was married. And when I saw that first red flag I felt a surge of desire to find more. I wanted Rose to be in a coercive relationship – preferably a violent one – because then the dissolution of her marriage would have moved faster. And I could be there as Nathan's antithesis, the man into whose arms she ran when she was hurt by the man she was with. I pushed, I pressed. *I* coerced.'

Leaning an elbow on the unforgiving wood of his desk, Saeed lets his head fall, rubs his eyebrows with finger and thumb, pressing them into his eyes as if to stem tears.

'It was what she needed at the time.'

'No,' he says, still not looking up, but calmer now. 'No. When a person is in a coercive and controlling relationship, they need an anchor in the storm. Not someone who tries to control them in the same way, pushing and coercing them to leave. They need you to be there for them, hold them steady, while they find their own way. Otherwise you are no better than the abuser. And I know better than that. I let my feelings for Rose get in the way of my sense. And that is something I will have to learn to live with, come to terms with.' Finally, he looks up but hesitates for a long time before adding, 'Rose is not ready. And I will not push her. She has been pushed around enough. After two abusive relationships, another man is the last thing she needs. She needs to heal. Find her inner strength. Learn to stand alone, please no one but herself for a change.'

'And then?'

'And then... it is up to Rose.'

'So you are in love with her, then.'

'Daisy...'

'Good, because that might be worth sticking around for.' I shuffle down in the leather and make a show of getting comfortable, as if I really am here to stay.

Saeed smiles.

He has a devastating smile.

I know why Rose loves him. And sometimes, in certain lights, with certain expressions, he reminds me of Luc.

I say, 'I bought the cabin, did Rose tell you?'

'She did. But Daisy…are you sure that was wise?'

'Maybe. Maybe not.'

'Will you go there? Could you go there without Luc and Alfie?'

'I don't know. There's only one way to find out.'

'Daisy? Will you at least try to stay in this world? For a little while at least?'

'Saeed – call me Maggie, will you? It's painful to hear and at the same time I miss hearing it sometimes. It's what Luc called me.'

'French for Daisy. You told me.'

'You remind me of him. I think I'd like it if you called me Maggie. Or Marguerite.'

'All right then. Marguerite… Will you try to live in the real world? For me?'

I like hearing Saeed say it with those soft, velvet tones. And I'll be hearing it every week for a long time, I suppose. And that's all right. This is still the only place I've ever been okay without Luc and Alfie. And it's not this office. Not this comfortable couch. Not the warm lights or the earthy smell.

It's Saeed.

With him, there's some chance I will be able to live in reality.

FIFTY-ONE

MAGGIE

I TRUDGE across the shingle towards the lake, my feet sinking beneath my body weight, as if I'm walking over soft sand. Sauntering around the waterline, Cairo at my heel, I scan the shore as I used to, stopping now and then to toe the stones, hoping to find the right one buried beneath the rest.

I've skimmed so many across the lake that finding the right one gets harder every time. So I bend down on my haunches and pick up a handful as if I'm panning for gold. Sieving them through my fingers, I toss aside the stones that are too big, too round or too jagged.

And there it is.

Smoothing my fingertip over its polished surface as I stand, I turn the pebble over and over, bouncing it on my palm to assess its weight and viability.

It's perfect.

The lake is mirror-flat and clear. In the distance, the sun sets as if it's dipping its toes in the water. I ready myself at

355

the shore…but before I skim the stone, something in my peripheral vision catches my eye.

Holding my breath, I turn towards the figure in the treeline, standing at the head of the path.

It's not a man.

The stag holds its majestic antlers high, smoke rising from its nostrils on the cold evening air.

We lock eyes.

Staring at each other, we maintain the stalemate for what feels like minutes but is probably no more than a few seconds. Then the stag lets out another cloudy breath before slowly turning and meandering into the trees. And, unable to tear my eyes away, I watch until it disappears from view.

I step closer to the water, bounce from foot to foot and bend low, arcing my arm to and fro, getting a feel for the motion as if practising a golf swing before the stroke. Then I snap my arm forward, releasing the stone at just the right moment.

It bounces across the water.

Alfie would have loved that. He would have jumped up and down in his cumbersome wellies, burbling screams of joy until I said it was his turn now. And, having already found his perfect stone, he would have bent down, stuck out his sweet little bottom and launched himself off the shingle while throwing both hands in the air. And only when his feet touched the ground would he have let go of the stone, which would have flown no more than a ruler's length before landing a few centimetres from his right toe.

But I would have clapped.

We would have laughed.

And I would have told him he'd be world champion one day.

We skimmed so many stones from this shore. Too many to count. I used to imagine a great pile of them in the centre of the lake, almost touching the surface. And I'd fantasise that, one day, I'd skim a stone that would bounce six times before stopping dead, coming to rest on the top of the pile as though it was floating on the glassy water.

Crunching the shingle, I make my way back to the cabin and Cairo follows me. An image of the sun setting behind me is reflected on the glass of Luc's study window, making it impossible to see inside. I pretend he's in there, sitting at his desk, a headful of dark hair sticking up from behind his computer screen.

At the foot of the porch steps, I stop for a moment.

Is this a mistake?

Saeed said maybe I shouldn't come to the cabin.

But it belongs to me now.

I hesitate for just a moment longer before climbing up to the decking. And at the door, I hold the latch for a few moments before pressing it down and pulling it open.

I step inside.

A fire roars in the burner. The room is toasty, welcoming, and Cairo jumps up on the sofa, clawing the fabric before tucking herself among the cushions and settling down. I stamp my feet on the doormat to shake off the lake water and then wipe them clean before standing there for a few extra moments, inhaling the familiar scent of wood-smoke.

Then I make my way across the lounge, up the two steps to the split-level floor, and pause at Luc's study door. As I take hold of the doorknob, my fingers tremble, and I have to tell myself he's not in there. That the window isn't broken and there are no bodies on the floor.

That didn't happen.

It was nothing but a bad dream.

Bolstering my courage, I open the door, step inside, and close it behind me. It's so quiet and everything is just as it should be, just where I left it. Following the rectangle of sunlight that spills across the floorboards and on to the rug, I make my way around Luc's desk to the window, where I watch the sun sink into the lake.

Breathtakingly beautiful, it burns the water gold. And in the centre of its reflection there's a small, black mark.

My stone.

It sits there.

Floating on the lake's glassy surface.

And behind me, a small boy giggles.

Dear reader,

I am a writer – I make up stories. I am not a psychologist and cannot offer professional advice. But I did write this story with the hope that it might help even one victim

When I wrote this novel, I was deeply involved in the life of someone very dear to me in a coercive controlling relationship with a man his own therapist described as a narcissistic psychopath. In order to help her get free – to be an anchor in her storm – I needed an in-depth understanding of what she was going through. I had to see her world through her eyes because, without being subjected to twenty years of brainwashing, her world, and her inability to just walk away, made no sense to me.

After reading and listening to dozens of books, lectures and podcasts, I was finally able to see her world as she saw it. And it terrified me. I saw just how coercive, subtle and cruel this behaviour is, and I realised how easily it could happen to any of us caught in the net of a narcissist.

And yet – impossible as it felt some days – I still had to sit back and wait for her to find the strength to overcome the sustained destruction of who she had been as a young woman and prepare to leave in her own time, on her own terms. Much as I was desperate to be, I couldn't be another coercer.

She has allowed me to share one story with you:

When she was ready to leave, she sought advice from a solicitor. Convinced her husband was tracking her phone and her car, we left both at her place of business. I drove her to a solicitor ten miles out of town and, within two hours, she was back at her desk. The next day, during a sunny stroll, her husband brought up in conversation, so casually it was chilling, the name of the business park that housed that solicitor.

I'd like you to imagine how that made her feel. How did he know? She hadn't taken her car, or her phone, and he was supposed to be at work himself. Did he have someone watching her 24/7? It left her stunned and terrified. But, of course, if she'd said anything, he would have laughed and told her she was crazy and paranoid, that it was a mere coincidence.

This is what coercive control is like. Each incident is so insignificant that to make a fuss would make you question whether you were irrational and paranoid. And yet, at the same time, you're chilled to the bone by things you can't clearly label as abusive behaviour. Coercive control emotionally destroys its victims, but it manages to do it without them even being aware it's happening to them.

I deliberately kept Rose's marriage to Nathan short because to extricate her from twenty years of brainwashing and coercive control would have taken far more than the 200 pages afforded to her character development. It took the person I love many years to get free.

Victims are not only women, and it is not exclusive to sexual relationships. I have seen these behaviours exhibited between mothers and sons, brothers and sisters, and even bosses and employees. If any of the behaviours in this book ring a bell for you – no matter how quietly it rings – please, please, very carefully and very cautiously seek out help.

I would highly recommend the following books and that you read them in secret. Do not underestimate a narcissistic coercive controller, and do not put yourself in danger by revealing that you may have figured out who they really are:

Why Does He Do That?: Inside the Minds of Angry and Controlling Men, by Lundy Bancroft.

The Verbally Abusive Relationship: How to Recognize it and How to Respond, by Patricia Evans.

Should I Stay or Should I Go?: A Guide to Knowing if Your Relationship Can – and Should – be Saved, by Lundy Bancroft and J.A.C. Patrissi.

POWER: Surviving and Thriving After Narcissistic Abuse: A Collection of Essays on Malignant Narcissism and Recovery from Emotional Abuse, by Shahida Arabi.

The Mind of the Intimate Male Abuser: How He Gets into Her Head, by Don Hennessy.

Healing from Hidden Abuse: A Journey Through the Stages of Recovery from Psychological Abuse, by Shannon Thomas.

Invisible Chains: Overcoming Coercive Control in Your Intimate Relationship, by Lisa Aronson Fontes.

Look What You Made Me Do: A Powerful Memoir of Coercive Control, by Helen Walmsley-Johnson.

Remembered Forever: Our Devastating Story of Control, Abuse and Domestic Homicide, by Luke Hart and Ryan Hart.

Why Is It Always About You?: The Seven Deadly Sins of Narcissism, by Sandy Hotchkiss.

If you suspect that a friend or family member is a victim of coercive control and wish to support them, I encourage you to learn how to be an anchor in the storm by reading *Helping Her Get Free: A Guide for Families and Friends of Abused Women*, by Susan Brewster.

And if you have the stomach to hear from the horse's mouth of a self-confessed narcissist, then read *Red Flag: 50 Warning Signs of Narcissistic Seduction* by H.G. Tudor (also *Fuel* and *No Contact* from the same author).

Stay safe.
With much love, Carrie

Eva has made a catastrophic mistake.
Her career is in tatters.
By day, she's tormented by nosebleeds and blackouts.
By night, her violent dreams leave her shaken.
They should. They hold a devastating secret.

The truth is more terrifying than her nightmares.
Confronting it demands an unthinkable choice.

Eva would kill for a baby. Now she may have to.
She has six seconds.

PICK ONE. YOUR HUSBAND? OR YOUR CHILD?

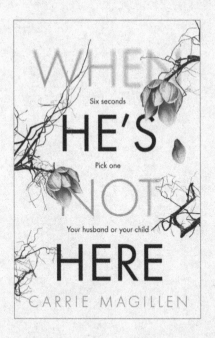

Read the first chapter of Carrie Magillen's
thrilling debut novel overleaf…

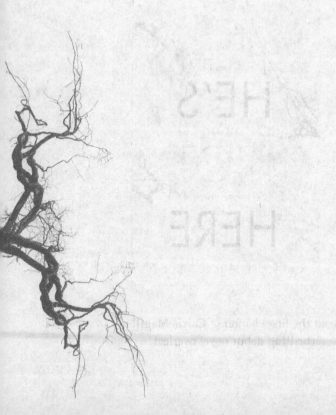

ONE

BEFORE THE BARREL of the syringe is even empty, I know I've killed him.

Lying side by side on the countertop were two syringes, each filled with yellow solution.

I've picked up the wrong one.

Yet the plunger continues to work its way down the barrel as if I'm not the woman pressing it. I don't stop. I can't. My brain is tangled up in the need to pretend this isn't happening. It can't be happening. I can't have killed Jack.

My mouth falls open as I look up from his body into Caroline's benign, unsuspecting eyes.

No words come out.

'Eva? Is something wrong?'

I stare at her.

'Eva?' And her eyes are no longer benign. They match mine.

Her terrified expression jolts me into action. I need to get him out of this examining room and into prep, fast. I scoop him into my arms and yell, 'Wait there!' as I struggle with the doorknob before bolting from the room. Her voice follows me down the corridor.

'Eva? Eva, what the hell's going on?'

By the time we reach prep, Jack's already drowsy and I run into one of the nurses at the door. 'Jenny! Thank God. I need help.'

She holds the door open. 'What is it? What's wrong?'

I can't tell her.

Jenny runs alongside me as I scream, 'Bron! I need help.' Bron is my boss, the most experienced surgeon at the practice, and she rushes to my side as I lay Jack on the operating table.

I want the words to stay trapped inside me. I don't want to say them out loud. Because as soon as they leave my lips I'll have broken things I'll never be able to mend. But they must be said.

'I injected him by mistake.' My voice quivers. 'Pentoject.'

'Jesus Christ!' Bron grabs her forehead. 'Jenny, hand me my stethoscope and get him on oxygen.'

'What can I do?' I ask.

'Step back!' Bron's voice is rock-hard. I break against it.

Jenny holds the oxygen mask over Jack's nose and mouth and pumps the compression bag while Bron shouts, 'Clippers. I need clippers. And a tube, get me a tube over here.'

Nurses run in different directions while I stand glued to the spot, staring at Jack's limp body on the table. I've been treating him for digestive problems since he was a year old. For four years now. And over the last six months I've seen him every fortnight. I've come to love him as if he were mine.

Now I've killed him.

'It wasn't the full dose...'

Bron ignores me. Her attention is on Jack. I can't just stand here and watch him die. I have to do something.

'Prep the crash cart,' says Bron.

'Bron.' I fight to keep my voice calm. 'There aren't enough nurses. Give me something to do.'

Bron stares at me for a moment. There isn't time to weigh up whether it's wise to let me help, so she relents. 'IV fluids and adrenaline.'

I don't wait for her to change her mind.

At the medicine cabinet, I stare at the vials. My vision blurs until every one is filled with yellow solution and every label reads Pentoject. Beneath the grilling strip lights, a dribble of sweat runs down my spine into the waistband of my trousers. My tongue is dried meat in my mouth and I swallow a surge of acid vomit. I close my eyes, shake my head, and open them again.

Pull yourself together, Ev. Pull yourself together.

I grab IV fluids and a vial of epinephrine, check and double-check the labels, and then prep two syringes of adrenaline: one low dose, one high.

Back at the table, Bron is sizing an endotracheal tube, while Jenny finishes shaving Jack's leg and chest before placing an IV catheter in his cephalic vein.

'Fluids and epinephrine.' I put them on the tray next to Bron.

She glances at me with her lips pressed tightly together before administering the fluids. I stare at her downcast eyes. Her eyelids are a wall that's gone up and I'm on the other side of it.

Jack's blood pressure spikes and then gradually declines. I watch in horror, unable to move a single muscle, as Bron barks orders at the nurses rushing around me.

I stand in the eye of the tornado.

Antiseptic fills my nostrils and coats my tongue. I swallow it down. It's a scent as familiar as the aroma of my own home. I breathe it in without even being aware of it, yet now it's thick. It takes up all the air in the room.

Jenny administers the first shot of low-dose adrenaline while Bron gets up on the table to begin chest compressions. Unless it's an exceptionally small patient, Bron always does this, because she's particular about her technique and doesn't think they're as effective leaning over a table. I've seen her do this many times, but it's never been so painful to watch.

My eyes track the twitching ECG as if I'm watching Jack's heart pumping inside his chest. I will it to keep moving, to beat on its own, and its slow pace drags mine into step.

After two minutes of compressions, Bron stops to check the ECG but there's no rhythm or heart rate. Jenny administers the second high-dose adrenaline shot, and she and Bron change places on the table. Chest compressions are tiring, mentally more than physically with a patient as small as Jack, so they switch to ensure they're maintaining the correct force and weight.

After another two minutes, Jenny stops to check the ECG.

Nothing.

'Adrenaline, amiodarone and atropine,' shouts Bron.

And before any of the nurses have the opportunity to beat me to it I run back to the cabinet and prep the syringes. The amiodarone is in case the defibrillator doesn't restart Jack's heart. The atropine is a last resort. It's unlikely to do any good.

Behind me, Bron shouts, 'Prep the crash cart to sixty.' And by the time I get back to the table she's removed the ECG leads from Jack's chest and is applying electrode gel to the defibrillator paddles.

I've never believed in God, but I pray anyway.

She places the paddles on either side of Jack's sternum and shouts, 'Clear!' before she shocks him. With no ECG connected, she has to check manually for a heartbeat. 'Nothing. Charge to ninety.'

I swallow bile.

Jenny and Bron continue with adrenaline, chest compressions and the defibrillator, but there's still no heartbeat. They administer amiodarone and shock him at a hundred and ten, but Jack's heart refuses to beat on its own. Finally, Bron shouts, 'Atropine,' and my eyes well up as I lamely hand her the syringe.

The next two minutes feel like the entire thirty-eight years of my life. I watch them buzz around Jack as they shock him again and check for a heartbeat. But nothing they do will come to any good. Jack was dead the moment I pressed the plunger on that syringe.

'It's been fifteen minutes,' says Jenny, and Bron pumps Jack's chest a few more times before stopping. Her shoulders slump.

I stare at Jack's lifeless body.

This can't be happening. It can't be.

The tight leash I keep on my life is snapping.

I snap.

'Get down!' I reapply the ECG leads and hurry Bron down from the table as I climb up to take her place. Elbows locked, shoulders over my hands, I begin chest compressions.

'Ev,' says Bron. 'We've done everything we can.'

I ignore her and carry on pumping Jack's chest.

'Ev… Ev…' Bron tries to pull my arms away and I fight against her but she's taller than me, broader. She wraps her arms around mine, pinning them to my side. 'Eva! Let him go.'

There's no use fighting her so I stop struggling, slump over Jack's little body and sob. Bron and the nurses stand around me. They've never seen me like this, never seen a chink in my professional armour, and now I'm in pieces none of them have any idea what to say to me. Eventually, it's Bron who speaks.

'I'll tell Caroline.'

'No.' I sniff and wipe away tears. 'No. I'll do it.'

I get down from the table, turn my back on Jack's dead body and walk as slowly as I can back to the examination room where Caroline is waiting.

Available now!

GRIPPING audiobooks for
When He's Not Here and *Stone the Dead Crows*

SLY

Could you murder in cold blood

TRAP
FOR A

to save the life of a stranger?

FOX

CARRIE MAGILLEN

WHEN

Six seconds

HE'S

Pick one

NOT

Your husband or your child

HERE

CARRIE MAGILLEN

STONE

Three sisters

THE

Two strangers

DEAD

One secret

CROWS

CARRIE MAGILLEN

ACKNOWLEDGEMENTS

THOUGH WRITING is a solitary endeavour, it takes a great number of people to get it into your hands, and I would like to thank the following:

First, as always, you, dear reader, for buying and reading this book. It's your imagination that breathes life into our stories and we're nothing without you. But also to everyone who bought *When He's Not Here*, left reviews, and propelled it to No.1 on the domestic thriller chart last year. It was a joyful day and all thanks to you.

There are many people without whom these thrillers wouldn't exist, but that's especially true of my wonderful husband, Darrell. Without you, I would still be sitting in an eight-foot-square cubicle with my soul dying a little every time I said, 'Have you tried switching it off and on again?'

Jenny, my loving sister and best friend for fifty years and, over the last two, part of our home as well. It will always be your port in the storm. You've shown us all the phenomenal strength of women in adversity and our whole family is so proud and so very lucky to have you as a sister, daughter and mother.

Linda McQueen, to whom this book is also dedicated. And here, even a writer gets lost for words. How can I properly convey my most heartfelt thanks for the incredible lengths you have gone to, to support me and my career? My editor since early 2019 and now a friend. I hope we'll work together until we're old(er) and grey(er)! E.L. Doctorow said, 'Writing is like driving at night in the fog. You can only see as far as your headlights, but you can make the whole trip that way.' That's true about every aspect of writing and publishing, but I've been lucky enough to have Linda jogging in front of my car with a flashlight pointing out every rock in the road.

Charley, for your meticulous proofreading. It's a joy to work with you and I hope we get to do it again and again. As I've said before, all errors are mine: the lovely Linda and Charley don't make mistakes, they just do their best to catch them.

Ayeesha, my dear, dear friend, for supporting me in so many ways, for talking over plots, for reading drafts, and for allowing me to bring your beautiful Cairo back to life on the page. But also, sincerely, for allowing me to share one of your most deeply personal experiences. If it means one woman doesn't have to go through what you went through, we'll have made a difference.

My incredibly supportive and talented writers' group: Shady, Madelaine, Elisa and Tilly. You beautiful ladies make me a better writer and, like a sturdy pair of crutches, you hold me up every time I wobble. But extra-special thanks must go to Luke, not only for feeding back on drafts but for staying up into the night to discuss plot in such excruciating detail you'd think my characters were real. Your probing questions force me to dig deeper and work harder and every book is better because of you. I owe all of you so much, my dear, dear friends.

The IAC for all your incredible and selfless support (particularly to Darren, Sharn, Stephen, Dan, Luke, and the extra-special Ken who makes me laugh all the time). A rising tide really does lift all boats and you buoy me up every day with love, laughter and your helping hands.

Mark Read for your beautiful covers and attention to detail. Seeing a new design is one of the highlights of publishing, and working with you is a real joy. But I'll be damned if I lose the sunflower competition this year. It's on!

Louise and Jo for putting so much of yourselves into the audiobook. These characters have been chatting in my head for two years, which makes it hard to embrace someone else's interpretation of them. But your phenomenal performances sound far better than the voices in my head and I can't thank you enough for bringing them to life with such realism, beauty and emotion.

The wonderful Douglas Kean (who's an absolute joy to work with) for putting so many hours into the audio and giving up your own time to produce remote recordings during lockdown. If listeners heard the transition from initial narration to seamless final production, they would be as in awe as I am.

Jacqueline and Elodie for your help with Luc's dialogue and the French recordings for the audiobook. Without you, Luc would have been more than un peu unconvincing!

Mum, Dad, Katie, Amy, Willie and Anne, Teresa and Stella, and all my other wonderful relatives and friends for being my biggest (and potentially biased) fans who lift me up every day with love, encouragement and support. I'm one incredibly lucky lady to be surrounded by such amazing, happy, funny people. Thank you all for reading drafts, buying books, and shouting praise I probably don't deserve from the rooftops!

And finally, as always, for Nick. Sweet girl, look at this... I got off my ass and wrote another one!

CARRIE MAGILLEN spent fifteen years as a computer engineer working for IBM and Sun Microsystems, all the while with a yellowing copy of *Plot* by Ansen Dibell on her bookshelf.

She left IT in 2006 and studied creative writing at Webster University in the Netherlands, Wollongong University in Australia, and Winchester University in England. She lives in Hampshire with her husband and two American cocker spaniels.

Her debut novel, *When He's Not Here*, was a No.1 bestseller in 2020. *Stone the Dead Crows* is her second novel.

Carrie loves hearing from readers and you can reach her via her website:

carriemagillen.com

9 781913 692087